BEST NEW AMERICAN VOICES 2008

GUEST EDITORS OF
Best New American Voices

Tobias Wolff

Charles Baxter

Joyce Carol Oates

John Casey

Francine Prose

Jane Smiley

Sue Miller

Richard Bausch

BEST NEW AMERICAN VOICES 2008

GUEST EDITOR
Richard Bausch

SERIES EDITORS
John Kulka and Natalie Danford

A Harvest Original • Harcourt, Inc.
Orlando   Austin   New York   San Diego   London

CONTENTS

PREFACE

Best New American Voices, now in its eighth year, is the only annual short story anthology devoted exclusively to new work by emerging writers. Its focus is the writing workshop. Why the workshop? Because the Best New American Voices series places a premium on the new, and on the pleasure of discovery, and because writing workshops simply happen to be the place where young, talented writers gravitate. Flannery O'Connor, herself a graduate of the Iowa Workshop, once wickedly wrote: "Everywhere I go, I'm asked if I think the universities stifle writers. My opinion is that they don't stifle enough of them." O'Connor's remark is sometimes incorrectly taken to be a disparaging comment about writing workshops. It is not. Rather it is a comment about her low opinion of commercial fiction. Indeed, O'Connor flourished as a young writer at Iowa, learning a great deal from such legendary instructors as Paul Engle, Andrew Lytle, Austin Warren, and Robert Penn Warren.

Most of the contributors to this volume are, for the present, unknown; a few make their debuts here. They are, generally speaking, young or young*ish,* though age is not a criterion for eligibility. These writers come from all parts of North America and from all walks of life—most of them born in the United States, but some not. They have little in common, probably, other than the fact that they have recently attended a writing workshop. Many but not all were enrolled in MA or MFA programs when their stories were nominated for the Best New American Voices competition. Some were taking classes in nondegree programs, either as writing fellows (in the Stegner program, for example) or as writers attending a summer writing conference (such as the Wesleyan Writers Conference). In the past, contributors have come to us from various community workshops; a few, representing writing courses sponsored by the PEN Prison Writing Committee, have been convicted felons.

As you might expect from such a diverse group of writers, they have different concerns, writing styles, and views on life. Having read many thousands of manuscripts over the past eight years for the Best New American Voices competition, we have observed certain patterns or trends—or at least we think we have. Greater reliance on the present tense. An avoidance of, and perhaps skepticism about, omniscient narration. More experimentation. A willingness to explore formerly taboo subjects such as bisexuality and transgender. Beyond such general and tentatively offered observations, however, we wouldn't be willing to say much. And we certainly don't wish to claim that such patterns have anything, particularly, to do with writing coming out of the workshops. If these observations are valid, then they must be connected to the development of contemporary fiction. The "workshop story," as far as we can tell, is a specious category. What do famous workshop alums Flannery O'Connor, Wallace Stegner, Michael Cunningham, T. C. Boyle, David Foster Wallace, and Kiran Desai have in common? In what meaningful sense can we call them workshop writers?

We do not accept submissions from individual writers for the Best New American Voices competition. Each year we invite workshop directors and instructors to nominate stories for consideration. We ask them to send us what, in their own estimations, were the best stories workshopped during the past year. Numerous programs across the United States and Canada participate in the annual competition. A directory at the back of the book lists all of this year's participating institutions.

For *Best New American Voices 2008* we received hundreds of nominations. We read every nomination at least once, as we do every year for the competition, and winnowed these down to a group of finalists that we then passed on to our guest editor, Richard Bausch. Richard has selected seventeen stories for inclusion in *Best New American Voices 2008*. The stories speak for themselves.

We would like to extend thanks to Richard Bausch for his many excellent editorial suggestions, for his alacrity and professionalism, and for his general enthusiasm for the Best New American Voices series. Without the continuing support of the many faculty, administrators, and workshop directors who nominate stories every year, this anthology would not be possible. To them we offer heartfelt thanks and congratulations. We would be remiss not to mention here, too, our contributors, whose book, after all, this really is (thank you, all of you, for your persistence and grace). To name a few others: We thank our editor Andrea Schulz for her continuing belief in this series; Lisa Lucas in the Harcourt contracts department for her ongoing attention to details; Kathi George for her careful copyediting; and our families and friends for their love and support.

—*John Kulka and Natalie Danford*

INTRODUCTION

Richard Bausch

One November night about ten years ago, I was driving Grace Paley around Washington, near the campus of George Washington University, looking for her hotel. We'd had dinner with a friendly crowd of PEN/Faulkner people and some members of Bernard Malamud's family, after the PEN/Malamud Award ceremony where, as that year's honoree, Ms. Paley had delivered a marvelous reading, and answered some questions from the audience. The two of us had parted from the others in a mood of happy gratitude for the good weather and the large turnout. And I was now completely lost, turning up one street and down another, trying to find the hotel. I had been the one to pick her up at that same hotel, at the start of the evening, so Ms. Paley, to spare me the embarrassment I was feeling, began to talk about short fiction as a literary art form, and some of the story writers she admired.

We got to talking about the resilience of story, the strength of it, the persistence of it. I had a story coming out that month in *The Atlantic,* and I remarked that Mike Curtis, the magazine's senior fiction editor, had told me he receives something like 3,600 stories every week. "A lot of people out there scribbling away," Grace said. I said something fairly pompous about how the refinement of the form had been an American phenomenon, really, and that we could say it is our contribution to the world's literary landscape. Ms. Paley, chewing gum, staring out the window at the chilly night, said, in her inimitable nonpompous fashion, "Fuck'n A."

I laughed very hard. We both laughed. And then we went on to talk about the fact that some magazine editors were calling fiction "the F word," and that the market seemed to be shrinking; we agreed that it has always been shrinking. I told her of a remark I heard at a conference way back in 1971, that the short story was dead. She had a memory of someone making such a remark, and someone else had said to *him,* "Sir, the short story will be at your funeral."

We laughed about that. I finally, almost by accident, found the hotel. She blessed me with one of her kindly smiles and a pat on the shoulder. I drove home thinking how, in that week, I had seen or spoken to Grace Paley, William Maxwell, and Eudora Welty. And then I started going down the names of great writers of short stories who were my elders, alive and well: Those three alone seemed an embarrassment of wealth. But then I thought of the others: Saul Bellow, John Updike, George Garrett, Ruth Prawer Jhabvala, Elizabeth Spencer. All of these were people of the generation preceding mine, which has its own set of gifted practitioners, too many to name here, all of them contemporary representatives of the vitality of the form. That November night, driving home from dropping off Ms. Paley, I had the thought that a hundred years from now, people, readers—if human beings are still curious and they still read—will look back on this time and marvel at the riches.

In the volume that you are holding in your hands, there are some new names, the fresh talents working in this superior form of entertainment, which for so long has so glibly been judged by the market types and the critics to be dying out. These emerging artists, inexperienced though they may be, naive though they may seem at times, possess startlingly original voices, and vivid, sophisticated sensibilities.

No doubt some of them are composing stories in the belief that they are serving a kind of apprenticeship for at last approaching the novel they hope one day to write. Some will only realize later, as I did, that the form requires its own attention. Yet, fortunately, the short story is elastic enough for us to work in it while having perfect disrespect for it. Because people like stories; human beings live in them, by them, with them, from earliest childhood on.

In each instance, here, the writer is striving to be absolutely splendid, trying, as every writer is, to make something lasting out of the confusions of living.

I think they succeed wonderfully.

What I was looking for was *imagining.* Or a quality of imagining—I have been saying for years that, for me, it is the *wayfaring* writer whose work I respect most. So now we have Jedediah Berry, Tucker Capps, Oriane Gabrielle Delfosse, Lauren Groff. Remember the names. Garth Risk Hallberg, Leslie Jamison, Razia Sultana Khan, Elizabeth Kadetsky. They come from all around the country, from every culture and subculture. Suzanne Rivecca, Sharon May, Stefan McKinstray, Jordan McMullin, Peter Mountford. They defy classification, and there is not one that is like another. Dan Pinkerton, David James Poissant, Christopher Stokes, Adam Stumacher.

In "Alice," a father and daughter try to deal with grief and with their own estrangement from each other; in "Inheritance," a man has to find some way to accommodate the fact that his father left him a beast as an inheritance—a beast that is never named, has hooves, but is gaining the ability of human speech; in still another, "Quiet Men," a woman recounts a series of empty relationships with men, after having been dumped by the one with whom she was in love. There is a story here about a failed concert pianist ("Men and Boys"), and one that begins at the onset of the flu epidemic of 1918, and moves on into the future, and ends with the sad lives of a pair of lost lovers ("Surfacing"). "Early Humans" is told to us by a none-too-sympathetic talent agent in trouble, who nevertheless earns our sympathy; "Men More Than Mortal" arrives through the voice of a woman bicycle messenger, who desperately needs a superhero. Then there's the one told by a Cambodian translator ("The Wizard of Khao-I-Dang"), and the one we hear through the voice of an Asmat native ("The Man Who Ate Michael Rockefeller"). Some stories have distinctly American settings ("Headlock," "Venn Diagram," and "Mouse"), while others roam farther afield ("Alms," "Horizon," and "The Neon Desert"). Still others cover the vast terrain of human emotions, as when the protagonist of "Uncle" struggles to overcome what the title character did to her so many years ago, or the disaffected youth of "No One Here Says What They Mean" try, sometimes desperately, to connect.

All this variety. All these riches.

We have all heard by now the objections of those who decry the writing programs as having some sort of negative influence on American writing. But let's look at those objections. First, there's the idea that writing programs have a kind of cookie-cutter effect, turning out writers who sound the same and who make all the same gestures. All right, so take Jane Smiley, Allan Gurganus, me, Joanne Meschery, and T. Coraghessan Boyle. We were all at Iowa at the same time, and all took our MFAs from there. That's five people from the *same* writing program, with the same teachers, and in the same time frame. And of course we are quite radically different from each other in all ways, in subject, treatment, stance, gesture, theme, and in tone, too, even liking and admiring each other's work. Between my novel *The Last Good Time* and Gurganus's *Oldest Living Confederate Widow Tells All,* there is little that can be termed remotely similar, except that both are made out of English prose sentences; and between those two and Boyle's *The Road to Wellville,* the obvious differences couldn't be more wide. And these three are nothing like Smiley's *Greenlanders,* or Meschery's *Gentleman's Guide to the Frontier.*

And of course the seventeen individual voices in this volume make their own argument revealing the essentially misinformed nature of the cookie-cutter objection.

The second major objection one hears is that writing programs coddle upcoming writers—this idea stemming from the shopworn and finally—say it—brainless idea that writers need great economic depressions, catastrophes, wars, all *that,* in order to develop properly. My god, the enormity of *that* misconception has always boggled my mind. Folks, the only thing a writer absolutely needs to develop is a lived life, anywhere and anytime, but preferably a peaceful time, with a lot of books around and paper and pencils; and also a writer needs for someone *not* to shoot or kill them.

Let us suppose, for instance, that Wilfred Owen, instead of taking a round in the chest in the trenches of World War I, had lived to a moderately old age. What might he have had to tell us about love, or family, or the hopes of his time, the sorrows and unexpected joys of his years, and all the stages of human living? What news of the spirit might have come to us from that talent? The war didn't make Wilfred Owen a great poet. It silenced him.

The fact is that the good writing programs in this country provide, in a loose institutional way, the kind of salon that writers have used and gravitated to from the beginning. Shakespeare and Marlowe and the crowd in the pubs of London were all talking shop over their ale and wine, folks. And Hemingway, Stein, Joyce, Fitzgerald, Pound, and that gang in Paris were, too. Even Faulkner, that famous loner, spent many days and hours in his formative time down in New Orleans among the artists and writers there.

It is my firm belief that future cultural histories will report that in one of the most heartening developments of the last sixty years of the twentieth century, American colleges and universities helped to establish an atmosphere for the release of literary talent, and for the support of literary art. And that art flourished, even as the culture around it embraced a terrible vulgarity, a tidal, sweeping, vast, rising wave of banality. Writing flourished and the books, the work, came forth anyway. Riches. Treasure.

To provide a place where writers may sit with interested others of their kind and discuss this arduous occupation and craft is a perfectly beautiful thing. It shows a shrewd understanding of how it happens with writers in any case. And so, why not provide the setting for the proliferation of new talent, as has been done with music and art since before the Renaissance? One isn't "teaching writing," one is providing a place for it. If one is teaching anything, it's the life: patience, trust in the thing itself, discipline, and stubbornness. Out of the steady persistence of these virtues, and the great elasticity and strength of the form itself, we are blessed to have these brilliant new expressions of the human news. Take a look inside this book and see for yourself.

BEST NEW AMERICAN VOICES 2008

TUCKER CAPPS

University of Iowa

ALICE

The surgeon on TV was inserting tubes into a man's shaved chest, a man my age, when I heard Alice, my daughter's chocolate Lab, coming down the basement stairs. Her paws ticked on each step—forepaw forepaw, hind paw hind paw—and I worried for her, because her legs were stiff as chair legs, the basement stairs were slickly varnished, and she must not have come down to the den since summertime.

But she made it all right, and when she got to the foldout couch she licked the arch of my foot and started pacing a wide oval between me and the TV cabinet. Over and over, she hobbled on this invisible rabbit trail from the wall, along the bed, to the other wall, then back along the TV.

"Alice," I said, as if saying her name would make her tell me why she was having this second wind after so many months of being an arthritic lump on the dining room carpet. It was a Sunday morning in December, an hour before dawn, and nothing was on but home shopping and a surgery show—open-heart. Tour de France, my bicycle shop, didn't open till ten. I'd get in my truck at nine.

I stubbed my cigarette on the funnies and looked back down at the newspaper article I'd finished an hour ago, wondering superstitiously if it had anything to do with her strange behavior. The article was about these scientists in Albuquerque who trained golden retrievers to detect lung cancer on people's breath. The thought of it— some dog in some lab sniffing me for cancer the way he'd sniff a fist for a Milk-Bone—jolted me more than any cigarette warning I'd ever read.

"You want out?" I asked her, talking from the side of my mouth while I lit another cigarette. "You didn't ring your bell." I was almost shouting to reach her deaf ears, but she kept hobbling past the TV, vulturelike, until I grabbed her collar at the foot of the mattress and made her lean against my knee, where she blinked her dark eyes, milky green with cataracts.

I led her out onto the driveway, but she came back a minute later and started doing the same damn thing. Pacing. On the TV they were opening the man's rib cage.

"You have something you want to tell me, Alice?" I climbed the stairs to the kitchen, but her mound of food was still in the dog bowl by the sliding glass door—one scoop dry, half a can wet. She'd nibbled some of the wet, but most of it still had the fork marks from when I mixed it with the dry. Her sporadic appetites and inclement digestion I had come to expect in her old age; this mysterious second wind baffled me, though. Alice was fifteen, eight years younger than my daughter, Leslie.

I unlooped her leash from its coat peg in the hall, feeling guilty I hadn't walked Alice since June, since Father's Day.

Leslie was why I took care of Alice. Not that I hadn't always adored the dog, or that I would have gotten rid of her. But Leslie was why I remembered to take Alice to the vet every spring and why I cooked bacon some Saturdays and fried eggs in the grease. Bacon grease and egg whites were supposed to keep the luster in her coat, even though her chin and chest had gone from chocolate to ash long ago.

My daughter usually visited in December, but we'd had a disagreement two years earlier, so she hadn't come the previous year. Our phone conversations, which we still arranged now and then, had been short and ceremonial ever since, always on Father's Day or one of our birthdays. I never had much to report. She had a whole life she thought she had to hide.

For a long time after she left Oregon I couldn't say my daughter's name. Saying her name wasn't a daily concern, but every now and then an old customer at the bike shop, usually a woman buying or repairing a midlife cruiser, would ask me about the daughter she'd met years ago, the cute little girl who sat behind the glass counter doing homework. Now, what was her name again? I could say it, and I would, but then I'd wonder if I'd slipped and said *lesbian,* as if that were all she was to me. The slip never happened, of course—I would've just laughed it off—but all that time thinking about her in New York, not hearing from her once that first year, made the two words slide together in my head, like cardboard boxes at the back of a truck. Not that I hadn't come to terms with her being a lesbian or that I ever had anything against lesbians. It had been six years since she moved out to the East Coast, seven since her mother died. Now she went by Les. I knew I'd get a call on Christmas Day. We'd exchange pleasantries—a bit about the shop, a bit about waitressing in SoHo—then she'd ask, "So how's my girl?" It was the only time she ever sounded enthusiastic on the phone.

On the way up the hill I stopped every few steps as Alice sniffed the asphalt. Windhill Estates didn't have sidewalks. Seen from above, as in the brochure, the streets spread like blood vessels from the top of the hill and split into cul-de-sacs. Windhill Lane, Windhill Drive, Windhill Way, Windhill Place, et cetera. Our house stood at the steep end of Windhill Court.

We stopped at the wooden entrance sign and stared across Germantown Road at the brick church, its lights on, watching the first cars pass by in the thinning darkness. Alice sounded a bit winded, her tongue throbbing under puffs of warm steam, so I sat on the curb and she lay on her side on the bark chips and weeds, licking my knuckles. As I rubbed and scratched her belly, I wondered how it would feel to have arthritis as bad as hers. I ran my thumb and forefinger down her spine. She let her head rest sideways on the bark, but when I reached down to knead her hind leg, she twisted around and snapped at my hand, biting the air.

I felt it on her haunch, on her hamstring, like an overgrown tick allowed to suck there for years. The tumor. It had its own rough skin, its own wispy hairs. It pushed out of her and flapped down, half an inch long and thick as my thumb. After I was done feeling it, she licked the fur there and grinned at me while I stood up. "Bet you don't even know what that is," I said, tugging on the leash. "Get up."

Alice started down the hill ahead of me, her tail swinging like a lazy brown flag. Maybe she knew what the tumor meant and didn't care. Maybe dogs didn't think about how the world would go on without them. Maybe they were always ready to die, even if instinct told them to snap and snarl like wolves. It didn't surprise me—old dogs are always walking around with tumors on their ribs, tumors in their paws, tumors between their teeth—but I wondered how Leslie would take the news. I wondered if I should tell her. I touched the phone on my belt, but didn't unclip it. I didn't want to disturb her if she was still in bed.

Alice rode with me to work that morning. She lay on a towel in the truck bed, closemouthed under the Datsun's hardtop. I didn't usually bring her to Tour de France. Never, actually. I just thought it would be good to keep an eye on her, see how sick she really was. If I didn't normally pay so much attention to her, it wasn't because I didn't love her like a member of my own family—I did—it was because she didn't seem to need it.

We'd just pulled off Highway 26, still early for Sunday shop hours, and were curving through fields of wheat and fog when I finally worked up the courage to call my daughter.

I could have driven those farm curves with my eyes closed, so I didn't mind the fog clouding over the road like smoke from my cigarette. A few weeks earlier I'd programmed Leslie's number into my cell phone, but now I couldn't remember how to access it, even though her New York number and the shop number were the only numbers in there. I hardly ever used the cell. I'd bought it for the same reason we bought the house at Windhill Heights—twenty-some miles from my shop in Cornelius, but only two miles from the nurses and doctors at St. V's. I bought it because my wife, Teresa, was ill. Why I never got rid of it I don't know.

Coming down the dip where the road crosses Gales Creek, I had Leslie's name on the screen, but when I looked up I saw a horse, thirty feet ahead, white against white fog. He turned his long muzzle as I stomped the brake pedal and skidded through ten, then fifteen, then twenty feet of thick fog.

My eyes shut as the impact slung me against the seat belt, raked his hooves out from under him, smashed his enormous bones through the windshield, and hailed safety glass across my knuckles, forehead, lap.

I opened my eyes again when I felt the truck stop, just as the white body receded a few feet from the passenger side and thumped into the gravel ditch. Burned rubber swept in on the cold air while I bowed my head against the steering wheel.

I shouldered open the door, stumbled, and sat down in the middle of the road. I could hear the horse breathing on the other side of the front axle, heaving fast through his nostrils, but I didn't want to look. I stared between my knees at the pavement. I was still trying to grasp what had happened, still shuddering at the image of the horse's white bulk as it fell toward me, suspended. I don't know how long I sat there before I realized that the double yellow line ran right under my palm, that at any moment a vehicle might swoop into the dip, the driver not even seeing me in the fog. My chest flooded with a sensation I hadn't felt in years—the giddy fear that clenched my lungs too many times as I leaned into the last painful curves of a rain-slicked road race, pumping too hard, leaning too far, knowing the moment before it happened that the leather-wrapped handlebars would give way, dropping me in front of a dozen other cyclists.

I brushed the glass off my jeans, and got on my feet.

The horse's slow collision had wrinkled the hood and detached half the fender, but hadn't managed to maul the engine, which turned over after two or three twists of the key. I revved in neutral, reversed, then pulled forward into the oncoming lane, steering wide because I didn't know where the horse was. When I finally saw him, he was just a white heap in the side mirror, his chest rising and falling under the gray, getting smaller and cloudier as I drove off.

I crested the steep hill, scraping the crooked fender on the pavement, and there, looking out over Gales Creek, was the ranch house I commuted past every day. On my way home I'd sometimes see the silver-haired husband and wife in their overalls and rubber boots, walking three horses from pasture to stable. Now the stable door was wide open.

Pulling onto their gravel drive, I heard the metal snap of a gun—one, echoing shot.

I got out and started down the hill. Only as I neared the bottom and stopped could I make out the dead horse. A spot on his rib cage was stained red, and a woman, the elderly ranch owner, knelt in the crook of his neck. She stroked his chestnut brow, trying to make the upturned eye stay closed, and her long silver braid quivered on her spine as she curled over him. The discharged rifle lay at her knees.

Before I could come close enough to speak, headlights pushed through the fog, and two sedans rushed past us. Then, from the opposite side, the woman's husband lumbered down the grass slope and limped across the road in his rubber boots, almost dragging his left leg, a streak of mud down the side of his overalls. He didn't notice me standing in the ditch. He knelt wearily next to his wife. She laid her head on his chest.

"Peter," she said, "you shouldn't be walking."

"Was he still breathing?"

They didn't hear my footsteps in the gravel behind them, so I kept walking until Peter saw me out of the corner of his eye. They both turned, and when the wife saw me, she sat back on her calves, shrugging off Peter's arm.

I stopped a few feet from the carcass. I said, "He was just standing there. I couldn't brake in time."

The wife maneuvered on her knees to face me, tears in her eyes. "How fast were you going? Couldn't you steer around him?"

"Anne," said Peter in a low voice, "look at the fog." He stared at me firmly, then back down at his wife. He said, "It's my fault Seth got loose—knocked me down."

I unfolded my wallet and passed him two cards: a spare insurance card and a business card. "Here," I said. "Now's probably not a good time, but—"

"You're suing us," Anne said, as if I didn't have any choice. She freed her arm from her husband's embrace and rose up beside him while he stayed on his knees, propping himself on the horse's shoulder. "If that's what you've got to do, that's fine—bleed us dry if you want to. Seth was our last horse."

"That's not why I'm giving you those cards," I said. "I'd be happy if we didn't have to report it at all. I just need to get to work." They watched me, waiting for me to say more, but how could they trust me? How could they know what had hit me while I'd sat there in the middle of the road? How could they know that, more than anything, I didn't want to be involved?—not with them, not with their dead horse, not with insurance companies, not with a lawyer. All I wanted was to get back in my truck, drive to the bike shop, and open for business at ten. I needed a new truck anyway.

"Why don't you come up to the house?" said Peter, using the horse as a platform to boost himself onto his one good leg. "We'll talk it over."

They poured me a cup of black coffee in their kitchen, and Anne drew up an informal agreement on a yellow legal pad, one copy for each party. When we'd finished signing our names, agreeing never to sue, I folded my copy and stood up to go. Peter offered to call a tow truck, but I said no thank you, knowing I had just four miles ahead of me on back roads. He stayed in the kitchen, icing his hip, while Anne walked me to the door. "Gene," she said as I stepped outside, "have we met you somewhere before?"

"Not unless you've been to my shop."

She frowned. "No . . . but was it you who used to ride by here on your ten-speed?" I nodded, and she rested her palm on her sternum, as if I'd caused her chest pain. "I thought so. You were a strange sight. How you'd come up the big hill like it was nothing, in that turquoise jersey. I could see you a mile off."

I nodded again as a memory resurfaced: overheating after a fifty-mile loop, cranking myself over the steepest part of the hill, then finding a much plumper, fifty-something Anne by the mailbox, her arm raised in a stiff but neighborly salute, her braided hair less silver, more brown. "That was twenty years ago," I said.

"It's the blue in your eyes that tipped me off."

"Well, I guess eyes don't change." I stepped onto the flagstone path, which cut through the crabgrass toward my truck. I needed to get going before there were too many cars on the road.

"That's not true at all"—she stepped back with the storm door, leaving it open a crack, and smiled at me through the glass—"sometimes they get sadder."

"I'm very sorry about Seth."

She pursed her lips, as if she couldn't accept an apology from me, but said, "We're still alive . . . you're still alive—that's what matters, I suppose."

My cell phone vibrated when I was a mile away from Cornelius city limits, scraping along at twenty miles an hour, my head out the window in the lifting fog. I pulled over to the side of the road when I heard Leslie's voice.

"I was going to call you but I guess you called first," I said.

"You did call. That's why I'm calling you back." She sounded as if she'd just made up her mind about something.

"I guess I did then." I struggled to think of a way to explain what had happened after I found her number on my phone.

"Dad, I'm at JFK. I'm flying to Portland."

"Today? You didn't tell me that."

"Will you pick me up?"

"Wait—how did you get a ticket if you didn't know you were coming?"

"I can't talk right now. I'm in line."

"Sure, what time should I be there?" While she was speaking, I stared at some tufts of horsehair stuck to the punctured safety glass. I thought of how she must imagine me right now—probably behind my cash register, waiting for customers—versus how I actually was— idling on the side of the road, hoping the cops didn't see—and the whole situation suddenly struck me as funny. I imagined the stares I would get clattering through arrivals in a totaled pickup, and laughed to myself.

"Dad?" She sighed. "Are you there?"

"Seven thirty, United. Wonderful."

As soon as her voice was gone, my wonderful grin felt stupid, mistaken. She hadn't planned to visit me at all, I realized. She'd planned to come and go without ever setting foot in Beaverton. A piece of her other life was in Portland. Her other family was there. The woman who thought it was okay to take in a sixteen-year-old and keep her from high school and parental discipline. The woman who taught her about herself when she was already learning plenty as a normal, heterosexual girl: Janet Ullman, PA. The name Janet made me think of hornets. Yellow jackets.

Alice whimpered behind me. She'd been so quiet since the accident I'd almost forgotten she was there. I got out of the truck and flipped open the hardtop window, half expecting to find her on her side like the mare, breathing her last breaths. She hobbled toward me from the towel, no stiffer than usual, and nuzzled my palm. Her bottom row of teeth was bleeding a little.

"We're gonna have to fix you up, or trade you in," I said, stroking her silky ears. It was impossible to tell how much pain she was in with her teeth, her tumor, her arthritis. She just seemed happy to be going for a ride.

It is sentimental to love a house, I know, but if the house is ugly at least you know your sentiment means something. The cedar siding, the brown garage, the half flight of stairs that made our one story seem like two, the green shingles I tarred myself, the square windows that never caught the sun, the wall-to-wall brown carpeting that we tore up and replaced with a deep blue, as if we wanted our lives and furniture to float on the Mediterranean. The house in Cornelius was the only house Teresa and I could afford while taking out loans to launch the bicycle shop. I think we were both surprised how, over the years, the house became ours, the low-ceilinged rooms getting softer around us, losing their corners and sharp edges. They softened with our first months of married lovemaking, with Leslie's toddling and tricycling, with Virginia Slims and red wine, with the puppy we got when Leslie was eleven and laid up with pneumonia. They rounded the way teeth on a chain ring will dull and shallow out after thousands of cranks, hundreds of uphills and downhills, dozens of days.

When Teresa got sick I didn't think twice about selling our little brown house. After fifteen years, the business had grown. It was the best bike shop from Hillsboro to the coast, and we had money for a better house, something closer to where she needed to be. I put the house on the market the day after the oncologist told us what to expect and where to pin our hopes. We thought the move would be perfect for Leslie. Her first year at Forest Grove High had been too easy for her, even with Advanced English and Accelerated Biology. She told Teresa, who told me, that she heard people having oral sex in a bathroom stall, that she saw a special ed student get flipped backward in his wheelchair, that she watched dopeheads huff glue from sandwich bags in the cafeteria, and that she heard one teacher tell another that home room was an excuse for faculty to catch their breath while fighting a lost cause. Beaverton High School promised to be better.

But it was Leslie who got worse when we moved to Windhill Heights in the winter. Those were the weeks when I'd find the downstairs sink stopped up with hair that she'd snipped off herself. Those were the weeks when she'd come home from school without any books in her camouflage bag, and I'd ask her why she smelled like orange peels, and she'd smile from one side of her mouth and then not come out of her bedroom unless Teresa felt strong enough to make dinner. Whenever I made tortellini and broccoli, or pork chops and plums, or other things she loved, she'd say she wasn't hungry.

She sought me out only when something didn't work and she wanted me to fix it. Rewire her stereo. Unclog her sink. Replace the silver antenna on the cordless phone. Once I repaired an eyelet on her army boot with my needle-nose pliers, and she offered to sweep the front hall and wash the dishes.

A year passed this way, the year of the nine-month prognosis. That January Leslie began coming home from school at ten or eleven at night, not listening to me anymore about homework and whose car she rode in. The doctors were trying a new drug, which, like all the others, killed any cell that reproduced too fast. Before the first dose of it, before we walked arm in arm to the Datsun, we secretly called the new treatment our Wünderdrug, which reminded us both of when we visited Hamburg for a race and, just for the hell of it, smoked a plug of hashish in our hotel room. But they administered too much Wünderdrug, and Teresa, whose body wasn't her own anymore—whose lungs were pointed at on screens, on transparencies, on steel tables, as if her mind and voice no longer mattered—said that her mouth was burning. I was at the shop while it happened, while the sores spread down her tongue and inside her cheeks as if she'd drunk hot oil from her bedside mug instead of honeyed chamomile.

Where was Leslie when I carried her mother from our bed? Where was she when Teresa, waiting for urgent care, cried into the heels of her hands—less from the pain, I think, than from the strangeness of her own skin. Where was she? Gone when we left Windhill. Gone that night when I called home from St. V's. Gone from school the next day. Gone from her friends' houses in Cornelius, which I dialed from an outdated list in Teresa's purse. On the second afternoon of life support and twenty-four-hour infection surveillance, I called Leslie's guidance counselor on a courtesy phone and persuaded him to give me Leslie's boyfriend's address. Ten minutes later I was there, talking to Gabe's younger brother, who led me down to the basement, where Gabe stood on a sleeping bag in his band's practice room, spraying aerosol potpourri to cover the smell of pot that hovered over his nest of guitar cords, textbooks, magazines, pillows, and blankets. "Is this where my daughter's staying?" I asked him.

I remember him sitting back against the soundproofed wall, letting his oily blond hair fall over his face, smirking to himself as if I'd asked why he didn't use shampoo. "She hasn't been here since Monday," he said. "We broke up." He raised his eyebrows without widening his eyes, almost smoked shut, and stared at the flap of sole coming off his shoe. "*She* broke up with *me*."

I was torn between taking my anger out on this miserable kid, who'd probably filched her virginity months ago, and feeling sorry for him. I asked where she'd gone, and he explained that she had called her doctor, who picked her up on Tuesday morning.

"She doesn't have her own doctor," I said. "We have a family physician." I couldn't imagine her calling Dr. Gregoire voluntarily. I couldn't imagine Dr. Gregoire driving anywhere for one of his patients.

"For art therapy," Gabe said impatiently. He could sense my confusion as I leaned against the door frame, not wanting to set foot in that room, with that sleeping bag. "Doesn't she tell you anything?"

Leslie, I learned, had been taking a Tri-Met bus into Portland every Monday after school. She made collages and acrylics with a woman named Janet in a therapy program—something Leslie's guidance counselor probably could have told me. I looked up the downtown hospital, talked to half a dozen administrators, and finally found one who knew about Imitating Art in Life—"Isle," the admins kept saying—and could give me Janet Ullman's home number. Janet Ullman, it turned out, was *not* a doctor and *not* a professional therapist. She was a physician's assistant who took time off to volunteer at IAL.

Janet's voice sounded younger than I expected, breathily therapeutic. She asked who was calling.

"Her father."

"Oh, it's you," she said. "Oh, god, I'm so sorry. I thought you knew she was here. She said she phoned you after school—but how's your wife doing? Leslie thought you might've gone to St. Vincent's on Monday night. She said you were gone when she came home."

"Please put my daughter on."

"Sure . . . I'll go get her. You must have been worried."

"Dr. Ullman—Janet—you've had my sixteen-year-old daughter in your house since Tuesday—am I right?—and she's missed two days of school while her mother's been in the ICU. Can you explain this to me? This doesn't sound like the therapy my daughter needs. This sounds like something I should be worried about."

Janet took a deep breath. "Yes. I can explain. Leslie had an appointment on Tuesday. That's why she wasn't in school. But if it's true she wasn't there today, you'll have to ask *her* what happened. I drove her to the parking lot and watched her go inside. I don't know what she did after I left."

"You said she had an appointment."

"You know, she might not want me to talk to you about that—and I *don't* think I'm your enemy in this situation. There are a few things you should know about your daughter, but you're going to have to ask her yourself. Hold on—"

There was a long silence, broken finally by a quieter, sleepier voice. "Dad, I don't want to come home yet."

"Tell me where you are. I'm picking you up."

"I'll take the bus," she said, and the line went dead. No answer when I called back.

I saw Janet Ullman, PA, through the windshield of her Volvo when she parked halfway down our driveway and held Leslie under the orange dome light, then kissed her good-bye on the forehead. Janet wore a green jacket over a maroon hospital shirt, and glasses with green rims that caught the light when she turned her head to follow Leslie across the wet lawn, not noticing our dining room window, where I stood waiting in the dark. Janet's cheeks seemed young enough, round and smooth enough, to belong to one of Leslie's friends.

Leslie slept in her own bed that night, and Teresa's white blood cell count was almost back to normal in the morning—I brought clothes in the afternoon and drove her home—but from then on Leslie had two households, and the old household was losing whatever hold it had left on her, nothing like the maroon Victorian on the East Side of Portland and the young, stethoscoped assistant who could divide her time and money between one guest and one Great Dane named Governor. There wasn't much I could do to keep Leslie in Windhill Heights. Not while her mother divided her daylight hours between the bed and the wicker chair. Not while her mother drew oxygen from a tank, measured her peak lung flow every hour, and nodded off with murder mysteries on her lap, the only books she could follow.

On the night when I carried Teresa to the Datsun for the last time, no one answered at Janet's house, so I drove to St. V's alone. In the waiting room I learned from a brochure that St. Vincent de Paul was a seventeenth-century French priest who founded the Order of the Lazarists. The brochure didn't explain who the Lazarists were, or why the hospital chose that saint and not some other.

I opened at ten, and at eleven fifteen Luis pushed through the shop door, bowed, and touched his toes. When he looked up from stretching and saw me dumping bike parts onto the workbench behind the counter, he unclipped his helmet and smiled.

"Working today?" I asked. Luis put in twenty hours a week on builds and repairs. It was a thirty-minute ride from Hillsboro, so I usually expected him when the weather was good, or whenever it wasn't raining.

He stepped behind the counter in his long-sleeved Olympic jersey and said, "You okay, man? It looks like you rode a tow truck to work this morning."

We walked out to the far corner of the parking lot, steaming in the cold air, and I told him about the horse.

"That's so fucked-up. How you going to get home?"

I was thinking I'd take a bus to the nearest rental lot in Hillsboro, or Aloha, but seeing Luis clack around the front of the truck in his cycling shoes, his thigh muscles taut like mine used to be, his biceps incongruously slender—seeing a nineteen-year-old who'd just started training when I met him a year earlier—I changed my mind. "Thought I'd ride," I said.

Luis gauged me to see if I was serious and then laughed. "To Beaverton?"

"Yeah. I own a bike shop, don't I? I'll take one of the used bikes. That Schwinn."

"The Schwinn's nice." He chuckled and plucked a tuft of horse-hair from the windshield with one of his full-finger gloves. He looked back at me, at my gut. "No whiplash?"

"What—you don't think I can ride twenty-five miles?" Luis had spent plenty of time staring at the two feet of shelf space where I still kept a few medals and trophies. He'd seen the clipping from a news-paper in Vermont. He'd seen the black-and-white photo Teresa took of me in the Pyrenees when I was in top condition, my hair still long.

"Of course, man. I've just never seen you on a bike."

We went back in the shop, and this time Alice got up from her towel behind the counter. She licked Luis's sweaty palm and tipped over sideways into his shins when he started rubbing her. "What about you?" he asked Alice. "You running behind him?"

"Alice is an old dog," I said. "She'll be fine here for one night."

"Okay, man. You're the boss."

Luis and I worked side by side all day, building new mountain bikes to restock Tour de France's holiday inventory for the fathers who would come in during the last five business days before Christ-mas. As my ad in the *Oregonian* announced, the Last Chance Win-ter Sale began the next day and ended on Thursday, the day before Christmas Eve.

Used to me not talking much, Luis put on the Rolling Stones and, as I was dumping out a second bike box, I remembered Leslie's first bicycle, the hybrid I put together when she was five and tall enough for a bike that would last her a while. One day Leslie had come into the shop with her mother. While Teresa and I talked, she picked at the thin rubber tire hairs on one of the boys' bikes. She moved between a BMX and a banana seat, fascinated by both, but bothered, I thought, that the boys' bike didn't have tassels on the handlebars or pink on the frame. Over Teresa's shoulder, I watched Leslie as she held the nubby grips and finger brakes on the BMX, as if they were the controls for a motorcycle that would sputter and come alive if she were to roll it from the angled fleet of men's bikes. It pleased me that she liked the Mongoose, because it was sturdier than the cheaply made girls' bikes, but I could tell she wanted something to match her dolls and jump ropes and white bears. In a moment of inspiration, after I was alone in the shop, I rolled both bikes behind the counter and started taking them apart. I swapped the horn and tasseled grips from the girls' candy-cane handlebars and slipped them onto the BMX handlebars. I swapped the boys' finger brakes for a freewheel that would brake when she pedaled backward. I peeled the flower stickers off the girls' frame and found some superglue. I went to the hardware store and bought hot pink spray paint. I thought for a while about the saddle and finally decided to toss out the banana seat, which wouldn't fit anyway. The result was a perfect crossbreed: a sturdy girls' bike that wouldn't rattle if you rode it across the grass in a park. Leslie fell in love with it on Christmas Day and was riding without training wheels before New Year's. Working side by side with Luis, I thought if I told her now that her first bike was to blame for her becoming a tomboy, that being a tomboy was why she chose to cut her hair short, that keeping her hair short made her less attractive to men, and that feeling less attractive to men might have had something to do with why she didn't feel so attracted to them—if I told her that, she would probably tell me to piss off.

After Luis finished the bike he was working on, he said, "I'm out of here. You want to ride with me halfway? Take Canyon Road through Hillsboro?"

"It's only four."

"So close early for once—you don't want to ride in the dark."

A woman came through the front door just then, talking on her cell phone, and I motioned for him to go without me. "Another time," I said.

"Okay, man. Have a good night."

I watched him change from a Tour de France shirt back into his racing jersey. Luis had charmed me the day he walked into the store with a clunky old Raleigh, a yard sale bike, and asked if he could test-ride a thirteen-hundred-dollar Cannondale hanging from a hook on the ceiling. After he returned the bike to the shop and took back his expired high school ID, I told him the way to get a racing bike like that would be to work in a bike shop and buy it straight from the factory. He came back twice before he asked me for a job.

"Luis," I said as he wheeled his Cannondale from behind the counter, "my daughter's flying in tonight. Maybe you could meet her tomorrow, come out to dinner with us."

He raised his chin and nodded, looking me in the eye. "Sure, man. Let me know."

I sold some helmets and gloves, changed clothes, and left at a quarter past five, shutting the door on the sound of Alice lapping up one of my beef soups. It was the first time she'd gotten off her towel all day. The second wind was gone.

I pedaled out onto Canyon Road and concentrated on the white line in the dark, breathing deep, pumping rotations as fast as my heartbeat. It started to rain when I got to the river valley by the community golf course. Cars sprayed past at sixty. Luis had ridden this way an hour before, when it was dry. I let myself roll on the gentle downslope, and when I got to the steep upslope I fought it with all my breath, as if Beaverton lay just over the hill, not twenty miles down the road.

I'd never ridden with so much flab on my chest—a gut that sagged over my thighs like a lawn-mower sack. My trachea burned, my temple dripped, my back didn't feel right. I crossed the median line as soon as I saw a U-Haul lot with its lights on. "We're closed," a man in a plaid shirt mouthed through the window, but I persuaded him to open the door and rent me a white van that said HAWAII on the side. Then I bummed a cigarette and drove off to meet my daughter. I didn't feel like turning around for Alice, driving back the way I came. I didn't want to be late. At least that much I could do right.

Her flight was early. I spotted her by the baggage carousel, by a white pillar, lying on the same army surplus duffel that she'd had for years. She seemed to be talking to the ceiling, gesturing to get her point across. Her hair was shaved short, its natural brown, and she'd worked off all the fat on her arms, which looked more muscular than I remembered them, flexing in her black tank top. She could have been on military leave except that she had on a pink bandanna that gave the impression she had womanly hair.

I stopped short of the pillar when I saw that she looked close to tears. I thought maybe it was Janet on the phone, that they'd had some sort of falling-out, so I went out the revolving doors and called from the curb, apologizing for being late even though I wasn't.

When she found me outside, it was as if she'd never been in higher spirits; as if nothing had ever been wrong between us. She shrugged off her green canvas bag, clapped her arms on my back, and kissed me on both cheeks, something she never did.

"First you weren't coming at all," I said. "Now you're greeting me like a Frenchman."

She forced a smile and hoisted the straps of the duffel over her neck and shoulder, hunching under its enormous bulk. "You've put on some weight!" she huffed.

"What's a little more?" I said.

On our way through the parking garage, I told her about the horse, and the gunshot, and the kneeling couple. The thought of the horse made her cover her mouth and gulp. "Fuck," she said. "The lady shot her own horse? What did you do?"

"What did I do? It was dead when I came back down the hill."

Leslie swung the bag off her hip and let it rest on the garage floor, breathing heavily. "No—I mean what did you say to the old couple?"

"Let me take that." I reached for the duffel straps, but she didn't let go. She bent her knees and slung it back over her shoulder.

"Did you apologize?" she asked. "Think if someone hit *our* one animal."

If someone hit Alice, it occurred to me, they might be doing us a favor, saving us some heartache.

We stopped by the U-Haul and Leslie dropped her bag below the stenciled palm tree and wave. "Hawaii," she said. "That's where you should move to get out of your prefab coffin. I hate that house."

As we spiraled out of the parking garage, she said she was hungry and I suggested Rose's. Rose's was where we had gone two years earlier when she visited, the Jewish diner with latkes and French pastries, our favorite when we lived out in Cornelius, when visits to Beaverton were a rare treat. Leslie would always order the same thing: strawberry blintzes and a slice of chocolate cake—two desserts, though Teresa felt that the ricotta in the blintzes brought them into the realm of dinner.

"Mmm...blintzes," said Leslie, eyes gleaming, "but Rose's is so fussy. I know where we can get blintzes—get off at Twelfth Street. This'll be great, I haven't been to the Roxy forever."

She directed me to downtown Portland, off Burnside to Stark Street, not seeming to realize that even I knew about the gay clubs, bars, and one-hour hotel rooms clustered on those angular blocks.

"*There's* a spot," she said, pointing to a parking space across the street where two men walked in tight black shirts.

"Leslie—Les—I don't want bar food."

"It's a diner, Dad. Diners are all the same, except some have blintzes."

"Rose's has sentimental value."

"So does the Roxy. Just park, okay?"

She led me into a smoky room that looked enough like a bar to me. We sat down at a booth, and a large-breasted, black-nailed woman in a black T-shirt brought us water and menus.

Now seemed like a good time to bring up Alice. Maybe after our food came.

"So...," said Leslie, stabbing a straw into her amber cup with a smile that looked like something she'd practiced in the airplane restroom. "I want to spend more time with you this visit. Let's do things together. Maybe—*what?*"

"I'm just wondering," I said, "if that's you talking, or some New York therapist."

She leaned back against the booth. "Dad, I don't even have a therapist anymore—why are you looking at me like that?"

Her phone whistled a Boy Scout marching song, and a look of dismay passed over her face before she saw who it was. "Janet," she said, reading my face for a reaction. "Order some blintzes, please, and a slice of black forest. I'll be back in a minute."

Thirty minutes later her strawberry blintzes and my overdone bacon burger were breathing off all their heat while I stared at a booth of young women in bowling and gas station shirts, all with short hair that feathered over their cheeks like sideburns, all with mugs of hot chocolate topped with whipped cream. At first I thought they were as old as the waitress—two kept extra cigarettes behind their ears, which reminded me of some French card players I used to know—

but when I made out what they were saying, I realized they were talking about one of their teachers. One kept insisting Ms. Hamilton was a dyke. The others thought it was funny, but kept coming up with reasons why she was just middle-aged and sexless.

I guess I stared too hard, because at one point the two with their backs to me turned and looked in my direction. After that, they spoke more quietly, as if I were going to stand in front of their booth, red-faced, and announce that Ms. Hamilton was my wife.

"I used to be one of them," said Leslie, patting my shoulder as she took her seat. "This is where we came when everyone else went to homecoming." Then she raised her knife and fork over her blintzes and grinned so widely, so childishly unaware of how cold the food was, that I couldn't help grinning with her. I wanted to tell her something, but all that came to mind was Alice, and I knew she'd hate me for what I had to say.

"You're letting your burger get cold," she said.

As I picked up the burger, I watched over her shoulder. Bellies full of hot chocolate, the sideburned girls had slipped off their shoes, drawn their socked feet onto the leather benches, and wrapped their arms around their knees. There was nothing sexual in how they paired off and leaned against each other, shoulder to shoulder. It was the sort of tenderness that Leslie had shown Teresa—I saw them sitting that way on Leslie's bed, spelling words aloud from a notebook-torn list—before friends introduced her to hand mirrors, Chap Stick, and everything else.

At the house, Leslie carried her duffel down to her old bedroom and shouted good night up the stairs, not a word about the dog. I took a shower, went down to the den, and watched some television before drifting off on the foldout couch. I thought it was the TV shouting when I woke up, some minutes or hours later, but I turned off the TV and heard Leslie in the dark.

She was cursing somebody in her room, and for a split second I believed it was me; that we'd just had one of our fights about the color of her hair, or the girlfriends she wasn't allowed to see, but did see, after they brought psychedelic mushrooms to our house for a sleepover. I heard just a few words clearly—"Don't tell me that. Don't give me that shit." Then there was a plastic clack, as if she'd thrown a Barbie at the drywall, and silence, the empty-house sounds I was used to. I started to drift off again, but a door opened and bare feet whispered through the den, up the stairs, across the kitchen floor, and deep into other rooms. I woke with Leslie standing over me in her sweatpants and tank top. "I can't find Alice," she said. "Did she die, Dad? Did you not call me?"

I rolled over on my back and said in a calm voice that Alice was at the shop, I'd bring her home tomorrow night. Leslie sat at the foot of the bed and sighed with relief. It seemed awful to tell her that Alice was fine and then to tell her tomorrow that Alice had cancer. "You know, though," I began, "she's not going to live forever."

"Why are you sleeping down here?"

"I always sleep down here."

"It's weird, Dad. Good night." She patted the mattress and I saw her white teeth in the dark before she walked down the hallway.

I called after her: "Who told you to be so nice to me all of a sudden?"

She laughed and her door closed without an answer.

I was pulling out of the driveway in the morning, in the U-Haul, when Leslie came running out with her black leather boots untied, swinging a shoulder bag. She flung open the passenger door and jumped in next to me. "Can you take me to Hawthorne?"

Hawthorne Street was where Janet lived, on the East Side. I had to be at the shop at nine. "Last Chance Sale begins today," I said, still idling in the driveway. "I thought you were going to sleep in."

She just raised an eyebrow, ready to be annoyed.

"Sure," I said. "I'll take you."

When we got to the maroon Victorian, which I'd been to once before, but had never set foot inside, Leslie brightened for a moment and thanked me for driving her. She already had the door open with her foot hanging out when she turned and asked, "Are you sure you don't want to come in for a minute, say hello?"

"I'm going to be late if I don't leave now."

Sighing, she ran her hand over her stubbly scalp and down the back of her neck. "Dad, you can't still hate Janet. You don't even know her."

"Maybe another time."

"Okay"—she unclipped her seat belt, making an effort to smile— "go sell lots of bikes. Last chance!"

She seemed to want me to surrender unequivocally, as if all my frustrations with Janet and Janet's way of being and Janet's buzzing around our family had never happened; as if I could forget everything up until the point when Leslie disappeared to New York, leaving behind a hand-scrawled letter that said *I* should pay for her to take classes if *I* was going to be her father. "Leslie," I said as she got out and stood with her shoulder bag. "I've been meaning to tell you—about Alice."

She climbed back up on the seat and let the door swing shut.

"She can hardly walk." I waited for Leslie to say something, but she let me go on. "You come to a point, I think, when you have to wonder whether a dog's life is what it should be."

"Of course she can't walk well. She's old. She's got arthritis."

"There's a tumor on her leg."

Leslie looked down at the radio knobs and gulped the way she had in the parking garage when I told her about the Datsun. "I didn't know that."

"You knew she wasn't going to live forever."

"Of course . . . but are you saying you want to put her to sleep be-cause—that's what you're saying isn't it?—because she's not happy being alive or because you're sick of cleaning up after her?"

"She's not enjoying life as much as she used to."

"Dad, if we went by that, who *wouldn't* we put to sleep? Mom wasn't exactly 'enjoying' life."

"No, she wasn't. But Alice is a dog."

Leslie had words she wanted to say but swallowed them, hating to argue after the shakiness in her voice made her weak. "Do whatever you want," she said, and slammed the door after her. Like old times.

After Teresa's cremation, Leslie refused to come to the house at all. I got letters from Beaverton High School saying she'd stopped attending, and she called me every once in a while, usually to ask for money, which I gave her. Then, one spring day, while I was at work, one more resident departed from Windhill Heights, and she took the dog with her.

I yelled Alice's name at the fork of Windhill Court and Windhill Way, thinking she must have escaped from the backyard, but then I noticed that her bowls, leash, and cedar bedding were gone also. Leslie had taken her to live with Janet's Great Dane in Portland, and I wasn't in the mood to make a fuss. Alice didn't belong to me any-way. Neither did Leslie, since she was almost eighteen.

The next time I saw Alice was on a warm evening near the end of the summer. I hadn't heard from Leslie for a couple of weeks, so I drove to Hawthorne and knocked on Janet's door. Another woman answered—this one a full-fledged doctor, according to her alligator-clipped ID—and described herself as Janet's partner. Janet patted the woman on her shoulder and stepped onto the porch to speak with me alone.

"You didn't get a letter?" she asked. Under the green-rimmed glasses, her face looked older than I remembered it. She stood on the welcome mat in her bare feet.

"I got one from her guidance counselor," I said, "if that's what you mean."

"Les was going to write you a letter before she left for New York."

"New York?" I leaned against the maroon porch column by the stairs. Janet scrutinized me as I took in this news.

"Three days ago, by train. I told her you'd be unhappy—that I'd be unhappy—but she's not in a reasoning state. She just wants to leave everything behind, which is too bad—it's not the way to mourn."

"You didn't even bother calling me?" I felt like punching the door-jamb next to her head.

"I didn't call you, Gene, because you've only been rude to me on the phone." Janet slipped her bare feet into a pair of dirty running shoes near the door. "Anyway, it's good you're here—we need to talk about your dog. She's out back with Governor."

Alice rode up front with me on the way home, droopy-eyed and morose, as if I'd interrupted her summer vacation. The next day after work, as Janet had warned me she would, Alice whimpered by the front door, expecting an evening walk. I grabbed her collar to pull her away, pleading with her to give me some peace, and that was when I found Leslie's letter. It was folded into a four-inch white ribbon and Scotch-taped under the buckle. As I cut it free with my pocketknife it expanded like an accordion.

Dad:

I didn't have time to go to the post office and I never even knew our address at the new house, so I hope you get this when Janet drives Alice back home. I should almost be in New York by then. I have a friend I can live with. She says she can help me find a job.

I need a change. But really what I need is to get as far away from you and that house as I can because ever since mom got sick you've been taking your anger out on me and now that mom is gone I don't want to be around you. You never let things drop. And I'll never forget what you said about my sexuality (I know you hate that word because it sounds like something Janet would say), I'll never forget how you treated my friends and Janet like shit. Like they weren't even human. And I'm not going to forget how you kicked my door in and told me I had to go to school when I was still recovering from my abortion that you want to pretend never happened, because if you admitted it happened you would have to admit that Janet helped me when mom couldn't and that my life isn't so easy either. Janet is the nicest woman I've ever met beside mom. She taught me more about myself than anyone else ever could. When I get settled and get a job, I'm going to take classes and get my GED and maybe take some college classes if I can do that while I'm working. Can you help me, dad? You should, because I know you're in debt, but you won't be forever, and the shop makes more money than you need for living all by yourself. If you want to be my father, you should at least support my education. I hope you don't mind keeping Alice. I can't. Janet and I have been taking her on walks, and it's making her happier. She shouldn't have to live like she's sick just because the rest of us have been living like that. I have to go now to catch my train.

Bye,
Leslie

When I unlocked Tour de France, the warm shop air hit me like the sulfur smell of a pulp mill. I'd cleaned up plenty of Alice's diarrhea over the years and had gotten fairly used to the weekly task of wiping the kitchen floor with crumpled newspaper, then mopping, then mopping again, but this was the shop, and overnight Alice had been incontinent more than once. I stepped over a pool on the carpet by the bike racks and walked right into another behind the counter on my way to get a rag.

Alice just watched me from her towel, alarmed enough by my cursing to lift her head from her paws, but not afraid or ashamed, as she would have been when she was younger. The navy blue towel beneath her, her gray jowls, and her calm, dignified stare all looked royal, untouchable. I wanted her to be afraid of me. I wanted her ashamed. I wiped the puddle near the bike racks and carried the grease rags right up to her nostrils and made her smell them like a bad puppy until she squinted and tilted her head down to her chest.

"Goddamn parasite," I said.

Luis showed up five minutes after nine and helped me clean up the rest of the mess with some window cleaner and grease solvent. "I had a German shepherd," he said, as he scrubbed the carpet. "That dog, he *always* took a shit when I climbed out the window to see my girlfriend. Every fucking time. They're not so stupid. They know things you don't think they know."

There were more customers that morning than I expected. The whole parking lot filled up at one point, and I told Luis I'd give him a commission if he left the bike he was building and made some sales.

But nobody was buying. They'd make one round of the store and walk right out. It wasn't until I took a smoke break and came back in that I figured out why: The store still smelled faintly like Alice's accident. I told Luis, and he pedaled to the supermarket for some rug shampoo, which filled the store with a chemical perfume.

Alice had spent most of the morning lying stiff on her towel, looking up now and then to watch from behind the counter—guiltily, I thought—but when a father walked in with his ten-year-old twins, both blond girls, she got on her feet and hobbled over to them. The twins hid behind their dad at first, then eased out, as Luis pointed to parts and listed specifications as fast as he could. Alice lay on the floor, and the girls squatted next to her, stroking her belly with their palms, in awe of her, as if they'd found a pygmy stallion.

When the girls measured for matching bikes were gone, Alice didn't go back behind the counter. Her joints were loose now, so she walked up to other customers, blessed their hands with her tongue, then kept walking around the store, pacing long, slow laps around the island of bike racks, grinning and pushing forward like a crippled old greyhound who still wanted to race. Luis thought it was hilarious. He took a red, flowery ribbon off one of the display bikes in the window and fixed it around her neck. The next customers who came in seemed to think she was part of the sale—a chocolate Lab mascot, trotting the Tour de France.

It wasn't long until she lost whatever had inspired her and passed out on her towel, but it was as if she'd christened the sale with champagne and balloons. Customer after customer walked out with a shiny new bicycle.

Luis, I noticed, had brought a backpack to the shop, and it made me curious because he never carried anything that would slow him down. While he talked to a young couple, I flipped open the main pouch, which was already unzipped. Inside lay a white, collared shirt and a pair of pleated slacks. Restaurant clothes. I dialed Leslie on the shop phone, but she didn't answer. I dialed again a half hour later and left a message: I would appreciate it if she would call me. At five o'clock, an hour before closing, I dialed one more time and said I was sorry—sorry we'd argued earlier. Still no answer, still no call back. At closing, Luis asked me what the plan was.

"Looks like we're not going out tonight," I said. "Maybe later in the week."

He nodded as if it was the answer he'd expected and gathered up the trash bags. When he got back from the Dumpster, he walked from the door to the register and leaned on his hands against the counter, just as he had the first day he'd come into the shop, as if he were going to ask me for another test ride.

"What's on your mind?" I asked, adding up the day's cash.

"There's a big race at Alpenrose," he said. "On the track. In two weeks."

"You should enter. I'm sure you're good by now."

"I was wondering," he said, "if you could sponsor me. If, you know, the shop could sponsor me."

I smiled and looked up from a stack of ten-dollar bills. "You mean so you'd have a jersey that says 'Tour de France' on it?"

"I'm serious," he said. "There's an entrance fee and—" He looked down at the shop rag hanging out of his pocket and used it to wipe grease off his hands.

"And what?"

"And it's on the velodrome, so I need a fixed gear and some new tires."

"Amateur class?"

"Men's intermediate. Eighteen to twenty-five."

"I'll think about it," I said. And I would think about it. More than he realized.

"Thanks," he said. "I'm moving out of my parents' house. I have to pay first and last month's rent."

On the drive home I stopped at a store on Canyon Road that advertised cigarettes by the carton. As I waited for the red-vested man to ring up my Virginia Slims, I was calculating how many days four cartons would last me. One row of one pack per day. Two rows per pack. Twenty packs per carton. Four cartons. The answer was coming to me when the red-vested man spoke. He looked about my age, maybe a little older, but wider and softer than me under his vest. More gray hairs. He took my twenty-dollar bills and said, "Nothing for you today?" Then he winked a gray blue eye, as if to say that he had a wife, too, and knew how it was, stopping by the store after work to pick up her Virginia Slims.

The assumption that Virginia Slims were *women's* cigarettes always surprised me. They were the only cigarettes I'd ever smoked; they were the cigarettes I found on the shelf in the garage. After Teresa's last carton was empty, I tried other brands, but none of the others had the right mixture of tar and nicotine and pencil shavings—whatever it was in the smoke that smelled so miraculous when I brought it into the den from the garage, one summer night after Teresa and Leslie were gone. Cigarette vendors had asked before, but something in this man's delivery—as if our wives dragged behind us like sandbags—something made me change my answer. I usually said, "No, I've got plenty of my own cigarettes at home." This time I looked the vendor in the eye and said, "My wife died seven years ago. These are for me."

When I got to the van, Alice was barking. I'd put her in the cargo area, which didn't have any windows, and she must have thought I'd forgotten her in there. I rolled open the side door and let her out to relieve herself, but she just sniffed her way to the middle of a handicapped spot and sat, grinning at me in her red bow. If I looked close enough I could see the sickly ribs under her fur, the dangerous lack of flesh on her whole body, the milkiness in her eyes. Even so, the bow made her look handsome, almost young. I led her to the passenger door and lifted her up, so she could lie near my feet and not be afraid.

Leslie's metallic green phone lay on the dining room table, but Leslie hadn't come home yet. As I boiled water for dinner, the phone started to whistle its Boy Scout march. I waited a minute for it to stop, not wanting to fool with it without Leslie's permission, but then two minutes later it started whistling the same out-of-tune notes again, so I picked it up to find the power button. The whistling stopped when I unfolded it. The screen read: *JACK.*

"There you are," a man's voice said. "Can we talk? Les? Hello?" He sounded hurt, strung out, like Gabe, the only significant other of hers I'd ever met. Was this the person giving her shit? A boyfriend? I clapped the phone shut, but it didn't shut right. The half with the screen slipped sideways, crooked on its hinge.

The phone was broken—broken from when Leslie had thrown it against the wall—and I knew immediately why she'd left it on the dining room table: She wanted me to fix it.

Over the loose joint there was a piece of plastic missing. Snapped off. I went down to Leslie's room, where I thought I'd find it, and noticed a nick in the drywall above her bed. I crawled across the bedclothes and looked under her pillows between the mattress and the wall. If I found the piece and superglued the joint, she would be grateful. For a while, anyway, she'd show me some kindness, some uncontrived kindness. And maybe things were ready to cool down between us now that she had this man in her life—this poor Jack, who obviously missed her—even if he had done something to make her throw the phone. Maybe if I fixed it, it would help her fix things with him.

As I crawled on one hand and pulled back the comforter with the other, I heard a tiny snap in my left fist, like a loose hair pulled to its breaking point. I raised the phone, unfolded it, and looked into the hole below the loose swivel joint. Inside, a ribbon of plastic thin as a spoke had split in two, baring three copper strips: the connection between the microphone and the speaker; the connection between the digital display and the number pad; the connection between the phone's mind and the phone's body.

I felt like throwing the thing against the wall myself, but then I heard the tick-tick... tick-tick... of untrimmed paws on the stairs. Alice had heard me and was coming down to smell her owner, the grown woman who had slept on the bed where I sat. When she reached the doorway, she stared at me, meek as a lamb in her red bow.

"Let me see that leg," I said. "You look like you've got another year in you."

I knelt beside her and pinched the tumor, and the more I looked at it, the more it looked like something that didn't belong on her, something that could be burned off and forgotten if it hadn't already infected her.

I could fix Alice.

I picked her up, carried her into the garage, and cleared a space for her on the workbench beside the vise. She lay docile on her side, as if she'd been expecting me to take her there. After cutting back some of the hair with my scissors, I let her down on the floor of the garage and went to get my X-Acto blades and some of Teresa's codeine. The margin, I remembered. Clear a margin.

Leslie came home at ten o'clock, while I was lying on the foldout couch, watching a carpentry rerun. I heard her up in the kitchen, where I'd left Alice on her towel. "What happened to *you?*" she asked in her dog-babying voice. "You look so *slee-py.* So *skin-ny.* You're just skin and bones—*aren't you?*"

"Dad?" she called from the top of the stairs, without a trace of cuteness, "can you tell me why Alice has bloody gauze on her leg? Dad?" When I didn't answer right away, she started down the stairs. She took each step slowly and heavily. She had Alice in her arms.

"Did you think I'd pay a vet to do that?"

"Do what?" She stood beside me with her hips thrust forward to keep her balance, under Alice, and watched the muted TV—an engine oil commercial. I wondered how long she could stand that way.

"I cut it off."

"Jesus, Dad—you cut off the tumor?" She dropped Alice onto the end of the mattress, as gently as she could, and sat down beside her. The dome of Alice's skull pressed against my calf.

"She's just sedated," I said. "I gave her some of your mother's codeine."

"You gave her *Mom's* codeine?"

I sighed. "So this morning you were mad at me because I wanted to put her to sleep. Now you're going to be mad at me because I tried to save her."

"Dad, you cut open our dog. What am I supposed to say?"

"I think I got it all. I thought you'd be happy. I'm sorry."

"No, Dad—thank you for trying to help her—I mean I don't know if—"

"If what?"

"I was going to tell you—"

"What?"

"You're right. She's *not* going to live forever."

"She could live another year."

"She looks like a skeleton."

"At least another six months."

"But what if she doesn't? What if she dies while I'm in New York? I want to be here if she's going to die. I don't want to hear about it over the phone."

"So what do you want to do?"

She didn't answer. I changed the channel to a local weather report. A few snowflakes, big white asterisks, bloomed on the map of the Willamette Valley. Snowfall on the coastal ridges. Some farther east, by Hagg Lake, where the three of us used to ride a lap around the reservoir—we'd start at the dam, go up the steep hill, through the forest, past the boat ramps, around the inlets on the far side, then back down again to the dam.

"I broke your cell phone," I said.

"That's all right. It was already broken."

"Who's this guy Jack?"

She sighed and raised her eyebrows at once. "Jack . . . is the last man I'll ever date. A persistent jerk."

She stood up to leave, and I flipped channels, hoping she'd say something more, or else climb the stairs. But as the four sports channels flickered past, I caught a glimpse of women running with bicycles on their shoulders down a muddy switchback, a Basque cyclo-cross race. The angle changed to a cameraman standing next to a long puddle and a low stone wall. Lead runners hopped over the wall, thrashed through the puddle, hefted their bicycles onto the paved road, and swung their legs over the top tubes, hardly breaking stride. The rest of the pack came, and the camera panned to where cyclist after cyclist leaped onto her saddle and wobbled until she straightened out and pumped faster and faster into the distance.

Leslie sat down to watch, and out of the corner of my eye I could see her chin and nose and forehead lit up by Spanish sunlight and the canary yellow jerseys, gliding around asphalt curves, down, down, around, through the foothills of the Pyrenees. Her eyes seemed to glow with admiration. Did she know I'd ridden that same road myself? Was she thinking of the races I medaled in before she was born?

"Well," I said, after the first woman crossed the finish line, "if he was a jerk, I'm glad you got rid of him."

"Thanks." Leslie patted Alice's hip and stood up again. "Let's wait until after Christmas."

The next evening, when I got back to Beaverton, we went shopping together at Washington Square Mall. We bought treats for Alice, and I bought Leslie a new phone with a camera lens. She tried to persuade me to buy one for myself—my old cell was too big, she said—but I told her it was fine, and I'd replace it when it broke, if it couldn't be fixed. She led me through men's clothing in the department stores and showed me what I should wear. On Wednesday she went with me to buy a new truck, a Toyota.

On Thursday, the last day of the sale, we went out to dinner with Luis, and after I told him he had a sponsor, he described winning the Alpenrose race so passionately, so vividly, that it seemed like he'd already done it. All week long Leslie made regular trips to Janet's house, and she spent the evening there on Christmas Day, with Janet and her new partner.

On the twenty-seventh, the last day before her morning flight back to New York, I thought Leslie had forgotten all about Alice, leaving the problem in my hands. She let Alice sleep in her bedroom that night, toasting beside the space heater, and said good night without acknowledging that neither of us had called the vet while we had a chance.

She shook me awake at six o'clock, whispering, "Dad, get up. I want you to come with me."

"Where are we going?"

"Janet's going to do what she did for Governor. Just get dressed."

When we walked outside in the dark, the new Toyota was already idling in the driveway, exhaust pluming across the taillights, Alice on the front seat. It made me nervous to let Leslie drive—she hadn't even known how when she left for New York—but she got us there in one piece, to a parking spot near the maroon Victorian. Alice panted and hobbled in front of us up to the porch, still limping a bit on her bandaged leg. I carried her up the stairs.

Janet greeted us at the door in her hospital scrubs and black tennis shoes, ready for work. She nodded to me, smiling professionally, and hardly said a word as she led us into her kitchen, which resembled an operating room with its stainless steel countertops and white walls. Two wooden folding chairs waited for us, but Leslie led Alice to the center of the kitchen, made her lie on the floor, and sat cross-legged next to her. Janet snapped on latex gloves. "So, you two have made up your mind?" she asked. "You're sure you want to do this." Her voice was gentle, like a pediatrician's.

Leslie leaned back on her hands and looked up, reading me. Alice wasn't ready to die. I saw that. Leslie saw that. But she also saw that it wasn't a matter of convenience or inconvenience. She saw, I hoped, what I hadn't wanted to tell her: that I didn't want to watch another slow decline.

I nodded to Janet.

"You have a choice. The drug that will put her to sleep is an anesthetic. A barbiturate. It won't hurt her. I'll inject it in her leg, and after about a minute her heart will stop. I can give her that right away, or we can start with a sedative. The sedative will make her fall asleep first." She looked at her wristwatch, probably calculating whether she could make it to work on time.

"The sedative," said Leslie. "That sounds more humane."

Alice, oblivious of everything except the gathering of warm bodies around her, looked happy to have her ears stroked. Her tail swept back and forth across the floor.

"Okay, so here's what I did last year, for Governor—I'll tell you now so we don't have to talk about it later. Alice will fall asleep, but when I give her the final injection, she probably won't close her eyes. They might twitch a bit. And then, just like with a person, there's the chance she'll have what's called an 'agonal gasp.' It might look like she's breathing, but she won't actually feel anything. It's just muscle spasms. Okay?"

We watched Janet work. First she used a pair of surgical scissors to cut away some hair below the white bandage, just above the knob of Alice's leg joint. Then she filled a bowl with soapy warm water and used a pink disposable razor to shave a patch of skin. She searched for a vein, a pulse, then took a vial and a syringe from the refrigerator. She filled the syringe, found the vein again, and slowly injected the clear liquid. Alice closed her mouth for a moment, but then started panting again, excited by our attention and Leslie's ear rubbing.

"Ten minutes," said Janet, getting to her feet. "I'll leave you two alone with her. You probably have so many memories."

I knew she felt she had to leave because of me. She was suspicious of me, that I might turn on her while she was doing us this favor. "You don't have to leave," I said. "You can stay."

She hesitated for a moment, and then, as if figuring out what a professional veterinarian would do, sat in the other chair, the one beside me, and crossed her legs. Nobody seemed to know what to say. I'd thought Leslie would be crying, but she wasn't. She stroked and stroked.

Alice closed her mouth now and then. Her tail swept slower.

"Did you read that article in the *Oregonian*?" I asked Janet. "The one about the golden retrievers they trained to smell lung cancer on people's breath?"

"No—no, I didn't actually." She looked down at Leslie, who didn't seem to mind that we were talking. "But that's amazing. They're pretty accurate?"

I told her everything I'd read. The 98 percent accuracy. The number of patients they tried it on. The ways they thought it might be useful. I told her what experts said. I described the photograph. I told her things I didn't know I remembered. And she listened, looking back and forth between me and Alice, who was closing her eyes now, breathing through her nose.

"That's . . . amazing." She smiled at me, and it had nothing to do with the article, or Alice. It was, in the best way, an unprofessional smile.

"Thank you for doing this, Janet. You've been so kind to my daughter over the years."

Leslie curled over Alice and began crying.

Janet stood up from her chair, squatted, and readied the second injection, squirting a thin stream on the floor. Alice was completely asleep. After the syringe was empty, we waited again, this time in silence. Janet sat on the floor beside Leslie and took off her gloves. Their elbows touched as they stroked the deep fur around Alice's neck, and when the agonal gasps came—quick hacks, deep in her throat, like a soul shimmying out between her sharp teeth—Leslie turned and put her arms around Janet and held her face against Janet's chest.

Hunched forward in my chair, my elbows on my knees, my face in my hands, I felt that I was the one who should be leaving the room. But I stayed and watched them embrace, and when I teared up a bit myself, it wasn't because of Alice—though I did love her like a family member and would miss her—it was because of Leslie; because she looked—her head shaved and uncovered—like a tall, tanned boy Teresa and I saw in Barcelona, on the wharf, before we'd even thought of having children. In his swimsuit and goggles the boy brushed past Teresa and dove off the end of a dock. He and his friends were diving for what looked like medals or gold coins that somebody had dropped there, twenty or thirty feet underwater, and when the two of us looked down from the dock, the other boys were coming up for air, but he was still deep below, rising toward us, his swimsuit a blur of white under the blue water. A beautiful boy.

At the airport Leslie gave me kisses on both my cheeks, thanked me for talking with Janet, and said she might visit over the summer. "But you should move," she said. "You should drive around in your new truck and find a place that you like. And call me when you do."

I left her realizing I wasn't going to make it to the bike shop in time. I drove home, dug a deep, round hole by our back fence, and laid Alice in it. As I looked at her curled in the shadowed soil that matched the color of her fur, I felt there should be some ceremony, but I found nothing to say and began shoveling dirt over her. The truth was that dogs should be dogs, should die like dogs and be buried like dogs. A dog could be in the family, but wasn't family. A dog was a reservoir for whatever venom and hunger and regret pass, or don't pass, between members of a family.

After the hole was filled, I unhooked my Peugeot from the wall of the garage. The tires were flat and the rubber had dried and cracked like mud along the rims, so I took the tires off the used Schwinn, swapped them, and slipped in new inner tubes. When I got to the entrance of Windhill Heights, across from the brick church, I was already choking and breathless. It was two miles downhill from there, past St. V's, then up and down on Barnes Road, flat along Highway 26, rolling after Exit 57. I didn't push myself. There was plenty of time and a high gray sky overhead. Pump followed pump followed pump. My back felt fine.

JEDEDIAH BERRY

University of Massachusetts, Amherst

INHERITANCE

At first they didn't talk about it, the beast Greg brought with him to the Saturday night poker game. He tugged the leashed thing down the basement steps and it sat cross-legged in a corner, muzzled, but more sad than mean. Greg said, "It'll stay right there, don't worry about it." And they tried not to, but it was a worrisome beast, its snout long and searching, head furry with woolly clumps around the ears, cloven hooves at the ends of its lean legs. Even harder to ignore were the almost human parts—the navel visible through wiry hair, the hairless brown nipples, eyes with something like a soul behind them. The beast perked its ears while Abe shuffled and dealt the cards.

It was Phil who finally said, "You think it wants a drink?"

"Hell, it might," Greg said, so off came the muzzle, off the cap from another beer, and Phil thrust the bottle into the beast's big-knuckled hand. It held the bottle up to the light, squinting at the brown glass. Phil showed it what to do—"Here, lift and swallow, partner, lift and swallow"—and it tried with teeth and tongue to get at the liquid inside, to hold the bottle's mouth with its bullish lips. Most of the beer spilled foaming onto its chest.

Abe, from the card table, said, "Christ, get the thing a mug and ante up."

So they sat down and played the next hand. But the beast, encouraged by all the attention maybe, stood and started to explore the basement, its hooves clacking against the slab. It had a dank smell about it, like moldering leaves, strong enough to overpower the smoke from Phil's cigarettes, Abe's cigars. It was taller than any of the men by a foot or more, and there were signs in its ragged fur they did not care to read: bare spots, and rings around wrists and ankles worn bald and red.

It found Abe's model ships. These were arrayed on shelves sponge-painted blue to simulate ocean waters. The ships were delicate constructions of thin polished wood, with thread for rigging and real cloth sails. Each had taken Abe a month to build, and there were nine of them, one for each month since Corey left him. The beast picked one up and blew on its sails. It was the *Bonne Homme Richard.*

Abe set down his cards and prepared to say something, but the beast got bored and carefully set the ship back on its custom-made stand. Then it ambled over to the table, as though wanting a closer look at the game.

It grabbed Greg's beer bottle and poured the contents straight down its throat without spilling a drop, set it down empty.

"Learns quick," Phil said.

The beast snorted and shook its head like it was in on the joke, and Greg thought, okay, maybe this *will* work.

Lilith was still up when he got home that night—Greg could see her through the front window. A black-and-white movie was on television, and in that light the living room looked black-and-white, too, with Lilith the perfect celluloid wife, her nightgown luminous, her pinned-up nighttime hair an illusion of elegance.

She would want to know how things had gone. It had been her idea to bring the beast to the poker game, "to socialize him," she had said. And that was when Greg noticed she called it "him." He had felt responsible for the beast the moment he saw it. But it was Lilith who took the beast into the backyard that first day and washed it, not with the hose, but with shampoo and warm water from a bucket. Lilith who had made a bed of old blankets in the garage, who peeked in on the beast while it slept. Greg had agreed to take it to Abe's, not because he thought getting the beast out of the house would be good for it, but because he thought it would be good for her.

They went in and the beast waited beside him while he took off his jacket. It watched each of his movements, making Greg more aware of them, too: down off the shoulders, left arm out, right arm out.

Lilith came from the living room and said, "Oh, god, he's bleeding."

She took the beast by the arm and led it toward the bathroom. Greg followed. When she switched on the light he saw the dark patch below the beast's right ear, remembered how it had bumped its head getting into the car. The blood had matted the fur down to its shoulder and was dripping onto the linoleum in red coins.

Lilith whispered consolingly as she searched for the wound with her fingers, but the beast didn't seem to know it was hurt. She opened the cabinet beneath the sink and found peroxide, cotton balls, scissors.

"Head wounds just bleed a lot," Greg said, "even small ones."

She didn't say anything, and there wasn't space for all three of them in the bathroom, so he went to the kitchen for paper towels to clean out the car. He couldn't find any. He filled a bowl with water, took the sponge from the sink, and went outside.

Only a little blood was smeared on the backseat, but Greg took his time cleaning it up. A light was on in the house across the street. He saw Mrs. Heck peering at him, her curled silver hair hovering at the edge of the lace curtains. Her husband, Bill Heck, dead fifteen years now, had been a friend of his father's, had fought with him in the war, and Greg remembered her at their house some Sundays, seated in a corner with a pair of scissors, carefully cutting coupons from the newspaper—*their* newspaper—and stuffing them into her purse. Greg had almost expected to see her at his father's wake the week before, sitting in the back row, cutting coupons. But she hadn't come to the wake.

Greg closed the car door so that the interior light went out—now he was invisible. He whispered, "Your move, Heck." The woman emerged from behind the curtains, realized she'd been caught, and quickly withdrew. A moment later her light went out. Greg got out of the car and poured the water onto the lawn.

Back inside, he could hear Lilith's voice coming from the garage. She wasn't singing, but the words had a lullaby quality.

He sat down and watched the movie while he waited. A pair of cops had just stepped out of their car in front of a big house on a hill. The house looked like his father's, not because of the hill but because of the old slate roof, the big porch, the broad woods behind it. The cops were business as usual as they climbed the porch steps and rang the doorbell, but the music suggested trouble.

Lilith came in and Greg said, "It went well tonight."

"I don't want a divorce," she said.

Five years together and neither of them had mentioned the possibility, so Greg said, "That's good."

Her hair was down, messier without the pins. He had no idea what she was thinking. Then she came across the room and straddled him where he sat, blocking his view of the television. She kissed him very seriously. The music on the television reached a crescendo and one of the cops said, "Oh, for the love of god," and the other said, "Get ahold of yourself, son," and when Greg kissed his wife he smelled in her hair that faint rotting-leaves scent beneath the sweetness of her shampoo.

Phil's son Gordon raised his hand in Greg's third-period history class and asked, without waiting to be called upon, if the monster was coming to school for Halloween.

Gordon's question came out of nowhere; they were talking about the bombing of Hiroshima. But Greg had expected the question, not just because Phil would have told his family what happened on poker night, but because all day Sunday the neighborhood kids rode their bikes back and forth in front of the house, hoping for a glimpse of their new lodger. And Lilith, not wanting to disappoint, dressed the beast in a pair of faded blue overalls and took it outside, even let some of them touch its fur. ·

Gordon went on, "I was just thinking, it's like it's already got a costume."

Greg rolled the chalk slowly between his fingers. "We'll have to see," he said.

On Thursday, skeletons, witches, and mummies poked their heads into Greg's classroom. Gordon was dressed as the beast itself, with pointed ears on top of his head and false hooves over his shoes. But Greg, himself costumeless, said, "Sorry, kids. It got a bad cold and couldn't make it."

Greg looked sick, too. He hadn't been sleeping well, he needed a haircut. He took his break in the teachers' lounge and Meredith, the assistant principal, pulled him aside. "Greg," she said, "you never took any time off when your father was ill."

It was true he hadn't missed any classes, but he'd thought that was a good thing. There had been only those long nights beside the hospital bed while the morphine doses were rising, Lyle muttering commandments regarding the upkeep of his lawn, hedges, and roof gutters. His father's face had been whiskered for the first time Greg could remember, and when he saw him again in the casket, he wondered who had shaved him, whether they had used warm water or cold.

Meredith said, "You could take some time now if you need it, Greg. It's just that some of the parents are concerned. I heard that you spent a week and a half on the Holocaust. The World War Two unit's only supposed to be a week long."

"A week didn't seem like enough time," Greg said.

"It isn't, but you know they get this stuff again in high school."

He was thumbing the school's copy of the local newspaper. Meredith looked at it and said, "Have you seen the letter to the editor yet?"

Greg turned the page and read aloud, his voice making the statement into a question: "Devious elements springing up around this town like mushrooms overnight?"

The author was anonymous.

"It's just one person," Meredith said. But as she left, Greg noticed a few of his colleagues, silent in their seats, exchanging glances.

Lilith was in the kitchen when he got home, the beast seated on the chair before her, waiting patiently while she trimmed off clumps of fur with electric clippers. "Sorry," she said to Greg. "You're going to have to sharpen these when I'm done."

He went to the office and graded papers until the buzzing stopped. When he came out again, Lilith was sweeping mounds of hair into the trash. The beast was gone.

"So it was nothing but fur after all."

She nodded toward the bedroom. "He went that way."

Greg loosened his tie and went down the hall. The beast was curled at the center of the bed, brown hairs shedding onto the white comforter. Pale flesh was visible under its coat now. Greg grabbed its arm. "Come on," he said, "off the bed."

It rolled glassy brown eyes at him and sank deeper into the mattress, wiped snot from its nostrils with its free arm.

"Up!" Greg shouted, and slowly the beast relented, rising from the bed and following him out of the room.

Lilith said, "You could let him rest, hon. He isn't feeling well."

Greg pushed the beast into the garage and locked the door. "*It* stays out *there*," he said.

She turned her back to him and stood at the sink, gripping its edge with both hands. The fancy pillows were on the living room couch, the camera mounted on the tripod. She'd been getting it ready for a family portrait.

Phil and Elise came for dinner and brought Gordon with them. Elise handed Lilith a bottle of wine, but was already peering past her into the house. Phil nodded toward the open kitchen door and said, "There's the fellow." The beast was crouched near the wet churning warmth of the dishwasher, watching them.

"I heard he was sick," Elise said, searching for signs of contagion.

"He's better now," Lilith assured her. "You should have seen all the get-well cards."

Gordon ran past them and into the kitchen, halting just in front of the beast, his arms raised. The beast inched away from the boy, blinking. "Now it knows who's boss," Gordon said.

"Leave it alone," Elise said to him, and Gordon went into the living room to watch television.

Greg and Phil stood with hands in pockets while their wives squatted beside the beast. Phil said, "Those wrists are looking better."

The beast quickly lost interest in the newcomers and resumed its game of rolling oranges across the floor. When dinner was ready, Lilith shooed it into the garage. The beast sat and gazed up at her as she closed the door.

"It's hard to keep up with him these days," she said, picking up the oranges off the floor.

"Asserting his personality," said Elise.

Greg didn't talk much during dinner. He drank a lot of water, always going into the kitchen to refill his glass. Afterward, he and Phil retreated to Greg's office, and Greg took out a stack of photographs of his father. In the pictures, all from the war, Lyle appeared as a taller, handsomer version of Greg, dancing with women in flared skirts, smoking a cigarette in front of the Egyptian pyramids, standing on a runway in England with his arms around his buddies, always grinning, sometimes pointing straight at the camera as if to say, "Hey, you there!"

"You going to sell the house?" Phil asked.

"As soon as I can," Greg said. "Got it pretty much cleaned out now. I found these in his dresser. He never showed them to me."

"And what about the big guy? Where'd you find him, anyway?"

Greg held the last photo—Lyle behind the controls of his bomber plane—and flicked it rapidly against his knee. "In the basement," he said. "There's a little room down there where they used to store coal, for the old furnace. It was just chained up back there. Dirty and half-starved."

Phil whistled and shook his head. "And he never mentioned it? Wonder where he picked the thing up."

Greg said, "For the last thirty years the man and I were strangers. Now he's dead and I feel like he's around me all the time."

From the next room came the sound of Elise's laughter. Lilith had commenced the nightly lesson. "A," she said, and then again, insistent, "A."

"Ahgg," came the beast's rasp.

"B," Lilith said.

"Ahgg," it said.

Phil said, "Elise told me you've got the kids studying the atomic bomb. Gordon's really into it. He was telling me about how people's shadows were left on the walls, you know, afterward. Pretty creepy stuff. Anyway, Elise is wondering how long you're planning to spend on that."

Greg put the photos away. "Not sure," he said.

Elise drank most of the bottle of wine she brought that night. She and Phil were standing at the door with their jackets on when she remembered Gordon. "Where is that boy?" she said. The television was still on but the couch was empty.

Greg went across the house to the garage. The beast was curled up on its bed of blankets and Gordon was crouched over it. When the boy pulled his hand away Greg saw the bruise on the beast's nipple.

"It isn't so tough," Gordon said.

"Your parents are leaving now," Greg said. He waited in the doorway until Gordon walked past him. The beast watched the boy go, then settled its head down with a sigh.

Greg and Lilith were coming home from the supermarket when a police cruiser came up behind them and flashed its high beams. Greg pulled over and watched in the rearview as the cop stepped out of his car. It was Abe. He waved as he approached, and Greg rolled down his window.

Abe leaned over and said, "Just got a call from Mrs. Connor over on Myrtle. Says there's a bear chewing on her barbecue grill. You want to come check it out with me?"

"Oh, Jesus," said Lilith.

Greg said to her, "You go home and check."

"No, I'm coming with you."

Abe got back into his car and Greg followed him around the block. The Connor place was dark when they arrived. The three met on the walk and Abe explained, "Said she didn't want to attract its attention."

They walked around the side of the house, keeping close to the wall. Dogs were barking from the neighboring yards, and Abe had his hand on the butt of his pistol.

At first they could see nothing but Mrs. Connor's rows of tulips. Then from the shadow of a tree came another shadow, bent and shaggy. The beast's eyes were bright in the moonlight.

"Nice and easy now," Abe said, like a television cop. He handed Greg his cuffs. "You want to do this?"

But Lilith walked past them, one hand raised. The beast seemed to catch her scent.

"Come here," she called, but the beast ignored her.

"Doesn't look good," said Abe.

"Come here to Mommy," Lilith said.

Abe shot a glance at Greg that he was careful not to return.

When the beast still didn't budge, Lilith said, *"Come here right this instant."*

It put its snout in the air and produced a gurgling sound, almost a howl.

"Yes," Lilith said. "A."

"Bahgg," the beast said.

"A, B," said Lilith.

It rolled its shoulders and came slowly over the lawn, stood before her with head hung. She took its wrist and said, "Okay, let's go."

They put the beast in the backseat and Lilith got in beside it, moving groceries out of the way.

"I'll call Mrs. Connor in the morning," Greg said to Abe.

"Gave her quite a scare. You folks going to be all right?"

"Just fine, Abe. Thanks for grabbing us when you did."

Abe tipped his hat. "Poker tomorrow," he said, and headed up the sidewalk to the house.

Greg got behind the wheel and met Lilith's eyes in the mirror. She held the beast's right arm and squeezed it gently. Greg couldn't see its face, but he smelled the earthy breath, felt it hot on the back of his neck.

They could have played on the dining room table, since Abe had the place to himself now, but it was tradition to take the cooler into the basement, check the progress of the model ship of the month, pull out the folding chairs, and pass around the plastic poker chips. Abe had remodeled the basement the year before Corey went back to Minneapolis. Using any other room would have been an insult to the man's craftsmanship, and too much like acknowledging his wife's absence.

That night, though, even in the sanctum beneath the house, nothing was right. The cooler leaked water over the floor, the pretzels were stale, and Phil, usually the risk taker, quickly folded almost every hand. Finally Abe said, "Have to close up now, boys. Early day tomorrow."

The men shuffled back up the stairs. As Greg took his jacket from the wall rack, Abe put a hand on his arm and asked him to stay a moment. When the others were gone, Abe's face went tight and he said, "Your father was a good man, Greg. He was a friend of mine."

Abe was older than Greg but younger than his father. Lyle had never joined them for their poker games, but Greg knew that he and Abe shared a few beers sometimes down at Cooley's.

Greg said, "He always spoke well of you, Abe."

"That's why I feel a little responsible, like I should look out for you. I think your dad would want that. Not that I knew him too well, mind you. But this much about him I had figured. Either he took care of business or he kept his business his own. You follow me?"

"You bet," he said.

"Good. Now this guest of yours, Greg, a beast like that shouldn't be taught to speak. Nobody wants to know what it would have to say. You just call me if you need help with this thing, okay? I'm always here."

That room was tidy, pristine, just the way Corey had left it. And there were Abe's white socks, sunk in the thick blue carpet.

Greg put his jacket on. "Thanks, Abe."

At the door they wished each other good night. The porch light went off as Greg got into his car.

Greg got up early, made coffee, eggs, toast. He took the beast out through the sliding glass door into the backyard, where birds twittered angrily from the trees. Greg tossed an orange into the grass, said, "Go for it, boy. Let's see your stuff."

It hesitated, then bounded after the orange, rolling it along with its snout while Greg sipped from his mug. "That's it," he said. "Keep it moving, keep it moving."

The beast snatched the orange in its teeth and flung it across the lawn. Greg put his mug down and went after it, tossed it back into the air. The beast caught the orange in its mouth. "Yeah," Greg said. "Now rip that thing apart. Just tear into it."

The beast shook its head and bit down, juice spilling over its chin. It dropped the remains into the grass. "All right," Greg said, and he took the beast back inside.

He arrived at school early, claiming the best spot in the parking lot. His lesson plan was the best he'd ever written. He filled the board with notes for first period, using four colors of chalk, then sat in the first row to admire his work.

Meredith appeared at the door, in shorts and a T-shirt. "Morning, Greg. What are you doing?"

"Just getting ready for another day of junior high school," he said brightly.

"But Greg, it's Sunday."

Even the sixth-grader seat felt too big for him. "Sunday?" he said. "Then what are you doing here?"

She held up a basketball. "JV practice." Her shorts were orange and blue, the school colors.

"Right," he said. "I guess I'll just keep these notes up for tomorrow."

"Let the janitor know," Meredith said, "or he'll wash it clean." She jogged down the hall toward the gym.

It was well after midnight, and under the harsh streetlights the block looked a little like a museum exhibit. Greg was watching out the window when Abe's cruiser came to a halt in front of the house. It was Mrs. Heck who'd called—he'd seen her light go on, seen her standing at the window with the telephone to her ear.

Greg opened the door to let Abe in, and Lilith asked if he wanted coffee.

"No, thank you."

Phil and Elise were on the couch with Gordon sandwiched between them. The boy's face was red and puffy, one eye already blackening. Greg had been awakened by the sound of the boy's screaming. In the garage, he'd found Gordon crumpled in the corner and the beast settling back onto its blankets, the old scab on its head opened up again.

"You see what that thing did to my son?" Elise said. "He could be dead right now."

Lilith said to Abe, "He stole the spare key to our house. He's probably the one who let him out into Mrs. Connor's yard last week." To Elise she added, "And what the hell was he doing in our garage, anyway?"

Gordon sank into the cushions and whimpered, "I just wanted to pet it."

Lilith stopped herself from saying something and went into the kitchen.

Abe said, "You want to get dressed, Greg?"

Greg had been standing in silence in the middle of the room. He went down the hall and put on the clothes he'd worn to school that morning. When he got back, Phil was saying, "Look, Abe, we don't have to make a big fuss out of this." Elise glared at him, but Phil went on, "Let's just work this out in the morning. We shouldn't have bothered you at this hour."

"You take your son home," said Abe. "School night tonight. Gordon, you gave the key back?"

Gordon nodded.

"We're all set here, then."

"What about this eye?" Elise said.

"Ice for the swelling," said Abe.

Phil ushered them outside and into their station wagon. A minute later the vehicle crawled away down the street.

Lilith exploded from the kitchen. "That little twerp had it coming."

"Lilith," Greg said.

"She's probably right," said Abe. "Greg, you better bring your guest."

The beast sauntered sleepily from the garage and allowed itself to be led outside. Its hooves clacked against the sidewalk. Greg saw Mrs. Heck's curtain swish closed.

From the door Lilith said, "I got him to say my name, Greg. Damn it, he knows my name."

They took Abe's car; the beast rode in the back. Abe kept the chatter of the police radio low while he drove to the edge of town, out to Lyle's place. Greg used to drive past the house at night, if he had to go to the store for something. And sometimes the kitchen light would be on, and he'd wonder what his father was doing in there—taking in a cowboy movie, probably, or a gin and tonic. But Greg never stopped and went in. Now the place was dark and a Realtor's sign was up in the front yard. But the hedges needed trimming, and the gutters would have to be cleaned before winter.

When the beast stepped out of the car, it snuffled the air and blinked.

"Knows its own home," said Abe.

Greg took the beast's arm. They walked up to the house, then past it toward the woods beyond. When they reached the backyard Abe said, "This is where I stay." He handed Greg his pistol.

Greg felt like he was sleepwalking as he went into those woods, the beast beside him, he dressed for school. Dead pine needles crackled underfoot. He found a clearing that looked familiar and sat down in the damp weeds. He'd built a fort in this spot when he was nine or ten, and his father had helped, bringing him twine to bind the wood, a piece of burlap for the roof. Greg slept in the teepee a few times that summer, but water leaked in when it rained. His father told him that next time he would have to use a deerskin like the Indians did, and when Greg asked where to get one, his father said, "Off a deer." Greg took the teepee down and never built another.

The beast had been wandering, nose to the ground. It came back to Greg now and looked up at him. It had pushed a pinecone across the clearing with its snout. It said something Greg couldn't make out—Lilith's name, maybe. Or his. He got up before it could speak again.

He didn't know how to fire a gun, but he fired it. Then he walked back to the yard and Abe took the gun and strapped it into its holster.

They drove past the school on the way back into town. The lights were on over the tennis courts, over the soccer field, too, and inside the school Greg knew his notes were still on the board. On the radio the police dispatcher spouted a series of codes, then said something about a stalled car abandoned on an overpass, and a woman with pains in her chest, and a couple who had woken the neighbors with their arguing, and a man who'd cut his hand trying to chip ice out of his freezer.

Abe silenced the radio. "Could use some quiet now," he said.

SUZANNE RIVECCA

Stanford University

UNCLE

She told three men. The first stopped sleeping with her right away. Not because she was tainted or anything, he explained. It just put images in his head that were counterproductive to sustaining an erection. He felt terrible.

The second man asked a lot of questions. She didn't want to tell him—this was on the heels of the first man's reaction—but he treated her like the burial site of an ancient civilization; he dug for clues with a sweaty-palmed reverence and did not stop until he held it triumphantly aloft, that sordid tidbit like a saber tooth. He was interested in breeding. He didn't want to marry into a flawed tribe; for months she wished herself dead and him weeping at her bedside.

The third man was different. He said it wasn't her fault. He said it had happened to him, too, although in less severe form: a random crotch-grab in a public restroom, the culprit a classic drooler in a trench coat with one rheumy eye. He had been fourteen and he punched the man in the face, fled the room, hid and cried, and told no one. He was, he said, ashamed. He should have run to the nearest authority and turned in the drooler. The unchecked drooler could be fondling innocents at this very moment. He was so vehement on this point that she saw his terrible question coming at her like the fin of a shark, and she shrank inside but there was no escape. "Did you ever tell the police?" he asked, and when she said no, he scolded her for being a passive accomplice to countless evil acts. "You know his name," he said. "You know his address. It's unconscionable!" He continued to ask, "Did you call the police yet?" until she refused to see him.

They were kind men. They deplored sexual deviance. The third one once said to her, "You know what I think of rape scenes in movies? It's like someone put a big, beautiful birthday cake right in front of me and took a shit on it. It's like someone shitting on my birthday cake," and she scoffed at him for trivializing the issue, but at the same time felt oddly defended and grateful.

They were all kind. But she decided never to tell another one.

It did not define her; the men never understood this. She did things. It was not the sum of her because she made herself do things, stitched a personality together out of extracurriculars and carefully chosen proclivities. She hated Christmas and proclaimed her aversion loudly. She ran in the ravine. She was a person who ran all the time and had complicated shin issues. She made a lot of tea and learned the names, origins, and fermentation processes of each varietal. She did crosswords in ink and finished nearly all of them. She read. She loved novels in which people were genteel in their desperation and drank a lot of tea and spoke with dispirited eloquence.

Even with all of these diversions, she often thought about what the third man had said. She couldn't help thinking of it, because he kept calling to reiterate it.

"Just tell me his name," he said over the phone. "Just a first name is all I need. I'll do the rest."

"The rest?" she said. She was stirring sauce on the stove.

"The rest," he said.

She switched off the heat and visualized the third man's lips close to the receiver and moving emphatically, like a cinematic tight shot of a villain demanding ransom. "If you're thinking of the police," she said, "it's pointless. We're talking about twenty years ago. I was in grade school. There's a statute of limitations."

"Doesn't matter," the third man said. "Whether he's actually *arrested* or not doesn't matter. The thing is to let him know it's not okay. To let him know he's being watched. It's a deterrent."

She remembered how the third man had once turned to her while she was reading and said in a voice flat with impersonal awe, "Your face is beautiful." He said it as if her beauty were the beauty of a dead thing, a butterfly framed and dried; it could do neither of them any good.

She said, "He isn't even around any little girls anyway." She kept stirring because she didn't know what else to do. "I was the only niece. He has no daughter, no granddaughter. He's not like your guy. He's not a roving weirdo running all over town." Her voice roughened.

They argued some more and she hung up, then poured her sauce over cooled pasta and vegetables and sat down to eat. She wondered why she was able to eat after this conversation, and if it meant something was wrong with her. Coiling the noodles around her fork was strangely absorbing. She became lost in the round green integrity of a single pea, cupping her attention around it like hands, and when she disengaged herself she realized her dinner was cold and the dining room window was dark.

She put her fork down and sat back. The people across the courtyard were celebrating a birthday. Their lives seemed constructed of smartly colored geometric shapes. Through a bright square of window she saw a woman walking like a bride while carrying a blazing wheel of cake. The man she was walking toward was grinning, receptive, saving up breath for his big part, and when she placed the frosted circle in front of him he reared back his head and extinguished all its light.

A month later, her lease ended and she did not renew it. She moved to a new apartment in a half-gentrified part of town that smelled of hops and oatmeal from the nearby breweries and Pillsbury plants. There were train tracks everywhere. Children dangled off corroded jungle gyms. The neighborhood had the carved-out, makeshift feel of a hobo camp and she found it oddly soothing, the shambling lullaby of the trains at night, their *click click click* hypnotically monotonous as a skipping record, the starchy soup of fog in the morning. She biked to work every day past an abandoned casket factory, rows of moldy Victorians, morning glories entangled in fences and opening their blowfish mouths in the light.

She told herself she had moved to escape the attentions of the third man. She enjoyed imagining him learning about her relocation secondhand and marveling at the ingenuity and resourcefulness it took to orchestrate an entire move without telling a soul or asking for help.

For a while she felt safe. But her new place—a big shotgun flat in a converted rooming house, with spiky stucco walls and bad wiring—was uneasily silent. No matter how often she made tea and how invitingly she decorated her bed, she was plagued by waves of heartsick edginess, like a passenger who'd waited hours for a train only to realize that she'd been in the wrong depot all along: a sickly, hollow dawning. She ran more than ever. In her dreams she kept missing crucial appointments by a slim margin of time, and woke each day with a sore jaw from grinding her teeth. She waited for the third man to find her, or at least send an emissary. But no one called.

When the phone finally rang, it was her mother.

"Do you still want those dishes?" her mother said.

She began to cry. As always during displays of emotion, a specter hovered in the cool lobby of her brain, waiting for the signal to step in and put a stop to it.

"Oh, honey," her mother said. "What can I do? Don't you like your new apartment? You were so excited about it."

She swallowed air and said, "It's dirty. It's so dirty here. I've cleaned and cleaned and I'm not the one who made it this way, you know I'm not a slovenly person, I don't live in squalor—"

"I know that, honey," her mother said. "You're a very clean person. Remember how you used to vacuum the whole house when you came home from school, before I got home from work? I remember how nice it was to come home to a freshly vacuumed house. Remember how mad you'd get when Dad would step all over the carpet with his shoes on and ruin your beautiful vacuuming job? You did such a good job."

She laughed weakly. "I was a weirdo," she said.

"No," her mother said adamantly. "You were a good person and a helpful person."

"I cared so much about the vacuum," she said, and she began to cry anew. The image of herself in the house where she grew up, making back-and-forth furrows like a plow horse, made her feel horribly vulnerable. She knew she was being self-indulgent, but she didn't want the ghostly bouncer to step in yet.

"Why don't I come over?" her mother said. "I'm going to stop by and we'll clean the place together. You just need some help, honey. You just need help."

"I do," she said. "I do."

The mother waited until after a great deal of cleaning had been done—the blinds taken off the windows and soaked in the bathtub, the baseboards scrubbed, the ceiling fans dusted—before telling her about the uncle.

"What I was told," she said, wiping her forehead carefully, "is that he got religion."

The daughter looked out the living room window, toward the casket factory and the Grain Belt brewery. The air smelled of refrigerators and leavening. "What sort of religion?" she said.

The mother looked down at the gleaming baseboards. "I don't know. That doesn't ever mean a particular creed, does it? 'Got religion'? It's sort of like a generic born-again thing I guess. Not some theology you actually study." She picked up a dirty sponge and tossed it aside. "All I know is, he's going to these churchy meetings and he's taking it very seriously. That's what Amelia says."

The stucco wall looked like white meringue whipped into stiff peaks. She sometimes felt the urge to put her tongue to it.

"I'm telling you this," her mother said, "because he may be coming here. He may seek you out."

The daughter laughed. "Seek me out?"

Her mother laughed, too, flailing one wrist in a minimizing gesture, loose with uncoordinated relief and anxiety. "I don't know. There's some emphasis on making amends. They talk in these strange pilgrimage terms. So Amelia says."

They sat in silence for a while. Her mother kept glancing sideways at her with anticlimactic intakes of breath, as if about to speak. Then she blurted out, "Grandma said once, 'If I were you I'd keep her far away from him. I just don't have a good feeling.' Or something like that. But you always wanted to be with him!" Her eyes stretched wide. "I thought she was just thinking the worst, you know how she is. She's always having a bad feeling about something and she's never right. I thought, 'The kid *wants* to be around him, what could he possibly be *doing* to her that's so bad?' She's the one who always said, 'Two signs a man will make a good husband: if he's good to his mother and kind to animals.' And he was both. My sister wouldn't have married him otherwise. He was both."

The daughter had once called her mother a bad mother and made her cry. She didn't want to do it again.

She said, "How does he even know where I live?"

Her mother flicked a foot up and down and did not answer right away. Then she said, "Amelia asked for your new address. I didn't really think twice; what was I supposed to say? She sends birthday cards every year, you know that."

In the silence the ceiling fan rollicked round and round, its unsteady revolutions oddly comic. It seemed to be winding up for a dramatic liftoff, and the daughter almost laughed. Then a thin peevish misery, runny as yolk, spread over her. It was all very banal. The sun was boring, bland with midday virtue; there were ants on the floor and the clicking of the trains was depressingly productive and brisk. She had a sense that this encounter was not what it should be. Things should feel sharper in general right now, and less like cardboard. Life should seem much less ridiculous, more urgent than it did when her mother finally looked her in the face, not reaching out but backing away now, each breath between words a frantic hand-flap, a shooing away: "I always wanted to know, honey, what *was* it? What could it have been? When you kept being around him. When you just kept going back!"

The daughter wanted to say, "I didn't."

But she had. She had gone back again and again: to pretend to understand his stories and laugh at what was supposed to be funny and to be lifted like a sack, with an affectionate casualness that proved her

lightness, her doll-like simplicity, the reassuring physicality of someone else's entitlement to her. She had never since been borne into the
air with so little ceremony.

What she said was, "Shut up." She imagined her own eyes pale
and lizardlike, looking at the mother. "Will you shut the fuck up?"
she said, her voice louder this time. The mother looked out the window and didn't say anything.

Over the next few weeks she thought a lot about handicrafts. At work
she was competent, researching government grants with the whimsi-
cal earnestness of the postgraduate. Her coworkers were progressive
women in their midthirties and avuncular, aging gay men; they all
liked her and indulged the precocious sass that emerged after her trial
period of anxious sweetness ended. Gainful employment was still a
dress-up game, one she was good at. Lately, though, she found herself looking forward to returning home as soon as possible in order to
devote her full attention to thinking about handicrafts until she
cried.

She couldn't understand the sudden poignancy of the subject. But
it was something she needed, in the artless prodding way of a food
craving: to be filled with a grief whose origins were both dubious and
concrete, to absorb the sad wobbly essence of these unloved objects
until she spilled over with it.

So each evening, as dusk curtained the house and the phone did
not ring and the boxcars trundled off to Santa Cruz and Burlington
and Alberta, she sat on the floor against the couch and inhaled the
sawdusty yeast smell and thought of body parts made of clay, baked
in kilns, and ineptly glazed. An impression of her seven-year-old
palm overlaid with a sheen of sickly lavender finish. They punched a
hole so it could be hung at holidays, a disembodied emblem of the
universal sign for *stop*. There was also a plaster cast of her right foot,

painted streaky blue with acrylics. And the clay bowl she'd grandly visualized as so beautiful had emerged lumpen, thumbprints baked into its clumsy sides. Her silk screens always turned out backward, as did her woodblock prints. She could not cross-stitch. Was so inept at making a friendship headband out of yarn that the Girl Scout leader, a horsey blond matron who volunteered her time out of an honest faith in the character-building properties of female bonding of the rustic and homespun variety, gave up and made one *for* her because everyone had to have one for the Friendship Ceremony and the situation was clearly hopeless.

She held each failed object, sharp with the crystalline sterility of an art-class slide, in her mind's eye and squeezed, extracting its emotional pulp: the ache of having tried too hard, aimed too high, wrapped up loose ends in a slapdash of despair. Thinking of the crafts all together in a gallery of shame made her weep as she had never wept before: loudly, with copious amounts of mucus she did not bother to wipe off. Nor did she hide her head in her arms. She just walked around the house like that, doing menial tasks and cooking dinner and brushing her teeth, all the while thinking of malformed crafts and bawling.

If she stopped for a second, she was unsure of what to do next. Usually the only thing that made sense was to go to her bed and make herself come over and over, not languorously, not ardently, but like a rat pressing a lever. Once in a while she felt a tiny sting of clarity right after she came. In these moments the stopper of her numb chemical bath jostled loose, and she would regard her hands with a sober appreciation for their perfection and dexterity. The sensitivity of their little hairs. Their cunning joints. Then she would remember the clay hand and start sobbing again.

She bounced back and forth between craft-weeping and masturbation, clubbing herself dumb with the crudest of sensations, until one day she couldn't. One day the crafts didn't make her weep any-more and her groin was too tender to touch.

It was a Saturday morning. She sat back against the headboard and assessed her surroundings with the grim, bloodshot closure of a drunk coming out of a bender. The body's capacity for dissolution had been exhausted. Her options fanned out cryptic as tea leaves. She called the third man.

"What the hell?" he said. "Your phone's been off the hook for weeks."

"It's not off the hook; it's disconnected. I moved."

He asked where and she described the trains and the factories and the bread smell. She made him laugh once or twice. Then there was si-lence and he said, voice dipping in a nakedly aggrieved way that made her feel scarily womanly and responsible, "Well, why are you calling me now? Since you didn't even bother to mention you were moving."

She stood up, put a hand between her legs, and was bemused by the leaping, responsive pulse of herself: a gamely wagging trouper under the rubbed-raw skin. Her body was a perplexed animal, ever ready to serve. It forgave everyone everything.

She said to the third man, "I have something you want."

"What?" he said, wary; she was never one to be coy about sexual matters.

She said, "A name. And an address."

His face had lost its customary zealotry. Stripped of it he seemed washed-out and sheepish: the mild-mannered alter ego of his former self. He wore a puffy coat she did not recognize.

"Is it really that cold out?" she said, gesturing toward the coat. He caught the screen door with his elbow and shuffled into the kitchen.

"I rode my bike," he said. "The wind." She stuck a tea bag in a cup of boiled water and told him to sit down in the living room; he did, sticking his hands between his thighs to warm them: an uncharacteristic and studied gesture.

He took the cup she offered and said, "How's the job?"

She said, "I'm doing a grant to stop world hunger."

"Has it stopped yet?" He sipped.

"No. It will." She had the sensation that someone who knew her well, a sister if she had one or a close high school friend, was watching this exchange from above and snorting in disgust at both of them.

The third man eased himself off the couch and sat cross-legged on a floor pillow. "This apartment's weird. Your other place was nicer."

"This is cheaper."

"It really does smell like beer outside."

"Yeah, well, it could smell like something worse."

The third man pressed his lips together and separated them with a popping sound. "So," he said, eyeing the cracked plaster of the living room wall, "you have a name for me?"

"Guess what it is." She deliberately flattened her voice so it wouldn't sound like some flirtatiously sassy challenge.

He shrugged. "I don't know. Larry?"

She shook her head.

"Bert?"

"No one is actually named that."

"Yes, they are," he said. "I've known people named Bert."

She looked at him and had the urge to go running, right then, in the ravine, past the rained-on mattresses and trembling footbridge, the graffitied rocks and the flashers, bouncing complicit glances off the other runners as her rib cage lifted and lowered, her heart giddy and always the awareness of her own breath as a precious and fallible commodity.

She said, "I don't think I'm going to tell you."

She expected a scene, but he shrugged. "Well," he said, "can't say I'm surprised."

She snorted. "What, you thought I just wanted an excuse to lure you over here?" She thought, *What an inane encounter,* over and over.

He stood up and dusted off his pants for no reason. "I don't know. It didn't really matter. I've been worried. I just wanted to see if you were doing okay, I guess."

She stared at him. She had the sensation she was shrinking. "Okay?" she said.

He nodded.

"You're not a vigilante anymore?"

He shrugged again. "I still think he should go to jail. But I'm done with the whole thing about me being involved in putting him there. I think I was kind of infantilizing you. You know? It's up to you to come to terms with this thing how you see fit, is what I mean." He spoke without looking at her, and fidgeted with the zipper of his jacket.

She had never hated him before; she did now. She hated him and wanted to see his old rage so badly. She realized now that his eyes were a temperate shade of blue she recognized as a popular hue for the shutters of tract homes on her childhood cul-de-sac. She scrutinized him for a trace of the taut, hunted shiftiness men's faces assume when they were driven to be with her and didn't know why. It was never sweet. They were never besotted—just stiffly, sullenly advancing as though shoved toward her from behind. Some had looked at her like an animal eyeing an untrustworthy trainer; others in a gauging, measuring way, like she was an obstruction they needed to lift and move to get what they wanted.

And although there was nothing of this in the third man's face, although he just stood there in her living room looking gamely uncomfortable, she came forward and pressed her palm against his crotch. She looked down at it. And when he put his hands on her shoulders and said, "What are you doing?" she fumbled with her belt buckle, heard its gratifyingly heavy clink, began to unzip.

Her breathing was perfectly even, as though she had been granted a surgeon's access to her own insides, lifting and lowering her rib cage tenderly with both hands and guiding breath in and out of her throat like a fire-eater directing flames. For a few seconds she knew the shamanesque power of them all: the man in the bathroom, the flashers in the ravine, the uncle with his wormy silk-sweater smell and his aura of raspy restless movement like a cricket's legs scraping, the ease with which he reached into himself and split the seam demarcating what he did from what he was. Then got up the next day and ate cereal. Petted dogs. Engaged in the poignantly vain grooming rituals of a middle-aged man: the inspection of gums, the sculpting of sideburns.

The third man peeled off her hand and said, "I'm not doing this with you." He sounded resigned yet rehearsed, as though he'd glumly anticipated having to say this.

She stepped back. "Then why the fuck did you come over here?"

The third man picked up his backpack and looped it over one shoulder, his shutter-colored eyes flat, his voice tight. "I told you. To see if you were all right."

"I'm better than you are," she said. "You're fixated. You belong on *Oprah*."

He was walking toward the door now. When he reached the big double oven he backed against it and looked down at her and said, "What happened to me wasn't much."

"Can't quantify it," she singsonged, wagging a finger.

He just kept talking. "What happened to you was bad, though. I used to think you should go get vengeance. Not just for yourself. For everybody. But I can't make you into this poster child. It needs to be under your own jurisdiction. Or it won't count."

"You're like a shitty fortune cookie."

He shrugged. She didn't remember him being such an inveterate shrugger. He had always been too incapable of concession to shrug even in casual conversation.

"I'm sorry," he said. Then he opened the door. She stood on the back porch and watched him cross the parking lot, his back sloped like a mountain climber's, a carriage both braced and slouchy. He swung one leg over his bike. She thought of his meditative, bittersweet ride home to his normal-smelling neighborhood, a sage's flinty smugness in his eyes, the wind in his righteous hair. She thought of several things she could yell after him. But all that came out was something she hadn't known was on the tip of her tongue: the uncle's name and address, over and over. Not yelled but simply thought, and long after he rode away.

There were three men and that was all. The third was the last one she told.

Eventually she saw other men, and kept her mouth shut through Oscar-winning movies in which innocents were diddled; through endless televised parades of Very Special Victims; through the initial ten seconds of sex that were always fraught with panic, her heart whinnying, pawing, walleyed. She gentled it down and kept moving. She did things, tending her body with the disinterested briskness of a nurse. To friends, she alluded comically to a three-week stint in which she cried nonstop about handicrafts. She omitted the compulsive masturbation and came off as endearingly vulnerable and daffy, even as her inner abacus clicked coldly with each deposit and return, each ally enlisted.

She recognized that she was a person of limited means.

About six months after the third man's visit, she was running in the ravine when a man stumbled out of the underbrush with his pants around his ankles. She stopped and looked at him. Birds chirped. The air around her seemed to soften, deliquesce with sweet rot. A mother duck and three ducklings glided through the Mississippi. The man had freckled thighs and was knock-kneed. His eyes, deep-set and brown as the river, met hers and he flushed, looked back and forth, and suddenly covered himself—not shamefully, but with a whiplash grab of self-preserving instinct. Then he turned about-face and blundered back through the brush, clutching at the waistband of his khakis.

He seemed less of an exhibitionist than an apparition, some feral creature separated from his tribe. She pictured more of them back there, hunkering fearfully and waiting for her footsteps to fade. She imagined what otherworldly powers they superstitiously ascribed to her by firelight, how they warned their young and disbanded camp at the scent of her. The next day she said to a coworker, "Some naked guy popped in front of me in the ravine, but soon as he saw me he looked all horrified and ran away. I didn't know flashers were so discriminating." The coworker, one of the funny gay men with whom she pored over celebrity gossip magazines in the lunchroom, said the flasher likely wasn't a flasher at all and that the ravine was notorious for illicit gay-sex trysts; didn't she know that? She shrugged. She was inexplicably disappointed.

The next day the uncle came.

Somewhere in her brain, she had mislaid his significance. His face, bobbing up the back porch stairs, was blandly ubiquitous as a television personality's. But then he said her name.

Conventional wisdom claimed smell as the beeline to memory, but for her it was the sound of her own name on someone's tongue: a calling card coded with sensory nuance, redolent of the nature of their claim on her and their preferred method of collection. He rapped on the screen door. It never occurred to her not to let him in.

The uncle made a fussy show of scraping his shoes on the doormat and clapping his hands against his lapels. He looked the same. She hadn't seen him in five years, having avoided family reunions and holiday galas since the age of eighteen.

"May I come in?" he said, although he was already in.

"Yeah," she said. She flapped an arm toward the dining table. She didn't know what to say next, so she said, "Want some water?"

"No, no, no; no trouble on my account, please." There was a charged subtext to this, employed like a flexed muscle.

She leaned against the sink, arms crossed. He stood by the refrigerator with his hands at his sides. "My mother said you might come," she said.

"Yes," he said. He kept looking at her searchingly. He wore a good-quality coat with a hood. It was beige and belted tightly. His hair was slightly grayer and his eyes were still round and harmless-looking, with jaunty little eyebrows like a dog's vestigial markings. He didn't smell the same though. There had been an acidic sharpness. It was gone.

The uncle cleared his throat. "I've been trying to start a clean slate with my life," he said. "Your mom may have mentioned it." He waited for affirmation. She said nothing. He went on, "It's a time of transformation, and part of that is trying to make things right with those I've wronged. And I know it must be upsetting for you to see me. And I wrestled with this, you have no idea; I asked myself, is it selfish to go to her, to dredge this up? Do I have any right? And maybe I don't. Maybe I don't. But this is not about reducing karmic debt; please understand that. This is not something to cross off a to-do list. This," he said, inhaling as if about to plunge underwater, "is the central black hole of my life."

She sneezed violently. "Excuse me."

"Bless you," he blurted. He seemed grateful for the opportunity to bestow this benediction.

"Look," she said, tucking her hair behind her ears, "this really isn't necessary."

He looked down. "Would you like me to leave?"

"I don't care," she said. "If this is a big thing for you, say what you need to say. Go for it."

"I appreciate it," he said. His constant head-bobbing and knee-jerk deference made her feel like a guru in a kung-fu movie, attended by a bowing, scraping apprentice. She smiled coldly. She articulated the action to herself as she performed it: *I am smiling coldly.*

"I don't want to just make a speech at you," the uncle said. "I was hoping we could have kind of a give-and-take." His voice tilted up. She recognized it, that cocksure wheedling.

"I don't think so," she said. The crispness of her own voice made her stand up straighter.

The uncle's round eyes began to fill up, taking on the hazy miragelike illusion of movement that preceded full-fledged weeping. Then he blinked the water away. "All right," he said. He looked down at his galoshes. She remembered how his vacated shoes and his socked feet used to give off an earthy, pungent odor, not unpleasant, the expansive warm smell of something tightly contained and suddenly freed.

"I just want to say one thing," he said. His round eyes were stricken. He extended an arm as though tempted to grab her for emphasis, but quickly withdrew it. "What I did to you," he said, "was not your fault. I know... I've read the literature. I know a lot of people grow up thinking there's something wrong with them. That they're to blame. And they are *not*. It was me, it was all... my sickness. It could have been anyone. You were there, and you were—accessible. That was it. That was *it*." He made a slicing gesture, then winced at his own immoderation.

She pictured him reading the literature. She had read it, too. Then she said, "I'd feel better if it did have something to do with me. Is that sick?" The uncle took a breath to speak and stopped short. He was at a loss.

He opened and closed his mouth. He took a step forward and back again.

Then he did a strange thing: He bowed his head and covered his eyes with his hand.

She leaned against the stove and watched him for a while, earnestly but without investment, the way children watch parades and inaugurations and tedious civic rituals in general. The uncle's fingers dug hard into his temple.

The niece thought of self-defense. She wondered if this was a dangerous situation; technically, there was a lawbreaker and a deviant in her home. But she could see that something in him had shut against her. And not only against her but a lot of things, and she was just one of them, an emblem he distorted at will, a monster disarmed. He had to turn her into this. And for a moment she felt that he had succeeded: Her hands were folded in front of her, her chin pointed down, and she thought she must resemble an old daguerreotype she had seen long ago in a textbook of a pioneer woman on a prairie— salt of the earth and grimly unsexed, frozen in the eternal posture of one who bears up, bears up, bears up, then dies.

The uncle was now sitting on a wooden chair as though a giant hand had dropped him there by the scruff of the neck. He rubbed his forehead with thumb and fingers. His flesh pleated and reddened. He was right there in front of her. She thought of him having sex with his wife. She stared at his hands. They were small hands, chapped and pinkish with spatulate fingers and broad nails, and the first time they touched her—the back of the neck, brushing—she had not been afraid.

She had never been afraid of him. What she felt now, what she had always felt, was collusion: uneasy, dead-eyed, and leaden. It began in the back of the throat and slowly sifted downward, dragging heaviness to her base like a punching bag with a weighted bottom, rooting her to the ground with the knowledge that she belonged in this kitchen with this man, that she was born here and would die here and that there was no other scenario in which she would ever be so wholly herself.

She coughed and the uncle looked up. He looked at the corner of the wall where two cupboards met.

"Well, I don't know," he said finally. "I don't know what you want to hear from me. I don't know if I'm just making this worse than it needs to be." He wasn't pleading now. He was just looking at her sanely and tiredly. He was trying to reason with a tiresome woman. She realized that he was wondering what he ever saw in her.

The niece started rubbing her own chest: not sensually, but as if she were applying an unpleasant-smelling but curative poultice. The uncle's face sharpened in genuine surprise. As she rubbed she said, "Do you remember that white cat that used to roam around Grandma and Grandpa's neighborhood, the albino one? And you told me about the ghost tigers and I didn't believe you. I thought you were making them up for the longest time. But then, and this was my first year at college, I saw some at the Toronto zoo. They were very ghostlike. It was like seeing a herd of unicorn. It was quite a shock."

The uncle opened his mouth and closed it. Her hands moved down to her groin and she rubbed that too and felt a small cheap hit of comfort. She concentrated on this.

She suddenly couldn't stop talking.

"Do you think about it?" she said to the uncle, flatly and nasally. "How many times a week do you think about it?"

"I don't—I mean, I think about what I did to you often—think about the *damage* of it, the—" The uncle lobbed the words, trying to stand his ground, squinting at her now as if he could force her back into focus, his focus, the one he'd donned that morning with his galoshes and muffler and pleasant cologne.

The walls of the kitchen seemed to narrow around them and she moved closer, feeling taller and wider, her shadow throwing darkness over him like a tarp.

"What are you doing?" the uncle said. She stepped forward, not rubbing anymore but just holding herself like she had to pee. She could think of nothing else to say so she just stared at the uncle's face, and after a few moments she found it, the look she'd searched for in the third man: the taking over and the leaving behind. The bullish emptiness of the eyes. It was there. Then it wasn't; his face seemed to skip a frame and he was turning around, the uncle, he was clutching at his collar with one hand, he was moving toward the door.

"I'm sorry," he said, not looking at her. "I'm sorry."

He did not sound sorry. He threw the words like baking soda on a grease fire.

He was another chastened, decent man who closed the door without slamming it and walked through the rain to his sad car. It was so stupid it was criminal. The car revved up and crunched over gravel.

The kitchen grew chilly. As darkness set in she took her hands off herself and wrapped her arms around her torso. She continued to stand there like that, because it was cold. Because she could hear the train's *skip, skip* like a bad heartbeat and she knew the morning glories were closing their throats for the night, and because it was hard, in that clenched fist of twilight, to imagine doing anything else.

CHRISTOPHER STOKES

University of Mississippi

The Man Who Ate
Michael Rockefeller

Half Moon Terror and I were talking politics at the edge of the swamp when the billionaire's son first appeared.

It was late afternoon, the sun spiking through a wall of brush on the far side of the lagoon, and just as Half Moon pointed to a pair of alligator backs unzipping the skin of the water—"What does the Local Council plan to do with *those* guys, right? Can you tell a water monster, 'Be *Catholic*?' 'Don't be a man-eater: Drop your dignity and your instinct and speak *Indonesian*?'"—just as he said this the forest began trembling with sound and the boat careered around a bulge of trees.

"Case in point," I said, meaning the boat. "Ready to receive the Eucharist, change your name?"

Half Moon grunted. He hardly ever wore paint anymore, but as he squinted at the noise I thought I caught the former warrior in him twitching with hunger for a good invasion. Then he sighed.

"Those aren't priests," he said. "It's Bringing Man."

The boat slowed. It was a big white catamaran with greenish windows and battered twin hulls. Touching shore, it coughed and gargled and went quiet. Things had gotten so that the hullabaloo of a motored catamaran posed little threat to an Asmat. Traders, missionaries, art scholars—they all got here by boat. What made this weird for Half Moon and me was seeing Bringing Man take such motherly care in getting a white visitor to shore.

Tossing a rope ladder over the side, Bringing Man climbed halfway down and then dropped thigh-deep into the water. The billionaire's son swung a thin leg over the railing. Bringing Man stood waiting to help him, one hand slightly higher than the other, his face a grimace of expectation. As he made reassuring sounds in a white language, the visitor's foot slipped. His body fell hard against the side of the boat, and he clung to the ladder desperately, his feet kicking the air while quick waves smacked our feet and lapped at the crotch of Bringing Man's military fatigues. Bringing Man cooed, and the visitor craned his neck to see the water below him. After a moment's hesitation, he flung himself away from the ladder and splashed into the swamp. They slogged to ground holding hands, grinning like bedmates.

"Mind if we pop in for a bit?" Bringing Man said.

"Is this one Dutch?" Half Moon Terror demanded. "Because if he is—"

"Not Dutch," Bringing Man said. "Not even European!"

Next to him the visitor beamed, breathing hard. He had slender arms, a pale forehead glossed with sweat, and childish pink lips showing in an unsuccessful see-through beard. Absently he gripped the handle of the large knife in his belt and looked around in wonder. The lenses of his eyewear flashed in the late sun as he took it all in: the darkening green swamp, the high forest jingling with bird sounds, the mud-smelling air, a stick hut near the water where some wallaby hides lay tanning, Half Moon and me naked except for the ornaments in our faces. Some hunters in the village had recently brought down a black pig, and from its pelvis I'd carved and imbued with magic a crescent to wear through my nose. This sharp-tipped moon was meant to bring fertility to my wife and me, and the billionaire's son stared at it without shame. Bringing Man clasped his shoulder and shook a quick laugh from him.

"This is Rockefeller," he said. "He's from a kingdom in America called New York, where his father is a major, *major* dignitary. In New York, remember, they have paper charms called *dollars,* and the Rockefeller tribe, well—they have quite a lot of these."

"What, like an armload?" Half Moon said. "Or like a pile on the floor, or what?"

"More like sands of a riverbed. That's what *billion* means, you savage. And to have this many paper charms makes one not only a king of sorts but also a *billion-aire.* Anyhow, there's a doctor with him, and a couple of helpers still on board—"

"BILL-yon," said Half Moon Terror. He'd been fiddling with the barb of ivory in his bottom lip, and he quit doing this to tug philosophically at his foreskin.

"Bill-yon-ERR," I said, and slapped the white man in the chest. Half Moon and I had seen paper before; we both despised its uselessness, and Rockefeller's love of it made him, among other things, a fool. Also that he would own a billion of anything, let alone *papers,* was a lunacy of surplus. One of the first things visitors learn here is that in Irian Jaya nobody owns more than the eye can absorb in a glance. "Take him back," I said.

"Hang on, now," Bringing Man said. "He's all the way from a palace of learning in his father's kingdom—*Har*-vard—where they're dying to show off your work."

"Bringing Man, I know what an archaeologist is," I said.

"Right, I know, but listen. He tells me, before we left Java, he goes, 'Take me to Papua New Guinea, because I want desperately to find the master carver who made *this*.'"

Bringing Man made a sort of hurrying gesture to Rockefeller, who, fumbling with his shirt pocket, took out a fold of paper. He handed it to me. Bringing Man grinned like a thief.

"He's totally monkey shit over your stuff. And so I tell him, 'Good man, I'll show you not just where to look, I'll take you to *the guy*— Designing Man himself.'"

I unfolded the paper and saw a colorless image, bisected by a lightning white crease: a clean-shaven Rockefeller, holding an Asmat neckrest patterned with cuscus tails and flying-fox feet, the heads of my father and grandfather carved into each end. I'd crafted it three or four seasons ago, but couldn't remember which missionary I'd given it to or if I'd traded it for tobacco. In the picture, Rockefeller wore a look of agreeable surprise, as though he'd been snuck up on and greeted warmly by an ancestor.

"You recognize it, right?" Bringing Man said. "You do, I can tell."

I gave Rockefeller back his picture.

"He's also got one of your ancestor poles, same design, and a shield. He's opening a museum in his kingdom. Says he'll pay anything."

I should point out here that Bringing Man was a Yali from the Central Highlands. All Yalis know in their hearts that money is the most worthless of all tradable things; its primary magic needs at least two people to bring it out, always in a tingling moment of exchange. When one is alone, in a dark immutable forest, it will lay forever inert, like a broken spear or severed hand. Bringing Man knew all this, but he'd grown up working with his father repairing telephones on the main island, where he learned not only that trade but also a handful of white languages and some white geography and the hex of white dollars on men without talent—who, he discovered, made up much of the outer world. He earned a living by showing them the unshown, tooling them around the Irian Jayan coast on his boss's catamaran, and therefore couldn't help his spirit's bending over in money's presence.

"Bringing Man, what if I told you I was on semipermanent sabbatical?"

"I'd say *semipermanent* is an expensive word for *temporary.* I'd say that you, Designing Man, are the poorest fucker in your village, and that your wife would appreciate a little extra sago, as you guys are—no disrespect—semipermanently childless."

This stung. I must have made a face, because Rockefeller looked hard at me, then to Bringing Man, who smiled fabulously and placed an assuaging hand on Rockefeller's chest. The two of them whispered awhile, and it was during this pause that Half Moon leaned close and kidded that we should take the billionaire's head.

In truth there hadn't been a beheading feast for who knew how long. We'd been a Dutch colony for ages, although lately Amsterdam had argued that we deserved to be a sovereign nation, complete with a striped flag and multilingual representatives in Jayapura. The Indonesians were about to adopt us as their own, believing we were the feral ancestry of their culture. What the Indonesians failed to acknowledge was that we Asmats, not to mention the Bauzi farther inland, the Korowai, Dani, Kamoro—even the Yalis like Bringing Man—weren't Indoanything. We were all the children of Melanesians from the South Seas, or so Bringing Man kept telling us. But it didn't matter. Already tribes at the edge of the mountains were dressing in pants like missionaries; their children were reading from brightly colored books and singing the French alphabet. The skull of an immortal's son could offer a cosmic boost in warding off more irreversible change. It was an edge against fate, and Half Moon adored such edges. I was considering all of this when Rockefeller spoke up.

"Designing Man," he burst out in my language, "it would be my greatest elbow to stay for dinner."

"You mean *honor*," I said. It was clear he'd asked Bringing Man for the phrase. I shook my head. "Not *elbow*."

"You mean *honor*!" Rockefeller repeated.

"Elbow," Half Moon Terror said, and grinned knowingly at me.

Our village sits in a clearing just deep enough in the forest that we can't see the water. We have eighteen huts in all, every one made of grass and sticks and vine and raised on stilts. They're identically cylindrical, with pointed round roofs, except for the long feasting hall where we took Michael Rockefeller and his retinue. By the time Bringing Man, Half Moon, and I had unloaded their gear, the air was darkening. My neighbors had gotten a fire roaring in the center of the village.

It was a decent blaze, with all manner of edible bugs swirling above the flames. The trees encasing the village towered black against a dark blue shell, my brownish hut flickering orange, a shadow man walking spastically under my feet, all this rippling color beating back the night and lifting me in a way that felt like the moment just prior to a discovery. My spirit was bursting in my chest. I rushed into the darkness of my hut to grab my headdress and sensed right away a breathing presence in the room.

Mad spirits are like this. They hover in the heads of trees and hang low over the dark water of the swamp, unable to reconcile the fact of their death with their own unspent energy. Occasionally an angry one slips unseen into the village. It is this sort of spirit, restless and bitterly afraid of being forgotten, that will shatter your glass trinkets from missionaries, smear feces on your oldest ancestor poles, or pounce crushingly on your chest while you dream. I could barely make this one out in the gloom, though by the chaos of feathers on top of it I could tell it had stolen my headdress.

"Go away, fucker," I said.

The shade jerked, and I heard my headgear hit the ground. A bad thing, as the centerpiece of its design happened to be the skull of my father. I let out a yell.

"Sorry!" My wife's voice. "Sorry, sorry, sorry."

"What—what are you doing?"

She was quiet for a long time. "Talking to your father."

"Ah," I said. "And what'd he say?"

"He said first of all don't be mad at me for putting on your things."

"I'm not mad, Breezy."

"He said you are. About a lot of stuff, only, you don't know it. He says you could be a little nicer."

"Can we pick this up later?" I said. "There's this white guy shown up from I forget the name of the place and Half Moon's waiting for me down at the lodge, trying to get a feast going."

She stepped into the light, wearing a grass skirt and nothing else. "Can I come?"

"It's not that kind of feast."

I gathered up my headdress and a dogtooth necklace I planned to give Rockefeller and left her standing in the dark.

My wife's full name is Long Breeze Rousing The Forest In Hottest Summer And Swooshing Down To Gladden Our Hearts. Her father gave me a tame black pig for marrying her, but I would have done it for nothing. In my opinion she's the most inspired basket maker we have apart from Half Moon's mother, and without a doubt she's the best cook. Her face is capable of the subtlest emotions, as well as a bounty of wry glances and reassuring smiles. We've been married eight seasons, but in this time the spirit world hasn't once seen fit to restore balance in our village by sending her a child, and people are starting to talk.

Every Asmat knows that the failure to receive offspring reflects a certain spiritual flaw in a woman, a displeasure among her ancestors, but to know Breezy is to understand how absurd this is. She's far too gentle and wise to rouse anger in this world, let alone in the realm of past fathers, and it's in her nature to use only good magic, and this strictly in the service of others. If women were permitted at a visitor's first feast, she would've enchanted Rockefeller. As I hurried to join him I had to remind myself that the dead, who see everything at once, know best when to gift the living with parenthood.

When I entered the feasting house the Governor had already installed himself next to Rockefeller, his doctor, and Bringing Man. Half Moon Terror was busy working the fire pit in the center of the room. The Governor had illuminated the contours of his face with swirls of starlike white dots, and his eyes were rimmed in red. His headgear contained an imperial riot of wild plumage. He beckoned with a look for me to come join him, and by this I knew Rockefeller had been grilling him about how business might be carried out, how much tobacco and rice and sago root it might take to get me to carve a load of treasure for him. I took a seat between Rockefeller and Bringing Man.

"He wants carvings," the Governor said right away. "As many as you can produce in three months, and you get to name the price."

I looked at Rockefeller, who smiled back at me. His thick eyewear showed a pair of fires in refracted miniature. I took out my dogtooth necklace and drew it over his head.

"Let's work it out after dinner," I said.

All night Rockefeller waited to see what we would do and then mimicked our actions like a little boy. We had skewers of plump sago worms, and when I held one over the fire, so did Rockefeller. Usually visitors tend to hesitate before biting the head off a grub, but Rockefeller threw himself recklessly into eating. He chewed carefully, with his eyes closed, devoting the whole of his spirit to the labor of tasting. There was fire-baked fish and roasted flying fox and partridge stuffed with sweet rice, and with each new flavor Michael Rockefeller slapped his knee and exclaimed something in outrageous delight. Half Moon distributed sago cakes, which contained bits of fish and dried plum, and Rockefeller anxiously watched me break off a bite and hand it to him. When he popped the morsel into his mouth, his face seemed to bloom. He looked at me, nodding gravely, and seeing that tears had come to his eyes I couldn't help laughing. Rockefeller leaned into Bringing Man for a phrase to express his heart in my language. He turned to me and clasped my hand.

"I am a *monkey fucker*," he said.

Bringing Man's face was struggling. He glanced at Half Moon Terror, who sat grinning and chewing.

Rockefeller took the bone-handled knife from his belt and tried giving it to me. "Monkey fucker? I," he tapped his chest, *"monkey fucker—"*

Bringing Man snickered.

"That's not funny," I said.

"Yes, it is," he said.

"Monkey fucker!" Rockefeller blurted.

"What was it he wanted to say?" I said.

"Just, you know, this was the greatest meal of his life, he wants to be brothers and so on. Look at him, though. He looks like the monkey type."

Next to him Half Moon sat glaring at me. He cut eyes at Rockefeller, and with dreamlike slowness dragged an index finger across his throat.

———

Rockefeller stayed four days, gorging himself nightly at four feasts, and left with a promise to return in three months, as we'd agreed. I vowed to give him the finest work of my life—ancestor poles, war shields, all manner of noble figures in whatever colored woods I could find. Then, two days after Rockefeller's boat pulled away to roam the coastline, our Governor was found dead in his hut.

There was no wound. It was as though he'd fallen down and his spirit had leaped out of him. The under-chiefs were furious: He'd talked at length with Rockefeller's doctor at the first feast, and a few of them speculated that this man had somehow hexed the Governor, or poisoned him. In any event, they insisted, our tribe and Rocke-feller's were now out of balance.

Years ago, before we were polluted by certain imported virtues, such an imbalance would have meant that someone of power in the rival tribe would have to part with his head. On our walks together, Half Moon wouldn't leave it alone.

"This means Rockefeller," he said at the edge of the swamp. "But you're the one who's got the deal going with him."

"What are you getting at? I'm supposed to say either way?"

"Designing Man, our Governor's dead. We're leaderless. Until a new one's appointed the entire council has to agree how we handle this—and you, Master Carver, are a key player in this council."

"You sound like fucking Bringing Man right now, you know that."

"I'm just saying."

"Look, however the Governor died, that man, Rockefeller, is no enemy. You can't prove it's Rockefeller's fault. Next to my own wife he might be the least injurious soul I've met."

Half Moon laughed. "What, because he's a fan of your work? Because he likes to *eat*?"

He had a point. I couldn't have said for sure what it was about Rockefeller that made me want to protect him, other than maybe his earnestness at the feast and his naive thirst for my brotherhood. But when I tried to imagine taking his head I could only see stars pouring out of his neck and a flock of enraged spirits descending on me in a scream.

"I'm voting no," I said.

Half Moon behaved coolly toward me for the rest of the day. On my way back to the swamp for new wood, I spotted him at the edge of the village holding court with two councilmen. They wanted an argument, it looked like—speaking harshly while gesturing toward my hut—and I was moved to see Half Moon working to calm them. Something inside me, an oppressive tautness I hadn't noticed, untwisted and went slack.

Early the next morning I was jolted awake by Half's warrior voice roaring of my full name.

Breezy lay sprawled beside me, sleep purring from her nostrils. I hadn't yet consulted her about the Rockefeller situation; the Asmat wife can be an unrelenting persuader in matters of beheading, man-eating, and magic, good or bad. For all her gentleness, I couldn't shake the worry that she'd disagree with me and then never let up. She sprang awake just as the cry came from outside.

"Mother?" she said. She looked wildly around the room. Then, comprehending where she was, she rubbed her eyes. "I had the most horrible dream, about—is that somebody calling you?"

I got to my feet and walked naked to the door. In the center of a ring of onlookers stood Half Moon Terror, painted in the style of his warrior days: his right side entirely black, his left, moon white. He had an ancestor shield—one of my creations—on one arm. Next to him stood his wife, her belly gigantic with Half Moon's forthcoming child, her breasts painted red and white like the eyes of an angry cockatoo.

"Great Designer And Carver Of Judicious Trees Into Forms Appearing Spirited Enough As To Respire And Know Our Fathers?" he repeated in a ceremonial tone. "With highest respect and goodwill I formally offer you, my brother, an exchange."

Half Moon knew he had me here. Our brotherhood ritual had taken place long before I'd married Breezy, before I'd become master carver. When we were skinny young men we'd devoured the back meat of the Korowai warrior who beheaded his father. We'd shared our bodies in pleasurable ways, vowed to sacrifice our lives to spare the other. For me to refuse trading him Breezy for his wife Plentiful would not only undo this brotherhood but also be considered a grave social infraction throughout the village.

"Oh, for fuck's sake, Half."

"Brother," he went on, "I hereby give you my Plentiful Bliss, Plentiful Season, for whatever you would give to me in return."

I went back inside to discuss it with Breezy. She was already stripping her torso in red, white, and black.

"Tell him to hang on," she said. "I'll be right out."

I stood there not saying anything. Breezy wrapped her waist in a new grass skirt. "Have you seen my fox fur headpiece? The red one?"

"Wait, stop," I said. "What about the pig? We could give him our pig?"

"A pig's a pig, Designing," she said. "Not a wife."

She remembered then that she'd loaned the headpiece to her sister. Taking up her old brown one, made of dog fur and tiny white shells, she walked past me without a word. I stepped outside, wanting to stop her, to murder my grinning brother, and saw Plentiful Bliss crossing the dirt to greet me.

"This is such an honor," she said. Plentiful had an enormous top row of square teeth, so her lips never quite touched. Her ears were small. The whites of her eyes were almost lost to her fat black irises, and her skin, I realized at that moment, was the exact reddish brown of the flying-fox headpiece my Breezy had been looking for. "Designing Man, wow."

"Let us all rejoice in this exchange," Half Moon said to the whole village. "This pact between families."

Everyone, the councilmen and their wives, the weavers and hunters and bedecked warriors, raised their voices in celebration. I stayed quiet, staring at Breezy. She was smiling meekly, with downcast eyes.

"Okay then," Half Moon said. "Back to what you were doing."

Soon as the crowd began to break, Plentiful reached between my legs and took hold of my shaping tool.

"Want to lie down?" she said.

Half Moon raised his shield to me in salute. He turned to go back to his hut, and Breezy followed him.

"I guess so," I said.

There is no word in the Asmat language for what the missionaries call "love." We've always had some inkling of the concept, though, even without a term to solidify it in thought, and this, I believe, has left the feeling as unspoiled as the Asmat people used to be, before the Dutch conquered us and the missionaries came and the Main Island decided to make us Indonesian. In the week following Half Moon's exchange ceremony I found myself awake nights turning this word over in my mind, tasting it, or trying to, the way Rockefeller had explored the manifold textures of a roasted sago worm. And yet each time I felt close to discovery, just shy of the riches in that basket of a word, Plentiful would roll over.

"The baby's still a little lumpy," she'd whisper. "I can feel it. Do you mind, just..."

And then shaping again. The lopsidedness of Half Moon's child proved to be the foundation of my new marriage. In her quest for excellence, Plentiful awoke with relentless cravings that, no matter how often we shaped through daylight, harried her well into dark. But it wasn't until the third or fourth night that she had the nerve to bring up Rockefeller.

"I've been meaning to ask if you've given much thought to that recent visitor—what was his name?"

She was reclining on her right side, one leg suspended by a hand gripping her thigh. I was shaping Half's baby from this angle with hard driving strokes, which took some pretending on my part.

"You want to talk about that now?"

"Well, it's just that things are *so* out of balance." Her voice quavered with the violence of my pelvis. "Don't you think?"

"I'm not thinking at the moment."

"Yeah, but, I mean we don't even have a Governor. Probably won't get one until—did Half mention this to you already?"

"Many times. Pick your leg up a little, please."

"I think it's a good idea. You know what I'm talking about?"

I stopped, breathless. "That's enough shaping for tonight."

"But what about the feeding? You can't stop before, you know, *nourishing* the baby, can you?"

"Yes, I can."

There were, all told, thirteen more nights of this, each one with an increasingly detailed assessment of the Rockefeller situation: the spiritual imbalance between tribes, the daily rotting of my character in the eyes of the village council, that my drinking of a billionaire's spirit could make *me* Governor, possibly even a better carver. During the day I couldn't focus on the work I'd promised Rockefeller. Then one night she changed her tactic.

"You have to be worried," she said, on her back, knees raised. "Sooner or later, he's going to return."

"What are you getting at, Plentiful?"

"Oh, I don't know. Just that everybody else is so *for* it. Think about it. You could wind up exiled if you don't come around, and they'll just do it without you."

I withdrew and spat on the ground. "Get up."

"I'm trying to *help*."

Taking her by the wrist I led her under starlight to Half Moon's hut. When we got there I saw Breezy straddling my brother, her spine glistening in the dark.

"Enough," I said.

Half Moon peered around my wife. "Enough what?"

"I know what you're doing, Half."

Breezy climbed off him and hugged her knees. Half Moon lifted himself on his elbows, his shaping tool bobbing stiff against his navel.

"What are you talking about, brother?"

"You've initiated an exchange ceremony under false pretenses, for one thing."

"False pretenses," he said.

"To install a harassing brainwasher in my home." I dragged Plentiful to where he was. "Take back your demon and I might not consider this a breach of our brotherhood."

"Am I going back with you?" Breezy said. She turned to Half Moon. "Are you letting me go?"

"Yes, he is," I said.

I collected her things, her headpiece and skirts, her necklaces and the fertility charms I'd carved for her that had found their way to Half Moon's hut. Breezy followed me out the door. She was silent until about halfway home.

"You know you have to kill Rockefeller," she said.

I put my arm around her. "I know it."

Entering the hut we'd shared for eight seasons I took her shoulders in my hands. Her face was such an inspired carving of beauty and real meaning that I had to borrow from another world to express it.

"Love," I said. "You are *love* to me."

Breeze stared at me in something like alarm, as though I'd confessed an ancient inner anger at her for a thing she didn't know she'd done.

For the next month my lost ancestors were silent to me, or I was in no mood to listen. Either way I got no further on the work for Rockefeller. I'd retreated from the company of my village. My belly was like a stone pulled black from a fire. Beneath my chest two cold hands pressed tightly together, and every morning I trudged to the swamp carrying the same fresh log of whitewood and a handful of tools only to find myself stymied by these hands in my chest, this smoking rock in my gut. Then, all at once, I tore furiously into the first carving.

She seemed to come from nowhere. I shaped her head, her delicate sleeping eyes. I rendered in lifelike detail the fat of her tiny legs and forearms, the flesh under her chin, the navel and folded skin of her sex, and then polished her with the tanned hide of a baby wallaby. Somehow I couldn't bring myself to show her to Breezy. It would hurt her, or maybe communicate something to her I hadn't intended, and anyway the carving wasn't hers. I had made this, with or without the aid of my lost ancestors. There's a small hut beside my house, a place for my tools and unfinished carvings, and I kept her hidden there. She was mine. When I realized this I also knew that I couldn't give her to Rockefeller.

He wasn't expected back for at least another month, but I still had nothing for him. With every failure I tried to imagine him grinning sorrowfully, looking away in sharp disappointment, but his face was a blur to me. One afternoon I took a block of striped teakwood to the swamp and waited.

Hungry and bored, I sat there as the sun rode its arc through daylight. The iron glare of the water, the breathing forest, the mud sucking between my toes, all put me in a calm, receptive mood, but I had to wonder if my heart had gone out of carving altogether. Was this how The Great Carver felt after he'd formed us from living trees at the beginning of time and then went silent forever? There were spirits moving over the lagoon, toward the sea where the dead hovered, and I looked as far as I could to find them.

"Speak to me!" I cried out. "I am alone in my life! Tell me what to do!"

At that moment, like a gift, there was a dark fleck on the water not far from where it meets the sky.

It took a long time to complete its approach. Growing bigger and more distinct, it came to the mouth of the lagoon. A man alone, swimming, made buoyant by a pair of floating metal baskets tied to his back. He called my name. It was Michael Rockefeller.

I ran into the water. Chopping through the distance between us, I could see his thin flailing arms ahead of me, muddy and white. He wouldn't stop yelling. When I reached him he tore at my face and yanked me under. Clutching at his open shirt I managed to climb back to the air and knock him unconscious with two blows to the head.

When I finally pulled him to shore I could barely stand. In his sleep Rockefeller breathed terrifically, and I fell on the mud beside him, touching his cheek, the hard jawline through his beard. This son of an immortal king was barely a man. His face hadn't yet lost that fullness I'd carved into my secret daughter. And yet Half Moon Terror would have him before first dark.

Rockefeller groaned. He still wore my dogtooth necklace and, in his belt, the knife he'd tried giving me at the first feast. I got to my knees to unsnap the sheath at his side and he came awake in a panic, but searching my face he seemed to relax, like Breezy after her nightmare. He said my name then, and smiled up at me in heartbreaking relief. I ripped the knife from his belt and held it to his throat. Rockefeller screamed. "Monkey fucker! I am a *monkey fucker*!" He clawed at my face, tried pressing a thumb into my eye socket, and I had to sever the cords in his arms that would permit his success in this. "Brother," I said. "You are a brother, *my* brother."

Then one more swift slice and he was quiet.

That was almost a year ago. News of Rockefeller's disappearance soon came by way of Bringing Man. He'd overloaded a dugout canoe with ancestor poles at a village somewhere east of us. A storm capsized him in the Arafura Sea near the mouth of the Eilanden River and, according to the guide who'd clung to the overturned boat, Rockefeller tried making the swim to shore. He was almost certainly dead.

"Crocodiles, probably," Half Moon Terror said.

"Guess that settles it," I said.

"Not the way I'd hoped."

Since then Half Moon has been elected Governor. Plentiful gave him a loud baby boy not long after, and two months ago word came down that we are now a province of Indonesia. We have a flag somewhere, and white-educated men deciding secret fates for us in Jayapura, but none of this matters. My ancestors have been appeased. They speak to me like never before, and they've even given up their anger against my Breezy.

Today I wake to the squeals of our first daughter. It's barely daylight, and this hungry voice is the sound of the sun breaking through trees, lifting the night like the lid of a basket. We have yet to agree on a name. There is only one word I can think to call her, a missionary syllable I've sworn never to harass my wife with again, so I've decided to let Breezy discover it for us. Taking the baby, she begins humming a song she made up about a charmed basket deep in the forest, just big enough for three to live in, woven to blend indistinguishably with the trees. They look so peaceful, so whole and inseparable, that I leave the two of them and strike out for my work hut.

The room is overrun with tools and noisy ghosts and half-finished carvings. Hidden safely in one corner, behind a stack of drying red logs, there waits a private vessel carved of marbled rosewood, and today my inspiration tells me to go here before getting down to work. I pull away the lid and look inside. At the bottom lies the skull of a noble, polished to a dignified shine, and next to this, my greatest creation. A child I carved to life one day, alone, under the silence of my fickle ancestry.

Their combined magic fills the room like a scent, and suddenly I remember where to begin.

LESLIE JAMISON

University of Iowa

QUIET MEN

HE was a poet who worked with intricate forms—villanelles and pantoums—but during our month together he spoke quite simply. He had an evident lisp, a thin wet breeze running through his words.

I met him at my regular bakery in May. While I was paying at the register, I noticed him palming chunks of fresh-baked bread from a tray of free samples. He dropped handfuls into his pockets. They sent up curls of steam.

A few minutes later he found me at a table near the window. "Thanks for keeping them distracted while I grabbed that bread," he said.

"I wasn't trying to distract anyone," I told him. "Aren't you supposed to take samples, anyway?"

"Not like I do."

I thought he might empty his pockets right there at the table to show me his loot. But he just fished out one slice—gingerly, extending two long fingers into his pockets—and ate it slowly, hovering. He had black ruffled hair and dimples so large they changed the shape of his face when he smiled.

"Are there walnuts in that bread?" I asked him. I sounded like a customs inspector.

"Dunno," he said. "But it tastes good."

We were silent for a moment. He kept standing there, chewing. I imagined following him home, tracking a winding trail of bread crumbs all through the Mission.

He flipped out one pocket and let the samples scatter across the table. "These would be useful in the woods," he said. "We could always find our way back home."

"I was just thinking that!" I said. Though I hadn't been, exactly.

He came over that night to see my fire escape. I announced this to my roommate, vaguely breathless: "I met a guy and he's coming to see my fire escape."

She said: "Sounds like a euphemism to me."

I shook my head. "It's not like that. He writes poems about fire escapes." Which he'd told me that morning. I wondered what his poems were like. Perhaps fire escapes *were* a kind of code for sex, for him. Perhaps all of his metaphors sounded like punch lines.

Half an hour after he was supposed to arrive, there was a knock at my bedroom window. He'd climbed up. He was holding a box of frozen fish sticks in one hand and a bag of gummy bears in the other. I opened the window and took them while he crawled in. I asked him how he knew which room was mine.

"I took a guess," he said. "Things could have been awkward."

I handed the box back. "I haven't had fish sticks since preschool."

"They'll be better than you remember."

"They were fantastic."

"They'll be even better this time. Trust me."

We burned them in the oven and washed away the taste of their charred edges with a bottle of cheap Shiraz, sharing my only real wineglass. We sat together on my small black couch, nibbling and watching late-night cartoons about mythological characters. In one episode, a shepherd boy went looking for gods. He was angry about something that had happened before we turned on the program. He called up the side of a cliff, "You don't know what it's like to be human!"

An old man with a white beard appeared at the top of the rocks. He was maybe Zeus, maybe not. His voice boomed when he spoke: "I had a mortal heart, but it broke."

The poet leaned his face close to mine. "This show is awesome."

I nodded yes and let him kiss me. His body was heavy on mine. I liked feeling his hands beneath my back. We slept together that night—just slept—and it was lovely to wake up next to him, an almost-stranger absolutely solid next to me, swelling as he breathed. His skin felt faintly feverish when I touched my lips to his neck.

Hours after he left, I wandered into the kitchen and found our oven tray in the sink. I picked off crusty flaps of burned breading and stood there for a minute, sucking crumbs from my fingers.

We spent the next four days together, reading at Tartine during the days and wandering through different neighborhoods at dusk. In Chinatown he bought me salty plums, wrinkled like wet skin, and showed me a bathtub full of frogs. We sat curbside on Stockton and shared a piece of fruit we couldn't name, with tiny bulbs of white flesh lining its bitter skin. On Fillmore we got a plate of cinnamon-spiced chicken and picked shreds of filo from between our teeth. The chicken was sweet, so tender it melted off the bone.

"I love it when dinner crosses the line," I said. "Moves into dessert."

"You say things that are awesome," he told me. "But you shouldn't feel like you have to."

"I don't," I said.

Around anyone else, it would have been a lie.

We spent every night together during that month. It wasn't something we discussed. It was what we wanted, simple as that. I started having terrible dreams: A man's voice would say "cancer" in the darkness but I couldn't see his face, only his gleaming teeth. Or my skin would peel into ragged strips, lift from the bones, and writhe like worms. I'd never had dreams like that before. I was compensating for an excess of bliss. I woke up suddenly one night, cold-sweating and shaky. He reached over to stroke my arm. "What's wrong?"

"It's these dreams," I said. "I'm not sure where they're coming from. Worms start appearing. Skin starts peeling."

He said: "I'll dream that with you."

"Good luck."

"In Spanish," he said, "they don't say you dream about something. They say *soñar con* instead: dream with. Like your dreams are their own world, where people can join you."

"I used to dream with snakes," I said. "Now I dream with worms. What next?"

"The phallus itself," he said. "You'll dream with the phallus itself." But he was mumbling. He was already drifting off. I wasn't ready to go back to sleep. I realized that I actually preferred my waking life. This had not always been true for me. It was something I felt proud of.

When he left for work each morning, he left a note on my pillow. They were usually speckled with exclamation points, often several in the same sentence. Sometimes they were quotes from poems. Sometimes they were stupid, silly things: *Marianne Mendez, I love when your name shows up on my cell phone.* He told me that he'd shortened it when he entered my number: MariMe.

"Whenever you call," he said, "it's like you're suggesting a wedding."

"Which wouldn't be so bad," I said.

He nodded. "Which wouldn't be so bad."

We decided to drive my station wagon to L.A. for the weekend, but we made slow progress down the coast. Everything seemed interesting, the roadside full of possibilities. Cardboard signs advertising farm-grown produce made us wonder: What if these strawberries are the best we'll ever taste?

We pulled off next to one sagging wooden stall and picked up flimsy woven buckets. We chose our own fruit and washed it with a dirt-lipped hose. He bent to drink from its rust-barnacled tip. I wanted to be fully inside our moments, but I felt myself slipping out of them, taking notes: The hose was army green, our fingers blood-shaded and sticky from juice. The man who took our money had only one thumb. Everywhere I turned, there was something remarkable. It seemed impossible that we could last, and impossible that we wouldn't, and in the meantime the hose water dripped cold from his stubbled chin, brushed my lips when I leaned to kiss his neck.

Back in the car, buckets tucked in our laps, we found the strawberries broke too easily between our teeth and tasted faintly metallic. But I was thankful for that, that they possessed qualities I would be able to remember precisely. Neil Young kept us company on the ride: "Think I'll pack it in and buy a pickup, take it down to L.A. . . . ."

We got a motel room in Pismo Beach and found a bar near the ocean: the Big Bluff, though there weren't any bluffs in sight. When we walked in, the middle-aged bartender, rail-skinny and blond, warned us the jukebox had something against monster ballads. "Seems like it always gets stuck on Poison," she said. "There's no good reason for it. Whole thing jams up."

Though I hadn't thought of putting anything on, I used my last four quarters to choose three heavy-crooning rock songs. In equal measure, I wanted the machine to play and I wanted to see it break.

The bartender grinned at me. "You're a dangerous woman, I can tell."

I nodded. "But I like my liquor sweet."

I ordered a vodka-cranberry, which made her smile. It was strange to watch. She had the palest lips I'd ever seen, thin and pink against her rosacea-blooming skin.

I gestured toward the poet, who was inspecting a wall of trophies. He had his sweatshirt tied in a bulky knot around his waist. "And a bourbon on the rocks."

She squinted at him, raised her eyebrows at me. "He's okay with well bourbon?"

I smiled. "You bet."

She turned toward the bottles, showing the back of her fried-out mullet. The poet came behind me and tucked his chin into the place where my neck gave way to shoulder, kissed the back-shadows of my jaw.

"Do you know they give out trophies for whale sighting?" He whispered, "Just for seeing?"

I smiled. I knew his face was close enough to feel my skin move. "There's a kind of trust in that," I said. "Or else it's just a prize for telling stories."

He said: "Which wouldn't be so bad."

I nodded: "Which wouldn't be so bad."

I went to the bathroom while he took our drinks to the patio. I didn't even dry my hands. I felt every moment of his absence as something missed, which would have sounded foolish to admit to another person. But that was the thing—I didn't have to say it to anyone. "November Rain" was playing as I walked outside, music drifting onto the patio from its own fierce world.

Sunset was just starting to light up the corners of the horizon. The ocean was huge and perfect beyond the patio railing, frothing across ledges of skin-colored sand. The salt air was rough, raising bumps along my arms, and the desire to touch him felt like a kind of humidity in the air. I thought of an essay I'd read about a guy who'd grown up seeing the Mediterranean in glimpses, flashes of blue between buildings during train rides. When he finally saw the unbroken sea from a hotel balcony—years later, as a man—he didn't know what to do with the sight. I felt that way with the Pacific. It had always been mythic, part of someone else's happiness.

I turned toward him. "I wish there were more words for what I feel with you."

He kissed me. "It's true," he said. "Maybe that's what we need nonsense for—a sort of broken language for joy." He paused. "Also, I ordered a basket of fried cauliflower."

From the jukebox, we could hear Slash launching into his solo. A small, secret side of me had always hoped this part could last forever, that the lyrics might never return.

"Slash owns the heart of this song," he said.

I nodded. "And mine, too." I said, "What kind of nonsense would we use for this?"

He took my hand. "And how would it change with one word of meaning? Fa la la guitar? Fa la la Slash?"

I loved seeing his mind veering into thoughts, each one an original moment. I felt something open in myself. It was right and possible to see the Pacific all at once, the whole goddamned thing. You couldn't see it at all without having it stretch farther than you could see.

The bartender came out with a red plastic basket full of breaded lumps, golden brown, oozing cheese and grease onto the wax paper below.

"This'll end your young lives," she said. "So much fat it's barely a veggie anymore."

When she left, he said, "Her whole life. You start." This was a game we sometimes played. It had to do with strangers.

I said: "Her mother wanted her to be a stripper."

He said: "When she was a kid, she'd sneak out to this broken oven in the alley behind her house. She'd sleep there all night long."

I said: "She loves gathering secrets from old men she'll never see again."

He said: "She crumbles taco shells into her sandwiches. Eats alone."

My inventions were like sketch marks, connecting dots to form a made-up life. But his inventions! They were different, as if he'd taken the vast surface of a childhood, an entire loneliness, and distilled it into a single object: Something almost invisible. Something inevitably sad.

I took him to my favorite museum in L.A., a dim and confusing place where the exhibits weren't related to each other at all. We wandered through cases of objects scavenged from various trailer parks: old milk jugs, used condoms, a crowbar speckled with warts of rust.

"Between the concepts of salve and salvage," he asked, "which do you like better?"

"I don't know," I said. "It's the difference between saving something from context and saving it from itself."

"I like it when you're smart," he said. "But I like it when you're stupid, too."

That night we found an old wooden lifeguard station and dangled our feet over the edge. Our shadows streaked across the sand-speckled concrete of the drainage creek below, long and wavering from the distant glow of a Ferris wheel on the pier. The breeze was heavy with salt, humid on our tongues. We watched two figures sitting on the deck of the next station. They cut sharp black profiles against distant flickering lights and when the man stood up, we could see quite clearly what was going to happen: The woman kneeled in front of him, unbuckled his pants, and leaned in. We watched her bend over the edge once she was done, nodding her head as she spit into the sand.

"I went through a phase where I wouldn't swallow," I said softly. I had something I was building toward.

"Did it have to do with feminism?" he asked. "Or with moods?"

"It was more like a mood. Definitely nothing like feminism," I said. "I had issues with swallowing anything."

"You were sick?"

I nodded. I'd been waiting for this moment ever since my disorder; the chance to show my wounded self to a man and feel him stare at it—stare at me—without flinching.

"I was anorexic," I said. "For a while."

I told him how my body used to be: ribs like a ladder above my tank tops, wrists that looked broken because the knobs emerged so steeply. I told him about the places I'd fainted: my hallway, my mother's bathtub, an old interstate rest stop. I used phrases like "appetite for sickness" and "bone-cold hunger." I felt like I'd lived all of it—the weakness and the throbbing bellyaches and the gaunt-faced crying sessions—so I could deliver it to him like this.

He took my hand. He nodded sometimes. Once I ran out of things to say about how my body had been—and how it was—we sat quietly. It felt different than our first silences, those long mornings steeped in cold sunlight, reading our books while his fingers grazed the bone of my knee.

I wanted to talk forever so we'd never have to see the unspoken straight on. I hated my own voice but I spoke anyway: of my ridiculous love for peanut-butter-and-bacon sandwiches, the thwarted course of my mother's open marriage. I talked about silly toys you could only buy in Japan. I listed the names of my childhood pets and explained their hidden meanings.

There was a familiar rhythm to all this, full of comments I considered clever, but it felt like putting on a dirty outfit—something musty and sweat-stained, long discarded, foul with the odor of my own body. I had been someone else with him: less full of anecdote, suddenly able to say "I feel this deeply" without giggling or looking away. I mourned that self, felt it like a ghost rib tightening across the heart.

He broke up with me two days later. This happened back in my apartment.

"I feel myself become less complicated in this kind of intimacy," he said. "The other facets dissolve. I'm left with something that feels too simple."

"I feel myself contoured by you," I said. "Like I'm in relief against another person. Like I would have to simplify myself for everything else."

He seemed to grow more decisive as the night wore on. My own panic, the rising pitch of my evident pain—these were things that made him realize what he did not want me to ask him to become. "I feel drawn to a lack of attachment right now," he said, which only made me want him more—not just to be with him but to be capable of his desires. I wanted to be whole, apart. But I felt huskish instead, throbbing at each place I had allowed him to enchant me.

It was quiet after he left. I waited for my body to stop existing or else get out of its chair. I took his glass of wine and threw it against the side of my fridge. I picked up one broken shell of glass and pressed it to the skin of my ankle—as I had done so many times in high school—but I couldn't summon the energy to cut. I said "hello" out loud, to check if I could still make sound. I ran my tongue against the streaks of red dripping down the fridge to taste the wine he'd drunk. I stayed awake until morning.

For two weeks, I couldn't fall asleep unless I was drunk, so I drank every night. I told everybody who would listen that I wasn't doing well. "You don't understand," I explained. "I'm not usually like this." But did it matter? This was who I'd become.

I sat on my fire escape for hours, listening to Slash's solo on repeat. I divided days into sections based on when I would smoke my next cigarette. I often drank alone, sipping Shiraz from teacups. I whispered affirming things to myself out loud—"Your pain can become something beautiful"—and tried to believe them.

I had thoughts all the time and I wrote them down on scraps of paper. Sometimes they were facts: *I had a wineglass and it broke.* Sometimes they were things I couldn't finish: *I had a mortal heart, but.* I saved them with his notes but made my sister keep them in her apartment so I wouldn't read them every night. I was going to put everything that reminded me of him into a box, but then I realized there was too much: my cum-stained sheets, my remote control, my entire refrigerator. If I'd really gotten started, I would have scoured my floor for fish crumbs and packed every single one.

KEVIN was a tennis instructor who wanted to give books an honest chance.

"Reading," he said. "I've always meant to do more of that."

He'd overheard me describing myself as an avid reader. We were at a summer solstice party in Pac Heights that seemed to demand the use of such phrases. There was an actual pyramid of champagne glasses in the kitchen and a little dog wandering around with a Credit Suisse T-shirt dangling off his tiny barreled rib cage. Nobody seemed eager to claim him. He spent a lot of time pawing Kevin's legs, sniffing at his pockets. I wondered if Kevin was the kind of guy who might keep a couple of chocolates stashed away. I hoped.

"Take it easy, Suisse-man." Kevin pushed him away with his palm. He turned back to me. "What do you like to read?"

It seemed important to talk about something that didn't matter at all.

"I've been reading about pigeons," I said. "Pigeon war heroes."

"Really?" he asked. "What's that all about?"

"Carrying messages. Strategy secrets and all that."

"I never knew much about birds," he said. "Or wars."

I nodded, kissed him on the lips. I sensed this would be an important skill for my evening with Kevin, figuring out how to end each of our conversations.

At midnight, Kevin started looking antsy. We'd been vaguely tethering each other for most of the party, circling and returning for more moments of awkward small talk and large, toothy smiles. "I hear the roof has a great view," he said.

I nodded. "Let's go."

Another important thing about Kevin: He actually looked like a tennis instructor, with blue eyes that seemed—impossibly—never to blink, and broad shoulders that felt solid beneath my fingers when I slid past him to find the bathroom. I powdered my nose, leaned close to the mirror to see the gleaming, feverish eyes beneath my velvet-shadowed lids. I looked, more than anything, vaguely startled.

We had to climb a ladder from the patio to reach the roof. Kevin carried my drink and told me I was beautiful before he unbuckled his belt at the top.

I scraped my knees on the gravel when I kneeled, took one last look at the lights of the city before leaning in. I could feel the flush of my bleeding knees, their small cuts crusted with pebbles of tar. He kept his hand on my head. I kept my teeth out of the way.

He tasted like they all do, only he didn't take as long as most.

Afterward, he spread his jacket and patted the space next to him, as if we were about to share a picnic. He pulled out two cigarettes and we smoked together, tapping fragile flakes of ash all over the fabric. He tilted his head. "What are you thinking right now?"

I have made a point, during the course of my life, never to ask this question. I paused for a moment, said finally: "Betrayed by perfection, I seek its opposite."

"You seem smart," he said. "Can I call you sometime?"

I knew this was just a gesture we'd both participate in. "Sure."

He entered my number into his cell phone and then stared at the screen for a moment, fingers poised over the keys.

"Would you like my name again?" I asked.

He said: "I would."

He said: "I hope you know this doesn't change how I feel about you."

I said: "I bet."

VICTOR was a joker and a holder of long, unbroken stares. He was my boss at a tutoring center for people with dyslexia.

"People with dyslexic *tendencies*," he clarified at my interview.

"I've got those," I told him. But he didn't break a smile. He liked to make his own jokes.

He was a short man with a shaved head. He had these wonderful piercing eyes and a body that looked fierce and unpredictable, as if he might break into a sprint at any moment.

He stared at me for a long while, rapping his knuckles against the desk. I thought maybe there was something unseemly on my face. I'd eaten an almond croissant in a rush that morning, with jittery hands, and wondered if some of the paste had smeared across my chin.

"Do I have flakes on my face?"

"No," he said. "I just find you attractive."

I pulled my sleeves over my hands. I do that when I'm nervous.

"That thing you do with your sleeves," he said. "It's a sign of low self-esteem."

"Well, I've got that," I said. "Low self-esteem, I mean." I wanted to tell him that if I knew how, I'd build a sturdy mesh helmet and a nest of wool scarves and store them both in a tiny handbag I could flip open at any moment, for hiding purposes. But how can you explain that to a stranger?

He said: "I thought you might say *slow flesh-esteem*. Get it?"

Oh, Victor! Like I said, he was a joker.

On Tuesdays I worked with Raz, my youngest and favorite client. He was six years old and refused to recognize the letter G in certain fonts, as if it were a country he didn't have diplomatic relations with. He didn't like it when the letter dipped into its second, lower loop. He'd say words like *string* or *goose* correctly, and then he'd stop himself midsentence to say them again wrong: *strin* and *oose*.

I let him speak as he pleased. I liked that he had his own version of things.

Victor didn't feel the same way. "You're supposed to correct them when they do something wrong," he told me. "Every correction is a little victory."

"I'll try harder," I said. "I promise."

But I couldn't try. Or else I wouldn't. The next day, Raz pushed away his list of reading words and turned to ask me directly, "If you found a half cow, half horse, would it make milk you could drink?"

What could I do? I said: "Sure. What do you think it would taste like?"

"Like sour cheese," he said. "Like my dad's old gym shirts."

That's when Victor popped his head in. "What vowel sounds are you guys working on today?" he asked.

Raz wasn't ashamed to say: "None."

Victor gave me a long stare. "If you don't mind, I'd like to see you in my office once you guys are done."

"Sure thing," I said. I was doodling something on the back of my hand. It had started as a single beak, curved and enormous, but I gave it tiny crow feet and little inky wave crests for landscape.

I turned my hand to show Raz. "What if you crossed a pelican and a pigeon?"

He squinted. "Looks like another kid attacked you with a pen," he said. His voice left no doubt: He had known this kind of injury, spent his own private hours at some sink, scrubbing away ballpoint atrocities.

He took out a blank sheet of paper and began to trace very large and deliberate letters. When he turned the page toward me, I could see what he'd written: Pigican.

There it was: The G. Its double loop. Its several curls.

I rushed into Victor's office half an hour later. "Look!" I thrust the page in his face. "It's a real G!"

"Pigican?" he asked. "What's that all about?"

"Doesn't matter," I said. "What matters is the little victory, right? The progress?"

He raised his eyebrows for another stare: "You'll have to rethink your methods," he said finally. "Or else we'll have to start thinking about whether you're right for this position."

"I had no idea," I said, "that we'd come to a point where—"

"Just *kidding*!" he said. "You really need to lighten up."

I laughed. It was feeble, sounded like I was trying to scratch an itch in the back of my throat.

He kept smiling: "How about we think about getting a drink instead?"

"Ha ha," I said. "Always the kidder."

"I'm not kidding around," he said. And he wasn't.

That Friday, we went to a kitschy bar off Union Square. It had once dreamed of being an old-time saloon, but tourism had fallen on it like a pile of dirty clothes. Visitors sipped glinting shots of Goldschlager beneath the speckled shadows of their huge straw hats, exchanging breathless reports about sourdough chowder bowls and the homeless guys on Market.

"Look at all these folks," Victor said, peering into his Miller Lite. But when I imagined spending my entire life with Victor—something I did with almost anyone I even kissed—I could think of us as nothing but perpetual tourists, tucking away our glossy maps and making fun of other people's accents.

After a second round, I told him I should probably get home. He dropped me off at my apartment. "This was fun," he said. "Let's do this again sometime."

"I'm not sure..." I let my voice trail off.

He put up his arms. "Hey! No big deal! Don't worry about it!" He stuck out his hand: "Friends?"

"No, I meant I'm not sure . . . I'm not sure I want to keep the job."

He grinned. "Why don't you let me handle the jokes?" He paused. "You're a little awkward with sarcasm."

"You're right about that," I said. "But I wasn't being sarcastic."

He didn't say anything.

"I'm not kidding around," I said. And I wasn't.

GUILLERMO was a Colombian chocolatier who liked to talk shop. From him I learned the dusky taste of unsugared cacao, its solid ridges against my fingers. Another man's prophecy made me pause at his doorstep. It was this homeless guy I'd passed in the street, leaning against a mural full of cartoon Chihuahuas contorted in all kinds of aerial positions. Spray-painted letters behind him asked: IS YOUR DOG BULIMIC?

"You're sad now!" the guy called out. "But I can see it in your future . . . things are gonna get real good."

I walked over and crouched next to him. "Say more," I said. "When?"

He glanced at a row of old-fashioned Coke bottles lined up in front of him, each one filled with a different amount of rusty-colored water. "I use these," he said. "Every time it rains I put one out to see how much it gets. They make a pattern. They make messages."

"If you could just give me some practical advice," I said. "What's my lucky intersection? My lucky gas station?"

I had become fascinated by the possibility of signs and signals. Every day I drove to an expensive parking lot in North Beach, with fortune cookie prophecies painted in every space, just to see which open space I'd find first, with words of comfort or caution.

"I can only tell you this much," he said. "It's gonna be sweet."

An hour later I pulled over next to a sign advertising the San Francisco Chocolate Factory. I'd never heard of it before. I imagined a warehouse full of tiny rooms where wondrous things were made at every moment.

Guillermo worked alone in the small second-story shop. He wore black jeans and a pair of those chunky sneakers with little glowing red lights. He kept his dreadlocks gathered loose at the nape of his neck. His features were sharp and his face looked carved out, as if its less precise contours—the extra shavings—lay scattered across worktables in a backroom somewhere.

He was eager to introduce me to the kind of chocolate he loved: 60, 70, 80 percent cacao. "Not this milked-down garbage," he said, gesturing at the products around him, mostly specialty bars whose wrappers featured San Francisco landmarks.

Milked-down? I liked the way he spoke.

"Taste this," he said. He unwrapped a square of chocolate and held it toward my mouth. The flavor came in smoky pangs as it melted between my shut teeth. I wondered if his fingers had left any trace of their taste on it.

"Come outside for a moment." He led me to a patio behind the shop, crowded with ferns and frail white orchids.

He took both of my hands in his: "What is your name?"

"Marianne," I said.

He bent to kiss my forehead. "I will be back in one moment."

I found myself alone with his plants. The fog congealed around my shoulders in drifts, wet scarves of thicker air.

After a few moments, Guillermo tapped my shoulder. "I want to show you something." He took me to a corner of the patio where the leaves shaded a broad glass case like you'd find in a museum. Inside was a miniature landscape: mounds of dirt with patches of silk grass and tiny chocolate tombstones jutting from their slopes. I peered closer. One slab said: GRETA. Another: MOLLY.

Guillermo stood behind me, wrapped his arms around my waist. "Women I could have loved," he said. He tucked a curved slab into my cupped palm and I could feel the raised etching of my own name, the cold edges of the M.

"I never asked you to love me," I told him.

"I know," he said. "But a part of me wanted to."

TREAT Skylord McPherson was an actor. He introduced himself with his full name because it was memorable and he wanted to be remembered. He'd sometimes joke: "I've got a friend named Snack." We slept together for a week.

We spent most of our nights eating cheap pho noodles at a nameless café on the deep-east stretch of Sunset. Afterward we drank gin and tonics at the Silverlake Lounge, where loud cover bands took away the need for conversation.

I was taking a break from San Francisco. For the first time in my life, L.A. seemed full of the kind of people that everyone assumed it would be: attractive networkers who weren't particularly kind but were looking to fuck.

Treat was an experiment. I wanted to see what cruel men were like up close.

Our first night together, I told him: "I don't want to be with somebody who wants to hear about my *emotions*."

"Good," he said. "I don't."

We'd just had sex. We were smoking on his bed.

"Perfect," I said, but secretly I wanted him to ask some questions. I wanted to discuss *why* we wouldn't talk about our emotions, and what it would mean, and how it would feel.

He had these metal placards lying on his desk, made to look like street signs. But instead of street names they had phrases printed across them. *Slut,* one said. Another: *So?* Treat liked to use them like sock puppets.

"I don't usually go in for casual sex," I told him.

He nodded, handed me *Slut.*

"That's cute," I said.

He shrugged. "You're not."

"Excuse me?"

"You're not that cute. I thought you were at first: kind of bookish, dull brown hair. That whole librarian thing. You think you've got a kind of stealth appeal. But you don't."

He rolled me over so I was lying on my stomach and reached for the back of my bra.

"It snaps in front," I said. But my voice got caught in the pillow.

"Fuck it," he said. He pulled the whole thing off in one motion, fast and rough, so that the straps tangled on the bridge of my nose, almost flicked across my pupils. He tugged my pants off and smacked my bare ass before he yanked at my thong with his fingers. He whispered in my ear: "Get on your knees."

I turned to face him: "You want me to give you head?"

"I want you on all fours," he said. "Turn around."

I shuffled my feet to push my jeans from where they'd bunched around my ankles. Then I let him fuck me from behind. I could hear the ragged rhythm of his breath, muffled like his whole mouth had gotten soggy, and I could feel the sweat of his palms where they cupped my breasts. I could imagine several expressions on his face— eyes squinted in pleasure, teeth clenched like he was angry—but I couldn't decide which one was more likely.

I liked the thought of him aroused by a woman he found unat-tractive. It reminded me of young fantasies I'd had about ugly men fucking me and then paying for it afterward. I used to imagine them sweaty and balding, corporate types with an abiding loneliness that I would somehow heal. I pictured them running their fat fingers along the knobs of my spine and whispering: "Baby, you were worth every penny."

I turned to Treat once he was done. "I think a lot of this has to do with my father."

"A lot of what?"

"Why I'm here, doing this with you."

"Oh."

Another man might have said *Oh?*

But Treat said: "Oh."

"My dad was always giving me compliments but it never felt like he meant them. This feels real, at least. He was only halfway paying attention."

He held up *So?* This was the sign he used the most.

"I treat you like a whore and you take it," he said. "You talk about your father and it's tedious. You talk about yourself and it's worse."

After a few nights, I decided to start telling Treat everything he didn't want to hear. It would be like pressing a bruise to produce a certain, predictable feeling. I was so sick of myself. I wanted someone else to say to my face, "I'm sick of you, too," and I knew Treat would offer that to me—with signs and sighs and certainly, sometime soon, a failure to return my phone calls.

I agitated him when he was trying to fall asleep. "It's hard, breaking up with someone important," I whispered one night. "All the stupid daily tragedies. You know the kind I mean—you don't like being alone anymore because you can only think the same ten things, over and over again. You watch women in the cat-food aisle and think: *It could be me! It will be me! I will have many cats and perhaps never again sex!*"

"You just had sex," he said. "With me."

"Yes," I said. "But."

I had a mortal heart, but.

I kept on going, just to hear the irritation build in his occasional throaty coughs. He found me boring, because I was. And there was comfort in that—the sense of being seen through.

"I'm drawn to different lyrics from the same songs," I said. "Like when Axl Rose gets bitter: *You're not the only one! You're not the only one!* He keeps repeating himself, but I'm always wishing he'd go on forever. I think I could actually go the distance with him."

Treat was silent for a while. I thought he'd fallen asleep until he spoke: "Maybe the guy who dumped you *was* the only one," he said. "Did you ever think about that?"

I laughed. If he'd asked, "What's so funny?" I would have said, "As if!" I might have repeated myself, for effect: "As if I don't think that every single day!"

During our first and only Saturday date, I could tell Treat had other places he wanted to be. Other places he didn't want me to go. Our noodle shack was dead that night, just a string of moth-congested lightbulbs gleaming down on empty tables. He was agitated all through dinner, full of accusations: "You use too much hot sauce. You always take all the bean sprouts."

"Sorry," I said. "I've got this thing with nests. I think the sprouts make the soup look like some piece of natural architecture, like how those bowerbirds in New Zealand make their elaborate—"

"You know what?" he said. "You probably like bird nests because they make you feel safe, or you've got problems with being *seen,* or problems with leaving home, or some fear of flying that really fucked up your first long-distance relationship. But I don't care about any of it. Maybe you talk about your nest thing because you're afraid to admit you've got food issues just like every other girl in this town. But I don't care about that either. I just don't."

Treat wasn't stupid. He just wasn't interested in much.

When I pictured the two of us, I thought of this story I'd read about a python at the Tokyo zoo. He refused his ration of frozen rodents so the handlers put a live hamster into his cage instead, some little guy named *Gohan,* meal. But the snake wouldn't eat him either. They became companions instead. They sometimes slept curled together among the cedar shavings.

I fancied myself a kind of *Gohan,* a meal belonging to Treat.

"Did you ever kill insects for fun?" I asked Treat. "Were you that kind of kid?"

"No," he said. "But I could kill an insect if I felt like it."

As if I'd been challenging him. As if anyone couldn't.

He reached up and cupped his palms around our naked lightbulb, trapping one moth between them. He pressed his palm to the table, flattening the moth beneath, and lifted his fingers until it showed, struggling beneath the edge of his thumb.

"Finish it off," he said. "I dare you."

He kept his thumb pressed on the wing while I took a wilted lettuce leaf from our plate of spring rolls. I looked away, pushed down and rubbed. The lettuce was cool and slimy under my fingers, and I could feel the moth parts underneath, gritty like sand.

"There," I said. "Happy?"

He shook his head. "This really isn't working for me."

He actually paid for my dinner that night, which was something he'd never done before. He walked me to my car and kissed me tenderly on each cheek. "I'm sorry I wasn't nicer," he said. Somehow, that made everything worse.

———

MAURICE was an auto mechanic of few and surprising words. The first thing he said to me was a warning: "Stay away from the corner of Post and Van Ness!"

He yelled this from the cavern of his repair shop at Harrison and Fifth, where he worked all the graveyard-shift tow calls. We were nowhere near Van Ness, and only slightly closer to Post. I was walking home from an all-night doughnut shop.

He yelled again: "A guy was killed there tonight!"

I could see him coming out of the shadows: His pursed smile. His red coveralls.

He got close to my ear and whispered: "With a shotgun."

"I wasn't headed to Post and Van Ness," I told him. "I was going home."

"Good," he said. "I'll walk you."

He was an attractive man and he knew it: short curly hair and foggy blue eyes. He lived on Treasure Island, halfway across the Bay Bridge. I hadn't known that people lived there, but they do. He did. Who could guess his many worlds? He was wearing a jacket whose brick-colored lettering spelled out SAN FRANCISCO FIRE DEPT.

"Are you a firefighter?"

"No," he said. "But I did some paramedic training with them." Another man—a firefighting Victor—might have continued his sentence: *And all I got was this stupid jacket!* But Maurice just told it straight.

"So you know how to fix people?" I asked.

"I know how to fix some things." He turned and stroked my cheek with three fingers. "I could fix your broken heart."

"Wow," I paused. "You actually said that."

"Yes," he said. "I did."

He gave me his telephone number on the back of a business card that said *Fleming's Auto Repair.* I tucked it into the front of my diary for safekeeping.

A few nights after we met, I stopped by his garage with a plate of brownies wrapped in paper towels. I liked how greasy splotches seeped through the paper, rose up like ghosts from the fudge beneath. His manager was working up front—a middle-aged Hispanic guy, tall and gaunt—and I told him I was looking for Maurice. He smiled: "I bet you are." He ducked behind the counter and came back with a handful of peanuts.

Maurice emerged from behind an orange and white tow truck and reached for the brownies with oily fingers. Dark streaks spidered from under his nails, as if the skin beneath were rusting. I liked that he ate before speaking.

"Want to answer some tow calls?"

I nodded.

"It's a good time," he promised. "I'll show you how to use the truck."

We rescued four stoned rich boys from the Inner Sunset, an area they claimed they'd never seen before, and helped the manager of the Hyde-Out change a flat tire on the steepest block of California. He promised us free beers at closing if we wanted to come back. For dinner, we picked up little savory pies that burned our tongues with their vegetable steam. At the register, Maurice had to rummage for change in his pocket.

"I live from paycheck to paycheck," he explained.

"My treat," I told him.

He ordered a Coke and a second sweet-corn pie for us to split.

"I get paid on Thursday," he said. "Maybe we could go to Reno."

"Maybe." I imagined early mornings of lost money and tender sex. He would probably want to call it "making love," which I wouldn't mind. He seemed like that kind of guy.

The only place we went that night was Treasure Island. He took me to his apartment, a dreary unit in a block of converted navy bunkers, and showed me his blind gray cat, his typewriter, his drag queen couch.

"Why do you call it that?" I asked him. The couch was pink with zebra stripes.

"I got it from a drag queen," he explained. "She took a liking to me."

"It's nice," I said. "When people like you." I was trying to practice saying things that were simple and true.

"Sure is," he said. "But I want a black couch. Always have." He paused. "I like thinking about the kind of apartment I want—with huge glass walls and black leather furniture and those big pieces of art that are just one color."

I nodded. To me, it sounded like a coke-lord pleasure palace from 1989, but I liked the image anyway: Maurice nursing a cup of hot chocolate while Boris the cat stumbled into Rothkos.

"Sometimes I get home all wired from work—three or four in the morning—and I'll stay up all night thinking about how I'd like to live. I write about it sometimes, just clacking away on this old type-writer I found in our backyard." He raised his hands and punched the air with his fingers. "Clack. Clack. Clack."

I could tell from his motions that he didn't know how to touch-type.

"I like to write, too," I said.

"What about?"

"Oh, I don't know . . . about love. How horrible it gets."

"It doesn't have to be."

"But it usually is. There's this poem I like about a drunk priest in the middle of nowhere who goes around saying: 'Love is a *terrible* thing, terrible!' He says it even when there isn't anyone listening."

"Maybe he's a priest because he got his heart broken."

"Maybe. But his island's pretty cool. It's got bright stars and glass lizards."

"Doesn't sound very realistic."

"It's not. But love *is* terrible. That part's realistic."

"Terrible," he said. "That's one of those words that sounds strange once you say it too many times. Terrible, terrible, terrible."

I joined him: "Terrible, terrible, terrible, terrible."

He kept going: "Terrible, terrible, terrible, terrible."

Who would stop first? For a moment, it was hard to say.

Then he put his finger to my lips. "What do you think is romantic?" he asked.

"Being quiet. And not minding."

"What do you like to do on dates?"

"All the stuff with your tow truck . . . that was pretty fun."

He shrugged. "Let's go for another drive."

He drove a Ford Explorer with a six-CD player tucked in the trunk. He asked me: "Do you like Seattle sound?"

"I don't know what that means."

"Grunge. The whole Kurt Cobain scene."

"I haven't listened to it much."

"You're in for a treat."

I've got a friend named Snack . . .

"I'm done with those," I said. "I hope it's ugly."

He punched some glowing buttons on his dashboard. They changed from red to orange to yellow and reminded me of a jukebox. I wondered how a guy who couldn't afford his own savory pastries had managed an SUV with a spaceship-style stereo system.

I said, "Nice car."

"Thanks," he said. "I lived in it for a while, before I moved to Treasure Island."

We pulled up to a picnic area overlooking the water. The skyline was made of tiny lights across the bay, looking lonely and cinematic. I started feeling antsy. Would we make out? Would it feel like high school?

"How was that?" I asked. "Living in your car?" My questions always seemed to show how little I'd lived.

"It was all right. You learn to park under trees so the sun won't wake you up in the morning. You find the right spot in Marin and suddenly you've got the best view in town."

I gestured at the windshield. "I like the city better when I'm not in it."

"I know what you mean." He reached for my hand. "I like you."

"It's nice," I said. "When people like you."

"You seem sweet."

"I'm not," I said. "I'm just passive." I wanted to tell him I was only seeing him so I could tell people I'd dated a mechanic, report back to my friends and say, "Check out my tailspin! I'm so heartbroken I'm going crazy!"

But I wasn't sure I believed all of that anymore. Any of it, even.

"Don't sell yourself short. You're a kick-ass listener."

"Thanks."

"What makes you tick?"

I could feel my eyes bloom with heat. "What makes me tick is a guy who saw me—saw me *completely*, you know?—and looked away."

"He dumped you?"

I hated those words. They made it sound like I'd stepped into the snail shell of someone else's life.

"I guess you could say that."

"I'm sorry. I really am." He stroked the tendons of my palm, hard like roots under the skin. I wanted to thank him for taking my hand, but I couldn't think of what to say. I unbuckled my seat belt and leaned over. I kissed his neck, his lips. Then I kissed his neck again.

He called me on Thursday: "Let's celebrate my paycheck."

I suggested a Cuban place near Mission and 19th. I said I liked their plantains. This was true, but it was also true that the poet lived a block away and ate there several times a week. I wanted him to see me, though I wasn't sure what I wanted after that. I wanted something to change. Anything. I couldn't stop myself from remembering him, but I thought perhaps . . . perhaps if I saw him, the remembering might feel different, might be difficult in some new way. Even that would be a relief.

I found Maurice at Fleming's and drove us to the restaurant, where I found a parking space in front of the poet's building. I checked his street-side window, which was dark.

Inside, we sat at the bar, where I could see the whole room. I ordered a pitcher of sangria and proposed a toast: "To your paycheck!" Too late, I realized this made it sound like I was asking him to foot the bill.

"Let's order plantains!" he said. "Let's order lots and lots of plantains!"

So we got three steaming platters and ate them until my throat felt oil slicked and thick with starch. We got a bacon salad so salty I could feel my lips begin to sting around their chapped edges.

When I poured myself the final fruit-clogged dregs of our third pitcher, Maurice laid one hand gently on my wrist. "Heya," he said. "Take it easy."

"Don't worry," I said. "I drink alcohol like orange juice."

Which didn't mean: I can handle it. It meant: I drink all day long.

I picked one wine-soaked apple wedge from my glass. I tried to smile.

Back at the car, I pressed Maurice against the passenger door and kissed him hard, wrapping my fingers around the back of his neck to keep his face in place. The poet's window was still dark.

After we'd kissed for a while, Maurice gently pushed me away. "I'm having fun," he said, "but it's a little chilly." I rocked back, tripping my back heel against the curb. I could feel the sickness rising. There was a sense of something heavy draped across the back of my throat, like wool that had gotten wet. Sweet saliva prickled across my tongue. I pulled away, lowered myself to the sidewalk, and tried to pull out a cigarette. I yanked too hard and it bent into a shallow V. I lit it anyway.

"I'll take you home." Maurice stretched out his hand to help me up, but I brushed it away.

"I just want to sit for a second." I took deep smoky breaths. After a few drags I started gagging. "Oh, Jesus." I dropped to my knees in the street and started retching. Maurice kept his hand on the small of my back. I glanced at the poet's window. It was still dark. "Do you even *live* here anymore?" I whispered. Maybe he'd gotten a job with different hours. Maybe he was sleeping elsewhere.

"What's that?" Maurice knelt down beside me. He gave me a tissue to wipe the spit from my mouth. It hung in glistening trails like bits of spiderweb.

"Nothing," I said. "I'm sorry." I turned his face toward mine and stroked my thumb beneath his eye. There was a tear on his cheekbone. I smoothed it against the grain of his pores. "We make homes in the air," I said. "In which being there together is enough." I was drunk. I knew I wasn't getting it quite right.

"He lives up there, doesn't he?"

"Yes."

"I thought this could be something."

"Maybe it can." I didn't want him to leave.

"I don't think . . . I don't think I care enough to keep on doing this, like this." He shook his head. "Is that an awful thing to say?"

I nodded. It felt awful. I would keep doing this either way. He was the one who had a choice.

"I thought I could fix it," he said. "I'm sorry." He kissed my cheek. I knew he could smell the vomit on my breath.

"Good-bye," he said, standing. I sat back on the curb and looked up. I could see his loneliness, the way it made his arms sag in their sockets. I imagined him going back to his island and punching simple sentences onto clean sheets: *Tonight I feel sad. Love is a terrible, terrible thing.* I imagined Boris staring off into his old familiar darkness.

I wanted to say: "I'm sorry if I hurt you." But I couldn't.

I shrugged. He shrugged. He walked away.

I smoked five more cigarettes, waiting for the poet to come home, but he never arrived. For once, I wasn't sure I wanted him to return. The desire had gotten so familiar, it was hard to tell if it was still there.

The next afternoon, I asked my roommate to do me a favor. "Could you help me move something?"

"Where to?"

"To the Great Outdoors. But you'll only need to come part of the way."

She rolled her eyes, already familiar with the way I spoke.

Together we dragged my small black couch down our stairs and halfway up the block. I paused a few times to make sure it wasn't collecting grit. We jammed it into the back of my station wagon, squeezing ourselves against the front fender of a police car whose side panels said: SEX SQUAD.

At midnight, I got in my car and drove up Market until it curved into the hills. I crested suddenly into a thick layer of fog. It felt like the outer reaches of the city were an ecosystem of their own.

All the way up, I could sense the couch casting its dark pleathery shadows across my trunk. I took the turns hard up Twin Peaks, palms slick on the steering wheel as I imagined making the call. Would I disguise my voice or not? It seemed absurd either way.

I was scared that the observation deck would be crowded with drunk boys and territorial couples, but it was just me and one sheepish pair of lovers, plump and tight-jeaned, who'd brought their sleeping baby with them. They looked younger than I was. I raised two fingers in a jerky salute. The boy tipped his Giants cap in reply.

I sat in my car and found a Rod Stewart marathon on the radio. I pulled out my diary but for once I wasn't planning to write in it. I fished around to find Maurice's card.

I dialed the number and hung up. Then I dialed the number and didn't.

The night manager picked up. "Fleming's Auto. What's your worry?" I pictured his bony face, his hidden bag of peanuts.

"I've got a flat and no donut," I said. "I need a tow."

"Our guy's answering a call in Russian Hill," he said. "But he can get you after he's finished. Where you at?"

"Twin Peaks. At the top."

He chuckled. "You're not alone, right?"

"Actually I am," I said. "Just me and my flat."

I turned on the heat in my car and waited. I watched the couple sitting near the telescopes, stealing kisses above the bundled form between them. Every once in a while they glanced back.

After "Broken Arrow" came to its woeful close, I turned the station wagon around so that it faced away from the observation deck. I popped open the trunk and dragged out the couch. It wasn't hard. The couch was more of a futon, really, made of things that didn't weigh much.

I repositioned it a few times, turning it at different angles to face different sections of the city, but finally I just straightened it out, a dark hulk between two darker telescopes.

The couple watched me from their picnic table, but they didn't seem particularly surprised or curious. The woman smiled every time she caught my eye. The man nodded at me once, as if he knew exactly what I was up to, then gave me a sudden thumbs-up, as if he approved.

Once I'd gotten the couch settled, I sat down and lit a cigarette. I waited for the flash of headlights to illuminate me from behind.

Maurice parked his truck a few spots away and hopped out of the cab with a box of tools. I was leaning against the hood of my wagon, waiting.

"Oh," he said. "Hello."

"Hey."

He paused, glancing down around his feet. "I'm sorry about, you know, your flat tire ... I mean. And all that."

"I don't have a flat," I said. "I just wanted to show you something."

"Oh?"

"It's a gift."

He looked past me. "I remember what you told me about the city," he said. "How you like it better when you're not in it." He paused. "I think about that a lot."

I didn't want to talk about the city or its distance, the residue of my own stupid words.

I asked him: "Do you want to see it? The present?"

He said: "Sure."

When we rounded the corner of the car, he said: "Holy shit. It's a couch!"

I said: "Have a seat."

We sat like grade-schoolers, barely touching. Neither one of us spoke. I pointed out the couple and we watched them change their baby's diaper against the fallen lights of the city. I felt the summer break into things I could hold in one palm: a bent cigarette and a steaming sweet-corn pie, my own tombstone carved in fog-chilled chocolate. A note saying: *Slut.* A note saying: *So?* There were ash-speckled jackets all over those days, and Coke bottles collecting rain. I had a glass and it broke. I crushed a moth and it died. I had a month, but it ended. I had a heart. It remained.

GARTH RISK HALLBERG

New York University

Early Humans

The phone rings as I enter the outer sanctum Monday morning—or okay, less equivocally, it ring*tones*. The Barber Adagio for Strings. The theme from *Platoon*. "Stanley Cohn-Feldt Associates, kill for the love of killing!" Bethel declaims into her headset, and there's a moment when I have no idea what she's talking about, when even my own name sounds like nonsense.

Then it comes back to me: I was the one who gave her this line, back when I still had a taste for blood. It was supposed to be part of a presentation, in this case the invulnerable, *Terminator*-meets-*Predator*-but-on-your-behalf-but-still-never-go-against-an-agent presentation. At thirty, when you're luring talent away from CAA or William Morris, you're expected to climb on your workstation and beat your chest a little bit and maybe howl. (Though I always stopped short of ripping my shirt. A crisp white shirt was my cassock and camouflage and bulletproof vest. It became a second skin.) Now, for months, every third call on the call-list equals termination. I stand accused of a certain listlessness, a certain lack of focus. Around the tables at the Dining Room and Mr. Chow, the Joshes are murmuring: *Don't get us wrong, Stan Cohn-Feldt is a close personal friend. But—and this is said out of love—we're frankly seeing some risk factors since Lucinda left him. Some warning signs. And one has to ask, how much did she take with her? Sure, the dude is still bright and decent and so forth, but is he vibey, is he flux-positive? Does he get it? That is the question.* I'm down to a single client, a pint-sized fire-breather named Carrie Khan, and any minute now, the Freytag line will reach its climax, Carrie-wise, and it will be my blood on the walls.

This is probably her right now, calling to unload on me. I make the series of motions that means I'm not here. I slit my throat. I hang myself. I raise a handgun to my temple and blow my brains out. Then I raise a finger to my lips and tiptoe past Bethel's desk toward the inner sanctum. She sighs into her headset. "I'm sorry, Stan's in a screening. Can he return?"

Per my instructions, she's oiled the intrasanctuary door, whose squeak was becoming the sound track to my desperation. The only sound it makes is a soft click when I pull it shut. Still, after a long weekend of convalescence and Dad-management, I'm finding the inner portion of the sanctum very not feng shui. Very whatever the opposite of groovy is, very un: the Man Ray print, the machine. The surgical-steel desk where I left my hands-free when I checked out on Thursday. (Dead is the opposite of groovy.) If the last few months have taught me anything, it's that I have approximately thirty seconds before Bethel knocks on the door to ask what the hell is wrong with me. In bulleting out her upsides and liabilities, no one would charge her with a lack of curiosity. Or is the word concern? I put on my headset and dial Weather, so that when she sticks her head in, I'll appear to be in midpitch, forcing her to withdraw again.

Except Weather no longer exists. It occupies that kind of already-obsolete-but-not-yet-retro zone, the zone where my head resides. These days, everything is broadband, iBagels and ePants. There's a key I can push on my machine and a famous black spokesperson will intone, "Monday, June the sixteenth. Hazy and sunny, with a high of ninety-three." (And he used to be a renowned Shakespearean. Does that make it better, or worse?) The guy unfortunate enough to have been recycled on the old Weather number is interrupting my ostensible pitch to tell me that his name is Dylan Polk. That he hasn't even *seen the goddamn script, man.* That he has *like zero concept* what I mean.

"I don't suppose you know the temperature," I say.

"No, I don't know the goddamn temperature, man. But so hey—do you really see a part in it for me? Because as a Gemini, I'm a double threat. I do comedy, tragedy, dancing, whatever."

I'm feeling the onset of epiphany, like a migraine. I hang up on Dylan Polk. I buzz out to Bethel and ask her to start mining for intelligence on the formerly renowned Shakespearean. I'm seeing a potential client here who's not being appreciated for the truth of his performance. And does he have representation?

To poach is not the most ethical of behaviors, but in the months since Lucinda left, Stan Cohn-Feldt, once the envy of Joshes, has become a one-man game preserve, purely poached upon. If I'm going to be supporting Dad now, it's time to reacquire the old sanguinary habits posthaste. As all mojo flows from the List; and as all I've got to flow from, at present, is the Khan; and as Carrie-space is unspeakably tenuous, the phone will have to be avoided. All covenants will be made in person. "Bethel," I say to the overcom. "I don't care who calls, babe, you've lost me. I'm in a canyon." Then I go and stand in the closet with the door closed. In the dark. Between rows of identical soft blue suits.

Darkness opens up interesting perceptual spaces. Back when I was still a man, the late P.M. was when my best thinking got done. Lucinda and I would lie out on the veranda in our matching deck chairs, skimming the trades by the gentle glow of the light pollution. For hours after she fell asleep, I'd run through Carrie Khan blueprints. *Carrie—can I call you Carrie?—what I am loving for you is a halftime show. I'm seeing a chariot carrying Carrie across the Rose Bowl fifty yard line. Or no, wait. A squadron of cowboys—that whole hunky-yet-wholesome, rah-rah-go-America gestalt. I'm seeing the Carrie-themed quiescent treat the masses have been craving. Carrie Garcia. I'm seeing commercials: the ice cream of the future, paid for with a credit card embossed with your likeness. The CarrieCard—are you hearing this? A credit card that, through its generous cash-back mechanism, will someday cure AIDS.* That surprise ending, that philanthropic angle—that was my trademark.

Now the deck chairs are not an option, and when I slipped out back after pizza last night, what was I seeing? I was seeing the Y of the HOLLYWOOD sign blazing above the roofline. I was seeing the window of the screening room, the erstwhile screening room that had become Dad's room as of Saturday morning. The window was yellow. Dad-space was active again. This Thursday, he would turn eighty-two. And what do you get for the man who will accept nothing? I lay on my back on the bare tiles, a tumbler of Campari near to hand, and pondered this timeless question. I looked for the blueprint behind the violet miasma of smog. The miasmic, almost cosmic smog. Violent. I couldn't see an answer. I couldn't even see stars. *You're the man,* I whispered. *Still the man, Stan.* But beneath that, I was thinking, *Silence, you fucking mouse.* I waited for the window to go dark before I headed inside. I paused in the hallway and said, "Pop?" But soft, so he wouldn't answer. Lately, wherefore I know not, I'm barely hanging on. No, wait.

Having had another, better epiphany, I sally forth from the shadows and clamp my headset back on. I activate the hands-free. From the inner sanctum, I dial the outer sanctum. "Kill for the love of killing!" she says.

"It's me. Stanley," I say.

"I'm sorry, can he return? I seem to have lost him in a canyon."

"I'm out of my canyon now, Bethel. I need you to say I'm in a staff meeting."

"I am your staff," she says. "The army of one, remember?"

"A meeting of my entire staff, except you, whom I have tasked with the answering of the phone. Terribly important meeting. Especially if Carrie should call. That was her just now, wasn't it? Or was it my dad? Don't tell me it was—"

"It was the copier guy. The copier's on the fritz again."

"Crucial staff meeting, Bethel. Say it back to me." I'm standing in front of her desk now.

She takes a long swig from the torpedo of water on her desk, and a tattoo peeks from beneath a short sleeve. "Whatever," she mutters into her headset.

"I can hear you," I say into my headset. For the first time since Thursday afternoon, our eyes meet. Hers are red-rimmed and tired and full of misgivings. I would have missed this—her whole huffy, go-ahead-and-terminate-me presentation. I'm wondering what would happen if I leaned forward at this very moment and planted a big, wet kiss right on her furrowed brow. If I Santa Claused her with a giant novelty check for a million dollars, which is what she's worth. But our accounts are inches from receivership, and I have forgotten how to give big love.

Pulling out of the parking lot, I slouch down behind the wheel, in case Carrie or Carrie's people are on the lookout. Only on Sepulveda, with the land stretching out around me, do I straighten up and put on my dark glasses. I'm still wanting to present the ideal agent as a machine-tooled bionic unit—bloodless, unfeeling, highly effective. With one eye, I scan the sidewalks and outdoor eating areas for rising stars and potential rising stars. With the other, I search among the fast-food signs and mirrored office blocks for this place I must have passed a million times without really ever seeing it. And after several barren miles, there it is: a poured-concrete Krakatoa, King Kong scaling an Empire State replica. In place of Fay Wray, he holds between his palm and opposable thumb a sign that says, ADVENTURE GOLF. ERUPTION EVERY HALF HOUR. TODDLERS PAY HALF-PRICE! Truly, this is deus ex machina.

I come in from the garage that night fully intending to tell Dad about the capital-F Fun I have planned for him, but he gets the first word. "You're late."

I recline on the sectional sofa. "And a prosperous afternoon to you, too."

"Don't be clever." My gaze follows his to the plasma TV I had rush-delivered Saturday, preparatory to his arrival. *Five hundred channels,* I told him. *More TV than you could ever want.* Now a low-speed chase is on; the dragonfly shadows of news-copters flit across the freeway. "Everything is tawdry out here," he says.

"Shall we consume, Dad? Shall we devour? Masticate?"

He takes off his glasses, closes his eyes, pinches the bridge of his nose.

I clear my throat. "Have you eaten?"

"Eat, what would I eat? All I see in that refrigerator is old milk and yellow broccoli. Look at you, you're wasting away."

I look instead at the gut debouched above his belt line. Clearly, he's projecting. "I'm in the very pink of health, Pop. We'll order in again."

"I bet there was food when Lucinda was here."

"Please, not Lucinda."

"The point is, if I'd known you were going to start living like a wild animal, I'd have come out as soon as she left you." He raises the remote, changes the channel. Montel is resting his chin on his fist to consider the plight of a guest who is Wiccan, or possessed, only her mother seems to know for sure. Montel is kneeling to take the mother's hand in his. At this moment, Montel is a model of probity, and I'm wondering how they're treating him over at Enterprise. Actually, I'm wondering what it would be like to have someone pat my hand and nod thoughtfully while I tried to explain. But Dad just repeats that he wishes Lucinda were around, what a good, sweet, forthcoming, and plainspoken person she was. *You met her only that one time, at the funeral,* I want to remind him, but my killer instinct flags. "We'll order in," I say again. As I push myself up off the sofa and head into the kitchen to take my pill, he's still talking about my ex-almost-fiancée, and how she reminded him of Mom.

As a high-energy, highly motivated, and performance-enhanced individual, one learns to run on little sleep. This requires quantities of caffeine. I've squired enough clients, among them the dread Khan herself, discreetly through the gates of Betty Ford, to recognize the rhythms of addiction, but even after every other appetite has abandoned me, I can't kick the habit. The office is in Century City, but on Tuesday morning, I elect to bibulate in El Segundo. The drive affords time to stratagem, and the staff at the El Segundo outlet is composed almost entirely of talent seeking representation. And because all wisdom, in the industry, flows from the margins inward, the worms that turn up in the suburbs—who's up, who's down, whose space is or is not currently meaningful—tend to be fresher than those that have made their way to Hollywood's aseptic core.

At nine A.M. the Queequeg's drive-through is choked with traffic, but it's better to be inside anyway. The coffee franchise is like a satellite Spago, abuzz with blue suits and the matutinal intelligence of the studios, and one can learn a lot just standing in line. I nod to the Joshes pacing, gesturing, spieling darkly into their hands-frees, like people hearing voices. *Josh? Josh here. Are we to understand that Lucinda R. is now a player in the Carrie Khan sweepstakes?* Then, to avoid the appearance of eavesdropping, I step toward the counter. Every Queequeg's is alike—minimalist, vaguely earth-toned, that bridge-of-the-Death-Star-only-crunchier aesthetic. What's beautiful, I've always thought, is the complete inter-Queequeg uniformity. This is the miracle of quality control, of the diagonally integrated delivery unit. The way every goose flying south in a November V will mimic the one ahead of it, save one. But something is off. I know Leon, who works the register. We go way back. But the redheaded barrista struggling to unlock the espresso pistol from the machine—her I've never seen before.

"Redeye, right?" Leon says. We do a handclasp, thumb to thumb, fingers wiggling, concluding with a snap. Silly to whatever degree it's not ironic. "Doppio espresso, venti dark?"

"How about iced? It's purgatorial out there." I roll out the big word louder than is probably necessary, working hard to sound like I'm not working hard to sound cool, because you can't work too hard. And what I meant was "infernal."

"You read my treatment yet?" he asks.

"The *Mad Max* meets *Dr. Doolittle 2*?"

"It's more of a *Lethal Weapon 3* meets *Gorillas in the Mist* thing. Unputdownable, is my girlfriend's verdict."

"BlackBerry it to me, bro." This has threatened to become a running thing with us, but today I actually mean it. "I intend to skim it as soon as I get to the office. Has this intelligence not reached El Segundo? The List is being restructured. The Cohn-Feldt effect is back."

"Dude. The mind of man hath not power to conceive."

To the woman, I suggest, gently, "What about the other way?"

Without acknowledging me, she reverses her grip. She puts so much torque behind it that, when the holder comes loose from the machine, she is spun all the way around to face me. Espresso grounds spatter the floor and strafe the front of my shirt. "Shit," she says. "Sorry." The accent is East Coast. In the moment between when she turns red and when she kneels to mop up the grounds, I ascertain that she has fine bones and skim-milk skin and no bustline to speak of and is completely, utterly, tongue-tyingly beautiful. ANNIE, her laminate says.

When she's done with the floor, she hands me a towel. She doesn't let go immediately, and for a second we're looking at each other, and I'm seeing her in the passenger's seat of a convertible and the wind is in her hair. Also the sun. There are birds wheeling whitely across a winter sky. I'm hearing a pop song, seeing her plug into the whole SoCal mystery of existence. But all I can manage is "Thanks."

Leon turns to fiddle with the espresso equipment. Over the ungodly whine of the steamer, she says, "He's letting you see the treatment, huh?" Her eyes narrow to take in the blue suit, the polished shoes. "What are you, an agent or something?"

I hand her back the towel. "We prefer the term bloodsucker. Are you needing representation? Because I could refer you..." The milk is steamed. There is a silence. Silence is terrible. "Actually, I'm always hungry for new talent. I'd be happy to give you my number." When I slide my card across the counter, she flushes again.

"God, it's called small talk. Heard of it?" Then, under her breath: "Jerk."

She's not going to last long at Queequeg's, I think. There's the rigid corporate courtesy code. Probably I'll never see her again. (Better, or worse?) Out loud, I say, "Um..." Then Leon has my redeye ready. I throw down a five and flee, forgetting the chai latte I've promised Bethel.

See, it's the uncertainty that kills you, or the fear of the uncertainty. No, honestly, it's the fear. You think you'll have a heart attack if the phone starts ringing, but the phone can be eerily silent when you've only got one client, and that client is four foot eleven of sheer fury, and her call continues not to come.

I waste most of Wednesday hunched in my Aeron chair, swigging Maalox, drumming on the glass desktop and awaiting the ringtone of judgment. A Carrie ringtone—theme from *Jaws*—might finish me off. An unidentified caller ringtone—*Platoon*—would mean there's life in me yet. And what about Annie, that whole meet-cute in the coffee outlet? It's absurd how much I depend on women. In the outer sanctum, Bethel riffles the pages of *Variety*. She's dying to know what happened to me last weekend, but she still hasn't asked, God bless her and her eyebrow piercing.

From the machine, a digitized voice announces, "The time is three o'clock." Bethel has informed me that the renowned former Shakespearean is quite happy with his current representation, that he's really raking it in on this time-weather blueprint, and that Montel is in Cabo through the end of the month. To make up for yesterday's chai latte oversight, I let her go early for the day. Once the noise of her motorcycle has dwindled to silence, I call and listen to the moviephone guy until I've exhausted the new releases. I try swiveling in my chair, the way I used to when I was a kid and Dad would take me to his office in the summer. I'd pretend I was an astronaut encountering g-forces, but positive ideation has been difficult of late.

I find myself empathizing with Carrie Khan as I wasn't able to when she backed-into-slash-ran-down that paparazzo with her Hummer, or when, in a rage blackout, she punched out the autograph-seeking flight attendant (who, to be fair, had been warned). I.e., I'm connecting on a meaningful personal level with the dowdy sweatshirts and ball caps she's taken to wearing—the ones I've told her shave twenty Benjies off her market valuation each time she appears in public. Maybe Stan Cohn-Feldt, too, should start dressing down, start letting himself go.

I double-click on Leon's treatment, about a hotheaded Bombay detective who has to go undercover to infiltrate a gang of urban monkeys. Right around the point at which the chief of police insists that the detective start wearing a wire, which should be a point of maximal interest and tension, the words on the screen go out of focus. I keep seeing Lucinda's face, the window of the moving van rolling up. It dissolves into the luminous face of the woman from Queequeg's. She was right, I think. I am a jerk.

And again Dad's opening gambit when I get back to the house is, "You're late." He follows up with "I don't see why you're back at work already."

Thursday afternoon, I'm creeping across the living room carpet, hoping to make it to his chair before he can notice I'm home early. On the five o'clock news, a woman is flashing a finger to photographers, shooting them a digitally blurred bird. I avert my eyes, not eager to know if she is who I think she is. I lay my hand on his shoulder. "Waaszaap!"

He shudders like a wet dog. "For crying out loud, Son, do you want to give me another heart attack? What does that even mean, anyway?"

"*Waaszaap.* Multipurpose word, dating to Cro-Magnon times. Like *shalom.* Today, it means happy birthday. I'm taking you out for a surprise."

He claps twice, and the screen goes dark. "If that's what you call a surprise, I don't want any more surprises. My heart can't take it."

"How about just a nice meal?"

He looks at me for a minute, eyes anthracite behind the plastic lenses of his glasses. Eighty-two and he can still outstare me. Then he grunts and pushes himself up out of the lounger I bought him, whose shrink-wrap he has refused to remove. When I offer him a hand, he bats it away. "I can take care of myself, thank you very much." The implication is, I think, clear.

I was in a taxi the previous Friday when the call came. I had gotten so used to the hands-free that I'd almost forgotten what it felt like to have the cell tremble in my pocket. Bethel told me she had my father on the line. Then, ignoring my pleas that I was taking a meeting, that I was on-set, that I was deep in the Mariana Trench, she patched him through. She must have known somehow that I needed to hear from him. "Hi, yes, how are you?" I asked. "Is everything okay, Dad-wise?" This was on the 405, coming back from the hospital. At any moment, he was going to ask what had happened. I prayed for a solar flare.

The next morning, he was standing in the pickup zone outside of LAX: a short man, rounder than when I'd last seen him, but still with all his thick black hair. Wearing a raincoat in the dazzling June heat. Very Eastern European. Very *Being There*. One small suitcase was all he carried—the old-fashioned kind, without wheels. Superlative, I thought; he was only planning to stay a few days. But true to his threats, he had settled in for good. Hadn't consulted me, had just decided, in his actuarial way, that moving in to keep an eye on Stan was the needful thing, and so had done it. Had never even been to L.A. before, but hadn't commented on the palm trees, the mountains, had just complained about the car and the smog and read every road sign aloud.

Now, getting back into my little Boxster, he makes these grunting noises, as though it is physically painful for him to put his body in this car. The complaints are static. Not enough headroom. Speakers too loud. What's wrong with a good old American car? What's wrong with a good old American car, I tell him, besides subpar emissions standards, is the signal it sends to talent. The aw-shucks presentation, the not-going-out, ascetic-because-all-my-focus-is-on-you-the-client presentation. These have been known to gain traction in the short term. But the big picture is that the patina of power and sex and wealth and pleasure is what attracts the talent. And isn't that what we're all after? Power and sex and whatever else I just said?

"How about joy?" (He's one to talk, I think.) "How about the simple joy of knowing you've done an honest day's work?"

"Every day you tell me I work too much, Dad."

He falls silent, stares out at the blur of billboards and the hills scrolling past in the distance, ocher and umber and sienna. It's a silence I've known since I was a kid, and therefore one of the only comfortable kinds of silence. The silence of being in a car with Dad.

I valet-park at the hip meatatarian restaurant that's been getting all the write-ups. No vegetables, no grains, just meat: mixed-beef salad with a creamy marrow ranch; a tofu-substitute made of fish. He stops outside the glass door. "This place is filthy. Look at the fingerprints on the door. I'm not going in here."

I can't see the fingerprints, but I know better than to argue. "Where do you want to go, Dad? Everything else is vegan." We end up at an In-N-Out Burger in Van Nuys. No glitz, no aspirations, no fresh blood. But no Genghis Khan, either.

We set our trays down across from each other and settle into our molded plastic seats.

He unwraps the first of three double hamburgers and digs in. When I unwrap mine, the top half of the sandwich falls off. A layer of bun has sponged up the grease and adhered to the surface of the patty. It looks nothing like food is supposed to look. It looks devoid of all-important mouthfeel, but you sell sizzle, not steak, and when your dad says "Eat," what is there to do but obey?

For a while, we graze in silence, broken only by the pop of his jaw-bone. This silence, too, is familiar, but I'm feeling the old familiar need to fill it with noise. When I can't take it any longer, I raise my sweaty paper cup and bump it against his. "Here's looking at you, birthday boy."

His mouth is full. He grunts. I wonder if he's depressed.

"You know, we don't have to dwell in this whole not-talking-about-things space. We could ask each other questions."

"Like what?" he says.

"Like how's work."

"How's work?"

"How is work? Work is not good, Dad."

"There's no problem so bad we can't figure it out between the two of us."

"This isn't the kind of problem you just figure out." I take a breath. "Okay, you remember that actress I told you about, the first client on my List? Carrie?"

"The one who threw the champagne glasses at the hotel concierge?" he asks. "The one who spent a weekend in Las Vegas with the male dancer?"

"Where are you getting your intelligence, Dad? Is this on the talk shows? Jesus. I should put you on payroll."

"The Carrie who's put on all the weight, you mean."

"That's the one. She's totally going to fire me."

"I say good riddance. You're lucky your limbs are intact."

"And when the call comes, that's it. Show's over for Stan."

He freezes in midbite.

"Jobwise, I mean. As of last Thursday, she's all I have left. I'm just sitting there all week, waiting for the other heel to drop."

"Why does she have to be the one to call? Why don't you call her first? Clear the air, like we're doing here."

"Is that what we're doing?" I take my pill, hydrate with the dregs of my soda. The doctor said it might be about a week before I felt something change. That was about a week ago.

Frankly, no one grows up dreaming of being an agent. No schoolboy doodles call-lists in the margins of his math homework. No mousy little boy goes to sleep in Gersh pajamas, between Kewpie Lastfogel sheets. You want to direct, or you want to act, or you want, God help you, to write. Or something else, something better. You want to be the pro golfer your father wants you to be, the Hebrew Arnie Palmer. You want to save people from burning buildings. You want to go to the moon. But your short game sucks, your courage flags, and your growth peaks out at five seven, too small for the astronaut suit. Working your way through college, you pick up some cash in a copy room, or as a script-runner. And you're excited just to be a part of it, the V, the glimmering matrix, the star-making machinery, the source of all meaning in the universe.

Like a bird on a thermal, you ascend. You'd find, if you thought about it, that it's getting harder to leave the formation. But you don't think about it. You're a part of it now, and there's a part of you that likes being a part of it. You bring down the buffalo. You drink the blood, consume the meat, collect the hides, go home and fuck the women, the women who want to be a part of it, too.

You're the man.

The man is not embarrassed to address visiting potentates as *bro* and *dude*—anything to close the deal. The man knows all the elaborate handclasps. The man listens exclusively to up-and-comers like M. C. Escher and Orange Julius, represents Orange Julius's interests on a made-for-television movie, catches on to a word like *crunk* before anyone else, throws it around like Silly Putty. The man takes up squash. The man is, if not respected, at least feared. By most of the people, most of the time. What is feared by all of the people is the mouse. The mouse must be rooted out and silenced, because a pitch like *Let me be your personal asshole* must be delivered in complete seriousness, and if anyone should hear the voice wavering, the mouse squeaking: Game, set, match. The only person who didn't fear the mouse was Lucinda.

In the beginning, what I was loving was how far outside the matrix she seemed, how unhungry, how smart, how thoughtful, how kind. And yet still passionate about films, which she called *movies*. The screening room was our room. We would close the door and watch John Ford Westerns with no clothes on and *fumar el marijuana* and forget about Mom's prognosis. Later, when the scripts began to pile up, we'd sit out on the veranda and read them. She had a gift. She was the one, in fact, who spotted *The Muppet Pentateuch.* She was only ten pages into the treatment when she looked up, that quick gray fire in her eyes. "What about Rachel?" she said. "What about Carrie Khan for Rachel?"

"I don't know if she'd agree to Rachel," I said. "How about Eve? Eve's the one who goes above the title. Without Eve, no Rachel."

She gnawed for a few seconds on the arm of her glasses. "But I'm loving Rachel for Carrie. Old. Long-suffering. Prosthetics, or she could put on some pounds. It could be a real stretch for Carrie. This could be her *Raging Bull.*"

I let the idea marinate. Maybe Lucinda was just jealous of the focus Carrie was commanding from me, maybe an ugly Carrie Khan was her revenge, but she was right. Sure, it took a lot of makeup work and steak tartare, it wasn't glamorous, but it got Carrie the support-ing actress nod. On the big night Lucinda and I dressed up. We sat near the back of the Shrine, where they stick all the Joshes, and squeezed hands. Everyone had told me you just hope to get a men-tion in the acceptance speech. What Lucinda didn't know was that I'd told Carrie to leave me out, to thank Lucinda instead. And then I was going to ask her to marry me. Except Carrie didn't win, and the moment passed. The mouse had reared its head.

Then Mom died, and Lucinda got the call from CAA, and sud-denly we were competing. She took the entire smart-thoughtful-kind presentation I'd loved and monetized it. And worked late. Some nights we ate separately. Some nights we only met one another in the dark at two A.M., when I'd come in from the veranda with a head full of glittering synergies. The Joshes remarked at how perfectly matched we were. The Joshes wondered how long it would last.

One night I wandered into the Jacuzzi room with my Campari and began to unbutton my shirt, and it hit me. "Campari!" I said. "*Carrie* with an *amp* in the middle. We could use this."

And she looked at me as she might a script guy and said, "I want to transition, Stan."

Normally, you carry with you a constant dread of transitions, of the calls that say, *Just so you know, in the interest of full disclosure and ethics and et cetera, I met with so-and-so at Endeavor today, because I'm feeling I'm not getting the kind of attention I need, the love I deserve.* But after Lucinda left, everything went flat. It was Christmas, and I couldn't even bring myself to Santa Claus. A box of artisanal cheeses sat smelling up the office until Bethel threw them out. "You are suck-ing, Stan," she said, and it was true. I was no longer in the shiny, plummy place I'd started out in. Which maybe signified something, justicewise. I spent so much time trying to figure out if any of it had been real, Lucinda or anything else, that I hardly noticed my talent slipping away, my List becoming her List. I guess you never realize how much you'll miss people until they're gone.

When we are still a few blocks away from the surprise, I ask Dad to cover his eyes. He grumbles something about being too old for this, but apparently my powers of persuasion haven't completely deserted me, because just as I begin to ratchet up my pitch, he raises his fingers to his face. In the strobe of the arc lights we're passing underneath, I'm seeing how papery the skin is. I'm seeing the liver spots. They remind me of Carrie's hands, when she played opposite George Carruthers, the goy patriarch of patriarchs. I had to be on-set twelve hours a day then, working for Carrie, meeting Carrie's needs, showing dedication to Carrie, giving Carrie my biggest love. Building a relationship, the Joshes called it. I wonder what Lucinda called it. When King Kong rises above the gas station next door, I reach over and pat Dad's leg. "Okay, you can open up."

"Adventure Golf," he reads. "What does this mean?"

"I thought we'd play a round."

The holographic dash clock flips to 8:30. On cue, the volcano begins to erupt. "This isn't golf," he says.

"It's on me. For your birthday. For old times' sake."

Inside the little tiki hut from *Apocalypse Now,* where you buy your tickets, I pick up a lime green ball. He chooses a white one, because *what's wrong with a good old white ball?* It takes him five minutes to select a putter. I don't have the heart to tell him that they're all the same, just different sizes. Then, on the first green, he insists on taking practice strokes. I tell the couple behind us to go ahead. It won't be the last time someone has to play through.

Dad had some aspirations of becoming a professional before he succumbed to the siren song of life insurance. The country clubs had their membership rules, but it used to be a ritual with us that, when-

ever I'd go home to Milwaukee, we'd play the municipal course together. I drove fine, but had problems with the short game. "You're
all knotted up," he'd scold. Now, with age and a bum heart, the short
game is all he's got left. I don't know how long it's been since he held
a club—this is one of the many things we haven't really talked
about—but he plays every hole as if it's the eighteenth at Pebble
Beach, as if his life depended on it. Ever the big-picture type, I am
continually dumbfounded by the nuances of the green. Several times
he invokes the six-stroke limit on me. "You're up there in your head
again, Stan."

Even after there is no chance of my winning, he takes his time setting up his shots. He analyzes the topography minutely, grumbling
all the while that this is gimmickry, not really golf at all. And every
time he makes par, he turns to me, as if to say, "How do you like
that?" He licks the pencil and keeps meticulous score. When the
audio-animatronic showgirl from *Showgirls* kicks his ball back at
him, the man in me cheers mousily, shamefully—it is his birthday,
goddammit.

Humidity swirls around the electric lights overhead. As Dad
stoops to putt on the seventeenth, I can see the sweat stains spreading across the Ban Lon of his shirt. All this walking has him breathing heavy, but when I ask him if he wants to sit down with me for a
minute on the deck of the miniature *Titanic,* he shakes his head.

The final hole boasts split-level architecture. You start atop a
poured-concrete cliff with a little replica of the mansion from *Citizen
Kane.* You putt into one of three holes, each of which is connected to
its own PVC pipe. The pipes spit your ball out at varying angles on
the lower green, a perfect, flat lily pad of a green, where you then
putt for the real hole, careful to avoid the sled. He makes me go first.
The green ball goes into the hole in the middle. He grunts. The
white ball goes into the hole on the left. I offer him my arm and help

him down the steps that lead to the lower green. When we get there, only my ball is visible: neon, fifteen feet from the cup.

"Where's mine?" he says.

"I think you got a hole in one, Dad."

He stands over the hole. "It goes all the way down."

"It goes back to the clubhouse. So people don't walk off with these extremely valuable balls. I think you just won us a free game."

I can tell he wants to frown at this. *Ridiculous. Who would steal a golf ball? Who ever heard of a free game?* But his cheeks, gleaming with perspiration beneath the fluorescent lights, are flushed with pride.

"Congratulations, Dad."

"You've got to putt out."

"There are people waiting." I wave up at the party scowling down on us from Xanadu.

"It's in the rules, Stan."

"There's no way I can beat you at this point."

"You think that ever made Jack Nicklaus quit? You think Ben Hogan gave up so easy?"

"Jesus." I address the ball. I'm in too big a hurry to think much about what I'm doing. I draw back the club, bring it through, feel a solid clunk radiate upward through the metal, into the meat of my hands. The ball rolls forward, pauses at the lip of the cup, and then, as if on a breath of wind, drops in.

"That's the way," Dad says. "You hang in there, Stan."

He puts his arm around me as we head back toward the tiki hut. He can afford to be magnanimous in victory, I guess. And though I am nearly bankrupt, financially and otherwise, I can afford to reward him. "Come on, old man. Dessert's on me."

I steel myself and cut the headlights. Through the windshield of the Boxster and the logoed plate glass, I watch her wipe down the counters, her red hair falling over her face. It is a face not unlike Lucinda's. It is America's-sweetheart hair.

"What's the holdup?" Dad wants to know.

"You wait here," I say. The only thing more daunting than facing the woman from Queequeg's again is facing her with Dad in tow.

"Guff. Air-conditioning will do me good. It's so hot out here, I don't know how anyone stands it." He's still panting from the miniature golf. I can't say no, and so, together, we go into Queequeg's.

"Hi," I say.

Annie looks up. There is no recognition in her face. So New York.

"We need one decaf mint mochachino, whipped cream and chocolate syrup."

"Need or want? I'm kind of closing up here."

"Need."

"It's my birthday," Dad croaks over my shoulder.

As she looks at him, a kindly smile lights her face like a paper lantern. Then her eyes widen. "Oh, my god, are you okay? Is he okay?"

I turn just in time to watch Dad go down, first onto his knees and then onto his back. I see myself kneeling beside him. A strange silence descends. Everything is moving very slowly, as if underwater. Everything is intuitive. I'm picking his head up off the floor, putting my hand under it to cushion his skull. "Dad, talk to me."

"It's this goddamn heart." His voice is raspy, halting, but irascible. "I knew it. Adventure Golf, I just knew it."

Without taking my eyes off of him, I tell Annie to call an ambulance. (At this point, the words practically roll off the tongue.) I lay my hand on his chest. "Your heart is still beating, Dad. Are you in any pain?"

He nods. I scan his big black eyes for some sign of whether or not he is going to live. "I'm going to die," he says.

"Not on your birthday you're not, damn it. Just save your breath now, Dad. Please."

I can hear Annie in the background, feeding the dispatcher directions. Maybe there are multiple Queequeg's in El Segundo, because she has to give the cross streets. Then she's draping a damp towel over my shoulder. "Two minutes." Not wanting to take my right hand off my dad's chest, I reach across myself with my left for the towel. I put it on his forehead. I clasp his hand in my free hand and squeeze.

"Stanislav," he says. "I have always taken joy in you."

"Oh, geez, Dad. Please don't try to talk. Please."

He turns to Annie, who's kneeling on the other side of him. "I worry about him, you know."

"Don't," I say. "Please."

"I told that nice secretary of yours, I worry you're going to try to kill yourself again."

For a man on the threshold between life and death, he is remarkably talkative. I glance up despite myself to make sure none of the Joshes are here, none of the personalities, slumming, none of the personal assistants ravenous for intelligence. There's only this woman I wanted so pathetically to impress, and she coughs into her fist and stands. "Jesus fucking Christ, Dad," I say, around the brass fist in my throat. "Why don't you say it a little louder?"

"It's nothing to be ashamed of."

"It's absolutely something to be ashamed of."

"You're right, it is. After all we've survived," he says, "you have to keep going."

"Awesome. I'll just soldier on because you're ashamed." His eyes close, and it hits me that these could be the last words he hears me speak. Then the water evaporates. Everything is speeding up again, to normal speed, to too fast. "Okay, Dad, I will. Just stay with me, and I will."

His eyelids open again; was this some kind of act? The eyes are lively, hard. Men in blue jumpsuits are hustling through the door. He squeezes my hand back. "Promise."

"I promise."

After checking him out, the paramedics seem to think this is all no big deal. They tell me as they load him into the back of the ambulance that, as he still seems to be lucid, it was most likely a little stutter brought on by the temperature shock. I can follow them in my car. Queequeg's Annie watches through the glass. On her face is the same mixture of pity and disgust Lucinda wore when she came to the house a week ago. Not that it matters anymore.

I need a second to calm down before I can drive. After climbing into the ambulance to tell him I'm right behind him, that I'll meet him at the hospital, that I'm sorry, that I love him, I sit out in the parking lot, on one of those concrete barriers that keeps the car from rolling through the space, and watch the flashing lights fade into the night. I remember, too late, what it means when we say "I love you" out here. My hands are still shaking when I get into the car.

Maybe if the light had been on in the car, or in the garage, I wouldn't have tried to exercise my option in the first place. Maybe if I'd been forced to see my actual finger on the actual button, the actual glass rolling down, actual keys in an actual ignition, I wouldn't have been able to see myself as a leading man, despondent, done wrong, having made a Very Big Decision. Maybe if Lucinda hadn't showed up last Thursday night in a moving van, to collect the last of her things . . . I hadn't seen her since New Year's, and as she directed the moving men toward the matching deck chairs, each calibrated by a team of yogis to our unique firmness preference, our sleep number, I spotted the diamond on her finger. She was moving on. And maybe if the California legislature hadn't been so green, maybe if a team of German engineers hadn't worked so hard to reduce the emissions of the Boxster, I'd be dead right now. I'm given to understand that it is relatively painless.

The fumes were rumored to be odor-negative, but as they filled the black garage, I kept sniffing the air anyway, unsure of what I was smelling. I was smelling the brand of facial mask Lucinda favored. I was seeing her at the funeral, in a thick black veil, tossing fragrant white flowers into my grave, along with that engagement ring, vowing never to love another. I was seeing Carrie Khan telling her analyst how like totally guilty she felt about all the trouble her antics had caused me. The autopsy revealed a nearly perforated ulcer, the therapist reminded her, just for good measure. Toxic levels of stress. Carrie's mean little face filled with remorse. No, wait. Lucinda's did. No, wait. It didn't. It filled with contempt again, because the autopsy revealed carbon monoxide poisoning. The autopsy revealed a fear of living alone. The autopsy revealed weakness and failure, abjection. Really, what I was seeing just before the fade-to-black was Bethel, curled up on the couch of her apartment, numb and bewildered, swearing never to forgive me. I was seeing my dad shake his head.

Reception in the garage had always been questionable, and I couldn't reach 911, but with the door open, I managed to raise Bethel on her cell. "I'm needing an ambulance to my house," I said. "Like yesterday." For once, to her credit, she didn't ask why.

The hospital headshrinker wasn't buying my accidental-exposure pitch. He was writing a prescription, he said, and would release me only on condition that I'd allow him to call my next of kin. "Which is who?" he prompted. *Lucinda Reede,* I started to say. Then I remembered she was gone. My next of kin was who my next of kin had always been. I was eight, in the principal's office for running my mouth in class. He was going to call my dad.

———

The morning after his birthday is a mess. My blueprint to reascend the food chain is in tatters, but who cares? I've spent all night at the hospital, at bedside this time. They'd given Dad something to help him sleep, and since he was mostly snoring, I could talk to him about things. About Lucinda. About Mom. There was a no-cell-phone rule on the wards, which meant I didn't have to worry about La Khan.

Then, in the afternoon, a call penetrates to the inner sanctum. The doctor is thinking pacemaker. She wants to keep him on the geriatrics unit while they run some tests. I'm seeing the sort of thinly disguised hospital entity the shrink had threatened me with a week earlier. I'm seeing beige or surgical pink, cacti on the sill of a window overlooking the parking lot. I step into the outer sanctum and tell Bethel I'm going for a drive. "Everything okay?"

"Not really. But it's okay."

"What should I say if anyone calls?"

"Say I went for a long drive."

"Can I say you'll return?"

"I don't know." On my way out of the office, I pause. "Hey, Bethel. You know how they say 'I love you' on the East Coast?"

For the first time in a week, she smiles. "Fuck you, Stan."

"Fuck you, too. And see if you can get me Carrie Khan on the hands-free."

It's early summer, and already the hills are tinder brown, tamping down kindling for the brush fires of autumn. This is the city's golden hour, when you can actually see the mountains and the sea at the same time, when the gaudy light diffuses and grows liquid. The sun gets caught up in it, in the shimmering net of it, and even the tire yards off the 110 strike a chord of beauty. Back when I was starting out, before we traded in the convertible for the Boxster, this used to be our favorite time. After lunch some days I'd play hooky and turn off the car phone so I couldn't be reached and would swing by the house for Lucinda. By the time rush hour hit, we'd be way up in the canyons, above it all, watching helicopters glide serenely as skaters across the surface of the valley, following another low-speed chase. I was thinking we might have kids.

It's been years, though, since I've really been able to see the golden hour from this angle. Having landed Carrie Khan, I found leaving work early not so workable, what with the traffic, what with the quirks of reception at that most imperative time just before the long silence of night. The golden hour became just a time to do food, to do drinks, to work the room at Piccolo Paradiso. To build relationships. Relationships were everything—thus sprach the Joshes.

I've just reached Mulholland when I hear the ringtone: good old "Ode to Joy," meaning Bethel.

"Stanley Cohn-Feldt's car, drive for the love of driving."

"I've got Carrie. Sounds steamed. She's in Monaco."

"As in Santa?"

"As in Europe. Should I put her through?"

"With all due alacrity."

There is the little crackle of transfer, as of the frayed ends of wires brushing against each other. There is a familiar voice on the other end of the line, bedraggled, its sharpness slightly pixilated by the satellites. "Goddammit, Cohn-Feldt, where have you been? Do you have any idea what time it is where I am?"

I admit that I don't.

"I'm paying you to know, Jew-boy. It's your job."

"Maybe you shouldn't pay me anymore."

"Very funny."

"I'm serious, Carrie. I'm calling to tender my resignation. I'm moving to New Zealand."

"Do you hear Carrie laughing? No, you don't. Why? Because it's four in the goddamn morning, Stan. This is not a laughing time for Carrie."

"What are you doing in Monaco, anyway?"

"Are we talking about me right now? We had better be. I'm not paying you to talk about you."

"Carrie, listen to me. I'm quitting. I'm getting out of the industry. I quit."

"It's always about you, isn't it, Stan? You you you. Stan Stan Stan. What about Carrie? What about Carrie's needs? And where the hell have you been all week?"

"You need someone who's going to be dedicated to you, babe. Who can give you more love than I can. I'm imploring you to let this marinate: I quit."

"I won't let you." This is a typically perverse maneuver, classic Khan, and I should have seen it coming. I should have asked her to renegotiate our contract instead; she would have transitioned in the blink of an eye. "You belong to me," she says. "You are my agent."

"And as your agent, I'm recommending you terminate me and go with Lucinda Reede at CAA. I know she's been talking to your people, telling them she's the one who found you every good part you ever landed. And she's right. She's going to be smarter, faster, and more focused than what you've been getting from me lately. Lucinda's a damn good agent."

"You make a compelling point, in terms of you suck. But I need you right now, Stan."

And suddenly, *mirabile dictu,* she's crying. Never in all our years together have I witnessed this. As Rachel, the once-barren leading lady blessed with child, she had to use onions. Now I'm not even seeing the mountains anymore. Just her chin and cheekbones, so much more angular than the screen makes them out to be, slick with genuine tears.

"Well, I didn't expect you to take it so hard, Carrie."

"Shut up." I hear her biting back a sob. "I'm pregnant."

"Oh, god." I remember the weight, the frumpy couture. "With the exotic dancer?"

"Rodrigo shitcanned me when I told him."

"Oh, Carrie. Are you keeping it?"

She starts crying again. "It hits the papers tomorrow, Stan. Colonel Larry said it was the last straw. Even my entourage quit. I can't handle this by myself."

"What am I supposed to do?"

"I don't know."

I'm suddenly remembering that she's only twenty-three, the poor thing. "All right, listen. Get on the next available flight. Bethel will call and find a house. We're going to figure something out, Carrie."

She sniffs. "You'd better."

"Together. Now before I go, do you want me to tell you what single motherhood is going to do to your bankability?"

"No."

"Good girl. Call me when you're on the ground, Carrie. *Ciao,*" I say. And as she *ciao*s back, it hits me: There is some power in this, this connection, this whole circle-of-life gestalt.

The geriatric unit is a long, low building, adjacent to one of the last undeveloped fields—not at all what I pictured. A nurse leads us to the end of a hall, where there's a sunporch with a sliding door to the wider world. Dad is sitting next to it, a wheeled hemostat monitor beside him. It's Saturday now, the first official day of summer, and beyond the open door a humid breeze sets the grass trembling. From the other side of the room, I hear the semis roaring by on the Santa

Ana. A woman carrying a naked plastic doll drifts by on a walker, pausing beside me. After a few seconds, I give up trying to ignore her and turn to look straight into her eyes.

"I love you. Very much," the woman says.

"Okay. Thanks."

She moves off. A shrill beep like the shriek of the world's largest hands-free startles me. I've left the outside door to the day room open for longer than the minute its timer permitted. My dad puts his hands to his ears, annoyed, but doesn't turn around. Maybe he hates being lumped in with these people, who remind him of his own proximity to the end credits. Or maybe he's seeing something out there. Maybe he's trying to hear Mom. Me? I'm hearing harps and trumpets playing the hallelujah chorus. I'm seeing him borne up to her by a flock of underwear models. Sooner or later that day is going to come, but I'm sure he'll know what to do when it does. Dad always knows what to do. I take a step toward him. "Pop?" I say. "There's someone here I want you to meet." Carrie has been hanging back at a distance, terrified by the walking wounded, but I motion for her to come forward. She reaches out. She takes my hand.

PETER MOUNTFORD

University of Washington

HORIZON

Lucy has come down to Sri Lanka after being away for nine years to help her mother, Anne, sell The Horizon. In the week since she came, Lucy's done nothing but sit in the shade of the hotel's decrepit tiki bar, reading Harlequin romances. She still hasn't even begun to broach the subject of the hotel's sale, or the related topic of what Anne should do afterward. Lucy believes that her mother should come back to Edinburgh, where Anne is from, and where she can be looked after as she staggers through her dotage, but Anne, now in her midsixties, has been down here, on the southernmost coast of Asia, for almost forty years, and will likely resist the suggestion that she should leave.

At breakfast, Lucy does her best to avoid the subject. "Mum, could you please put them away?" she says, referring to her mother's breasts. Anne has always sunbathed topless, but these days she's also taken to strutting around the hotel all day, bare-breasted, and smoking Burmese cheroots that smell like horse dung.

"Don't be such a prude," her mother says. "It's just tits."

"It's indecent, Mum, and unseemly. Gives the impression that you're going dotty." The truth is if this was once the subject of gossip among locals, it has long since exhausted itself. Lucy knows this, and still it's difficult. The most mortifying thing of all is that her mother has developed the habit of absently tugging on her left nipple.

"Nobody cares, Luce. I'm old and sexless, like a child." She has a puff from her cigar. "Oh, I forgot to tell you," she says, and winces at her daughter, "Mrs. Vanderheyden is coming tonight and will be around for a while." Her mother, who has developed a near Singhalese patience, that trait often mistaken by expats for laziness, didn't forget to tell her about Mrs. Vanderheyden's visit at all; she's just using her languor as a cover.

"Well, it'll be good to see her," Lucy says. It's certainly true that her mother's friend will, at least, absorb some of the time mother and daughter would otherwise spend driving each other mad. The Widow Vanderheyden is witty and hard, a cantankerous old hag, and the two widows, who are very close, cut a striking pair: one an earthy ex-hippy, the other an old colonial shrew. It's often the case, Lucy's found, that expatriates who'd have nothing in common in the first world are tight friends down here. The only problem with Mrs. Vanderheyden coming tonight is that it will make raising the subject of her mother's retirement and return to Scotland all the more difficult.

After a pause her mother once again steers the conversation to the subject of Lucy's recent divorce. Lucy and Simon were married nine years, and the last time she came down was for their honeymoon. The systemic problems of their relationship were, in essence, twofold: She didn't want to have children, he did, and she didn't want him to sleep around, but he did.

"Certainly it was for the best," Anne says, pausing to relight her cigar. "When I met him, Simon seemed cowish, I thought—useless.

Your father was useless, too, but at least he was entertaining. Your father also slept around, but it was a vice I came to appreciate in the latter years, because it spared me the burden."

Lucy winces. This mention of her father is deliberate. She should have come down when he died three years ago, but she was busy trying to resuscitate her marriage. She's only come now because her mother called last month saying she couldn't run The Horizon alone anymore. In that conversation Lucy found out that her father, who had allegedly died in his sleep, had actually died of a brain aneurysm while screwing his mistress in Cabin #5.

"Well, Mother," Lucy says, tempted by this candor to bring up the postretirement plan, "now I'm alone in Scotland and you're alone here. All of our men are gone or dead and we only have each other. We need to do a better job of being a family."

"Is that so?" Even after all this time away from Britain, her mother has a talent for inflecting her comments so dryly, so archly. "I thought we were doing a fine job."

"Very funny. And, just so you know, it wasn't Simon's infidelity that caused the divorce—that was just a symptom. The trouble was that we loved the *idea* of one another, not the reality."

"Oh my! Love and reality?" Anne says, with strained delight. "Since when did those two have anything to do with each other? Life requires plenty of imaginative interpretation, Luce. I wonder if you got all this Protestant angst from St. Leonard's." Then, flicking dark cinders onto the sand, "What a foul place—so full of righteous and puritanical nonsense."

Lucy rolls her eyes, and her mother grins in a way that reminds her of Jordan—mocking, but too charming to be hurtful. When they evacuated in 1983, during the violence of Black July, she and Jordan, her twin brother, deceased now, sat in the backseat on the drive to Colombo. Jordan challenged Lucy to a thumb war, and when she refused he smiled just like their mother—as if to tease her for her timidity. Overnight, ethnic strife had bloomed across the tiny tropical island, and now the Singhalese majority was out in mobs, going door to door, hacking entire Tamil families to pieces, burning their corpses, their houses, their cars.

None of them spoke during the drive to Colombo. When they entered the city the two children stared at the haphazardly piled bodies on the streets. Black columns of smoke lifted symmetrically, tilting in the coastal breeze. At the British High Commission's lobby, Anne's body quaked as she stood, squeezing the forearms of her blond, barefoot, and freckled twins.

In Scotland, the two of them, who were thirteen at the time, were given the choice to stay and enter a boarding school, or return to Sri Lanka for more homeschooling on the beach. By then The Horizon was already, for Lucy, a place marred by her isolation, and she wanted a normal life, even if she didn't yet know what that would be like. Visiting St. Leonard's the following week, she found hundreds of normal adolescent girls and she knew that each one could be her friend or not her friend—at least they were prepared to be curious, which was more than any other girl she had met could offer. While in Scotland she discovered television, lager, sweaters. For the first time in her life she shivered in the cold. Interviewing at the school, she begged them to take her.

The following week her brother visited Fettes College, which was nightmarish: a colossal Gothic building with jagged black spires. Boys in shorts looked as sallow as Dickensian orphans and everything was rigid and austere. Jordan wanted no part of it. At thirteen, the dangers of a country torn by ethnic strife must have seemed impossibly remote to him. His decision turned out to be a fatal one. The violence in Sri Lanka would claim his life in less than a year.

When he was still alive, but just after she began at St. Leonard's, the war escalated. The Tamil guerrillas, once a ragtag militia fighting to annex the eastern edge of the island, responded to July's slaughter by becoming an organized army of terrorist insurgents. Lucy heard about these developments in her mother's weekly letters, but from the safety of St. Leonard's, the violence was incomprehensible. Because travel was expensive, Lucy spent Christmas in Scotland with the Donalds—university friends of her parents who never had children of their own. During holidays in the coming years she grew very close to them. In fact, she still spends her Christmases at their house by Pitlochry.

This afternoon, the memories, stirred by familiarity, swirl in her mind as she sits in the tiki bar, gradually edging away from the sunlight as it inches across the floor. The day is oppressively calm. She and her mother have not spoken since breakfast, and her mother's words are still ricocheting around her mind. Occasionally Lucy glances up from her book to the waves falling short and hard against the shore, churning up foamy brown water, and beyond, to the sunlight sparkling on the sea. Around her the bar's bamboo is spotted black with rot, and overhead the sun has bleached the hay roof. Her legs are warm with sunburn. The thighs that she normally avoids looking at are pink and cellulite-pocked; thin varicose veins crack beneath her skin like distant blue lightning. It's almost dinnertime, and tonight, even though the Widow Vanderheyden will be there, she plans to address the subject of her mother's retirement.

Bored by her book and too listless to do anything else, Lucy watches her mother and Raju, the cook, play chess. To judge by the deliberate pace of the game, they are evenly matched. Huffing in concentration, her mother leans forward until her sweat-beaded upper lip is inches from the chessboard and her pendulous breasts sag to her thighs. She chews on her lower lip, twirling a lock of hair around her index finger. In her flat in Edinburgh, Lucy has a black-and-white photo of her parents on their wedding day. Examining her mother now, Lucy finds that she somehow understands the giddy nymph in the wedding photo better than she does the aging mother she only thought she knew. When Raju stands and lifts the chessboard, Lucy puts down her romance novel, and straightens her sari. It is time to pretend that everything is okay. She projects a grin and walks over. She sits down. "You have a nice day, Mum?"

"Of course. Every day is nice here. Are you hungry yet?"

"Yes, but—" Lucy lets the pause dangle. "Shouldn't we wait for the Widow?"

"Such manners!" Her mother pretends to be impressed. "Don't bother with her, Lucy, she'll be fine. She can fend for herself around here."

After showering, they reconvene in the dining hall attached to the lobby. Anne is wearing a shirt now, Lucy's happy to see. She tells Lucy that the Widow Vanderheyden has arrived and is taking a nap. Flames on torches bob in the breeze, and the rich odor of kerosene wafts through the open-air hall, mixing familiarly with frying fish.

They eat curried prawns with rice and a flavorless radish salad. Ceiling fans spin feebly. A moth the size of a sparrow darts through the rafters. Waves explode in the distance. Though aware that this is her opportunity, Lucy can't manage to bring up the subject of her mother's possible return to Scotland. The dining room is mostly empty. Only two families and one couple are staying at the hotel, and Lucy wonders if business has slowed since the Tamil Tigers blew up a bus in Colombo last month. She thinks to ask her mother, but does not say anything.

Instead, Anne tells Lucy the same heavily embellished stories she recites to her guests: when the ailing mongoose stumbled into the dining hall, and when Pierce Brosnan came to the hotel for lunch, in

1989, and kissed her, and so on. They drink gin and tonics and do not touch a basket of freshly fried poppadoms that glisten under the yellow lights. Poppadoms were Lucy and Jordan's favorite, but they're too greasy for her now. The two children would sit every day on the stoop of the kitchen and eat hot poppadoms with bottles of Fanta, which they took from the old refrigerator behind the bar. As children they had an unlimited supply of Fanta. It was one of the few benefits of growing up at The Horizon. That refrigerator is still around and it occasionally grumbles awake and begins buzzing loudly. When they were children chilly vapor would cascade out of it, but now its light does not work and it barely keeps anything cold. The rubber seal on its door is disintegrating.

While her mother continues her storytelling, Lucy's mind wanders. Childhood for the twins was difficult. They had five hours of homeschooling each morning and spent most of their afternoons at chores: raking debris off the beach, sweeping floors, making the guests' beds. They worked together and played together, wary of the other children who were soon to leave and unlikely to return. Those children had toys and televisions, whereas the twins had neither and had to rely on one another for entertainment. Mostly, they played "pirates," a game that involved stockpiling shells and guests' lost trinkets in an old ice chest they hid in a small cove north of the hotel.

The water there was tranquil and the tourists never came around because the rocky path was too treacherous for them. The twins fenced with pieces of bamboo and waded through the cove's shallow waters, trouser legs rolled up, hunting for treasure. Heavy sand giving underfoot, they scanned the floor, where lines of reflected light shimmied. The treasure they found included a digital watch with a broken band, a sea horse's exoskeleton, a silver ring with a cavity that once held a stone, many seashells, and an old ceramic chalice—possibly a genuine antique. Once, for Christmas, their parents added to their trove a pile of antique coins they'd bought at Galle Fort. Later that year Jordan removed the teeth of a beached hammerhead and, weaving palm fronds around a section of fishing twine, made Lucy a tooth-studded tiara.

The fantasy sustained them until puberty, which arrived first for her, then for him. The change in him was pronounced. He lost interest in their games and began spending his time hanging around the kitchen, waiting for the daughters of the staff. He crawled under the cabins and peeked through the floorboards at girls changing into their swimming suits.

After finishing his chores, he'd spend his afternoons in the rough waves in front of the hotel. These waves would thrust his gangly body to the seafloor and spin him like a sock in a washing machine. At dinner, he'd describe the experience rapturously, explaining how, in order to enjoy it, you had to let your body go limp and trust it would float up. "Once you relax, it's heavenly," he said. At the time, she thought there was nothing holy about this. It was an easy thrill, like peeking at naked girls. Their fights were incessant, and vicious. Still, she continued playing pirates alone until the day Jordan pulled the teeth from her tiara and made a necklace for himself. He told her she could keep "the rest of that so-called treasure."

After they have finished dinner, Mrs. Vanderheyden descends from Anne's apartment above the office, where she has been sleeping. She and Lucy kiss hello. Mrs. Vanderheyden is gecko-faced: She has a wide mouth and bulbous eyes, a flat nose with perpetually dilated nostrils. A flap of skin hangs beneath her chin like an inverted cockscomb. Older than Anne, she has been on the island for forty years. She still calls it Ceylon and talks about the "natives" as though they were another species.

"Aren't you pleased to be back home?" Mrs. Vanderheyden says, and grins, exposing a row of tall bottom teeth that teeter in her mouth. Her accent has an affected poshness that reminds Lucy of Katharine Hepburn, where a single phrase will often be half purr and half caw. "For all of its troubles," she says, "Ceylon is a lovely little nook. The sun does wonders for one's health. I was at the Hill Club last week, visiting the plantation, and the cold was unbearable." The tea plantation she inherited from her late husband can be traced back to the early days of British occupation. "I can't imagine how you exist in Edinburgh, Lucy. Isn't it the most dreary place in the world?"

"Not at all. A lot has changed in the last half century."

"Nonsense, Luce, it's miserable," her mother says. Then, turning to Mrs. Vanderheyden, "She hasn't said it yet, but Lucy wants me to return with her. I just know it. Can you imagine me there? Another pasty and bloated pensioner with stockings bunched at the ankles? Lucy would put me into one of those old-age compounds that they call *assisted living*—a poor euphemism for *guided dying*. It'll be her revenge on me for sending her to St. Leonard's—that dungeon for unwanted children."

"St. Leonard's saved my childhood," Lucy snipes, if only to disagree.

"It is a gulag for little girls and it ruined your childhood," her mother replies, "though it may well have saved your life."

As soon as the words are spoken, a heavy silence descends on the women.

In mentioning Lucy's survival, Anne has accidentally recalled Jordan's death. Lucy looks down at the floorboards and then, lifting her head, gazes at the darkness, where white foam marks the edge waves. Palms wheeze in the wind and grains of sand are kicked out of her hair, stinging her sunburned chest.

Having finished their meals, the guests have retired to their cabins. The women are alone at the tables. As the waiter clears the plates, the women remain silent, waiting until he is out of earshot before resuming.

Anne chuckles, grimaces weakly. "I'll languish there in assisted living—slurping cafeteria food among a constantly dwindling group of senile codgers, while the nurses stand by, defibrillators poised."

Mrs. Vanderheyden laughs too forcefully and her mirth disintegrates into a lung-rattling cough. Recovering, she gives Lucy a look with eyes so cold they might as well be dead. "Nonsense, Anne," she says. "She'd never dream of taking you away from us."

"I won't be able to fend her off for long," Anne says, and her daughter, for the first time, can hear the full weight of the sorrow in her voice. "I'm reaching that age when I'll have to do whatever she wants. It'll be diapers and baby food all over again."

"Please don't talk about me in the third person," Lucy says, then lifts her glass and finishes her gin and tonic. The ice is all melted and it tastes watery. She takes a breath and looks out at the darkness. It was ridiculous to think her mother would ever be convinced to return to Scotland. In fact, she wonders now if she ever actually believed it would be possible, or was it just something she told herself to make this visit seem less final.

Anne sighs and tosses what is left of her cigar out onto the sand. "With the money from selling the hotel," she says, "I could buy a house in Galle Fort and live out the remainder of my life there, happily. Apart from the occasional incident in Colombo, the war is to the north and the east now."

"You know as well as anyone that the war is everywhere that Tamils and Singhalese live side by side," Lucy says.

"Well," says the Widow Vanderheyden, reaching a shaky liver-spotted hand toward her cocktail, "the best insurance for a woman here is a Singhalese man. Maybe you could take a husband in Galle? One of the widowers?"

Lucy stares at the Widow, dumbfounded. Then, finding her voice, she says, "You'd have my mother shack up with some stranger? That's a wonderful idea! Let him have his way with you and spend your savings, show you off as his white trophy—all this in exchange for what, protection from the very tribe he is a part of? It's disgusting and embarrassing and I won't have it! Not *my* mother."

"Don't be so dramatic," Anne says, rattling the ice in her glass. "She has a point: this man, whoever he is, would enjoy the status I offer and, of course, the financial security, but no man would want to fuck an overweight old hag, white or not. And even if he did want to fuck me, it's nothing I haven't dealt with before. Your father and I had a similar arrangement."

"Bullshit, Mother, you *loved* him."

Now both widows laugh. "Yes, I suppose I *did* love him—I think that's why I came down here, a lifetime ago." She laughs more. Then she takes out a cheroot and turns it in her fingers, sniffs it, and puts it down. "The love expired when you were young. Then you went off to St. Leonard's and Jordan died, and your father got drunk. He fell in love—or something like that—with Anura. He told me she made him feel young, and I told him to look in the mirror." The widows laugh again. "Anyway, they shared a bed for most of the last twenty years, and it was for the best. Early on, he'd come to my bed occasionally. And, you know, he kept his things upstairs, and we carried on for appearances' sake. But he was her problem, and I was thankful to her for it."

"Is she the one he was with when he died?" Lucy asks.

"I made a point of not asking, not my business," Anne says, lighting a match. "But I hope so—otherwise Anura would have been very upset."

Lucy watches her mother light the cigar. Mrs. Vanderheyden lights a cigarette. A cloud of smoke lingers in the air then vanishes in a breeze. Lucy has heard the rumors about the widows from Raju, who told them to her in confidence. It is said that since her father died Mrs. Vanderheyden has visited often. It is said that the widows share a bed. Lucy is prepared to believe it, but knows that if it is true it is not what the gossipers hope. Raju agrees. The widows may require comfort, even the warmth of a body to sleep beside, but it is not sexual. Since her own divorce she has done the same more than once. Life is cruel enough without people reproaching a woman for what she must do to fortify herself against the darkness.

She looks at her mother. "Isn't the new guard Anura's son?" She is not angry, but curious. It seems bizarre that the security guard at the hotel might be her half sibling. That he might be her only living sibling.

"Gopal is not new," her mother says in a tone of weary resignation that signals the end of the evening. "You wouldn't know it, but he's been with us for years."

"I'm sorry I've not come sooner. But I am here now, and I want to help."

"Then don't presume to know what I need, or want. You don't know me."

The music has stopped and the kitchen light is off. The beach where they once had nightly bonfires is empty. The waiter has gone home. Now the refrigerator kicks awake and quivers, humming a dull tune they all recognize.

"Well," her mother says, "we'll leave the dishes out."

Lucy watches her mother's hand rise to her left breast and lightly touch the nipple, and then something occurs to Lucy, and she speaks before she has time to think: "Did you breast-feed us both at the same time?"

"Both?" Anne says, then—understanding Lucy's implication—cocks her head to the side, and stares at her daughter with mute rage. It's a look that Lucy hasn't seen for decades. Another expression that

Jordan used to have. The anger doesn't last—it wilts into something softer, more heartbreaking. Anne smiles and rubs her eye, clears her throat. "Yes, I often breast-fed you both at the same time, and I know what you're thinking, and you're right: Jordan took my left breast and that is probably why I fidget with it sometimes. Are you impressed with yourself now?"

Lucy does not answer. Mrs. Vanderheyden doesn't speak either. The refrigerator won't shut up.

"We should talk about all this in the morning," Anne says again.

"Excellent idea," the Widow Vanderheyden says.

Lucy nods. "I'm sorry, Mum."

The three stand. Lucy offers to clean up and her mother says that she should only do the glasses. Lucy picks up the glasses and brings them to the sink behind the bar and, while she washes them in the tepid water, her mother and the Widow Vanderheyden walk to the stairs behind the front desk. Though she can hear the old ladies, she does not watch them enter the apartment above. Before turning off the lights, Lucy makes herself one last gin and tonic.

Standing beside the swimming pool, she sees that only one of the tiki torches is still burning. The pool is rectangular, its concrete lip stained green with chlorine. It seemed so much bigger before. So much about the hotel seems modest now. By comparison with the sleek hotels to the north, like The Neptune and The Triton, The Horizon is an eccentric place, appealing mainly for its dotty, archaic mood. Although she could move down and save the hotel—as her mother certainly wants her to—she believes it'd be a mistake. She'd just end up a frailer version of her mother: alienated and struggling to sustain the dreams of the dead.

Lucy walks out onto the beach. The moon is jaundiced and half full, rising in the north. Its light reflects in a line that crosses the sea only to diffuse in a shimmering yellow cloud near the shore where the crests of the waves rise, pale and ragged. She sits down and digs her feet into the sand, feels the coolness beneath. A wave thuds into the shore, spraying briny mist into the calm air. She remembers the listlessness of the monsoon season when they watched typhoons gather in the distance, followed by the rain, a ceaseless torrent, and gales that ripped the palms' fringes away and rattled the shutters while they sat, mesmerized, waiting for a flare of emerald phosphorescence to light the otherwise gray sea. She glances around and spots the cluster of tall coconut trees between the cabins and the bar. In 1984 her father cut down three trees that stood right there.

That year the Tamil Tigers struck often and directed their energies to undermining Sri Lanka's fledgling tourism industry. When they raided The Horizon, they beat Lucy's father unconscious and raped several guests, including a little girl. Jordan and two Singhalese men were executed on the beach by firing squad, their dripping bodies strung up from palms. In the morning Lucy's father cut down the bodies and then the three trees where they had hung, and he made a pyre from the wood and on that pyre he cremated the three. When the tide rose it took everything away.

Sitting and looking out at the distant lights of fishing boats, she feels worn down by regret and the knowledge that she used the tragedy as an excuse to avoid her family. Even as a child the excuse seemed weak, but it did the job. Now, though, she has made a life for herself in Scotland: She has friends, and—in the Donalds—something like a family. The Donalds live a carefree life outside Pitlochry in a refurbished seventeenth-century inn. They keep geese in a coop in the back, and grow raspberries, mint, and cucumbers in their garden. A handful of sheep are penned in beside a front lawn with two hammocks and a croquet set. The lawn ends at the rocky bank of the River Tummel, beyond which a field stretches to the base of Ben Vrackie.

The summer of 1983, after the family visited boarding schools, the Donalds threw a party for them at that house. There was a bonfire on the lawn near the river. Almost a hundred guests came. They rolled the upright piano outside and a drunk American man played while they all sang and danced. Lucy and Mr. Donald—who had a huge black beard then, which is mostly white now—ran around shooting each other with cap guns. Seven months later, at Christmas, when Lucy's parents couldn't afford to bring her home, she spent the holiday with the Donalds, who had a party that went on for a fortnight. The same American was there with his family. He played the piano every night, and Lucy kissed his sparkly-eyed son in the barn. It was her first kiss. She's still friends with that boy, who is now a man, a married lawyer who lives in Philadelphia. They both remember that Christmas, when by day they'd ice-skate on the frozen pond, and in the evenings they'd drink mulled wine, eat roasted venison, and listen to the adults' stories. That year, on Christmas Eve, Mr. Donald set off fireworks over the river.

Four months later Lucy's brother was killed, and she spent a few weeks back in Sri Lanka. Everything at the hotel seemed bizarre and foreign. The mood was desolate and more than ever before she felt alone. At night she sat on the beach, in the same spot she now sits, and stared at the black stain where the pyre had been. With her feet buried in the sand, she thought about her new friends at St. Leonard's and how she loved Scotland and never wanted to return to Sri Lanka again. When she thought about Jordan she wept. She cried not because he was gone, but because he had taken part of her with him, and left her with a gaping cavity and an intractable lesson in the scope of permanence.

Lucy stands and walks down to the firmer sand and feels a cool wave rush past her ankles. As it retreats her feet sink slightly. She watches a green coconut roll out with the water only to be cast back up by the next wave. She knows she will never return to Sri Lanka again. Her mother will never return to Scotland. In a perfect world these two, abandoned by their men, would fortify each other against the world. But the shifts are irreversible. And so, Lucy decides, tomorrow morning she'll go to Galle and find out about houses for sale. While there she might visit the lighthouse. And there, on the fort's ramparts, she'll buy presents for friends back home: antique coins, fragile portions of coral, and maybe a Sri Lankan flag for the Donalds. After lunch she will return to The Horizon and she'll step out into the Indian Ocean for the first time in twenty-one years. She will wade to where the waves break. Inevitably, a wave will knock her over and hold her underwater, and there—spinning in muffled obscurity—she'll relax and trust herself to float upward, and when she feels the sun touch her face she will inhale, open her eyes, and try to enjoy what is left.

LAUREN GROFF

University of Wisconsin–Madison

Surfacing

He is at first a distant wave, the wake-wedge of a loon as it surfaces. The day is cold and gray as a stone. In the middistance the swimmer splits into parts, smoothly angled arms and a matte black head. Twenty feet from the dock he dips below the water, then he comes up a moment later at the ladder, blowing like a whale.

She sees him step onto the dock: the pronounced ribs heaving, the puckered nipples, the mustache limp with seawater. She feels herself flush and, trembling, smiles.

It is March 1918, and hundreds of dead jellyfish litter the beach. The newspapers this morning include a story, buried under the accounts of battles at the Western Front, about a mysterious illness striking down hale soldiers in Kansas.

The swimmer lifts his towel to gain time, wondering about the strange, expectant trio that watches him. The man in the clump is fat and bald, his chin deeply lined from mouth to jowl. His shave is close, his clothes expensive. A brunette stands beside him, the wind chucking her silk collar under her chin. The fat man's young wife, the swimmer thinks, mistakenly.

Before them sits a girl in a wheelchair. The swimmer's glance brushes over her and veers away when he sees her wizened child's face, the diluted blond of her hair, her eyes sunken in the sickly white complexion. A nothing, he thinks. That he looks past her is not his fault. He doesn't know. And so, instead of the lightning strike and fluttering heart that should attend the moment of their meeting, all the swimmer feels is the cold whip of the wind and shame at his old suit, holey and stretched out, worn only on the dark days when he needs nostalgia and old glory to bring him to the water.

The swimmer is a famous man. He is an Olympian: gold medalist at the 1908 London Olympics in the 100-meter Freestyle, anchor on the 4 x 200 relay. Triple gold in the 1912 Stockholm Olympics: 100-meter Freestyle, 100-meter Backstroke, anchor again on the 4 x 200. He was on the American Swim Association's champion water polo team from 1898 through 1911. He is, quite simply, The World's Best Swimmer.

His name is L. DeBard, though this was not always his name. He was Lodovico DeBartolo, but was taken from Rome at the age of six and transplanted to New York, where the Ukrainians, the Poles, the Chinese couldn't pronounce "Lodovico." He reworked his last name when he discovered in himself literary agility and a love of Shakespeare.

He is a swimmer, but he is other things, too. A forty-three-year-old with a mighty set of pectorals, one chipped front tooth, and a rakish smile; a rumored Bolshevik; a poet, filler of notebooks, absinthe drinker. He knows a number of whores by name, though in the wider world, the feeling is that he is a bit queer, his friendships with the city's more effeminate novelists and poets a mite too close. He has been alone in the company of Tad Perkins, C. T. Dane, Arnold Effingham. There is something suspect about a man-poet, anyway, and many of his critics ask each other, pursing their lips lewdly, why he is not in France, fighting for the Allies. The reason is that his flatfeet make him unfit for battle.

And today, he is one last thing: starving. Poets and swimmers are the last to be fed in these final few months of the Great War.

The fat man steps forward. "L. DeBard?" he asks.

L. wraps the towel under the straps of his suit. "Yes," he says, at last.

Then the girl in the wheelchair speaks. "We have a proposition for you," she says. Her voice reminds the swimmer of river rock: gravelly, smooth.

The girl's name is Aliette Huber. She is sixteen and a schoolgirl, or was before her illness. She won her school's honors for French, Composition, Rhetoric, and Recitation for three years in a row. She can read a poem once and recite it perfectly from memory years later. Before the polio she was a fine horsewoman, a beautiful archer, the lightest dancer of any of the girls at the Children's Balls society had delighted in staging in the heady days before the war. Her mother died when she was three, and her father is distantly doting.

She knows L. from his book of poetry, which she read when she was recuperating from her illness. She feels she knows him so intimately that now, freezing on the dock, she is startled and near tears. She has just realized that to him, she is a stranger.

———

And so, Aliette does something drastic: Moving the Scottish wool blanket from her lap, she unveils her legs. They are small, wrinkled sticks, nearly useless. L. thinks of his thin sheet and the dirty great-coat he sleeps under and envies her the blanket. Her skirt is short and her stockings silk. L. doesn't gasp when he sees her legs, her kneecaps like dinner rolls skewered with willow switches. He just looks up at Aliette's face, and suddenly sees that her lips are set in a perfect heart, purple with cold.

After that, the swim lessons are easily arranged. When they leave— the brunette pushing the wheelchair over the boards of the docks, her trim hips swishing—their departure thrums in L.'s heels. The wind picks up even more and the waves make impatient sounds on the dock. L. dresses. His last nickel rolls from the pocket of his jacket as he slides it over his yellowed shirt. The falling coin flashes in the water.

At night, Aliette lies in her white starched sheets in her room on Park Avenue and listens to the Red Cross's trucks grinding their gears in the streets below. She puts the thin book of poetry under the sheets when she hears footsteps coming down the hall to her door. When the book slides from her stomach to the gap between her useless legs, she gasps with sudden pleasure.

Her nurse, the brunette from the dock, enters with a glass of but-termilk. Rosalind, only a few years older than Aliette, looks as hearty and innocent as Little Bo Peep, corn-fed, pink with indolence. Aliette tries not to hate her as she stands there, cross-armed, waiting for Aliette to drain the glass. The nurse's lipstick has smeared beyond the boundaries of her lips, though she has clearly reapplied it. From the front hall, Mr. Huber's trilling whistle resounds, then the butler says, "Good afternoon, sir," and the door closes, and Aliette's father returns to Wall Street. The girl hands the glass back to Rosalind, who smiles a bit too hard.

"Do you need a trip to the water closet, miss?" Rosalind asks.

Aliette tells her no, that will be all. As Rosalind's footsteps fade, the girl retrieves the book of poetry from under the covers where it has nestled so pleasingly. *Ambivalence,* the title says. By L. DeBard.

While L. and Aliette wait to begin their first lesson the next day, the mysterious illness creeps from the sleepy Spanish tourist town of San Sebastián. It will make its way into the farthest corners of the realm, until even King Alfonso XIII will lie suffering with symptoms in his royal bed. French, English, and American troops scattered in France are just now becoming deathly ill, and the disease will skulk home behind them when they demobilize. Even King George V will be afflicted.

In New York, they know nothing yet of what is to come. L. eats his last can of potted meat; Aliette picks the raisins from her scones and tries to read fortunes in the dregs of her teacup.

They use the natatorium at the Amsterdam Hotel for the lessons. It is a lovely pool of green tile, gold-leaf tendrils growing down the sides, and a bold heliotrope of yellow tile covering the bottom. The walls and ceiling are sky blue. They cannot use it during the guest hours, and so must swim either in the early morning or at night.

L. hates to take so much money from Mr. Huber for so little work, so he insists they meet twice a day. He comes early for the first lesson, marveling at the beautiful warmth and crystal water. He leaps from the sauna to the pool, laughing to himself. His mustache wilts in the heat.

When Aliette comes in, steaming from the showers, her hair in a black cloth cap with a strap under the chin, L. lifts her from her chair and carries her into the water. Rosalind sits in the corner by the potted palm and takes out her knitting, then falls asleep.

In the beginning, they don't speak. He asks her to kick as he holds her in the water. She tries, making one tiny splash, then another. Around the shallow end they go, three, four times. Rosalind's gentle snores echo in the room. At last, Aliette slides one thin arm around L.'s neck. "Stop," she says, panting with pain.

He brings her to the steps and sets her there. He stands before her in the waist-deep water, trying not to look at her.

"What is wrong with Rosalind?" he asks. "Why is she sleeping?"

"Nothing is wrong," says Aliette. "Poor thing has been up all night."

"I trust that she was not caring for you? I assumed you were healthy," L. says.

Aliette hesitates and looks down. "She was caring for me, yes— and others," she says. Her face is tight and forbidding. But she then looks at him with one cocked eyebrow and whispers, "L., I must admit that I like your other suit better."

He is wearing a new indigo bathing costume with suspenders, and he looks down at himself, then at her, puzzled. His new suit cost him a week's wages. "Why is that?" he asks.

She glances at the sleeping nurse, then touches him where a muscle bulges over one hip. "I liked the hole here," she says. Then her hand is under the water where it looms, suddenly immense. She touches his thigh. "And here," she says. Her fingertip lingers, then falls away.

When he has steadied himself to look at her face, she is smiling innocently. She does not, however, look like a little girl anymore.

"They were only small holes," he says. "I am surprised you noticed."

"I notice everything," she says. But her face grows a little frightened; her eyes slide toward Rosalind, and she gives a great roar as if he's told a stunner of a joke. This awakens the nurse, who resumes her knitting, blinking and looking sternly at the pair. "Let's swim," cries Aliette, and she claps both of her hands on the water like a child.

During the late lesson that night, as Rosalind again succumbs to the heat and damp of the room, Aliette watches with amusement as L. tries to hide his chipped tooth from her by turning his face. He has waxed his mustache mightily, and the musky fragrance of the wax fills her head. She laughs, her face in the water. He thinks she is only blowing bubbles.

By the end of the first week, Aliette has gained ten pounds. When she is not swimming, she is forcing herself to eat cheese and bread with butter, even when she is not hungry. She loosens her corset, then throws it away. At night, though exhausted from swimming, she climbs out of bed and tries to stand. She succeeds for one minute one night, and five minutes the next. She has a tremendous tolerance for pain. At the end of the week, she can stand for thirty minutes and take two steps before falling. When she does fall, it is into bed, and she sleeps immediately, L.'s poetry beating around in her brain like so many trapped sparrows.

All that week, L. paces in his apartment. On a cloudy Friday, he kicks the notebooks full of weightless little words, watching them skitter across the floor. He decides that he must quit. He will tell Huber that he has another obligation and can no longer give lessons to Aliette. Blast her pathetic little legs to hell, he thinks. L. stands at his window and looks down into the dark street, where urchins pick through boxes of rotting vegetables discarded from the greengrocer's down-stairs. A leaf of cabbage blows free in the wind and attaches itself to the brick wall opposite L.'s window, where it flutters like a small green pennant.

"*Porca madonna,*" he says. Then, as if correcting himself, he says in English, "Pig Madonna." It doesn't sound right. He is completely unable to walk to Park Avenue and quit.

Late that evening he sits by the pool. He touches the place on his thigh where, a week earlier, Aliette's finger had touched him. He does not look up until he is startled by a throat clearing and looks up to find himself staring into Mr. Huber's face, the fat man's hand resting on his daughter's capped head.

"Papa is going to chaperone us the nights that Rosalind is off," Aliette says, her eyes bright with merriment. L. tries to smile, then stands, extending his hand for a shake. But her father doesn't shake his hand, just nods at him and then rolls the cuffs of his pants over his calves. He takes off his shoes and socks and sticks his white, hairy legs into the warm water. "Go on," he says, "don't let me get in the way of your lesson." He takes a newspaper from his pocket and watches them over the headlines as L. carries Aliette into the shallow end.

L. is teaching her the frog kick, and she holds on to the gutter as he bends both of her knees and helps them swing out and back. When her father's attention is fixed on an article, Aliette takes L.'s hand and slides it up and over her small breast. By the time her father has read to the bottom of the page, L. has removed his hand to her neck, and he is trembling.

As Rosalind sleeps under the palm the next morning, Aliette tells L. that her father didn't say one word to her in the cab home. But when they were coming up in the elevator, he asked her if something wasn't a little funny about L., something a little girlish. And she laughed, and related to her father the gossip about her swim coach's *bosom* friends.

"Very subtly, of course," she says. "I am not supposed to know of those things."

She tells L. that later, as she was drinking her last glass of buttermilk before bed, she left out his book, open to a poem titled, "And Into the Fields the Sweet Boys Go."

L. interrupts her, face dark. "That poem is about innocence, my Lord, I'm not—"

She puts a hand on his mouth. "Let me finish," she says.

He shuts his mouth; his face is set angrily. She tells him that she heard her father and Rosalind talking about L. in the morning, and her father called him *that nance.*

L. drops Aliette unceremoniously into the water. She swims, though, reaching the wall in three strong strokes, her legs dragging behind her.

She says, grinning, "You didn't know I was a nixie, did you?"

"No," he says, darkly. "I am amazed. And for your information, I am *not* a—"

"L.," says Aliette, sighing. "I know. But you *are* a fool." Then, very deliberately, she says, "The nances of the world have many uses, my dear coach."

When he says nothing, trying to understand, she droops. "I'm tired," she says. "This lesson is over." And she calls for Rosalind and will not look at L. as the nurse wheels her away.

Only later does he realize that this means she has read his book. He cannot look at her that evening, he is so flattered and fearful of her opinion.

Sunday, his day off, L. goes to Little Italy for supper with his family. His mother holds him to her wren's chest; his father touches his new linen suit with admiration. In Rome, Amadeo was a tailor; here he is a hearse driver. He mutters, "Beautiful, beautiful," and nods at his son, fingering the lapels, checking the seams. L.'s older sister is blind and cannot remark upon the visible change in him.

But in the trolley home, his stomach filled with saltimbocca, L. thinks of his sister when she touched his face in farewell. "You have met a girl," she whispered. Lucrezia has never seen her own face and cannot know its expressions—how, at that moment, her smile was an explosion.

In late April, the newspapers report a strange illness. Journalists blunt their alarm by exoticizing it, naming it Spanish Influenza, La Grippe. In Switzerland it is called La Coquette, as if it were a courtesan. In Ceylon it's the Bombay Fever, and in Britain the Flanders Grippe. The Germans, whom the Allies blame for this disease, call it Blitzkatarrh. The disease is as deadly as that name sounds.

Americans do not pay attention. They watch Charlie Chaplin and laugh until they cry. They read the sports pages and make bets on when the war will be over. And if a few healthy soldiers suddenly fall ill and die, the Americans initially blame it on exposure to tear gas.

L. has gone tomcatting with his writer friends only twice as spring rolls into summer. The second time, he has had only one martini when he pushes one very familiar redhead from his lap so roughly that she hits her head on the table and bursts into tears. C. T. Dane comforts her. When Dane leaves, the indignant redhead on his arm, he raises an eyebrow and frowns at L.

From that night on, his friends talk about him. "What's eating old fishface L.?" Tad Perkins asks anyone who will listen.

Finally, someone says, "He's writing a novel. It's like having a mistress. Once he's through with her, leaves her on the floor, weeping for more, he'll be back."

And the friends laugh at this. They raise their glasses. "To the mistress," they cry.

Aliette's cheeks grow plump and her legs regain their muscle tone. By May, L. is being driven crazy by her touches: leg sliding against leg, arm to knee, foot moving across his shoulder. He immerses himself in a cold-water tub, like a racehorse, before coming out to greet her.

Then one spring day it happens. Dawn pinkens in the clerestory window, and L. lifts Aliette's arm above the water to show her the angle of the most efficient stroke, when his torso brushes against hers, and stays. He looks at dozing Rosalind. Then he lifts Aliette from the water and carries her to the men's room.

As she stands, leaning against the tiles and shivering slightly, he slides her suit from her shoulders and slips it down. To anyone else, she would be a skinny, slightly feral-looking little girl, but he sees the heart-shaped lips, the pulse thrumming in her neck, the way she bares her body bravely, arms down, palms turned out, watching him. He bends to kiss her. She smells of chlorine, lilacs, warm milk. He lifts her and presses her against the wall.

When they reemerge, Rosalind still sleeps, and the pool is pure, glossy, as if nobody has ever set foot in it.

Aliette leaves her wheelchair behind and begins to walk, even though at first the pain seems unbearable. She loves the food she loathed before, for the flesh it gives her. She eats marbled steaks, half-inch layers of butter on her bread. She walks to the stores on Madison, leaning against a wall when she needs to, and returns, victorious, with bags. On one of her outings, she meets her father coming home for lunch. As she calls out and runs clumsily to him, his eyes fill. His fleshy face grows pink, and the lines under his mouth deepen.

"Oh," he says, nearly weeping and holding out his arms. "My little girl is back."

In the hot days of the summer, the pool sessions are too short and the days that stretch between them too long. In his anxiety to see Aliette, L. writes poetry. Those short hours of relief aren't enough, so he walks. But on the streets everything sparkles too brightly: the men selling war bonds smile too much, the wounded soldiers seem too filled with gratitude, their wives too radiant and pregnant. He hates it; he is drawn to it.

To forget her need to be with him, Aliette keeps herself busy. She takes tea with school friends at the Plaza, goes to museums and parties, and accepts dates to the theater whenever she can. But if her dates lean in to kiss her, she pushes them away.

Five times in the Amsterdam before July: that first time in the men's room; in the lifeguard's chair; in the chaise longue storage closet; in the shallow end; and in the deep end, in a corner, braced against the gutter.

All this time, Rosalind sleeps. The days that Aliette suspects she won't, she fills her nurse's head with glorious evocations of the cream puffs that are the specialty of the hotel's pastry chef. Rosalind, she feels certain, will slip out at some point during the lesson and return half an hour later with a cream puff on a plate for her ward, licking foam from her lip like a cat.

The second wave of the illness hits America in July. People begin to fall in Boston, old and young alike. In a matter of hours, mahogany spots appear on cheekbones, spreading quickly until one cannot tell dark-skinned people from white. And then the suffocation, the pneumonia.

Fathers of young families turn as blue as huckleberries, and spit a foamy red fluid. Autopsies reveal lungs that look like firm blue slabs of liver.

Aliette slips away on a day that Rosalind is visiting a cousin in Poughkeepsie. She takes a cab to the dark and seedy streets where L. lives, so enthralled by her own subterfuge she doesn't see the dirt or smell the stench. She gets out of the cab, throwing the driver a bill, and runs as quickly as her awkward legs will allow to L.'s apartment door.

When she enters, he stands, furious to see her in this hovel. She closes the door.

It is only later, sitting naked on the mattress, dripping with sweat and trying to cool off in what breeze comes from the window, that she notices the bachelor's funk of his apartment, the towers of books and notebooks lining the walls like wainscoting, and hears the scrabble of something sinister in the wall behind her head. That is when she tells L. her plan.

That night Mr. Huber chaperones. L. pays his friend W. Sebald Shandling, another starving poet, to sit by the pool. Shandling is foppish, flings his hands about immoderately, has a natural lisp.

"Watch me like a jealous wife," L. says.

And his friend does as he's instructed, growing ever more grim, until, by the end of the session, when Aliette comes to the wall and touches L. on the shoulder, he paces like a tiger, glaring at the pair. Mr. Huber looks on with an expression of jolly interest.

In the cab home that evening, as the horse's hoofs clop like a metronome through the park, Aliette asks her father if L. can come live with them, in one of the guest bedrooms.

"Daddy," she says, "he told me how disgusting his room is. But he can't afford to live elsewhere. And I've decided to train for the New York girls' swimming championships in September and need to add another session in the afternoon, at the Fourteenth Street YMCA. It's just easier if he lives with us."

"You two have become friends?" he says.

"Oh, we get along swimmingly," she laughs. When he doesn't smile, she adds, "Daddy, he is like a brother to me."

And her father says, without much hesitation, "Well, I don't see why not."

On the July day that he leaves his hovel, L. stands alone in his room one last time. When he hears children playing in the alley below, he goes to the window. Two girls skip rope, chanting.

"I had a little bird," they sing, rope clapping to the words.

Its name was Enza.
I opened the window.
And In-Flu-Enza.

They shriek and fall to the ground, clutching their chests, giggling.

L. has entered a world of privilege. Now there are servants, people calling him *sir,* any food he likes at any time of the day, the palatial apartment filled with light. And, of course, Aliette's midnight visits to L.'s bedroom and free midafternoon siestas in the cavernous cool apartment, as the servants sit in the kitchen and gossip about the war. In mid-August, L. is deemed chaperone enough, and Rosalind stays home when they go to the Amsterdam or the Y. If Aliette's father leaves for work a bit later than usual on those mornings, the servants' bland faces reveal nothing. Rosalind begins wearing a long strand of pearls and French perfume. She takes to sitting on Aliette's bed, combing her hair, and asking the girl about her dates with Ivy League boys. Her voice is rich and almost maternal.

Aliette tells her father that she no longer needs Rosalind, that she is healthy, and he can let the nurse go. Then Rosalind becomes *his* nurse, for he has discovered gout in his toes.

One golden night at the end of September, they all listen gravely to the radio's reports of war dead, eating petits fours in Aliette's father's study. Mr. Huber and Rosalind go into his bedchamber to treat his gout. Through the walls, L. and Aliette can hear their murmuring voices.

L. takes the cake from Aliette's hand and lifts her skirt on the morocco leather couch. She bites his shoulder to keep from screaming. Throughout, they can hear her father moving about behind the wall, Rosalind's heels tapping, the maid dusting in another room.

When Rosalind and Mr. Huber return, Aliette is reading a novel and L. is still in his wing chair, listening intently to the radio. Nobody notices the pearls of sweat on his forehead or, when Aliette stands for bed, the damp patch on her skirt.

The marvel is, with all she and L. do together, Aliette still has the time to train. She does, growing muscles like knots in her back, adapting her kick from the standard three-beat to a lightning-quick eight-beat flutter better suited for her weak legs.

At the competition in September in the 200-meter Freestyle, she draws so far away from the other girls that she is out on the diving platform and already wearing her green cloak when the other girls come in. She also takes the 100-meter Freestyle.

The captions below her picture in the *Times* and the *Sports News* read, "Heiress NY's Best Lady Swimmer." In the photo, Aliette stands radiant, medals gleaming in the sunlight on her chest. If one looked closely, however, a slight bulge around Aliette's waist would be visible.

The slow rumble of influenza becomes a roar. September drips into deadliest October. In Philadelphia, gymnasiums are crowded with cots of soldiers healthy just hours before. America does not have enough doctors, and first-year medical students, to treat the men. They, too, fall sick, and their bodies are stacked like kindling with the rest in the insufficient morgues. More than a quarter of the pregnant women who survive the flu miscarry or give birth to stillborn babies.

Aliette's stomach grows, but she does not tell L., hoping he'll notice and remark upon it first. He is in a fever, though, and sees nothing but his passion for her. She begins wearing corsets again, and she makes a great show of eating inordinately, so that her father and Rosalind will think she is simply getting fat.

When the plague hits New York, trains rolling into the boroughs stop in their tracks as engineers sicken at the controls. After 851 New Yorkers die in one day, a man is attacked for spitting on the streets.

Mr. Huber sends his six servants away, and they are forbidden to return until the end of the plague. Three out of them won't return at all. Mr. Huber, Aliette, Rosalind, and L. remain. They seal the windows, and Mr. Huber uses his new telephone to order groceries. They buy their food in cans, which they boil before opening, and their mail is baked piping hot in the oven before they read it.

During the second week of quarantine, Rosalind becomes hysterical and makes them drink violet-leaf tea and inhale saltwater. She paces the apartment wildly and forgets to brush her hair. They cannot convince her to make up the fourth for bridge, so they play Chinese checkers, backgammon, and gin. Mr. Huber suddenly unveils his collection of expensive liquors, and dips into them gladly. When he has had too much, he and Rosalind go into the servants' quarters and hiss at one another. At those times, Aliette sits on L.'s lap, and presses her cheek against his until the shape of his mustache is embossed into her skin.

Two months later Rosalind watches from a window as a coffin falls from a stack on a hearse, its inhabitant spilling to the ground. She goes nearly mad. She breathes into a paper bag until calm and makes them wear masks inside. She forces them to carry hot coals sprinkled with sulfur.

When Aliette and L. kiss through their masks, they laugh. And when Aliette comes to L. in the night, she swings her coals like a priestess swinging a censer.

On a lazy day of snoozing and reading, L. gets a letter from his mother. He doesn't bother to bake it. He tears it open, Aliette watching, hand over her mouth.

In three sentences, in her shaking hand, his mother tells him that his father, the hearse driver, was one of the rare lightning deaths. Amadeo toppled from his horse and was dead before he hit the ground. Two hours later Lucrezia fell ill, her knees wobbling, joints stiffening, the fever, the viscous phlegm, the cyanosis, the lungs filling.

L. understands only years later that when his sister died, she died of drowning.

He stays in bed for one week and does not weep. He lets Aliette hold his head for hours. Then he rises and shaves off his mustache. Its outline is white on his tan face and looks exceptionally tender.

In the first week of November the crisis slackens. People emerge into the street, mole-eyed and blinking, searching for food. In some apartments, whole families are found dead when their mail can no longer fit through their slots. Rosalind, however, will not let the Huber household leave the apartment. L. reads the baked newspapers, saddened. In addition to his family, he has lost his novelist friend, C. T. Dane; his fellow swimmer and the long-distance champion Harry Elionsky; the actress Suzette Alda, with whom he once danced for an entire night.

But life picks up again, though some new cases are reported, and the horror is not completely over. More than nineteen thousand New Yorkers have died.

At four o'clock on the morning of November 11, the streets burst into triumphant rejoicing in victory. Sirens blare, church bells ring, New Yorkers pour into the streets, shouting. Newspaper boys run through the sleeping parts of town, shouting "The war is ovah!" An effigy of the Kaiser is washed down Wall Street with a fire hose; confetti pours down; eight hundred Barnard girls snake-dance on Morningside Heights; and a coffin made of soapboxes is paraded down Madison, with the Kaiser symbolically resting in pieces within.

Many people still wear masks.

A mutiny occurs in the Huber apartment, and Rosalind wrings her hands as the other three rush into the street to join the celebration. They are all in their nightclothes. Mr. Huber dances a jolly foxtrot with a dour-faced spinster. When a blazing straw dummy is kicked down the street, L. turns to look for Aliette. She is standing on a curb, clapping her hands and laughing. As the dummy passes, the wind picks up and billows out her nightgown. Through the suddenly sheer garment, he sees how her belly extends above her thin legs.

When Aliette sees him swaying there on the sidewalk, his face pale, she puts a hand on her belly. A soldier and his girl pass between them, but they don't notice. When she turns, L. is beside her, gripping her arm too tightly.

He drags her into the building and to the doorman's empty room. A thin wedge of light falls across her flushed cheek.

"You didn't tell me," he says. "How long?"

She stares at him, defiant. "Since May," she says. "That first time, I think."

"My god," he says, then leans his forehead against the door, above her shoulder. She is pinned. He rests his stomach against hers and feels a pronounced thump, then another. "My god," he repeats, but this time with awe.

"A good swimmer, I'll bet," she says, daring to smile a little. But he doesn't smile back. He just stands, leaning against her, until he feels another kick.

They wait until a December day when Mr. Huber has returned to Wall Street and Rosalind has gone shopping.

They pack only what she needs. In the cab to Little Italy, she squeezes his hand until it goes numb.

"You're kidnapping, you know," she whispers to L., trying to make him laugh.

He looks away from her, out the window. "Only until we can figure out what to do. Until you have him and we can be married."

"L.," she says, ten blocks later. "I don't want to be married."

He looks at her.

"I mean," she says, "I would rather be your mistress than your wife. I don't need a ring and a ceremony to know what this is."

He is silent at first. Then, L. says, "But your father does. And that should be enough."

His mother, aged with grief, meets them at the door. She looks at her son, and touches his lip where his mustache was. Then she looks at Aliette, and holds open her arms to embrace her.

The detectives don't come looking for Aliette for a week, unable to discover where L.'s mother lives. When they knock at the door, L.'s mother hides the couple in her bedroom, then opens the front door, already talking. The detective who knows the language passably becomes confused by her quick jumble of Italian. He turns tongue-tied, then shamefaced when he tries to tell her why he is there. "L. DeBard," he says. "*Noi cerciamo* L. DeBard."

She looks at him as if he were the greatest fool in the world. "De-Bartolo," she cries, hitting her fist on her chest. She points to the card in the door. "DeBartolo." She throws her hands to the skies, and sighs. The detectives look at one another, bow, and leave.

In the bedroom, L. and Aliette listen and press tightly together.

The next day, Aliette goes into labor. Though the baby is more than a month early, Aliette is very small, and the birth is long and difficult. From morning until late at night, L. paces down the street, finally going into a bar. There he discovers Tad Perkins drinking himself into a stupor, alone.

"Isn't that old fishface L.?" cries Tad. "My god, I thought you damn well died."

"You're not that lucky," says L., laughing with great relief. "You still owe me thirteen dollars." He sits down and buys Tad and himself four quick martinis.

Later, staggering slightly, he goes out into the street. The moon is fat above. When he reaches the apartment, all is still. His mother sits beaming by the side of the bed, where Aliette sleeps. In his mother's arms he sees a tiny sleeping baby. A boy, he knows, without being told.

When Aliette awakens, she finds him sitting where his mother was. She smiles tiredly.

"I am thinking of names," L. says, hushed. "I like Franklin and Karl."

"I have already named him," says Aliette.

"Yes? What's my son's name?"

"Compass," she says. And though he presses, she won't tell him why. At last, grinning, he accepts the name, vowing to nickname him something more conventional. He never does. After the child is a few months old, he will find the name suits his son to perfection.

They have a month together in that tiny flat. L.'s mother bustles about and looks after them, feeding them elaborate meals, and rocking the baby while L. reads Aliette his new poems.

"You are growing into the best poet in America," she says.

"Growing?" he jokes. "I thought I already was."

"No," she says. "But now you might be." And she lies back, letting the words from his poems sift into her memory. She looks a little ill. She doesn't complain, but L. can see that something is not right with her. He worries. At night, he hears a soft rasp as Aliette grinds her teeth in pain.

———

Soon the detectives return. L.'s mother does not let them in this time, but their voices grow loud in the hallway. They shout and rage at her. At last they leave. L.'s mother is shaky and collapses into a chair, then puts a cloth over her face and weeps into it, unable to look at the couple for fear.

L. turns to Aliette. "I am taking you back," he says. "I'll keep Compass with my mother."

Aliette says, very quietly, "No."

"Yes," L. says. He tells her that he knows she is ill and her father can afford physicians that he cannot. If she returns without Compass, her reputation will not be tarnished, and no one will know about her pregnancy. Later, when they marry, they can adopt him. Their argument is quiet, but goes on for many hours, until Aliette finally succumbs to her illness and pain and his arguments. She has been afraid that she is growing worse, and so she allows herself to be convinced into doing something that if she were stronger and less frightened she would never have countenanced.

L. stops the cab half a block from Aliette's father's apartment and leans close to her. Their kiss is long and hungry. If they knew how often they would remember it, for how many years it will be their dearest memory, this kiss would last for hours. But it ends, and she climbs out, wincing with pain, and he watches her walk away, so lovely, the feather in her hat bouncing.

When Aliette walks back into the house, her father is sitting in the parlor, head buried in his hands. When he looks up, he clearly does not recognize her. She looks at the mirror above the mantel, and sees herself: pale and skinny again, hair dun colored, her face above her fur looking a decade older than its age. When she looks back, Rosalind stands in the doorway, the tray in her hands chattering. Her face is pinched with unhappiness, while a broad, bright smile spreads across her father's red face.

Only years later does Aliette trace the pieces of her loss in the evidence scattered through her fever-addled memory. Her father's expression when he looks at her as she first walks in, a mixture of hurt and relief. How the doctor asks probing questions about her delicate parts until she admits to the pain and allows him to examine her. How her father's expression changes after conferring with the doctor, how he looks at her angrily. And a year later, she will hear him shouting at Rosalind one night when drunk. "Nobody, nobody abandons a Huber," he'll say. "We were right to do what we did."

Two nights after Aliette has returned to her father's house, L. is restless, anxious to hear of Aliette's health. He decides to take a walk in the wintry streets, to kick through the snow and work off his anxiety. He leaves Compass with a kiss in his mother's lap and hurries down the dank stairwell and into the night.

He does not see the shadows detaching from the alleyway, or how they steal close behind him. He feels the sudden grip on his arms, then the handkerchief with the sour stink of chloroform pressed over his nose and mouth. The gas lamps flicker and darken, the street becomes wobbly, and a snowdrift catches him as he falls.

Much later, L. can see a golden light growing between his lids. His head is bound with pain. His eyes open slightly. He lies on the hard wooden floor of what appears to be an office, a vast mahogany-paneled room with bookshelves, paintings of ships. His fingertips lie on what feels like rubber.

Two unfamiliar faces loom over him. "He's waking up," one says. The men back away, and in their place stands Mr. Huber, transformed and dangerous with rage. Beside him is Rosalind's brunette head, her face covered by a mask, her eyes filling with tears. L. suddenly feels cold. He is naked, he realizes, a window is open, and snow is pouring in and powdering the rug.

"You deserve this, and more," says Mr. Huber.

L.'s lips move but he can't say anything. He closes his eyes.

"Rosalind," says the fat man. "Give it to me."

When L. looks again, Rosalind's eyebrows have come together above her mask in a frown. But she hands Mr. Huber what he wants, something that appears to be a blade, glinting. Aliette's father stoops closer. Through his numbness, L. can feel hands grasping his legs roughly and pulling them apart.

"Bastard," Aliette's father breathes in his face. L. has only a moment to smell his sour breath before he goes out of L.'s line of vision.

He hears a thunk. Then such pain that L. blanks out again.

Time runs fluidly through the rest: the discovery of the fiercely bleeding L. in the snowbank by a police officer on patrol. The rescue and delivery to the hospital. The doctors unveiling his wound, vomiting, the cauterizing of the hole between his legs. And, at last, the fever that makes him delirious and lasts for months.

His literary friends come to visit him, and out of kindness they do not tell him that the newspapers are full of the story of his gelding. When L. seems unlikely to survive, W. Sebald Shandling visits L.'s mother. He finds her holding Compass; the baby is chewing on his father's most recent poems. In an act of uncharacteristic selflessness, Shandling convinces a publisher to take the collection, to provide something for the babe in case his father dies. And L.'s fever rages long past the time when the world shifts into treaties and recovery. It rages still while President Wilson is struck by influenza and then recovers in time to sign at Versailles.

Just when his fever begins to dissipate, L. catches one of the last strands of the flu.

For three days, the only thing he can hear is the gurgle of water in his lungs. He doesn't think he'll live. When the worst passes and he can sit up again, a young doctor whose face is prematurely lined comes to see him. He looks as if he might begin to cry.

"Mr. DeBard," he says. "I am afraid that your lungs are so damaged you will never swim again. They're so bad, you won't be able to walk far unaided." Then he gives a curious half sob, and says, "I followed your swimming, sir. When I was a boy, I admired you greatly."

L. looks at the doctor for some time before closing his eyes and sighing.

"Frankly, Doctor," he says, at last, "of all the many things I do extraordinarily well, it is not the loss of swimming that upsets me."

By the summer, L. is still recovering, walking about weakly. His mother leaves Compass with a neighbor when she visits, but brings a photograph of the boy that L. stares at for hours and keeps in the breast pocket of his pajamas when he sleeps.

In all the time he is in the hospital, Aliette does not come to see him. She pays dearly for her transgressions, supervised day and night, allowed only to go to the pool and only when accompanied by her new female coach. She is not allowed to see Compass, though two or three times she tries to slip out at night, only to be collared by her coach or her father. She is not allowed to keep the baby blanket she took, and is not allowed to send money for his care. Rosalind and another nurse follow her, even to the bathroom. She spends her rage in the water, holding her breath until she almost drowns.

———

L. comes home on the day his new book sells out in one hour. His detractors, however, claim his success is due to the shocking nature of his story, the scandalous tale. Compass cries when he sees this strange man, but slowly grows used to him, and in a fortnight he tugs on L.'s reinstated mustache and touches his cheek in wonder.

At last, after its third time around the globe, the pandemic burns itself out. By the end, whole villages have been wiped clean from history; in a single year, more Americans die from it than from all of the battles of the Great War.

L. and Aliette never meet again. She holds her breath every time she sees a man walking a little boy down the street, and goes home so agitated she will be unable to speak. She begins letters that she will never send, and with every new one she tears into confetti she hopes fervently that L. and Compass will understand.

But at first L. doesn't understand. Her absence aches. He knows that if they were to meet, they wouldn't be able to look at each other, burdened with shame and loss, but he doesn't understand how Aliette could give up her own son; it seems a horror. Then, Compass begins to speak and to develop his own little grave personality, and on the boy's fifth birthday, as they sit on the glowing grass of the park and eat cake together, L. looks at his son, kicking his legs at the sky, and in the fullness of the boy's presence and his delicious joy, L. realizes what Aliette has done. She has released Compass to him, an exculpatory gesture, a punishment. He imagines her in the city somewhere, staring out the window on her son's birthday, and knows she is dreaming of the child.

By then, though, no other life is imaginable, and Compass never tells L. he misses having a mother, for the older the boy becomes, the more his father comes to depend upon him. And yet L. still becomes drenched with sweat every time he smells lilacs or sees a tiny blond from afar.

L. reads about Aliette's small rebellions in the newspapers. How she is arrested for nude bathing at Manhattan Beach when she removes her stockings before swimming, and how through this act and its subsequent uproar, women are liberated from having to wear stockings when they swim. He reads of how, with an escort of four strong matrons, she goes to bombed-out Antwerp for the 1920 Olympics, and wins every gold medal in women's swimming, breaking world records in that estuary, more mud than water. He saves the papers for Compass, for when the boy is older. And L. attends opening night of her water performance in the Royal Theatres, but leaves when he sees the falseness of the smile pasted on her face. When he wakes up the next morning, his heart still hurts.

And it is in the papers that he notices her one last rebellion, when she is arrested for swimming at night in the pond in Central Park, but the mayor intervenes and from this incident comes a good thing: New York's first public swimming pool. She sinks quietly back into her life, coaches a few women's swimmers to the Olympics, and has no children, as far as he can tell. He hopes, as he watches Compass grow, that she is happy.

Aliette watches him, too. She follows him as he grows famous and reads every one of his new books. She leaves them strewn so conspicuously in her home on nights when she holds soirées that her high-society guests, most of whom have never read a line of poetry, cite him in interviews as their favorite poet. She reads the profiles of him in the papers and watches Compass grow and become his father's amanuensis, his nurse, his friend. Compass follows his father to Harvard when the university offers L. a lectureship, and then he enrolls. He graduates with a degree in English, and posts three school records on the pool's walls. Later, when the interviewers can induce the boy to speak, he smiles his serious smile and says, "I can't imagine a better life than that I live with my father." Aliette snips this quote and carries it in a locket that hangs from her neck.

One night she turns on the radio and hears L.'s dear voice reciting some of his oldest poems, the ones from *Ambivalence*. He gasps slightly with his troubled lungs as he reads the lines, "I have dreamed a dream of repentance / I have known the world eternal." She listens, rapt, and when she switches off the radio, her face is wet.

She sees him only once, in all this time. They are both old, and he has just published his twelfth book of poems. He stands on a stage, behind a lectern. His hair is white, and he is stooped. He reads deliberately and well, stopping between poems to catch his breath.

He does not notice the plump woman in the gray cloche and chinchilla coat at the back of the auditorium. He doesn't see how she mouths each word he reads, how her face is bright with joy. When he has shaken the hands of his admirers and stands alone with Compass in the theater, she has already left. Though he has not seen her, he has felt all evening a change in the air.

He walks on the arm of his handsome son onto the cool New York street that glistens with rain. Outside the theater, he tells Compass to halt. L. lifts his face to the drizzle, and closes his eyes, breathing deeply once, twice. When he lowers his face, he is grinning.

Then he tells his son, "This feels like that breath you take after coming up from a long swim underwater. The most gorgeous feeling, that sip of air you feared you'd never have again." He looks at Compass and, touching his son's cheek, he says gently, "Surfacing."

DAN PINKERTON

Pennsylvania State University

Headlock

Mr. Marsh prided himself on his spotless safety record and on his title, "Instructor of the Industrial Arts," which gave a certain Parisian flair to the varnished lamps his students assembled, with their pump handles and misdrilled holes stoppered with putty. He alone favored the longer title—even his colleagues had resigned themselves to being "shop teachers," though they surpassed Marsh in terms of ability, gutting small engines and timing themselves on the reassembly, teaching the upper levels, assigning advanced and individualized projects that called for runs to the Auto Parts Emporium. Mr. Nero and Mr. Hastings and Ms. Weatherall were the ones who earned the lasting respect of the kids they mentored through custom paint jobs, engine modifications, drug addictions, and relationship snags. Marsh, whose lamps emerged from a pattern, was often treated as a nonentity by his fellow industrial artists and by the students themselves. Didn't they realize he provided the framework, teaching the merits of precision, a basic apprehension of tools, and workplace safety? He wore earth tones. They called him Swamp Gas.

The nickname he could abide; nicknames at least implied the recipients were worthy of a certain level of attention. What irked Marsh was the recent trashing of school property. One morning he found his precisely measured lamp components broken in two. The boards didn't look as though they'd been sheared by shop hardware, and Marsh found no telltale sawdust near the tools or bins. Rather, the two-by-fours appeared to have been crudely split, as over someone's knee. Marsh stood holding the wreckage, feeling betrayed. He was always the first to arrive in the morning. The silent shop smelled of pine and engine oil and the chlorine that drifted in from the pool next door, where Marsh could hear the insistent whistle of the swim coach even now. He went to one of the bays and threw it open to admit a silvery, depthless light into the room. Frost coated the grass outside, the air smelled of freezer burn, and on the track that ringed the gridiron, a solitary figure, Principal Dees, plodded along, sweat suited, keeping time. Marsh wanted to flag Dees down, make his complaint, but, intimidated by Dees's newfound obsession with jogging, he managed to calm himself instead with some Neil Diamond on the shop transistor and set about loading the broken two-by-fours into the back of his Subaru wagon.

That day, as the teens measured and cut, glued and varnished, Marsh watched in a covert and clinical way for evidence of the vandal: a telling smirk, some underhanded laughter. He had a few suspects: Toomey, with his omnipresent leather jacket, taking Woodshop I a second time; O'Casey, skinny, remedial, always drawing hateful symbols on himself with a ballpoint pen; and Brunk, who wrestled. Marsh automatically distrusted any kid engaged in gladiatorial combat: the strange, spongy ankle-length shoes, the tight outfits resembling Betty Grable swimsuits, the gnarled ears. Brunk looked albino-y with his white blond hair and eyebrows, red lips that gashed his pale face like a wound. But it was too early to lay blame. Marsh would wait and see how things played out.

That afternoon when he returned home, Marsh found his wife jogging in place in the living room, measuring her pulse. Cara was training for a marathon. "Some jerk snuck in overnight and broke all the lumber for the lamps," he told her.

"That's terrible," Cara said, still jogging, legs hard and sharp. The legs had appealed to Marsh when the muscles sprang from their prior fleshiness like a sculpture emerging from a marble slab, but now they'd begun to clip him in bed, becoming more like weapons under the covers. Even Cara's libido had turned spearlike and aggressive.

"Yeah, I'm not sure whether I should make a big deal about it, maybe talk to the kids tomorrow. Could you stop moving for a second? I'm having trouble focusing."

"I was just getting ready for a run." Cara stopped jogging, but still shook the stress from her arms and tilted her head from side to side in a pugilistic way.

"How about you?" Marsh asked. "Your day go okay?"

"Yeah." Cara, a 911 dispatcher, shrugged. "There was a suicide— pills—but get this: Some girl calls in and requests an officer because the parking meter ate her change. Can you believe the nerve of people?" She glanced at her watch. "Wow, I've got to get going."

"Me, too," Marsh agreed, rising from the recliner for his afternoon ride. Their son, Thomas, swam competitively, so when Cara began making her long-distance runs Marsh had decided, reluctantly, to complete the triathlon troika. He loaded up his bike, changed into his shorts and jersey, and, as usual, drove to a neighboring town, fearful of a colleague or student spotting him. Marsh felt, perhaps, that teachers of the industrial arts had a certain reputation for rugged masculinity that spandex failed to convey. As he rode, Marsh shed the images of cleaved lumber and began thinking instead of the push mower he needed to buy. Then, across the median, he glimpsed a carload of kids laughing and pointing. Usually Marsh gave a bony shoulder and pumped hard in another direction, but this time he thought he saw someone he knew—yes, Brunk's ghastly, Casperish face in the rear window. What was he doing? Gesturing. A karate chop. So that was the score. Marsh had been right in his lineup of suspects, though wrong when it came to mode of attack. His boards had fallen prey to martial artistry.

The next morning he arrived at work to find another load of lumber turned to kindling. Eyeing the mess, Marsh even broke a few boards of his own. Then he sat down to wait for Nero, Hastings, and Weatherall. The trio, however, was largely unsympathetic. No one wanted to involve the police, which might risk shutting down the shop when students were at crucial stages of their projects. No one wanted to tell Principal Dees about the dilemma. "Let's handle this internally," Nero said, without elaborating.

"Maybe we could do some kind of stakeout," Hastings said, followed by silence, the type where one hears machinery humming.

"I've got a video camera I could set up," Marsh said, "for surveillance." The others quickly affirmed the plan.

When Marsh got home he found Cara stretching, her hair pulled up and tied over a headband. Stepping around her, he began rummaging in the hall closet. "Have you seen the camcorder?" he asked.

"What do you need it for?" Cara skimmed past him to the bedroom, returning a moment later with the camera.

"What was it doing in the bedroom?" Marsh said.

"What do you need it for?"

"I'm trying to catch the punk who's been breaking my lumber." He opened the cartridge that housed the film. "Where's the tape?"

"Needs a new one." Cara was in the finishing stages of her calisthenics, bent at the hip, grasping an ankle. Marsh caught himself scratching the underside of his rib cage, simian-like.

The next morning he borrowed a tripod from Skimmick in AV and set the camera up in his cramped office overlooking the shop, careful to lower the blinds around the lens. At day's end he pressed the RECORD button before leaving, proud of his handiwork—so pleased, in fact, that when he got home he felt a bit randy. Thomas was away at a friend's house, and when Cara entered from her run, Marsh, barnacle-like, attached himself to her. "The house is ours," he said, his arms fixed around her stomach as he kissed her salty neck.

"You don't want to come near me before I have a bath," Cara said, wriggling away. "Trust me."

"Maybe I could use a bath, too."

"Maybe." Cara smiled her way out of the living room, vanishing down the hallway, and when Marsh tried the bathroom door he found it latched. There was the modest complaint of a tap being turned, then running water on the far side. Marsh stood there, investigating. More sounds: of leisurely limbs plying the water, the scratch of a razor over stubble. Finally Marsh went into the kitchen and settled down at the table with the word jumble, which he battled unsuccessfully for a while before starting on dinner.

Marsh's camcorder—his Christmas gift to his wife, the instrument with which they planned to document their excursions to Yellowstone and Glacier, their son's swim meets, Cara's marathon—was gone. Though his office door remained locked, the window had been shattered, a neat spidering of glass.

Principal Dees seemed frustrated that his morning orbit of the football field had been disrupted and kept checking his watch, pressing buttons, eliciting meaningful beeps as Marsh spoke. "You shouldn't have tried to handle this yourself," he said when the shop teacher finished.

"Yeah, well, my colleagues thought it might be a good idea."

"Your colleagues? Don't listen to those guys, Marsh. I thought you had more sense than that. Between you and me, they're a bunch of idiots."

"Yes, sir."

"Now that camera—was it expensive?"

Marsh nodded.

"Tell you what. I'll give the police a call, get someone down here to ask the kids a few questions, and we'll conduct some random locker checks." Dees made air quotes around the word *random.* "You have any idea who might have done this?"

"I'm pretty sure it was Brunk."

"His father's on the school board, you know."

"I know," Marsh said.

"He's a lawyer."

Marsh scratched his head. "Huh."

"Yeah, a good one from what I hear. The son's a real shit, though."

"Yes, sir."

"Now if you don't mind, I'd like to get back to my jog."

Everyone was running, biking, swimming, frenetic hivelike motion—except, apparently, the slack young cop who showed up midmorning and stood shooting the breeze with Hastings. The officer was a former student. Marsh remembered the kid, who had even looked like a cop back in high school, with his crew cut and close-set eyes. A few set questions were put to the students in the shop. Afterward the officer wandered among the table saws and miters in a reverie of nostalgia.

Dees wandered down after lunch to tell Marsh they'd rifled Brunk's locker and found zip in the way of contraband. The case was stagnating.

Though spring had arrived, Marsh hung his bike on its hooks in the garage. He couldn't risk Brunk, the enemy, seeing him in another of his garish cycling outfits. Finding the house after school filled with a judgmental silence, however, Marsh felt the need to do *something*, so he climbed into his Subaru and eased out of the driveway with no particular end point in mind.

Ms. Weatherall lived in the country and raised horses, so Marsh thought he might drive out and see what was happening on the ranch—not much, it turns out, though he was pleased to see the horses cantering. No sign of life from the house, and Marsh wasn't about to stop. He had a feeling Weatherall lacked fundamental respect for him. Back in town, Marsh passed the houses of Nero and Hastings, then on impulse headed over to Principal Dees's split-level and, as he floated by in the wagon, saw Dees open the screen door and hold it chivalrously for a woman. Dees prided himself on his bachelorhood so, curious, Marsh tapped the brake to get a better look and caught Cara, hard to miss in her lavender shorts and flower-patterned tank. He took in the twin burls of her knees, the slender legs, the already-tan arms, the sharp ferrety face topped with a tangle of dark hair that, untied, looked like part of a disguise. He didn't know what to do. Apparently, neither did she. Marsh idled there on the street, Cara froze on the top step, then she turned and Dees once again ushered her into his house.

Marsh's heart beat hard as he searched for a song that might echo his current state. The radio fed him nothing but commercials. Back at home Thomas was in his room, door shut. Marsh went and stood in the bathroom, trying not to look at himself in the mirror. There was a chance he might be sick; he felt it as a real possibility, yet he also felt empty and was afraid that if he kneeled down at the toilet the only thing to emerge would be a dry seal-like rasping, so he went out and drove again. His hands were fluttering as he made his way to the Barnes & Noble at the edge of town, in the plaza with the other immodest superstores. There was something about the warmth of the place, the amber light, the unhurried affluent calm of the browsers inside, their heads glowing like the heads of saints in Renaissance paintings. Marsh wandered over to the history section. He wanted to know about Charlemagne and the fall of the Roman Empire and the Treaty of Versailles. He wanted to know why Custer charged down the bluff, why Truman dropped bomb number two. Books filled his basket, spines brilliantly smooth, pages fragrant and crisp. He took them over to the counter in the café that faced out on the parking lot and read until hunger overtook him and he paid for his books and left. The rush he experienced from ownership quickly passed, followed by the ballast of remorse. The books, which had set him back considerably, would go mostly unread. In the store they had glimmered with promise, but now, scattered in the back of Marsh's car, they seemed utterly useless.

Marsh drove, refueled, grew tired of driving, sat in the parking lot of a hot tub warehouse and tried to cry before settling finally at the town sports complex, his headlights playing over chain link and steep sentinel-like lampposts and a boarded-over cinder block snack hut before he shut off his car and climbed in back, where he passed the rest of a fitful night. In the morning he was awakened by the alternating blue-red lights of a cruiser, the same young officer from before tapping on the glass with the butt end of his flashlight.

"Mr. Marsh?" the kid said, squinting in, after Marsh had scrambled to the driver's seat and turned the key in the ignition to let down the window. "Taking that camcorder theft pretty hard, aren't you?"

"No, it's not that, I was just..." How could he explain? "I didn't feel like going home."

"Well, you can't sleep in your car like this. That's called vagrancy."

Marsh sat up. "You're right," he agreed, scratching his head. "I need to get to work."

"Alrighty," the cop said. "We'll keep you posted if we get any leads on that vandalism case."

Yes, Marsh thought. The vandalism case.

He didn't much enjoy showering in the swimming pool locker room, where he was forced to disrobe at a wooden bench bolted to the floor, stash his clothes in one of many identical yellow-painted lockers, and step barefoot through the pools of collected, fungal water on the tile floor. The first of the swimmers came in to find Marsh smoothing his hair with his fingers before the mirror, yesterday's shirt half-buttoned. He lacked toothpaste. The only thing that calmed him was the scent of chlorine, reminiscent of his son's swim meets. Then he realized that he needed to be gone before Thomas arrived for practice.

After school, Marsh sat in his Subaru, at a slight remove from Brunk's Mustang in the lot. Brunk was at wrestling practice—a week of vital training that led to the district meet on Friday, which would determine the state qualifiers. Eventually the kid came out, hair still soggy from the shower, putting his hands on his fellow wrestlers in a pawing, leonine way that irritated Marsh. He decided to follow Brunk to his house, a brick-and-cedar monstrosity half hidden behind a partition of trees.

Nothing much happened that night. Brunk stayed indoors while Marsh sat in his car, parked on the street, periodically running the heater. Finally, late in the evening, Marsh drove to the Holiday Inn Express by the interstate and rented a room.

Though Cara left messages for Marsh the next day at work, he didn't return her calls, and in the afternoon she showed up in the shop doorway. Marsh killed the drill press, nested his safety glasses atop his head, and called to Nero, who was flipping through a *Motor Trend*. "Can you watch my class for a second?" Nero nodded, rose slowly from his chair, and plodded over. Marsh and Cara converged at the door of Marsh's office. Both could see the taped-over gash through which the camcorder had been extricated. Cara had been doing some crying.

"Come home," she said, once they were inside.

"I don't know," Marsh said. He found he was having trouble really looking at her.

"I made a mistake." Her tone sounded more irritated than contrite. Ten years earlier Marsh would have asked for a divorce, but at this stage of his life he wasn't so quick to condemn. Really it was a choice of betrayal or loneliness, and he couldn't decide which was worse, though he figured he might try loneliness for a while. Cara inserted herself nearer to him.

"Come home," she said again, more urgently. "I'm done with Dees. I'm done jogging."

"Don't give up jogging," Marsh said, and then, "I'll come home." Mainly he said it to retain some distance. She was close to him now; he could smell the stuff she put in her hair. Clearly Cara wanted him to touch her, but instead he took some safety quizzes off his desk and held them in his outstretched hands like official decrees.

Marsh did not go home that evening or the next. Rather, he kept tailing Brunk, trying to catch him at something. Brunk was a busy kid. He went in and out of houses, drove to the bowling alley and the Cineplex. Everywhere he went he seemed to attract little satellites, kids who didn't mind how he manhandled them. Brunk traveled with a lithe ninety-eight pounder, Chrystal, a bleach-blond wearer of low-slung jeans, lip gloss, and a tattoo (a Japanese character) on the small of her back. They spent much of their time engaged in fog-windowed mischief in the back of Brunk's Mustang as they parked at the very sports complex where Marsh had earlier passed the night. Marsh kept a log of their activities, though to what end he couldn't specify.

Cara left messages with the school secretary, who delivered them with unseemly enthusiasm to Marsh. After his last class he bought a few changes of clothes at Sears and a toothbrush and paste from a vending machine at the hotel. He was in the middle of a quiz show on a Thursday night, wind heaving sheets of rain against the window, when the phone rang, startling him.

"Ken, you've got to stop this," Cara said.

"Stop what?"

"Staying away. Come home—for Thomas's sake."

"Don't bring him into this," Marsh said.

"But he's worried about you."

"Did you tell him what happened?"

Cara paused. "Yes."

"Are you sure?"

Another pause. "I'll tell him."

Marsh hung up on her. It scared him to do so, yet the act seemed somehow merited. He sat on the bed, TV muted, waiting for the phone to ring again, but it didn't.

That Friday night Marsh bought a sack of popcorn at the concession stand and entered the high school gym, climbing the sneaker-scored bleachers to take a seat behind Brunk's girlfriend, Chrystal, who held Marsh's camcorder brazenly on her lap.

Someone was calling his name. Looking around, Marsh spotted Hastings, waving and trampling his wife's feet in an effort to make his way over. "I've never seen you at one of these before," Hastings said.

"You're right, this is my first match. I thought it might be fun."

"Meet," Hastings said.

"What?"

"It's a meet, not a match."

"See," Marsh said, "I'm learning things already."

Hastings had his hand on Marsh's shoulder and leaned now, bearing down, to speak into his ear. At close range his breath smelled of whiskey and Wrigley's spearmint. "I'm sorry to hear about Cara."

Marsh was surprised. "How do you know about that?"

"Oh, well, the rumor mill—you know how it is. Hey, why don't you come sit with us?" Hastings had a plump, pockmarked face and a nose that looked as though it had been bitten off and reattached. His wife, Vivian, wore some sort of purplish velour leisure suit. As a pair, they embarrassed Marsh, who hoped to sit alone, keeping tabs on Chrystal. He knew, though, that he needed allies, so he joined Hastings and Viv.

Marsh didn't much like the way the wrestlers slapped each other's thighs, the way they sometimes seemed to mount one another from behind—"Par terre," Hastings explained—so instead he examined the crowd, the officials, the distracted cheerleaders sitting cross-legged at the fringe of the mats. Chrystal was occupied with the camcorder, *Marsh's* camcorder, while Brunk strutted around in his singlet, readying for his match. He seemed a grotesquerie to Marsh, though he assumed the proud parents, the attorney and his wife, were somewhere in attendance. Maybe that's what bugged Marsh: that Brunk was so clearly loved. Marsh's own son's door was always closed; his wife was porking his boss. Marsh felt he was experiencing some sort of deficiency, an emotional beriberi.

He nudged Hastings with his elbow. "See that girl over there?"

"The one with the camera?"

"Yes—that's mine."

"You're kidding me. Are you sure? I mean, those things all look alike to me." Hastings laughed nervously.

"I'm positive."

"What are you going to do?"

It was a fair question, and Marsh paused to consider. "I guess I'm going to go take it from her." That said, he set out on his mission, edging past spectators until he stood in Chrystal's line of sight.

"Get out of my way," she snapped.

Marsh snatched the camcorder. "This," he said, holding it out of reach, "is mine."

"Like hell it is," Chrystal said. "My boyfriend gave that to me."

"Did you ever think to ask where he got it?"

Hesitation marred Chrystal's smooth face for a moment. "Give it back!" she screamed. "BRUNK!" Brunk had just finished his match, a brisk pinning of his opponent, and was leaning now, hands on knees, catching his breath. When he heard his name called he lifted his head and saw Chrystal waving and began making his way up the bleachers, removing his mouthpiece and savagely unclasping his headgear. Chrystal continued berating Marsh, drawing the attention of nearby spectators. Marsh merely hugged his camera and prepared for his confrontation with the 171-pounder.

On spotting his woodshop teacher, Brunk stopped short. "Hey, Mr. Marsh," he said. "What's up?"

"For some strange reason, your girlfriend had my video camera. Why do you think that is?"

Brunk glanced at Chrystal. "Beats me."

"You know," Marsh began, "the shop is filled with some very dangerous power tools..." The appearance of the school's security guard kept him from saying more.

"Is there a problem, Mr. Marsh?"

"I don't know," Marsh said. "Maybe you should ask Brunk."

"Well?" said the guard.

"We found Mr. Marsh's camera and were returning it to him." Brunk seemed perfectly at ease except for a single nostril that flickered of its own accord. He didn't even bother wiping away the sweat that pooled above his eyes.

"Is that true?" the guard asked Marsh, who paused before nodding.

Once the guard was gone, Marsh turned to the delinquent and his girlfriend. "This is the end of it. Right?"

Now it was Brunk's turn to nod.

That evening Cara visited his hotel room. Marsh had no reason to shun her, but once he'd opened the door to find her standing there, he returned to his indentation on the bed and to the movie playing on TV as she waited in the doorway for him to ask her in. "I can't understand why you're doing this," she said, looking not so much at him but into the closet near the door, at the small ironing board and steam iron and the handful of cheap clothes dangling from cedar hangers.

"This is *my* fault?" He didn't look up from the TV.

"No, but I said I was sorry."

"Maybe it's not that easy for me." So, had he settled on loneliness? The two of them pretended to watch the movie for a while.

"I see you found the camera," Cara said, nodding at the camcorder resting on top of the entertainment center.

"You were filming yourself with Dees, weren't you?"

Cara said nothing.

Finally Marsh looked at her. "If you give me the tape, I might consider coming back."

"Why do you want it?"

Again Marsh turned away. "I don't know," he said.

Cara wasn't satisfied. "Tell me," she said. "Would you watch it? Would it turn you on?"

Marsh made no reply.

"Well, I destroyed the tape." She was lying: Marsh was convinced of it.

"No deal then."

"Okay," Cara said, semirelenting. "I'll think about it. I don't think it's a good idea, though."

"It probably isn't," Marsh agreed. But he felt that watching the tape would affirm some idea of his marriage or maybe teach him a lesson. It was a form of self-flagellation, a pixilated hair shirt. Cara remained in the doorway a few minutes before leaving, wordlessly, and Marsh didn't know she was gone until he heard the door hiss shut and click.

Marsh continued following Brunk around, continued keeping a log. It became an adventure, or a compulsion. He had to admit that maybe he was living vicariously through the amorous goings-on he witnessed between Brunk and Chrystal in the cramped backseat of the Mustang. Once he'd ascertained their hiding spot and a rough schedule of their interludes, Marsh began planting himself among budding rhododendrons with the camcorder, recording what he saw. Later in his hotel room he would watch the videos—grainy and dark-edged and revealing little but a mass of nebulous movement— until he felt so leaden with sadness that he turned them off and tried to sleep.

The Holiday Inn would bankrupt Marsh before long, so he planned a return trip home. There were no other options. Maybe he'd set up a Hide-A-Bed in the basement. He kept the news from Cara, hoping she'd deliver the tape before his surrender, which she did on a warm spring evening, knocking at the door as Marsh lounged on the bed, trudging through one of the histories he'd bought, the window open to admit a breeze that rippled the pages of the book. She drew the tape from her purse and tossed it on the bed beside him. The camcorder was plugged into the back of the TV, the tapes of Brunk and Chrystal stacked on top of the entertainment console, and Marsh cursed himself for his carelessness, resolving to destroy them the next morning.

He did not, could not, destroy the tapes. Instead Marsh stayed on at the Holiday Inn, taking leave from work to lie in bed watching them—first the films of Brunk and Chrystal, then the tape of Cara and Dees, alternating like that. Brunk and Chrystal, Cara and Dees. His examination—at first bloody, with a metallic taste on the tongue—turned clinical. Notes were jotted in the Brunk file. There was something about Brunk. Marsh considered interviewing Brunk's friends and relatives. He could claim to be making a documentary.

He didn't hear Cara knock, wasn't even sure how she'd gained entry, but she was suddenly there, standing beside the bed, squinting at the screen.

"What's that?" she asked.

Marsh started; luckily he was not naked. Once he'd tried masturbating to the Brunk tapes, but the act seemed too off-kilter, so he had quit midway through. Luckily, too, the footage at this point in the film was surpassingly grainy. "That's the subject I've been following."

"Those are people? I thought they were wild animals or something."

"No," Marsh said, pausing the tape. "That's the kid who stole our camcorder."

"But you got it back."

"True, but the kid's a delinquent. He was vandalizing the shop."

"He's still doing it?"

"No, not recently. He's lying low right now."

"Ken," Cara began, "I just wondered if you're planning on coming home. I mean, Larry has been pursuing me and I'm...confused." Her gaze fell on Marsh's notes. "What's that?"

"This?" Marsh said, shutting the composition book. "Just some poetry."

"Poetry," Cara said, her interest piqued. "Read me some!" She sat on the bed and straightened her skirt in one fluid movement. She was wearing a new perfume.

"I can't," Marsh hedged. "It's embarrassing. Really it's just my thoughts. It's not developed or anything."

"Come on, Kenny, don't be like that." She edged closer.

"Fine," he said, and began flipping pages as though searching for a particular piece of work. "Okay, here we go." Marsh marked the page with his finger and began desperately inventing. *"In my youth I was two-fold, / one part transmission, one part manifold, / but as I grew older the parts changed / wore out, became rearranged, / and now I'm a car that sits on blocks in the yard."* Marsh smiled, pleased with himself.

"You just made that up," Cara said.

"No, I didn't."

"Yes, you did. It was nice, but you made it up."

"How could you tell?"

"Your eyes weren't moving."

"Oh, yeah," Marsh said. "Duh." The two of them laughed.

"So what's really in the notebook?"

"Poems," Marsh insisted. "Little poems. Poem-thingies."

"Let me see," Cara said, reaching. Then she was stretched across him, hand nearing the Brunk files, skirt riding up, blouse and body making inadvertent contact. Marsh got an erection. Embarrassed, he surrendered the book and turned his back to Cara in bed.

She began reading. "*3:45–4:45, weight room. Coach Lorenzo tells me that Brunk does squats and calves, then works his delts and finishes up with bench press—three sets of 10 reps at 180 lbs.*

"*4:50, Brunk buys an energy drink from the vending machine in the student lounge. Can't tell what it is, but I think it's Gatorade. Grape-flavored...*

"*...7:40, picks up Chrystal. They see a Jackie Chan movie but leave early and drive over to the Hy-Vee on Eighth Street. Meet a guy in parking lot (should confirm identity), give him cash, he comes back with Old Style Light, which seems to be Brunk's favorite. They take Highway 6 out into the country east of town, tossing beer cans out window...*" Cara began turning pages. More of the same. "Ken," she said. "What is this? Tell me what this means."

"It's nothing." Marsh still had his back to her, eyes closed, trying to envision polar bears and biker gangs until his boner subsided. He tugged the bedspread tighter around his shoulders.

"You're stalking this kid."

"He's very popular," Marsh muttered, as though that were an explanation.

"That's not right." He felt the bed shift as she rose, then knew from the noises in the room that she was gathering up the tapes and putting them in the garbage, cinching up the sack. "I'm taking these," she said. Marsh turned to look at her. What was this embargo of his? Why couldn't he return to her?

"Cara," he began, "are you still running?" It was all he could muster.

"Yes," she said. "I'm committed to it."

"That's good," Marsh said.

"Is it?"

Pep rally day. A warm spring afternoon, late in the week. On days like these, craftsmen, nodding off, lost a digit or two to the band saw.

The bleachers filled with students while teachers leaned against one wall as though preparing for a game of bombardment. Principal Dees and Skimmick from AV messed with the microphone up front, making sure it was flipped on and feedback-free. His Brunk log under one arm, Marsh watched for signs of the 171-pounder while the band struck up the school's fight song. Cheerleaders performed their minor acrobatics. Everyone had come to applaud the wrestlers advancing to state, namely Brunk and one other sad sack with a last name like Bursitis or Encephalitis who came forward wearing, of all things, his headgear, as though ready to wrestle anyone who might question his odds at state. Dees called Brunk's name a couple times, allowing silence to accumulate in the cramped gym. Where was he?

Marsh had seen him only an hour before. The audacity—to skip an assembly held in one's honor—irked Marsh, who went searching. He passed through the major corridors, checked the shop and the music room, the student lounge, then headed outside to hunt for Brunk's Mustang in the parking lot. The car was there, which surprised him. Standing, baffled, squinting in the sunlight, Marsh gazed back at the school and by pure chance happened to glimpse a figure standing distantly on the gymnasium roof, a shadow figure, and a second climbing the maintenance ladder.

Marsh took off at a run. Afterward he'd realize he should have fetched the security guard. Instead, he started climbing. As he neared the roof of the school, the breeze picked up and the gridirons and diamonds gave way to checker-squared fields; Marsh could see why the ladder might be a temptation. The sounds of the student population beneath him grew strangled and remote. Then he was atop the flat gravel roof, where Brunk and Chrystal had already begun some light petting, a pair of jackets spread beneath them. Suddenly Marsh wasn't sure what to do. He knew he should call out—should stop them—but he'd become so used to observing their behavior from afar that now, close up, everything seemed somehow too normal, the way a clown looks without his makeup.

Chrystal finally turned, saw him, and gasped. Brunk paused, looked up, then leaped to his feet in one lithe gesture reminiscent of the way in which he had risen from the wrestling mat after pinning his opponent. There was an animal grace that Marsh admired. But now the feral, predatory gaze was upon him, and it occurred to Marsh that Brunk might push him off the roof. He set his feet and said, "Don't do anything stupid, Brunk," which was like asking a baby to change its own diaper. Brunk kept coming. He then had hold of Marsh's arm, quick like that, before Marsh could prepare, and got around behind him. Marsh's legs were swept from under him and he fell.

Brunk had him in a headlock. The grip was tight. Though he could breathe without effort, he could not move, except for his arms, which flailed like an insect's blind antennae.

"Stop following us," Brunk said, squeezing tighter for emphasis.

"Stop being an ass," Marsh replied.

By this point, Chrystal had shaken the gravel from their jackets and wandered over. "What are you going to do with him?" she said. Though he couldn't see Brunk's face, he felt him turn quickly to look at his girlfriend. Brunk had not planned out his movements.

"I don't know," he admitted.

"You may as well let him go. We're already busted."

"Don't worry," Brunk explained. "My dad will get us out of this."

"Whatever," Chrystal said. "I'm leaving."

"How are you getting home?"

"I guess I'll take the bus or something. This is stupid."

Marsh knew that Brunk had turned to watch her leave. He, on the other hand, could see only the flat expanse of the gymnasium roof, some treetops, the contrail of a jetliner that had passed overhead without his hearing it.

Brunk adjusted his hold in a bored way. "How long have you been married, Mr. Marsh?"

"Twenty-one years. But I'm probably getting divorced."

"How come?"

"My wife was unfaithful."

"So was Chrystal."

This surprised Marsh. "Why are you still with her?" he asked.

Brunk was silent a moment. "I don't know," he said finally. "I guess I should be pissed, but it's like once I knew other guys wanted her, I wanted her even more."

Marsh's arms finally found a purchase, and he clung to Brunk's neck. "When my wife cheated on me," he grunted, "I mainly felt startled. Then I knew that things would be different afterward. I didn't really give it much thought, though. Maybe things don't have to be different."

Brunk tightened his grip and Marsh felt the muscles flex under his chin. His breathing became labored; he started clawing. "I'd like you to stop following us, Mr. Marsh," Brunk said. "Can you do that?"

Marsh let out an indistinguishable sound—a gurgle, a babble. He was forced face-first into the roof, released, and when he turned, Brunk was gone, already halfway down the ladder.

Marsh tried to speak, but nothing came. He tried again, a single word. "Home." Then he repeated the word, again, again, testing it to see how it sounded.

JORDAN McMULLIN

University of Maryland

MOUSE

When I was a young boy of nine, I began taking piano lessons from a woman called Mrs. Hanolin. As are many students of their piano instructors, I was frightened out of my wits by her. She was neither a bad person nor a bad teacher, but every Wednesday night as I entered her home through the garage door—after bestowing upon my mother in the driveway a spiritless wave meant to induce guilt—I felt as if I were passing into a mildly haunted space, the air heavy with the sad traces of an ordinary life, its ordinary sufferings, and all I could not know about them.

I was small and corpulent and I went to Catholic school. I wore a red polo shirt and pleated gray wool pants. Over the polo shirt in the colder months I wore a gray vest, and that's how I see myself now, thinking back on it: swaddled and sniffling.

First the snow crunching under my mother's car tires, then an orange songbook pressed against my chest. Rubber boots would lead me onward, as if against my will. Mrs. Hanolin's highly organized garage, with its shelves of cardboard boxes labeled in green: X-MAS ORNA-MENTS, RUG SALVAGED FROM FLOOD. A dark laundry room cluttered with shoes. A mustard-colored kitchen stuffed with food smells that nauseated me simply because they were not ours. Finally a thickly car-peted staircase that opened into a finished basement, where the grand piano stood, and on the stool in front of it the older, pimpled girl who had a lesson before mine and who never played anything other than "The Spinning Wheel Song," and beside her Mrs. Hanolin her-self, running her fingers through her necklace so that its glass balls clacked together, underneath the melody.

Photos and paintings and Things Within Frames hung from every possible wall surface in the basement piano room, so that it was im-possible to say what color the walls were underneath, or if there were walls at all. I studied the images, and the odd choices for their layout. A few stand out in my memory. A black-and-white photograph of a man with a handlebar mustache who seemed profoundly annoyed to have one growing there, right in the middle of an otherwise dignified face. A small portrait of a girl with a horse chin. A painting of a man holding a woman's giant bottom against his groin. The man wore a top hat, the woman a shabby blue dress. She was fat with bright red cheeks, her hair was coming undone, and she puckered her lips in a way that begged me to reach out to them, to give them an experi-mental push.

I never did. Mrs. Hanolin didn't have to tell me that I was not to touch anything. She didn't have to tell me that I was to wait patiently on the couch at the opposite end of the room while the pimpled girl's lesson ran overtime. She didn't have to tell me that, while I waited, I was to flip through the wicker basket of falling-apart children's books next to the couch. At first these didn't interest me as much as the Things Within Frames, but I found in the wicker basket, eventually, my one and only consistent pleasure at Mrs. Hanolin's: a book called *The Lives of Dinosaurs.* Halfway through, on page thirty-three, was a drawing of a T. rex and a stegosaur in battle. The T. rex was roaring, its eyes wild. It was clearly winning the fight, claws poised for another strike, but it had suffered a gash in its neck that spilled bright red blood down its haunches. The gash surprised me. It was deep and wide, flapping open like a lazy mouth. The stegosaur retreated through a shallow stream, its neck contorted in a last, desperate attempt to defend itself. Blood dripped from its tongue. Soon, I imagined, it would stumble and fall.

I sketched in my mind the next picture in the book: water from the stream, blue and white, frozen in a splash around the stegosaur's fallen body. I wanted to draw it myself at home, but I had no artistic talent of any kind. I merely had the ability to imagine something vividly and to nurture it there in my mind.

I longed for effortlessness, genius. I longed for this in everything, including the piano. At night in the dark of my bedroom I listened to Pachelbel's "Canon" on a hushed cassette player. I had a vision: me alone on the stage of the school gymnasium, beneath a spotlight, my eyes closed, the notes bursting forth from my fingers as if they were my only language. All around me were dilapidated sets from plays of long ago—it looked as if someone had taken a hatchet to them— and when I looked up from the keys to gauge my audience's reaction, I wasn't surprised to find them all in dresses, even the boys and the male teachers.

But I never learned how to read music adequately. I fudged my way through two years of lessons by managing to figure out one note at a time, learning only by rote where to place my fingers. I began well enough. I could play the first few bars of any song perfectly, but after a few moments everything would fall apart. Under Mrs. Hanolin's gaze—under *anyone's* gaze—I had no sense. My fingers landed on the right note or they didn't, and most often they didn't. I watched my fingers as if I were watching a centipede on its back trying to right itself.

If given the choice, I'd have waited forever for my lesson to begin.

Every week, I waited in the same way. With the cheerful, unthinking melody of "The Spinning Wheel Song" as my disjointed sound track, and the couch cushion swallowing me into its buttocks-shaped bowl, I would linger over each page of the first half of *The Lives of Dinosaurs*. I studied the brontosauruses lazily chewing ferns. I studied the pterodactyls hang gliding over a black lake. As I began to finger through the book I felt an insistent desire to skip to page thirty-three, but I felt an even stronger, grating satisfaction in denying myself the page—in keeping my love for the T. rex and stegosaur in check. Finally, at the right time, I'd allow myself to look. I'd stare until the T. rex grew blurry before me, until its gash was nothing more than a distant red fireworks burst that I saw when I closed my eyes at night. I would look until I knew with another swelling in my throat that my waiting was over. Mrs. Hanolin's long brown fingernails would click against the piano stool as she adjusted it to my height, her hand swirling it in circles as if swirling through pond sediment.

The old upright piano in our own home was horrifyingly out of tune. I'd never have known had I not heard the same songs played on two pianos every week. How different they sounded! Ours clunked its notes out, indistinct. Mrs. Hanolin's shimmered with sound—with *correct* sound. At my very first lesson, Mrs. Hanolin had given me a demonstration. She played a song as it was meant to be played, and she took up the whole piano while demonstrating, her arms outstretched to high and low keys, complicating a simple beginner's tune with extra chords and flourishes, her fingernails clicking against the keys and her torso swaying back and forth. My heart thumped as she played. I listened, transfixed by the rolling movement in her shoulders, by her feet, which depressed the mysterious pedals. I told myself that if I were Mrs. Hanolin, with such a striking ability, I would never leave the piano stool at all. I'd been tricked by her demonstration. Tricked into longing.

Although my mother was clearly disappointed by my seeming inability to learn even one song well, she insisted that I stick with the piano lessons and display, as she put it, "follow-through." I wasn't entirely persuaded. Like most adults, my mother was filled with vague, passed-down notions of a child's mettle and what was good for it. When I accused her of signing me up for piano lessons merely because it was what mothers did to their sons, she closed her textbook, used a fingernail to scratch at the remnants of the sticker announcing it was USED, and said, "But you seem to *like* the piano so." I could not explain to her then that I was also terrified of it.

My mother was a thoughtful woman, who loved to brush her hair on the back porch in the summertime and hold the stray hairs out to be carried off by the wind. She worked in an office and was studying to become a nurse. She had her own longings then, for the ordinary. Every Wednesday, after escaping from Mrs. Hanolin's laundry room into the biting gray air, my heart would jump with relief at the sight of my mother's dim headlights in the driveway. I could read hope in her shoulders—in the defiant way she held them back as she drove us to the Dairy Queen. Her eyes darted around, blind to the demands of the road. They moved as if they watched an imaginary scene before us. Whether it was a ballet or a battle, I couldn't tell.

Tuesdays were for practicing and dreading—moaning and begging. I would rest my forehead on the keys. I would roll my head from side to side, depressing them gently enough so they made no sound. "Just play me what you can," my mother would say, and I would set my fingers on the keys and rattle off the first few bars of a sonata. Then I would stop and look at her solemnly, knowingly. It was a look that said, *You know we are not these people.* Then she would stand by the stool and lean over me, squinting. "Well, what note is this here?" she would ask, and I would say that I knew perfectly well what note that was, thank you, and even if she let me quit piano lessons this very instant, it would never erase the irreparable trauma of having played so poorly, and for so long. My mother would rub her hands on the dish towel tucked into her skirt and look worriedly at the floor. Her perfume bothered me, on Tuesday nights.

"I will not thank you someday," I would add.

I dreaded Handel, Mrs. Hanolin's old gray tabby, perhaps even more than I did playing poorly in front of my teacher. The cat had blackberry-jamlike goo in the corners of its eyes. Usually by the time I got to page thirty-three in *The Lives of Dinosaurs* and the pimpled girl was playing for the tenth and last time "The Spinning Wheel Song," the cat was already transferring copious amounts of fur to my pant legs. My mother often complained about having to use the lint brush on them, and so, one Wednesday night in the dead of winter, the night that everything began to converge and then unravel, I batted away the cat as politely as I could.

Mrs. Hanolin caught me. She appeared in the basement quite suddenly and silently, after having made the untypical effort of walking the pimpled girl to her waiting car.

Fear gripped my heart, and I closed the dinosaur book in my lap. Mrs. Hanolin tilted her head, as if to reassess my identity. I'd long sensed that tolerating other people's pets was one of those unfortunate human duties—one of those crosses every decent person had to bear—and there I was failing at it, right out in the open.

Mrs. Hanolin smiled a little. She fiddled with the beads on her necklace and said, "My little man."

I thought for a moment she was referring to me, and I swallowed.

Then she said, "He's telepathic, you know. Senses everything about the person inside."

Handel sidled up against my leg again, undeterred. I began petting him profusely. "Really?" I said.

"Well," she said. "It's a complicated gesture, isn't it? All that rubbing and demanding. Obscene, even."

The cat butted its ears into my shin. "Yes," I said, "it is."

"I was crying yesterday and he found me," Mrs. Hanolin continued. "From all the way across the house. He came right to me. Right into my lap."

I looked at Mrs. Hanolin's midsection. It was securely contained within navy blue pants, then partly covered by a big, tentlike smock. I looked at the cat again. He opened his jaw in a mute meow.

I sat through the lesson conscious of the fur on my pant legs.

In the car on the way to the Dairy Queen that night I experienced the typical half hour of joy that followed each release from Mrs. Hanolin's domain, but this time it was tinged with wonder. What on earth did Mrs. Hanolin have to cry about? The thought made me uneasy. Mrs. Hanolin lived by herself in a large development of identical ranch houses. Why, I considered for the first time, was she called Mrs.? I had trouble imagining her crying, or doing much else besides playing the piano. I couldn't even imagine her in another part of her house, separate from her Things Within Frames. I tried to imagine her sleeping, but I couldn't picture her lying horizontal.

My mother ordered a vanilla cone, I ordered my usual strawberry, and we took them back to the car, parked in the far corner of the lot that overlooked a go-kart track. Our weekly trip to the Dairy Queen was our way of apologizing to each other, without actually having to do so. Me for my complaints and lack of ability. She for having misplaced my father.

Though a small woman, my mother was a voracious eater. She finished nearly twice as fast as I did and then shoved the small, ineffectual napkin into the ashtray. The heater breathed on us, and the radio played country music songs.

I turned to her and said, "Are we happy or sad?"

She didn't answer right away. She looked in the rearview mirror at her reflection. Then she said, "Sometimes it's hard to tell, isn't it?"

Our car bumbled back along familiar roads, headlights cutting through snow. We were returning to our own ranch house in our own development with our own dogwood tree out front. Ours was just like all the others on the street but it was different because it was *that one*—with the greenish shutters. The one that smelled, on the inside, just the way we smelled.

Were we happy or sad? Sometimes it was hard to tell. There was so much we could not talk about. We could not talk about school and its various miniature atrocities. How I feared and hated eraser duty, when I was made to walk with another student, usually female, into the dark, dank janitor's room, where we smacked the erasers together, my shirt always getting covered with white—and me choking on the nauseating dust. And what could she not tell me? She could not tell me what happened after she put me to bed and she remained in the living room for hours, with her glasses of wine and her textbooks and her country music albums and a faraway look on her face. Whatever it was she thought about, she was not thinking about me.

The next week, I opened the door into Mrs. Hanolin's laundry room and didn't hear a thing: no "Spinning Wheel Song," no Mrs. Hanolin saying "allegro here—*here.*" I glanced around for some kind of sign, then noticed a man with a bald spot like a little white saucer sitting at Mrs. Hanolin's kitchen table, staring out the window at the naked trees. He turned his head when my feet hit the linoleum. He

smiled and lifted half his palm from the table in a lazy hello. I nodded, then proceeded to the basement.

The pimpled girl was gone. A black-haired sloucher had taken her
place on the stool, arms folded tightly against Mrs. Hanolin's diagram explaining musical chords. The sloucher was a girl: She wore a
dark gray T-shirt way too big for her, all the way down to her knees.
I saw that the songbook open on the piano was purple—the color of
the *Beginner's Volume*—and I decided that this must be her very first
lesson, that this must be the new Girl Who Would Always Be Here
Before Me, when I entered Mrs. Hanolin's house every Wednesday.
Neither she nor Mrs. Hanolin looked up as I slid into the couch,
looking at a scuffed-up canvas book bag crumpled next to the wicker
basket. There was a small button attached to the front pocket that
said WHO CARES.

I pulled out *The Lives of Dinosaurs* and, with a nervous heart,
opened it. I kept my eyes on the title page throughout the lesson,
glancing up at the girl only when Mrs. Hanolin clacked the glass
balls of her necklace and said to her, with finality, "Let's go upstairs
to talk with your father."

She didn't listen. She waited until Mrs. Hanolin was gone and
then swiveled around on the piano stool, leaned her back against the
keys without hitting any of them, and began to swing her legs back
and forth violently. I was surprised to be left alone with her and quite
frightened, for when she spun around I saw that she was much older
than I'd originally assumed.

She made eye contact with me, and I immediately looked at the
book in my lap. "What grade are you in?" she asked.

"Fifth," I said softly, and then again—"Fifth!"—but louder this
time, in case she hadn't heard.

She nodded, her legs swinging. "I'm in eighth."

"Okay." I turned back to the book. Without looking up I could detect her rising from the bench, walking toward me. In an instant, the couch cushion was responding to her surprisingly significant weight. She smelled of peaches.

"Do you go to St. Stephen's?"

"Yes."

"Too bad for you."

I wasn't sure how to respond to this. I flipped a page in the book and was struck instantly by the fact that I'd never before, until that very moment, bothered to look past page thirty-three. In front of me was a drawing of a little crocodile-like thing escaping from its shell, pushing itself into the waiting world. I immediately flipped back to the title page.

"How long've you been coming here?" she asked.

"One year and ten months."

"Sucks," she said. "You must be good, though."

A kind of pride swelled in my cheeks. Because her lesson was before mine, she would never have to witness my clumsy and halting performances.

"Why does she make us come in through the garage?" she asked.

"I think so our shoes only dirty the laundry room."

"Why does she have so many stupid pictures up?"

The wall in front of me seemed to throb, causing a surprising sensation in my gut: defensiveness. Mrs. Hanolin's Things Within Frames were mine, too. I could have closed my eyes and given the girl almost the entire layout of the wall in front of me. I knew that right below the framed photograph of three shirtless men in a motorboat was a pencil sketch of a nun in full habit, her body stretched to cartoonish length, pulled taut as if by a pack of mad dogs in a tug-of-war, which the artist hadn't bothered to depict. I loved this sketch precisely because it didn't fit in with the rest of the Things Within Frames, emitting their separate auras of determination, declaring against all better knowledge, *I am real.*

"My dad is making me take lessons," the girl said. "My mom's dead."

I looked at her, for the first time, right in the face. It was a round face, with olive skin stretched tight and shiny over high cheekbones. Her nose was flattish, her eyes far apart and almost black. Her face looked strange to me, and I was concerned that my reaction betrayed this. I looked away.

"My dad's dead," I said.

This wasn't true. My father was somewhere in California, and every now and again we would receive a package from him that contained a check and a letter that my mother snatched away before I could see it, along with a random selection of gifts packed in Styrofoam peanuts: organic jams and jellies, silk scarves, and once for me a pair of leather cowboy boots I didn't have the nerve to wear outside my bedroom. I was ashamed of the way I waited for these packages. It had been months and months since the last package. Another would never come.

Handel entered, ears bent back, agitated by the change in routine.

"Get outta here!" I said, startling myself.

"Aw," the girl said, "we have a cat." She extended her hand, palm up. She tisked and smooched, but the cat wouldn't come. It paused ten feet away and sat, watching us with a twitching tail. "Whatcha reading?" she asked.

I closed the book so that only the back cover showed. There was evidence of years of youthful abuse: chocolate smudges and poorly executed doodles. I'd never noticed those before, either.

"Nothing," I said.

"You're too old for a picture book."

"Shut up," I whispered. My teeth grinded. "This one isn't for children." With shaky fingers I searched for page thirty-three. "Look."

The girl took the book into her own lap, tucked a loose strand of hair behind her ear. "Huh!" she said. She handed back the book. "Can I show you my scar?"

I looked at the T. rex—at the injury that might eventually kill it, despite its victory. "I don't know," I said. "Where is it?"

She stood in order to pull up her T-shirt. She lifted it as far as her dingy white brassiere. Her stomach was paler than her face, and it spilled over her jeans a little, jiggling. Across her midriff—from one side clear to the other—was a straight line of pink scar tissue, puffy and thick as a piece of licorice.

"How'd that happen?" I asked.

"Not telling," she said. She dropped her T-shirt, but it refused to lie correctly, bunching up around her bottom. She yanked at it until it covered her thighs once again. "It was worse than that dinosaur, though," she said.

"Let's go!" came a man's voice from upstairs. I jolted on the cushion, and the cat scurried off to hide under the ottoman.

"All right!" the girl yelled, her voice powered by the kind of annoyance reserved for the familiar. She shrugged at me and I shrugged back, realizing that a shrug was not a gesture I coolly employed.

She grabbed her book bag and took off up the steps, decided and booming.

I ran straight to my bedroom when I returned home. I studied my face in the mirror above my dresser. How did I look? What did I look like to the black-haired beauty with the scar on her stomach? I did not have a face with noticeable features, like hers; when I stood in front of a mirror I saw eyes and nose and mouth and nothing more. Face.

My mother knocked on the door. "Sweetheart," she said, "what are you doing in there?"

My door had no lock—not even a doorknob. Instead there was a big hole we'd always meant to put a doorknob in, but somehow we never got around to it. Through the hole I could see the tiny blue flowers on my mother's dress. She pushed open the door, then had nothing to say. I realized that I had enjoyed, for just a moment, being apart from her.

In the world I fashioned for myself in the darkest dark of my bedroom, the girl was welcome. There I talked to her freely. I told her that somewhere in California there were sea lions on rocks like concrete slabs and beaches with piles of rotting kelp that the dogs were fond of urinating on. In my visions the girl wore braids that fell over each ear, just past her shoulder blades. I played Pachelbel's "Canon" for her, and it came out right. In a dream, she stood next to a giant egg. She said to me, "But the stupid thing's heart is still beating!" and I answered her coldly, "I *know*." In reality I wanted her to speak to me again, but I was also worried she might say something I couldn't un-hear.

The next Tuesday evening I practiced with something like gusto. I was learning an old church hymn, and every time I finished playing what I knew—the first six bars—my mother would mumble, "Oh, I just love it," and scurry into the kitchen to stab at something inside a Crock-Pot.

This was a special day for my mother, though she hadn't told me anything about it. When a knock came at the door, my mother ran to answer it. A man entered. As far as I could remember, a man had never been admitted into our home. I turned on my stool and looked from him to my mother, who—it then dawned on me—was wearing one of her special dresses. The man had a bouquet of baby's breath pressed to his chest, and he wore a bright red checkered shirt and a blue blazer. When he said hello to me and used my name for the first time, his voice caught on some phlegm and he harrumphed into a wet cough. He cleared his throat throughout the next hour in the living room, and then throughout dinner. When we sat down at the kitchen table, my mother pulled up an extra chair that was far too low for her. She was cut off from view nearly at the bust, and she looked nervous, but she laughed at almost everything the man said and she poured a bit of wine into a teacup for me. When I drank it, it made my cheeks hot. By the time we were eating Oreos off of plates, the man was sweating.

"Play for us, sweetheart," said my mother.

I stared at her for a moment, confused.

"Play us your song," she said. "You've just been doing so great."

I shook my head, fast and sure. I glanced at the man, who had been placed, unfortunately, right next to me, making it difficult to stare as much as I might have liked. The man had big shoulders that quivered when he chuckled. He was chuckling now. "A request from Mom," he said.

I found this an odd thing to point out. I had found all the man's conversation odd, for it was comprised merely of observations of the obvious, which my mother inexplicably appreciated. I had never known my mother to be so simple. I pulled apart an Oreo and shook my head once more. "I don't know the song for tomorrow yet," I said.

"Well, how about a song you *do* know?" asked the man.

My mother laughed. "Yes," she said. "Sure."

I looked at her. Perhaps I could knock her over with the force of my shame.

She smiled blankly and nodded. She picked up her wineglass and took a sip, then nodded again. "Go on," she said.

I stood up and pushed my chair away from the table as loudly as I could. I walked to the piano, vision blurred, and sat on the stool. The songbook was open in front of me, displaying the notes of the sad church hymn. My hands squeezed into fists, and then my left hand began to pound out a familiar bass clef: bum-bip, bum-bip, bum-bip. The start of "The Spinning Wheel Song." I had learned it at the end of my first year with Mrs. Hanolin and was surprised I remembered it. Bum-bip, bum-bip, bum-bip. My right hand descended to begin the optimistic melody. Out of the corner of my eye I could see my mother twisted around in the short chair, watching me with steady shoulders. My hands made it through the first ten bars of the song and then stopped, dead.

"Ha-hey!" exploded the man, clapping in the oppressive way only a big man can. I rose from the stool and ran from the room, down the hallway, into my bedroom, where I closed the knobless door and fell upon the bed, pressing my face into the quilt, trying to imprint my features there.

I waited for my mother to knock. I tried to hear what was being whispered in the kitchen. I woke at three o'clock in the morning, the lights still bright and my school clothes still on. The house was eerily quiet around me, the air heavy with new meaning.

On the way to school the next morning, I did not speak to my mother. I ducked into the school building without turning to wave. I ran to the bathroom after lunch to vomit up my Wednesday carrots. Then, after school, I waited in the parking lot for my mother to appear as she always did, and when she didn't I began to believe that she had left me forever. And wasn't that the right thing? I was nothing but a fatherless ingrate who couldn't even play the piano.

Finally, when the children swarming out front had disappeared into cars and buses and vans and I stood shivering and alone but for the teacher waiting beside me, I saw my mother's car slowly barumping into the lot. Her face was tight behind the windshield. The teacher gave my mother an admonishing salute and then headed to her own car.

I settled into the passenger's seat. I was compelled to stare at her. Her lips were rimmed with pink, and she was not dressed appropriately for the weather. She had forgotten her coat; her shoulders looked pointy under a thin sweater. She did not seem sad or happy but buzzing, her knuckles white on the steering wheel. It was as if she'd been plugged into some kind of generator that had set her skin alight.

"You aren't a little boy," she said.

Outside, the air was frozen. The trees seemed posed for another life. "Okay," I said.

The man never came back to our house, and neither of us ever mentioned that there had been one Tuesday, different from all other Tuesdays.

By the time we pulled into Mrs. Hanolin's driveway I was bursting with anxiety. I wondered if the girl had left—if I'd have to wait another six whole days to see her. I burst from the car and hopped the oil puddles in Mrs. Hanolin's garage. Just as I was about to open the door to the laundry room, it opened on its own. The girl emerged, wearing a puffy blue jacket that hid her body. Her black hair was pulled into a high ponytail that was so tight the corners of her eyes strained. "You," she said, slamming the door shut behind her.

I tried to catch my breath. Out on the street everything was turning dark. I inhaled.

"How was your lesson?"

"I did good." She looked past me to the driveway.

"Where's your ride?" I asked.

"I dunno."

"I'm late today."

When she didn't respond, I thought I must have been boring her. I moved to open the laundry room door, but she put a hand on my chest, flat and forceful, catching me off balance and causing me to stumble a step backward.

She laughed. "I got you something," she said. She stuck her arm out and twisted her back so that her book bag slid down her arm. She unzipped it. My mouth went dry with anticipation and dread.

She pulled something out of her book bag, flipped it around, and the scene before me became distorted for an instant. It swelled and then shrank again, as if it had taken a breath. *The Lives of Dinosaurs.*

I opened my mouth.

"Here, dummy," she said, holding out the book.

I put my hands in the air as if to surrender, and that's when I realized I'd forgotten my songbook in the car. "No," I said.

The girl glanced around quickly, then pushed the book toward me. "I snatched it for you," she whispered.

"Where will I put it? She'll see me walk in with it."

"You figure it out."

I watched my hands receive the book. They were red and cold and my fingernails needed clipping. I stuck the book, suddenly huge to me, under my armpit and said, "Thanks."

She put her finger to her lips. "Quiet as a mouse."

I nodded, unfeeling. "Can I go inside now?"

She snapped her ponytail around. "Yeah," she said, "whatever."

I went inside and stood in the yellow light of the laundry room, breathing. The dryer was working on a load, rumbling away, zippers and buttons clicking against its sides. It was a familiar sound, but it was accompanied by the smell of a strange detergent that accosted my nose. I listened intently for any sounds, above the noise of the dryer, which might come from downstairs, where Mrs. Hanolin was surely beginning to wonder about me.

I pushed my body into the small space that separated the dryer from the wall. It was impossible to walk downstairs with the book in my hand, but I also could not bring myself to hide the book and then retrieve it on my way out. *The Lives of Dinosaurs* would never belong in my home, would never belong to me. I had no interest in looking at the book now, under the yellow light, crouching low. As if I were a criminal. The dryer hummed beside me, warm through my coat. I waited, not sure how much time had passed. My legs cramped and my nose began to run. I nearly yelped when the dryer let off a buzz and came to rest.

I held my breath. The house was still, and in the silence that followed the dryer's shutting off I could see, really see, the laundry room for the first time. The walls were mint green and completely bare of pictures. Exposed. In the corners of the floor, which I had a particularly good view of, there were balls of lint caught on bits of peeling-away linoleum. From downstairs came the faintest sound of a piano. Mrs. Hanolin was playing a song—a sad, forgettable song. I stared at the mint green walls and listened. It wasn't the song she'd played for me at my first lesson.

Eventually, I heard my mother's car engine idling in the driveway. I stood, my legs pinching. I unzipped my coat and slipped the book inside. I would never return to Mrs. Hanolin's. I would take the book home with me and, without having read it once all the way through, I would destroy it.

RAZIA SULTANA KHAN

University of Nebraska, Lincoln

ALMS

Kanta poked her head through the kitchen door and said to the shadow moving inside, "*Adab Amma.* How are you today?" Salma, busy with her after-lunch routine, glanced at the beggar woman and nodded. Kanta took this as an invitation and sat down on her haunches, just outside the wooden jamb of the kitchen door. A smile played around her dark leathery face with its mesh of fine wrinkles, as she watched Salma, the mistress of the house. Kanta had worried that Salma would be resting and she'd have to go away empty-handed. It wasn't always the case that she arrived at such an opportune moment, when the lady of the house was able to exchange a few words with her. Eyes half shut, she took a deep breath. There was no suggestion of any earlier cooking: only the spicy smell that pervaded most Bangladeshi kitchens. She released her breath slowly, a little vexed.

"What does it matter? For a woman it's all the same. Beggar woman or queen." Salma's voice was low, but Kanta caught the words. She took this as a very congenial beginning to conversation and let her sharp, bony bottom slide to the floor. An "Aaaaaaah . . ." escaped her lips as the doorjamb took some of the pressure off her sore back. Cradling the sole of her left foot in both her hands, she massaged it, the bones of her fingers rolling up and down, as if coaxing a tune from an off-key harmonium. A layer of dirt and dust caked the calloused sole, the heel edged with vertical cracks, some as long as three-fourths of an inch. One, deeper than the others, showed a thin red line as Kanta gently squeezed it. There were few lanes in the old part of Dhaka city that these feet had missed in the last few years.

But Kanta had seen better days.

"I wasn't born a beggar, you know," she would say to anyone who listened. "I was a housewife. Yes, a farmer's wife, with cows in the shed, a barn brimming with rice and yellow lentils, and fields golden with grain." Her voice would fade, the light in her eyes dim. At other times it would be, "Fate! It's all written on this four-fingered width of space." She would join the four fingers of her right hand and cover her forehead with it. "Just four fingers." A few sharp taps to the forehead to emphasize the point, and a wise nod or two. "If it's written in your forehead, nothing you do will erase it."

Most people are familiar with the story. It's a common one in Bangladesh. A flood that washes away the land from under your feet, taking everything that stands on it—fields of rich soil, barns full of animals, babies sleeping beside their mothers. You're left thrashing in a quagmire.

"Not satisfied, it then took my husband . . . and my three beautiful children." At times a wail broke out of her cracked lips; at other times, she sat oblivious to her surroundings until someone with a kind heart brought her back from her refuge to the real world.

After losing her family, she turned to the reality of her life: no education, no skills, no money, no one to support her. There was nothing to do but go to work as a farmhand for her neighbors. People who knew her lowered their eyes and nodded when she joined the able-bodied men queuing for seasonal jobs. And if planting the little shoots of paddy at sowing time took longer, or if the buckets of water she carried to the thirsting plants were smaller than the others, the landowners turned a blind eye, knowing she would complete the work even if it meant working late into the evening, long after the other farmhands were home and in bed.

She watched with surprise and pleasure as the little plants turned into lush green fields rippling in the summer breeze. As a farmer's wife she had mostly stayed on the homestead, keeping an eye on things. She stored the surplus grain to ensure there would be enough for the rest of the year, entertained relatives and friends, and, of course, looked after the needs of her family. What had she to do with a farmhand's job? Now she was in direct contact with the land and the grain.

She liked winnowing the best. Holding the bamboo *kula* high up in the air to one side of her head, tapping it, letting it create its own music, adjusting to the rhythm of the other five or six women who stood in a semicircle. The rhythmic motion lifted the chaff, making it dance in the wind before it snuggled down on the rectangular cement floor in the yard. So what if the paddy did not belong to her and she was not the one giving orders? She was content being one among others, content to come to her empty hovel at night, too exhausted for the ghosts of the past to torment her.

Once the winnowing season was over and the grain stored or sold, there wasn't much left for Kanta to do. The farmers settled down to live off the surplus and she was out once again looking for work. The only available work now was in the houses of those who could afford hired help—washing, cleaning, and scrubbing. She never said no to any work, not even when Munni's mother tentatively asked her if she wouldn't mind carpeting the kitchen floor with a water-and-clay paste, to return the sooty floor to its original freshness.

One year the monsoon was exceptionally long and Kanta could not keep her hands dry. They were wet at work and wet when she stayed home. They started to itch, and one day she noticed a few water-filled bubbles in the spaces between her fingers. Scratching brought relief, and she scratched with abandon until the bubbles burst and a burning sensation started, as if someone had rubbed chili paste on it. A few weeks of this and her fingers were covered in angry red sores. She squirmed with the itch when she scrubbed pots and pans or mopped floors.

Gradually, fewer people offered her work in their homes. In the beginning it didn't bother her much. She thought, *Good, I can rest my hands.* But the monsoon continued and the blisters spread to her arms.

The day came when she finished the last of the broken rice she had saved. The next morning she left home early to look for work. She walked farther than usual, but with little luck. Finally, stricken by hunger pains, she sat down on the steps of a building. Cars honked by and rickshaw bells tinkled as if jeering at her, but she sat oblivious to her surroundings. She didn't notice when a car stopped in front of her and a lady in a shimmering silk sari got out. She passed Kanta, then stopped and retraced her steps. She opened her bag and dropped something in Kanta's lap.

Kanta's eyes focused. It was a ten-taka bill. She looked at the money, puzzled, unsure what was expected of her. Then she felt her face become hot and flushed with shame. She picked up the money to thrust it back at the owner. But didn't. She closed her stiff, sore fist over the bill and with it the door to her pride. The hunger pangs had won.

It was traumatic at first. She felt the full force of her moral and social degradation. A beggar; the lowest of the low. What if she met people she knew? What if...? But she needn't have worried. Nobody recognized the skinny beggar pulling her faded and torn sari over her averted face.

A new life began for her. She left her village early in the morning and walked to the old part of Dhaka city, about a kilometer and a half away. Once in the crowded city, her footsteps slowed. She brought out her clay bowl and went from house to house calling out, "Ma! Give to this poor beggar. Allah will bless you."

Once the poshest area in all of Dhaka, Old Town was now a famine-stricken replica of its past. Formerly paved roads had become pockmarked lanes, through which ran the decaying entrails of Old Town for all and sundry to witness. A putrid smell hung over the whole area like a dense fog. The original residents were long dead; their heirs had moved to more affluent residential areas: Gulshan, Banani, and Bashundhara. Only those whose condition reflected that of Old Town stayed on, becoming synonymous with its putrescence.

Kanta's surroundings did not affect her in any way. If anything, she liked it. Here, people were more traditional, clutching closely to the religious rituals shed by the upwardly mobile as they moved to more respectable parts of the city. Here, people still believed that giving alms to beggars was a form of charity, and doors were left open so one could at least enter the houses without meeting the baleful glares of the guards or being shoo-shooed away like a thief or a vagabond.

Kanta had to learn many things afresh. She found herself floundering in a world of *mastans*, pimps, thieves, and dishonest police officers. She didn't know whom she feared more—the few earnest police officers who thought they were doing their jobs by periodically rounding up beggars and ferrying them to a distant place and expecting them to start a new life there from scratch, or the dishonest ones who turned a blind eye to almost everything in exchange for a few takas. Every inch of the large city was chalked out into sections that were controlled by self-styled *mastans* who thought they owned the beggars or whoever else happened to be in "their" areas.

She had learned from her mistakes, and each mistake had cost her dearly, in terms of work and money, but eventually she had been able to establish her own route. Now she made sure she kept to a strict schedule as well as her own space. One important lesson she had learned early on was to live for the day. Saving for the future was a futile activity.

She was amazed at first at how easy it was to move from house to house, and from lane to lane. And after all the time and energy she had spent begging, it seemed to her as good a profession as any. Certainly she worked much harder as a beggar than she had ever worked as a farmer's wife, and she knew she had never been lazy. None of the women she begged from worked as hard as she did, and after ten years of begging she had accepted her fate.

Weaving through the lanes and alleys, Kanta became a familiar sight in Old Town. In her travels she encountered all types of people, about whom she told stories for those who gave her alms. She learned to add a little here, polish a little there, sometimes changing or adding a character or two. Her stories were as good as any written by a published author. The women and children in the houses she visited listened to her with wide eyes and open mouths. She savored those moments more than the rice and money she collected.

On Fridays her route led her to Agasadeque Road and Salma. Friday was a good workday, since most people reserved their moral obligations for the holy day. Then, rich aromas would come wafting from their kitchens. Perhaps the thought that a succulent meal awaited them while the dregs of society went trudging from door to door induced people to be more generous.

One of Kanta's favorite stops was 606 Agasadeque Road. She'd been coming here for the last eight years, since the time of Salma's mother-in-law. Over the years a bond had formed between the two old women. Perhaps each could see a reflection of herself in the other. Each could so easily *have been* the other. Both widows were dependent, one on her son and the other on society.

When Salma came to Agasadeque Road as a new bride, she resented the beggar woman who sat and talked with her mother-in-law, imagining herself the topic every time they became silent at her entrance. But when her mother-in-law passed away, Salma took on the yoke of the household, and it appealed to her sense of authority as the lady of the manor to treat Kanta with kindness. She kept up the tradition, making sure Kanta did not go empty-handed from her door.

Also, Kanta brought news of the outside world. She told Salma where she had been and what she had seen. She would dwell minutely on what Kazi Sahib's wife had cooked the other day, or the fact that sixty-year-old Amir's second wife, just twenty, was pregnant again. Salma's eyes would sparkle as she listened to events from outside the walls of her house, so near yet so out of reach. The passing years had brought these two women closer despite the difference in their ages.

"How can you say that?" Kanta now said in response to Salma's comment that the life of any woman, beggar or queen, was the same. "You're a lucky housewife belonging to a rich household. Be grateful for what you have."

Her ploy worked and Salma snorted, "And what do I have, pray? I work from sunrise to sunset and for what? Heartbreak, that's what I have." Kanta nodded, happy in her role as a sounding board.

"But let's not talk about my problems. What about you? I haven't seen you for a while. What have you been up to?"

"Believe me, I must have seen the whole of Dhaka since the last time I saw you. Wasn't that the Monday of the new moon? And it was *amabasha* yesterday. It was pitch-dark when I walked home."

"You overdo it. You're not getting any younger you know."

"True, I must be at least sixty-five. Could even be seventy. I was five years old when we had that great flood and our whole village went underwater. And I've been on foot since sunrise. I've picked up some rice here and there, but I won't be able to cook it till I get home, and God only knows when that will be."

Salma took a red plastic bowl from a shelf, and went to a wooden cupboard in one corner of the kitchen. Blocking the view of the interior with her body, she put her hands inside and took out a few handfuls of puffed rice from a large rectangular container and pushed the door shut. She poured the contents of the red plastic bowl into Kanta's clay pot. The wall of white, foamlike pellets cascaded into Kanta's clay bowl with a reassuring patter.

"May Allah bless you! May your cupboards always overflow with food!" Thanking her loudly, Kanta took a fistful of rice, raised it over her face, and poured it into her gap-toothed open mouth. She chewed the crispy grains with relish. It was amazing how different the food from the cupboards tasted from what was left aside for beggars.

"Your *muri* is the tastiest in the whole of this area. And I should know. It's your intention, I say. If you have a good heart and give happily, the food is bound to taste good."

Kanta's sharp eyes had spied a large chunk of *gur* that was sitting on a plate near the earthen *chula*. Her eyes kept darting toward the date-palm molasses, until Salma finally caught the look. She went up to the *gur*, broke off a piece, and plunked it on the bowl of puffed rice. Kanta's eyes lit up, and she crushed the rich brown chunk between her fingers to break it into small crystalline bits and spread the sweetness.

Salma's face became thoughtful as she toyed with Kanta's boast that she traveled all over the streets of Dhaka. She looked at Kanta, wondering how far she could be trusted. She went up to the kitchen door and looked out. There was no one about. Then she came close to where Kanta was sitting and whispered, "Will you do something for me?"

Salma wasn't sure what first made her suspicious. Perhaps it was the unfamiliar fragrance she caught one day as she was washing his clothes. Or the realization that he had missed dinner three times in a row. Or perhaps the fact that she could not really recall the last time they had sex. Salma's husband was a director at the Taxation Office. They'd been married eight years now and so far she really had nothing to complain about. He was a good father to their four children. Seldom at home, he always managed to be present when the children were ill or needed his attention. She tried to pinpoint when he had changed. When had the late nights started?

When he was a junior officer at the insurance company he had come straight home after work. Then the promotions began. A promotion meant greater responsibility and more work and he had started coming home late, an hour one day, two the next. Busy with the children, Salma had been grateful for his hard work and the extra money. Then another promotion, and soon his job was taking him out of town. Sometimes to Mymensingh, sometimes to Rangpur or Sylhet. The overnight stays had lengthened to two, then three days until he was gone for weeks at a time. Her gratitude slowly turned to concern.

She remembered the first time she had asked him why he needed to be away for such lengths of time. It had resulted in a big quarrel. He had walked out of the house, only to return three days later with a beautiful *jamdani* sari. Instead of putting her mind at ease, it only fueled her worries. Why had he bought her the sari? Because she had questioned him? Because he had stayed away? Because he was sorry? However, she learned not to voice her concern, going about her daily chores as if all were well.

After Salma finished her household tasks for the day, she would lie in bed beside her husband and wonder if all marriages were like this. Was he bored with her? Was he interested in someone else?

She started noticing little telltale signs. Instead of running the comb through his thinning hair in the absentminded way he had, he now stood fiddling with his scalp, debating between parting his hair in the middle or on the side. The bathroom shelf, which had contained one bottle of Tibet Snow and a family-size container of Johnson's Baby Powder, boasted a colorful new row of bottles of aftershave lotions and jars of cream. When she took timid sniffs at them in his absence, exotic masculine fragrances played with her senses and escaped into thin air. In the tiny wardrobe that they shared, lemon yellow, sky blue, and salmon pink shirts vied for space with the white and buff-colored ones. For the first time since their marriage, he was now the proud owner of an embroidered silk *panjabi*.

"You know things are not all that well between my husband and me," Salma now continued hesitantly. No response was necessary. Kanta had been picking up bits and pieces during her visits.

"Can you help me?"

A grin spread over Kanta's wrinkled face.

"Just ask me and see," she replied.

"But you're not to tell anyone!"

"I'll die before my lips reveal anything."

"No, swear. *Kasam khao.* Swear on Allah's name."

Kanta hesitated, but only for a second. Realizing it was important to Salma, she put down her bowl and gave Salma her full attention.

"I swear," she said, her voice solemn.

"I think he visits someone." There was no need to give the "he" a name. Another long pause, and Kanta wondered what her role was going to be in this.

"I want you to find out where he goes."

Kanta continued chewing carefully, but mumbled, "That won't be a problem. I will let you know when I come next month."

Salma wondered if she had understood the gravity of the situation. "I want you to come the moment you have some information." She said each word separately, putting a little stress on each.

Kanta looked down and started separating the few grains of rice that had failed to pop. It took up all her attention.

"I can't come before finishing my rounds," she said, "I'll miss my clients and then some won't want to see me until next month."

Salma turned to Kanta; her eyes narrowed, but Kanta seemed not to notice. Salma paused, not sure what she expected. Then she rolled her eyes and said, "Wait here. Don't move." She shot a look around the kitchen before she left, taking in the position of everything, making certain nothing of value was left lying about.

Alone, Kanta looked around her. There was a little boy in the yard, but he was some distance away, playing marbles. With speed that gave lie to her age, she darted to the cupboard and tested the door. It gave way, and in the twinkling of an eye, she was scanning the darkness inside. Her eyes zoomed in on the large tin of *muri*. She thrust her right hand in and with one swift motion ran her splayed hand through the *muri*. Her fingers closed over a hard ball, the size of a small grapefruit. Everyone knows that the best place to preserve *gur* is inside a tin full of *muri*. The dry puffed rice absorbs the moisture from the balls of date-palm juice and keeps them hard and fresh. In a second she'd removed the large ball, replaced the lid, pushed the cupboard door shut with her shoulder, and was back at her place, outside the kitchen door.

She looked around her and, secure in the knowledge that no one had seen her, loosened one end of her sari and tucked the *gur* in one corner, tied a knot around it, and then another, pulling it tight, testing its strength. She stowed the sweet *gur* within the manifold recesses of her flowing garment. The ball became part of her amorphous sari-clad form.

"Allah have mercy on us!" She gave a long sigh, her eyes twinkling, a smile hovering on her *pan*-stained lips. She thrust a few grains of *muri* into her mouth. It tasted so good!

A minute later she heard the soft *slosh slosh* of Salma's sandals hurrying back. Salma stopped at the door, and her eyes roamed the kitchen. It looked undisturbed, just as she had left it. Her eyes glinted when she saw that the door of the cupboard was slightly ajar. She shot Kanta a look, but Kanta was absorbed in her *muri*.

"Here." Salma dropped a ten-taka bill, folded and refolded into a tight wad, into Kanta's lap. Kanta's chewing paused as she unfolded the bill and looked at it. With the side of her palm she ironed out the creases.

"I'll try, but I don't know how far I'll be able to walk." She let out a tentative cough. This brought on a series of longer, wracking ones, and she gasped, "I haven't been feeling too good the last few days. Remember how hard it rained last week? I was drenched twice in one day. Brought on a temperature... and you know, at my age..."

"I'll give you more when you bring me some news." Salma's voice was hard, not the pleading one she had used earlier.

"I know you will. If people like you, who God has blessed, don't look after us, who will? What will become of us?" She put the remaining rice and *gur* in the sack she was carrying. The money she carefully placed in a little worn-out black silk pouch. The painted golden butterflies on the material had faded, but the cloth was still strong. Tucking the pouch into another fold of her waist, she took a couple of sniffs. "What are you cooking? Smells nice."

Salma turned her back to Kanta and started chopping green chilies. "It'll be a while yet. You had better go. There is much that needs to be done."

Accepting that the visit was over, Kanta picked up herself and her clay bowl in one motion, and then trudged out of the kitchen, with a cheerful, "Allah Hafiz, Amma."

Days passed and then weeks. At the sign of any beggar, Salma rushed to the door. She worried that Kanta would turn up when her husband or someone else was at home, but there was no sign of Kanta. Four weeks passed before she heard the familiar voice.

"Amma, are you there?"

Kanta had chosen her timing well. The house was empty.

"Well?"

"Oh! My feet are killing me. I must have walked ten kilometers today."

"Well, sit down. But tell me, do you have any news?"

"Do I have news!" Kanta stopped.

Inside the folds of her sari she fingered a hundred-taka bill. She could feel its crispness and weight against the soft worn-out material of her sari.

"Didn't I say that you were a lucky woman? Your husband has a *pir*. He goes to him almost every night and prays for your well-being and that of your children."

Salma stood still for a few seconds, puzzled. She peered at Kanta, but Kanta was looking out far into the distance as if reminded of her own family. Salma's face relaxed; a smile broke out.

Kanta closed her eyes. But she could not get rid of an image, an image of a small redbrick house. A man standing inside in a blue checked *lungi* and *ganji,* very much at home. Behind him stood a young woman carrying a small infant. He did not recognize her and her begging bowl. But she recognized *him.* Salma's husband. And she made sure he knew who she was. She gave a loud and long "Salaam! Sahib." She then blessed his child.

What would be the use of telling Salma? It was done. It was written on Salma's forehead. A four-fingered width of space. And knowing would not change things. And what would she, Kanta, get out of it? How much more would Salma give once she knew the truth? Her husband, on the other hand, would be generous. He had already shown that. She was old and on her own. She was getting tired of walking the streets of Dhaka. It would be nice to have a fixed source of income every month. She was not going to be greedy. Just enough to survive, and maybe a little extra for her *pan* and betel nut.

"I'll be on my way," she said rising wearily. Without waiting for the money that Salma had promised her, she let herself out into the damp and grimy street.

ELIZABETH KADETSKY

Wesleyan Writers Conference

MEN MORE THAN MORTAL

I.

We are pulsing, we bicycle messengers, inhaling with a single breath. We play the surface tension above the pavement like mosquitoes on water. We are expectant, scofflaw. It is only the hundred taxis soaring through the intersection that hold us, tantalized, behind the crosswalk. The red light reflects demonic in our hundred gleaming eyes.

A black guy with an Ace Messenger bag and a Kryptonite chain around his waist nods at me. "You go, girl." His voice is low and gravelly. A Mexican guy scans us both with sleepy eyes. He wears his chain slung over his shoulder. The light flickers to green and Ace pulls ahead, his bicycle swaying from side to side, dipping close to the pavement on the right and then the left as he sails through one red and then another down to Union Square.

This is how it is in the week since I split from Smith. When you want the warmth of a man this bad he makes sure to put distance between you.

For my first run of the day I cruise downtown. I am fleet, skimming over the pavement, airborne. I have lost ten pounds. I was never a good candidate for the heartbreak diet. I was doing fifty miles a day on the bicycle before the diet and now I look wan and thin and probably even Smith, especially Smith, thinks I'm no longer beautiful. *If only I could grow back my breasts,* I think as I coast someplace high above St. Mark's.

A hangover buzzes my head. I was up drinking Jameson till two with the friend who's putting me up, Gus. Then I lay on the futon in his living room, thinking, *After five years of marriage, you break up. Two days later he fucks someone else. New life. Bang. Change now.* Sleep would have been a gift. Insomnia was not the anxiety kind, worrying about a good night's rest. Don't even wish for a moment's sleep, just for time to transport you forward.

In the morning I strapped my lock around my waist and took off on my bicycle for Manhattan. I was halfway across the Williamsburg Bridge before I realized I'd forgotten my helmet. Without the helmet I am even lighter. Some combination of streets got me to Godspeed Messengers in Midtown. Biking, thinking, *There is nothing left of Smith's desire.* I couldn't have traced back the route.

At Godspeed there was an e-mail message from Milo. *Come to India,* it said. *I'll book the ticket.*

For Milo I will grow back my ass, I thought as I glided away from the office on my bicycle and across the Atlantic, the Arabian Sea, racing to India, to Milo. This time I would let him make me pregnant. Or we'd miss but I'd go back for Christmas and try again. We'd have a back and forth, New York and India, a transnational child. Five years ago my life took a wrong turn. There was Milo.

There was Smith. I turned at the wrong intersection. Now I'd like to leap back over.

The only thing keeping my bicycle fixed to the pavement is the weight of the lock around my waist. My chain is 11.4 pounds. With the chain I weigh more or less what I used to without it. The chain, if nothing else, will keep me planted on the ground, ready to bear new life.

I turn and see a van behind me. I swerve left, out of its way, and lose balance as the van speeds alongside me. My front wheel angles sharply to the left and jackknifes. The bike skids. Everything stops but me. I fly for real now, over the handlebars. In the air I think, *I have no helmet.* I think, *I weigh so little.* I land in a racing dive on the pavement, riding forward shallow and long, belly down, traveling several yards eastward. The van screeches. My cheek scrapes. I wait for the van. I am ready. Take me away. I open my eyes and see pavement, see that I am still of the earth.

I sit up, wrap my arms around me, cry into my knees. Feeling alive has never brought me so close to death. The contents of my messenger bag are strewn along the gutter—pens, a large manila envelope for delivery, lipstick. My feet look frail and tentative resting on the pavement.

The driver gets out of the delivery van. "Are you all right?"

"I'm okay." I'm not okay. I want to jump into his arms. "Thanks for stopping."

He puts an arm around my shoulder, tries to lift me. "You okay?"

"Thanks. I'm so sorry. It was my fault. I didn't sleep. I forgot my helmet."

It's too much information. He looks at me quizzically. I was midway across the Arabian Sea, but that doesn't matter to him. There's a taxi honking behind him. "You see this bullshit?" he asks, fuck-you gesturing to the taxi.

"It's okay. I'm really sorry."

The driver shrugs. He looks from me to the taxi and back to me again before he goes back to his driver's seat. The van shrinks in the distance, moving low and cautious, steady and deliberate.

After a while I pick up my belongings and move along myself. I'm scraped up, a little bloody, but nothing's broken really.

2.

I arrive at my delivery a half mile farther and rest the bike on a street sign. I ride with three locks: the chain around my waist, a U-lock, and a thin wire combination cable. The chain attaches the front wheel to the frame to a street sign; the U-lock secures the back wheel; the cable stays the seat.

My chain is a Kryptonite New York lock, the single most effective deterrent against our city's ubiquitous bicycle poachers. They travel in delivery vans, the bicycle syndicates, nitrogen-freezing U-locks, collecting bicycle frames that they overhaul and sell right back to you. They pilfer seats, pedals, wing nuts; they would steal your grandmother.

The New York lock is the last line of defense. According to the manufacturer, it is a triple-heat-treated boron manganese steel chain with a plastic-encased disk-keyhole padlock, seventy centimeters of four-sided steel chain links resistant to saws, hammers, files, and bolt cutters. It is an unseverable, no-trick shackle, like Houdini's last handcuffs, solid like Superman.

I look over my creation. It will be sturdy as jail. I feel in my pocket for my keys. Nothing.

This week when I moved out from Smith, I put most of my belongings in plastic garbage bags and left them out on the street. I spent that night on the futon in Gus's living room thinking and barely sleeping, and then got on my bicycle at five A.M. and rode by our place. The bags had been lifted from the pavement. Smith's bicycle was gone, too.

The next day I asked him where he'd been.

"I went to sleep early." In fact he was with some woman.

"Last night I dreamed you were curled up and sleeping in the doorway," I told him.

"You can find someone better, baby. You don't want a man who's sleeping in the doorway."

"You were like a dog."

"I just want to move forward. I want us both to move on. It's not me or you. It was the space between us. There was no future there."

And this is how it is now. Breaking up is not gradual. One day he rolls on top of you in bed and nuzzles your neck. Two days later he's with Miss Whoever.

In one of those garbage bags left on the street beside the ghost of Smith's bicycle were my extra keys. I never registered those keys with the Kryptonite Corporation, so I have lost the only key to the padlock to the chain that is around my waist.

The chain weighs heavy as I wander into the office building for my drop-off. It clanks as I near the security guard. "Nice belt," he comments. "That the fashion?"

"Sure is," I say. I give him glimmer eyes. "Will you watch my bike?"

Upstairs, a Kryptonite representative informs me over the telephone that I am daft for having thrown out my extra keys and never having registered the key number. That said, there's nothing she can do for me.

"It's around my waist," I whisper. I imagine my plea as Kryptonite, a chunk of sizzling ore.

"Your what?"

"My waist."

"Why?"

"That's how we ride."

"*We?*"

"Messengers."

"New York City?"

"Yes."

Her voice goes cold. She knows our kind. We are the poster-child patrons of the New York lock, sure—but mostly, for them, an insurance risk.

"So, can I break it?"

"Nooo," she says, drawing out the word. "If you wanted to break it why would you buy the New York lock? It's triple-heat-treated boron manganese steel."

"Yes. Can I talk to the chemist, please?"

"The who?"

"Chemist?" I try. "Or the welder?"

"The what?"

I change the subject. "Why would you name a lock after a piece of odor-emitting metal that disempowers Superman?"

"Excuse me?"

I am disgusted. "The lock should evoke the charisma of the superhero, not the magically imbued lump that makes him wither. These rings are petty crooks, don't you see?"

"What rings?"

"The bicycle-theft syndicates. They just have tools. Superman always prevails. Even Kryptonite can't thwart him, ultimately. If you call your lock Kryptonite you invite the gangs to imagine they're Superman. You should call the lock Superman."

"Thank you for calling Kryptonite Corporation."

"Don't you get it?" I am shouting into the phone. "Superman *always* wins. The lock has to be the superhero, not the gangs. Otherwise the gangs will win."

She rings off. Me, with my lock around my waist—I am the superhero. Kryptonite holds me in its snakelike strangle. I survive.

I ride back to St. Mark's. The street is empty and clean, with the particular midmorning desolation of a late-night district at the wrong hour. It's a cyclist's dream, well paved and empty and neat.

My keys are nowhere to be seen. I peer down into a sewage grate and think of the Hitchcock movie *Strangers on a Train,* in which a man uses a magnet to collect a silver watch from a New York City gutter. I think of magnets with extraplanetary pull; magnum wire cutters; superhuman, iron-bar bending musclemen.

3.

I am cruising up Sixth when I alight on a plan. I call Smith from a pay phone. I get nothing. He was my husband. *Husband.* The word once reassured me. Smith was strong. He once told me to be more like him, "more solid."

"You have to rely on yourself better, baby. I feel burdened sometimes, by your needs. You talk about wanting a child. It doesn't seem real. You're a child yourself. I don't want to take care of you. I don't want to take care of anyone."

I felt blank when he said it. Smith was a man who stood firmly on the ground. He is a sculptor, he works in heavy materials. "You don't have to," I lied. But I was thinking of a painting I saw once, of a man standing on the ground with his arm in the air framed by vertiginous swirls of clouds. Attached to him at the hand was a woman in a flowing dress, floating up above him in the clouds. It was true, I'd imagined myself that woman. I never told him.

"I can stand on the ground," I said instead.

"If you'd figure out how to take care of yourself you wouldn't be so confused about what you want in life. A baby is not what you want. You have to find yourself first." Smith wanted me to discover my art. In Smith's eyes, I was a bicycle messenger for only as long as it took me to discover my art form. "Find your bliss." He was quoting Joseph Campbell.

"I hate that line. Bliss is sex, or heroin."

"Bliss is creating something."

"I thought bliss was passion."

"Bliss is making your life work for you so you can get what you want."

"I prefer to think it's flying along the length of Manhattan Island collecting small parcels from random locations and depositing them minutes later elsewhere. Maybe messengering is my bliss, Smith. Messengering and loving life."

"You're not talking about bliss," he said then. "You're talking about passion."

On this street in New York City summer, I see no passion, only survival. I rest my head against the Plexiglas of the phone booth and peer into the urban landscape. There are taxis—fortified metal caskets that look like creatures from the apocalypse.

But then I make out, huddled among the taxis like small bursts of fresh growth in a decrepit wasteland of concrete, a strange and lively procession. The taxis have edged it into the narrow margins of the avenue: a Vespa carting two women in matching wedding dresses, each with long, unbrushed, hay-colored hair that lifts behind her in tangled strands. The wedding dresses are billowy and soft-looking, cut down low, all the way to the small of the slender back of the girl at the rear. Each wears white pumps, the one in back balancing hers on either side above the wheel cage so her knees are bent in close. Her stance is animal-like, erotic. White balloons ride the air currents behind them.

This might be a double wedding, but the motorcade that follows gives me the distinct impression that the brides are each other's. A woman on a three-speed with a basket and no helmet pumps her bicycle hard, like it's a rickshaw. A beat-up Toyota pickup emblazoned with shaving cream and glitter follows. Then a guy in a tux snakes by on a scooter; he holds his handlebar with one hand while grasping a large bouquet of lilies in the other. The pageant floats along as if on wisps of cloud. They move into the distance, through the next intersection and then off into the greenery of Central Park.

I love weddings, but Smith and I never had one. Smith preferred to do it at City Hall. Shortly before, I'd met Milo at just the kind of wedding I'd always wanted, but Smith and I were engaged by then.

The wedding where I met Milo was at a ranch in the Pasadena hills. Guests got dressed up in costumes, with boas and stocking caps and rusted hubcaps dangling from their bodies, items gathered from thrift stores and scrap heaps. Milo was the minister. He was a Catholic, direct from Italy via India, but a year in California had cured him of religion so quick he mailed away for a minister's credential from the Universal Life Church.

I stood next to an artist who worked in urban debris collected from the sides of freeways and homeless encampments and concrete tunnels that give on to the L.A. Riverbed. That artist turned out to be Gus. He'd made a float out of found objects, and the couple rode in on it to the huppah, really a wrought-iron contraption constructed by Gus to look like an arbor made of metal daisies.

Then Milo delivered the service. "Do you believe in the love?" Milo shouted to the crowd, his words round and generous in his thick accent.

"We believe in the love!" Gus and I and everyone called back. Gus squeezed my hand and I felt something hot shoot through my body, but it was Milo I was feeling. The image of Milo under the wrought-iron huppah lodged someplace deep inside me. The guests jumped and yelled and I watched him. Someone exploded firecrackers. Sparks flew wildly, in random paths. One raced toward me. I didn't flinch as I watched the growing red ember approach me. If it went off in my face it would take me someplace thrilling. That was all that mattered.

Before that wedding I'd believed marriage marked an entry into something stable and knowable. It closed out options. But at this wedding there was the feeling things could turn violent. This day could change all our lives in unspeakable, unthinkable ways. We leaped to danger together.

Hands gripped me from behind, Milo's. He kissed me roughly up and down my neck. I wanted to make love, to embrace him and flee off into an unknowable darkness. In the parking area, balloons and ribbons rose from all the vehicles. We got on Milo's motorcycle and sped off with balloons trailing out behind us. I held on tight as Milo raced through curves down out of Pasadena's craggy hills. We had no helmets, and I held him knowing he could kill us both.

That night Milo and I made love. I never told Smith. I held on to Milo tight, and a floaty euphoria overtook me. I imagined I was wafting above him like diaphanous cloud matter, my hair flowing behind me. I would peel away from him unless I held on tighter, so I clutched him until we both drifted up into the clouds and turned to swirl patterns.

I traveled with Milo on his motorcycle for two weeks afterward. Then I went back to Smith.

4.

Milo was returning to a job assignment in India, where he had a girlfriend. She was pregnant. He loved me. But there was the baby.

When I saw Smith again, we made love, but I didn't feel it and we both knew it. After, I cried. "Smith, I can't do it. I met someone. He wanted to marry me."

Smith turned white. "So?"

I gave Smith the *I love you but . . .* line.

He came to dinner with me and ate nothing. Finally he told me, "Don't leave me. I want you. I feel it in my body."

"I don't feel passion."

"I want to feel passion."

"We're too calculated. We try too hard."

"I know."

Something happened to me over the *arrabbiata*. The oil turned gelatinous over the sauce, and the noodles seemed oozing and thick, overripe with juices. My life would take a very wrong course with Milo. We would move from motorcycle accident to motorcycle accident. Eventually, we'd flame out. "I want you to stay," I told Smith.

We never brought up Milo again. I spent the next two months curing myself of loving Milo as if it were a disease. I charted my progress daily, aching with secrecy.

I was a little bit less in love each day. At first I thought of him every five seconds, thought of his skin, of lying in bed pressed up against his back. The next day the thoughts came only every ten seconds. After a week I had pared down the thoughts to four or five an hour. Within a month I was remembering Milo only at night, when I crawled into bed and loosely held Smith in his T-shirt and tried to train myself back into loving him.

Now Smith says we never had passion. I told him that when I met Milo. What was I hanging on to?

Smith and I'd been living in a loft that shares space with his sculpture studio. He's still living there; I am on Gus's couch until I find a place of my own. Our loft is off Delancey Street, in the shadow of the Williamsburg Bridge. This block is immortalized in the noir film *The Naked City,* where after giving heinous car-, bicycle-, and subway-chase through the Lower East Side, our villain, Willie the Harmonica, races past the Bowery Savings Bank and onto the ascent to the Williamsburg Bridge only to elude his pursuers by catapulting through three stories of metal grating and stairwell onto the sidewalk before Smith's and my very entryway. Then the voice-over coins the now famous saying, *There are eight million stories in the naked city. This has been one of them.*

I chose Smith because he was solid. He could use welder's tools. He could break down your door if he had to. He is still my husband, still that word that's as firm as pavement.

I rest my bicycle against a street post that rises from the very stretch of sidewalk where Willie the Harmonica met his ugly fate. Through the window into Smith's studio I see him nod somberly into his welding saw, which he's holding before the delicate-looking calf of his current nine-foot-tall socialist-realist android in progress. He wears goggles and earphones. A flash of fire erupts from his welding torch, illuminating his face and creating lightninglike reflections in his goggles. I slide my fist through the metal window grates and rap. He releases the flame from the welding gun so the reflections in the goggles slowly ebb, lowering across the lenses like two setting suns on movie screens.

When the reflection goes black he recognizes me. He smiles in reflex, but then fixes his face in a frown.

He lets me in. "What's up?" Cold. I try to remember that we are "moving forward." His eyes settle on the scrapes on my elbow and shins. "What happened to you?"

I sit on the couch fingering the padlock at my waist. Outside, there has been a thick expectant humidity all day, but now the air begins to cool as pressure breaks. Through the window grates I see black bulbous clouds. "I'm locked inside my chain."

He looks at me long. "Allison. What did you do?" This is a new name for me, not *Sweetie* or *Honey* or *Love* or *Baby*. The whole time I've known him he's never used my name. The word wraps itself inside my skin like a layer of ice.

"I lost the key."

"Where are the backups?"

"Kryptonite can't help me."

"What do you want me to do?" He's looking at me blankly, so all I can read in his face is what I imagine there—disgust, apathy, not a trace of desire.

"The torch?"

"You'd have to take off your clothes." He looks me over again.

I was once beautiful to you! I scream inside. "I think you've seen me naked."

I go into the bathroom, look at my body. The scrapes along my legs and forearm still have raw blood streaks, and bruises are beginning to blossom beneath them. My face looks tired and ugly to me, though on the street just yesterday men turned to me with expectant momentary hellos. Looking back at them, searching their faces for desire, I saw the men swallow their hellos back inside them. I pull my hair back into a tight knot and take off all my clothes. This way, I look like either a pubescent ballerina or a girl in a face-soap ad.

Smith holds me by the tops of my shoulders and presses down, his arms locked at the elbows to maintain maximum distance. Smith's android sculptures dominate the studio—larger than life, bulky and strong, weighty in a way humans could never be.

Naked like this, except for an 11.4-pound chain around my waist, I feel like an angel who dropped into the wrong universe and got stuck there, a nymph whose wings got traded for boron. I am trapped in the realm of Smith's nine-foot-tall androids. One of them peers at me. Under its gaze, I am particularly aware that I am naked. She or he or it is angular and machinelike. I wonder how superhuman beings ever muster the emotion to act.

Smith carries over a roll of heavy plastic Mylar and unscrolls four or five feet of it. It catches the light so the sheet turns iridescent, an effect I try to think about as he pushes one corner through the chain and then the whole sheet, then wraps me like a chicken on a spit. I feel hot sharp darts along my skin as the Mylar scrapes against my cuts and bruises. Then Smith takes an aluminum plate from the rear of his studio and slides this between the Mylar and the padlock.

"Okay?" he asks.

I will my feet to stay bolted to the ground. I hold my breath to make my waist smaller inside the chain.

Smith lowers his goggles and points the torch away from us. It lets out a mean orange flame. He makes the flame narrow. I can see the slits of his eyes through the goggles. "Don't move," he says.

I am getting smaller. The flame moves toward my middle. The plastic casing on the padlock melts in less than a second. In another second I feel a heat like a sharp knife. I cry out.

Smith stops, tries the lock. Nothing.

We do this ten times before he gives up. The chain hasn't registered a nick.

Smith shrugs. "This really isn't my job anymore, Allison."

Once more the ice sheath forms like lacy snowflakes beneath my skin. "I know."

"I don't know what to do. Can't someone else help you?"

5.

Gus is also a metalworker. He is a master welder, metal shaper, arranger of iron flowers. Gus has tools, not to mention heavy magnets with which, if all else fails, to excavate the crevices of Lower Manhattan's sewage canals like the character in *Strangers on a Train*. Gus came to New York shortly after I met him at the wedding in Pasadena and found studio space and an apartment just down Delancey and over the bridge in Williamsburg. Smith never liked him.

I bike there now, thinking that my bike makes my body whole again. I push through wet, expectant air.

"Hey," Gus says, looking me over.

I try to erase my grief face. I want to play a role. I laugh. "I'm screwed, Gus." I point at the padlock. I am a normal healthy happy human being who has a world opening up in front of her, a place of possibility and limitless options. I just happen to have a chain permanently affixed to my middle.

Gus touches the lock at my abdomen. "Come here." He tugs on the chain, lifting me slightly. "Sit down." He slides his palm in the tight space between the Kryptonite and my belly, then eases his wrist through.

I would like a man to make love to, any man.

Gus unlooses my shorts with one hand and tugs them down from behind with his other. "Come here." He pulls me by the Kryptonite to his bed. *Triple-heat-treated,* I think. "I have some tools," he says. He rushes to his studio and comes back holding another cable, this one from his own bike.

"What are you doing?"

"What do you mean?" He laces the cable through the Kryptonite, attaches it, and me, to the bedpost.

"You locked me up."

"What do you mean?" He's pulling off my underwear.

I've never been into S/M, never made love with chains or whips. Now I am locked to the bed and Gus and I are having sex. I'm not thinking about the locks or the cables, the packages owed or the day at work tomorrow that might never happen. The sky crashes; rain pummels Gus's courtyard.

Later, though, not a single tool in Gus's workshop can match the triple-heat-treated boron manganese New York lock. His magnets, on the other hand, look potent enough to rouse a city of rats. We take off on our bikes over the Williamsburg Bridge, move silently through endlessly intersecting patterns of metal railings and gratings and stairwells, overpasses and underpasses, shadow lines and spotlights. All the intersecting angles make me dizzy. Looking down, I have the distinct sense that I, alongside Willie the Harmonica, am crashing down toward the bottom in a great spiraling leap.

Once more the rain starts up. First it is just a few drops, pelletlike and stinging. The drops keep up their velocity and gather in density. They get thicker and heavier, until they feel like mercury beating down on us. Their force is the force of a lashing. The pellets seem to break up into small metal BBs as they crash onto the pavement and tumble down through the sewer grates. Soon the sewers will be stuffed with thousands of raindrops packed like mercury balls transubstantiated to solid. I imagine them congealing, and everything below the New York City pavement becoming frozen and stuck.

I sob as I ride. I peer into the street but can barely make out the potholes through the curtain of rain and my tears. Gus, riding at a clip in front of me in black T-shirt and jeans, has been swallowed by the darkness. Water pools in the gutters. I call to him—"You're invisible!"—but the rain devours my words. We are only blocks from the sewer that may have eaten my key, but the downpour has by now washed it to the East River. I imagine my key floating in a puddle of iridescent green water. The key is luminous, shining as it lifts to the sky. It blinks down at us.

6.

This is how I solve my problem: Two weeks later, I have found a place to live for now, and I have settled into a life that is in all regards normal, except that there is a chain around my waist. I am still eating less. The chain grows loose around my waist as I drop weight.

One morning, I stumble outdoors to make my way to Godspeed. My bicycle has not fared well either. Without the New York lock it has become instantly more vulnerable. Someone stole a pedal, and as the bicycle has settled into its decrepitude, the bicycle marauders have looked upon it less kindly. The brace for the U-lock has disappeared, as has the frame for the water bottle. The seat vinyl was slashed a week ago, and a few days later the chain links that secured the seat to the frame were sawed through, the seat pilfered. I replaced the seat, but by then my bicycle was marked as easy prey.

I walk outside and react with cool resignation when I see that the bike, finally, has been lifted. A wave of calm washes over me.

Suddenly, everything makes sense. There is an ecosystem composed of New York City bicycles and the syndicates that stalk them. It is in the bicycle shops where there are sage observers who chart the habits of this microclimate. They read the city, the bike-shop guys; they understand the order of its food chain. The manufacturers of the New York lock don't get this.

I walk to the bike shop. The guy who sold me my Kryptonite is not hard to find. He has long wavy bangs and dark circles under his eyes and speaks to me in grave tones.

I explain my predicament.

He reacts without a trace of surprise. "They'll get you out of there," he advises me. "No lock can deter the bicycle rings forever." He's directing his words straight into his chest, so it takes a second before I realize that he's nodded out. He stays blank for ten seconds before picking up again midthought. "It used to be Kryptonite insured the old-fashioned U-lock up to a thousand dollars and no one could break it. Then the gangs devised the nitrogen freeze. The Kryptonite Corporation reacted by reinforcing the metal bar of the U-lock, and so the theft gangs devised pincers that could break it open through force applied inside the middle." He looks at me long. "The company is always one step behind the gangs. The gangs are superhuman."

"Superhuman," I repeat. "Like Superman." I feel cold. "The gangs will win?"

He nods grimly. The cat and mouse between the corporation and the syndicates inspired Kryptonite's New York lock, the 11.4-pound, seventy-centimeter triple-heat-treated boron manganese four-sided steel-link and padlock chain. The stakes will rise indefinitely. He reaches a hand toward me and lifts up the padlock in his fingers, drops it down again against my abdomen. "It's only time before they crack it. They have the tools, tools with extraplanetary powers. Any bicycle is safe for only a grace period."

"You believe this?"

"I know this."

He tells me more things. The locks exist because there are people who can outsmart them. Without their antagonist, the locks have no purpose. Lurking somewhere in the shadows of New York City, there are a dozen or three dozen or five hundred men who know how to cut through Kryptonite boron. No one ever sees these men. No one knows who they are. But they are out there, clinging to the shadows at the corners of buildings at night, creeping across sewage gratings, skulking through the Financial District in windowless Econoline vans. They thrive in New York's underbelly. They live out their existences underground, perfecting their craft—their bliss—daily.

I, too, understand it perfectly. Eventually, mystical invisible packs of thieves pinch your bike. They lift all the bikes of New York, one after another, and then slowly reseed the streets with them. And soon enough, they pinch those, too. The bike-store guy has been telling me something that should have been clear all along, something crystalline and obvious that I have seen but overlooked.

That night I lie awake until three and finally crawl out of bed. I hold the boron chain and padlock in one hand as I dress, and then I step out to the subway. There are a good five inches of give in the chain now, and I have to hold it in both fists to keep it at my waist. Someday I will be so thin I can step right out of it. But not soon enough.

I ride the train to Wall Street and step out to the desolate sidewalk. In the morning it will bustle with the excitement of stock deals and bond trades, but at night it is a graveyard. I hold the chain tight and close my eyes, listen. There is a low rumble far off. It seems to come from all sides. It is the pulse of the city, the heartbeat of an underworld.

I scan the streets and see exactly what I expected. Chained to street posts and parking meters there is not a single intact bicycle. There are sad and decaying specimens—a rusted frame bearing nothing but a flywheel; a U-lock attached to an inner tube; a flattened aluminum wheel rim. Not a single uncorrupted bicycle. The thieves have scammed them all.

I stride to a parking meter that has nothing dangling from it and place my front up close. Then I lift myself on tiptoes and, holding the lock as high as I can in front of me, so it digs into my back on the other side, I ease the lock over the head of the parking meter. It's tight going down, but sucking in my stomach I can just fit the meter head inside the circle of chain alongside my waist. Now I lower the chain so it circles the meter post at my abdomen, and then I swivel my body so the post is to my rear. Then I slide to the ground so I am sitting cross-legged with the post running along my spine.

I wait. I listen for the whisper of the men. I listen for Milo's motorcycle. The men will rip me from my chain. They will steal me. I will fly.

ORIANE GABRIELLE DELFOSSE

Sarah Lawrence College

MEN AND BOYS

Gideon, Paul, Thom, Nathan—it's the fifth day of the trip and counting has become a tic, a way to feign control and seem valuable. Bugs thicken the already muggy air, and Jane gives them a vague swat as she counts heads. Annie trucks toward her across the campsite, pausing to help Margot and Lily with their tent. Gideon jabs at Paul with a pole and the two engage in a sword fight. Jenna and Grier, like responsible citizens, stake four corners into the ground.

Annie is scowling when she reaches Jane. "Where's Justin?" she asks. Annie has little tolerance for Justin: the disrupter, the problem child.

"I was just getting to him," Jane says. She hops her pointer finger through the air, exaggerating the motion so that Annie will see she has been taking note.

"Justin's the only one not here," Annie says. "Henry's his tent mate and look"—she points to delicate, spindly Henry who stands before a pile of tent equipment—"he's working alone." There is nothing in Annie's tone that berates, but Jane feels useless just the same. Though she doesn't lack for things to do, Jane feels trivial on this trip. It is Annie who engages the group in team sports—ultimate Frisbee, tag football—Annie who enjoys easygoing relationships with the kids built on a spirit of camaraderie one might have learned from playing on a team. Jane doesn't understand this. She grew up on a piano bench, not a soccer field. She has never thrown a Frisbee.

"It's time for his medication," Jane says, almost to remind herself. She slaps at a mosquito on her calf and silently curses Nova Scotia summers. The kids spray bug repellent on every inch of their skin and clothes and her throat seizes as she spots Gideon aerosolizing Paul's face.

"Christ," she mutters. She is the medic on the trip, a label she chose during training, but her certification has not prepared her for the odd ailments she must nurse—vague muscle pains, bulbous bug bites, a sweeping purple rash that she douses in calamine. For most problems she offers condolence and the kids, though grouchy, accept it. Officially, her job is to administer medication. Benadryl is popular, as is Pepto-Bismol, particularly with Henry who seems to like the taste. And Justin, whose sheet states that he suffers from attention-deficit/hyperactivity disorder, takes pills twice a day. His mother, a bossy woman Jane has spoken to on the phone, insisted he be given these pills discreetly. *He's very sensitive,* she said. *He cares what people think.*

Don't we all? Jane wondered. This daily exchange has created a rapport between them in the eyes of the others; in the unspoken division of tasks, Justin has become Jane's responsibility.

Jane props up the bikes the kids have thrown down in the field and then heads toward Henry, who labors to fit together two poles. The grass is dewy and sodden and the tents scattered about the clearing have taken on a glistening sheen. Most are only partially erect; they sag in a pathetic huddle, and Jane glances up at the darkening sky.

"Hurry up, guys," she says. She spots a dim star overhead, the first of the night. "Setting up these tents gets a lot harder after the sun goes down."

She scans the clearing, ringed by a wall of trees. For a brief moment, the entirety of the scene—the kids, the bugs, the tents, the poles—seems part of a chaotically choreographed dance. Movements are staged and exaggerated. Henry drops his poles, wearing a skewed expression of fear and glee. Jane peers through the burgeoning twilight, and then, like a specter, Justin appears, running toward her, something wrong with his mouth, his lips cupped as if gargling, his neck tipped back, his palms turned upward to the sky in supplication.

"Vrah!" he yells, and his mouth is foaming. Liquid bubbles and cascades down his chin into the bowl of his palms. "Vrah! I'm rabid!" he shouts.

Jane stares at him, her own mouth agape, and then quickly clamps it shut. He has dark features and long arms, which he now flings about in frenetic appeal.

"Ha!" he says, spitting a mouthful of foam onto the grass. He jogs in merry circles around his audience and spits again.

"He ate Alka-Seltzer," Margot tells her, "but he didn't eat it. I saw him. He put it all on his tongue and then he drank some soda and then it fizzed up like that." She points at the bubbling foam on the grass and sighs in an overly adult manner. It reminds Jane of herself, tangled in the sheets, watching Boris dress, his hurried buttoning, a sharp glance at his watch, and Jane sighing as she swept her fingers over the crushed, moist islands of mattress, a sigh to remind him of what had just come before. She glances down at the top of Margot's head, disconcerted by the girl's tone.

Justin has run out of foam and now casts nervous looks in Jane and Margot's direction. The other kids are all wrestling and swatting at the flies and mosquitoes. They yank up handfuls of grass and throw them in each other's hair. Margot squeals and joins them as a clump skims in her direction.

"Time for a meeting," Jane says, snagging Justin's sleeve as he darts by.

"It was funny, wasn't it? I was rabid. I really looked like I was rabid."

"I didn't need to be convinced," Jane says. She leads him toward the forest. The mosquitoes have intensified with the onset of dusk and it takes all her effort not to flail and swat like the others.

Justin is breathless, bounding through the muck, scratching and swiping the air. "You didn't know. The look on your face. Look, Gideon's whacking Henry with a pole." His gaze skitters from her hair, to the trees, to the tents at their backs. He babbles until Jane stops next to a log. He is her height, but growing. Every day he takes up more space. He expels a long deep breath and blinks in Jane's direction. "Jane, are you mad?"

Jane reaches into her satchel to pull out his medicine. "No, Justin," she sighs, reluctantly. "I'm not mad." She shakes two pills into her palm and the motion sets him shifting from foot to foot. "But you know that was inappropriate." In fact, she thinks it rather clever, the type of brainy antic she would like to have pulled off. "You can't just do whatever you want whenever you want."

"Why not?" He shrugs. "It's a free country." He kicks a rotten log at their feet, releasing a swarm of ants. "Bugs!" he says brightly.

"It's not," she says distractedly, brushing at the ants that now crawl over her sandaled feet. "I mean it is, but it's not, here, in Nova Scotia." She hops on one leg. "On this trip, it's not. There are rules and you—"

"Rules, rules, rules," Justin sings. He wipes his nose on the back of his sleeve like a messy child. "Other people aren't following the rules."

"What does that mean?" She flicks at the remaining ants. "The truth, Justin."

"You can't handle the truth!" he shouts. He stomps the log, then dances on it. "Jane, Janie's got a gun," he sings.

"Stop dancing," she orders.

He stops, makes his body pencil thin. "No dancing allowed," he says and stamps his foot like a soldier. Jane regards him wearily until he finally relents, his body coming loose as if unraveled. "Aw, I'm just joking around, Jane," he says, shaking out his arms. "I'm just trying to get you riled up." He shrugs innocently, boyishly.

"Take them," Jane says. She hands him his pills. "And stop killing bugs."

They bike. Through Halifax, past rows of colored houses, then out of the city into rural terrain. There, the houses are on cinder blocks and mailboxes lean at odd angles into the red dirt road. It is quaint, everything small, so small it eventually disappears; then the land turns soggy and there are no houses at all.

Marshland and mudflats, inlets and fjords. Jane spots a great blue heron stilled in the crabgrass. Sparrows start from the fen as the group rides by.

Jane points all this out to the kids, but they don't care; they are fifteen, distracted by each other. They jabber as they bike, swerve dangerously into the two-lane road. After a few days, Jane doesn't care either. Who has time for scenery? The kids form their own landscape of demands, every moment a decision. Can we eat? Can we rest? Can I have some aspirin? Benadryl? Lactaid? Can we stop for milk shakes? Can I call my mom? Can we swap duties, switch tents, skip dinner, play Frisbee? Can I spray bug stuff inside my ear? Jane answers these

questions haphazardly, vaguely trying to adhere to the rules and prin-
ciples governing the camp, and it is only later, in the dark of the tent,
that she wonders how she should have done it differently. Then Jane
thinks of Boris, wonders how he deals with his own children. He has
three, all girls, and a wife Jane knows he will never leave.

She met Boris in her third year at the conservatory. He was her
professor, and famous, with large hands and a talent at Rachmaninoff. His fame filled her with a sense of accomplishment and when
she watched his crashing performances it didn't matter that she had
no prospects for grand performances herself. It was enough that she
had a secret, an intimacy inside her, and that intimacy was him.

Two months ago, after an audition that she bombed for all the
regular reasons, after calling and calling Boris at his office, pacing her
apartment and then calling his home—the haptic memory in her
fingers finally returning, finally pulsing as they should have hours
earlier onstage—after his wife picked up the phone and Jane heard
her voice for the first time, firmer and stronger in pitch than she
expected, after she hung up and slumped pityingly in her armchair,
realizing, not for the first time, that she would never possess the necessary courage for a career in piano, or the ability to swallow her own
mediocrity—really swallow it, choke it down—after heading to the
practice room to crash out her own Rachmaninoff, which was actually Liszt's *Transcendental Études,* and jamming her pinky finger in
the process—after all of that, determined, exhausted, with no purpose or love in her life, she suddenly had quite a bit of time on her
hands. The job as Outdoor Adventure Leader had seemed the perfect
way to begin an exciting and different career. That was what the ad
had said: "Exciting and different career!" She learned CPR—saving
lives was important!—and from that came certification in all manner
of rescue techniques. Certification courses were everywhere, at rec
centers and swimming pools, and they taught an actual skill. Plus,

they concluded with a self-affirming certificate and a wallet-sized card, which Jane found neat and tidy. By the time she answered the ad, she officially could splint a torqued leg using a toothbrush, a snow-shoe, and some string; stab someone in the thigh with an EpiPen, though the meaty resistance made her gag; and drag a plastic manne-quin from the depths of a swimming pool, press hard into his unfor-giving lips, and bring him back to life.

None of these skills have proved particularly useful on this trip, and now on the seventh day she feels more like a sounding board for Justin's bizarre rants. All morning he shouts to her about natural dis-asters and deep-sea creatures and hydrothermal vents found along cracks in the ocean floor. They stop for lunch in a grassy patch by the side of the road.

"The water from the vents is so hot it smokes," he tells her. He speaks one decibel too high, as if the wind were still whipping through his ears. Jane spreads bologna, ham, turkey, chicken, cheese, bread, cookies, apple slices, crackers, granola bars, peanuts, and raisins on a tablecloth she has laid out on the grass.

"Hey, Justin," Gideon says in an exaggerated whisper as he sidles by, "we can hear you." He raises an eyebrow and puts a finger to his lips before heaving himself down on the grass beside Lily and Margot.

"Anyway," Justin continues, crouching down with his back toward Gideon and changing his tone to a lower, more conspiratorial level, "it's like three hundred and fifty degrees, but all this crazy stuff lives on the vents, like giant clams and tube worms—"

Jane weighs a jar of peanut butter in her hands, considering whether or not to set it out. These kids devour everything, every crumb, every granule, and she might need the peanut butter for an afternoon snack.

"—and the worms live inside this tube, just the very end pokes out—"

Jane hides the peanut butter in a sack and spots Thom and Henry hovering nearby, gradually inching their way toward the food.

"Back away from the tablecloth!" Annie shouts from where she has been distracting the kids with a game of Hacky Sack. "Do not touch the food before we say go!" Thom and Henry slink back a few feet, eyeing the ham, which Jane now folds in triangles and fans out in a half circle around a platter.

"And they have roots, extensions of their bodies!" Justin presses, his voice back up again, filled with an urgency about—what? What is he talking about? Tube worms? His voice trembles and pitches, and he has shredded a corner of the paper tablecloth into a scattering of bits. "They're the oldest living creatures and they're, like, six feet long!"

"God, Justin, you are *so* disgusting," Lily moans.

"Repulsive," Margot echoes. Her leg drapes casually across Gideon's thigh, the weight of it carrying just enough suggestion to make Jane squirm. Any kind of sexual activity is grounds for dismissal but the thought of having to enforce this rule, the thought that it would be broken, fills Jane with dread.

Justin stands and grins down at Margot and Lily, his lips twitching a little. His gaze lingers on Margot's outstretched thigh. "They grow a couple feet a year," he says. "You know in Africa people eat them and then puke them up and it's like one long string of worm they have to keep pulling out of their mouth."

"Ew!" the group screams in unison, covering their faces with their hands. Gideon rolls around on the grass and gags.

"Justin, we're about to eat," Jane says, though she is relieved that Margot and Gideon are now separated.

"*When* are we going to eat?" Gideon moans, jumping up and raking his eyes over the food.

Henry stands behind him, as if hiding in his shadow. Henry, so thin he is translucent, so fragile, like a fawn. "I'm so hungry," he whispers in a deadpan, almost desperate voice.

"Have a peanut," Jane offers.

Henry recoils. "I hate peanuts."

"Why are you folding the bologna?" Justin asks.

"I'll take his peanut," Gideon says.

"Look," Justin says, jabbing the others with his elbows, "she's folding it up all pretty when we're just going to eat it in a second." He dances a jig and forces a shrill laugh. "Pretty, pretty bologna!" he coos.

"Justin!" Jane snaps.

The boys surround the spread, peering down. She has divided the platter into quarters: bologna, ham, turkey, chicken. Her fingertips are now coated with a creepy film. She stares down at the platter. Once, halfway through a piece at an audition, she stopped playing. Just stopped. Hung her head and heard a faint, awkward cough from the back of the room as she contemplated whether to start the piece over or just get up and bow.

She folds her hands in her lap. "Dive in," she tells the kids, and they do.

After lunch, Jane pulls Justin away to give him his meds.

"Jane, are you mad at me?" he asks.

"Stop asking me that," she says.

"You seem mad." The sun is fierce, and she squints to make sure there are two pills in her hand and not three.

"I'm not mad. I'm tired," she says.

"That's 'cause you're old."

She laughs but this comment throws her for a moment. "I am not." She holds out her closed fist.

"I don't want them." He crosses his arms over his chest.

Jane is surprised. Usually he scoops up his pills without a word. "Why not?"

"I just don't." He shrugs. He looks back toward the group with an expression of indifference, but his breath quickens and his fingers clench along the cuff of his wet and dirty sleeves.

"Well, you have to." Jane jabs her fist toward him. The shells of the pills are beginning to soften in her palm. She wants to get rid of them before they disintegrate.

"I won't take those, Jane." His tone borders on threatening, though there is an imitative quality to it, as if this is how he has heard older men speak.

Jane thrusts her hand closer to his arms. "It isn't up to you and it isn't up to me," she says. "I can call your mother and ask her if you'd like, but I have a feeling I know what she'll say. Should I call your mother and ask?" This is her only weapon, the only thing Justin seems to fear.

"No." Justin's arms, folded tightly across his chest, drop to his sides. A truck rattles by on the road but he doesn't turn to look. "No one has to know, Jane," he pleads. Like that, his fierce edge is gone. "Don't tell my mom."

Jane takes his curled hand and places the pills in his palm. He frowns at them with self-pity. "I get a little woozy after I take these." He glares. "I hope I swerve and get hit by a truck."

Jane hands him a bottle of water and watches him drink them down.

Justin sulks the remainder of the day. He distances himself on his bike and does not snack when they stop for breaks. He is listless during dinner, but silent, for once allowing the group to have discussions that are not dominated by his pranks and diversions. They sit around a picnic table like a large pioneer family, rubbing elbows and stealing off each other's plates. After dinner they hike along a wide dirt road to a nearby lighthouse. The road is tree-lined, shadowy, lit only by a low moon. They walk in small groups, hooting ghost sounds, pushing each other amicably. Annie creeps up behind Henry and Lily, whispering to the other ones, *Shhh,* and howls suddenly in their ears. Lily jumps and Henry shrieks like a woman, and everyone laughs. A few of them charge Annie, attempting a vain tackle, but she remains upright as they pull at her arms and shoulders and then she lifts them, like free weights, up off the ground.

"Annie's so strong," Lily announces and her voice resonates in the stillness of the night. They near the point now and the waves can be heard crashing on the cliffs nearby. "And Jane," she glances back as if to size Jane up in the dark, "Jane's so—Zen."

"Yeah! Zen!" Gideon agrees, crowing the word. "Like so Zen she's not even here." The kids find this uproarious and they cackle and burst into the clearing, where the lighthouse, tall and striped, projects up out of the ground.

"Why do they think I'm Zen?" Jane asks Annie. They stand together at the base of the lighthouse, the earth crumbling into the ocean below.

"They don't even know what Zen means," Annie says. She shakes her head. "Probably because you don't get rattled."

Jane, who is all in pieces, cannot believe this is how she appears to the outside world. Though no one here knows that she quit the conservatory, or that she sleeps with a married professor, or that she used to suffer from weeks of despair after a performance, crippled by self-doubt. "Did you do trips like this when you were a kid?" she asks.

"I went to a camp in the Adirondacks every summer," Annie says. "Not quite like this, but there was canoeing, camping, hiking." She slaps at a bug. "Archery. You?"

"No," Jane says, "not really." The few times she went camping as a child were not in the rustic style of this trip; they visited campgrounds with lawn chairs, barbecue pits, and RVs. This was before piano guilds shuttled her to neighboring counties, then cities, then states. From these musky nights, she remembers objects: a blue-topped cooler, bricks of ice, beef patties, a flashlight. She wanted to hold the darkness, heavy and stolid, to charge through it toward the children in the neighboring campsites and join them in their clusters beyond the grills. And she would, the breeze jetting through her hair.

But somewhere along the way she lost that charge, or it got all turned around somehow. She fingers a knot that has been growing like a nest in her hair. "I threatened Justin with a phone call to his mom."

"Good," Annie says. "Except this time we should call her. Kick that monster off the trip."

When Jane is silent, Annie glares at her. "Don't buy into his manipulative bullshit, Jane. He threw his bike helmet into the road today and when Henry went to get it for him he called him a faggot."

"When did that happen?"

"I dealt with it," Annie says.

"I thought they were friends."

"Yeah, well." They stand for some time in the dark. The lighthouse is defunct, a fact that suddenly fills Jane with a strange sadness.

"Listen," Annie says, putting a hand on Jane's shoulder, "I need a fucking cigarette. Can you cover me? I'll be five minutes."

"Of course," Jane says with a wave of her hand. She didn't even know Annie smoked. She is glad for this opportunity to share something with her, a secret.

After Annie disappears, Jane listens to the sounds of the waves and the shouts of the kids and the wind across the rocks. A dreary place, Nova Scotia, a place that spurns false hope. She should move here.

Live with no expectations for a life outside the corner store and the fishermen and her small house with the mailbox askew; this is what truly takes courage: contentment.

Justin emerges from the darkness to stand next to her. Both are silent. "Jane," he says, kicking his feet in the dirt, "what do you do when the summer is over?"

Jane squints at the moon. She does not want to go back to playing hotel bars or weddings; she isn't sure she wants to play the piano at all. Better to do more substantial things, she has decided, less abstract. Pour concrete. Fish lobster. Hammer a nail.

And yet, when she tumbles through a piece, adding dimension and mass to each note in a way that is all her own, when she thinks, *This belongs to me,* then it is worth it. But this only happens in the practice room, or in front of Boris, never at auditions before the people who matter. Onstage, she freezes up. Her fingers become leaden, bricked. Technically precise, a man in a blue suit told her at her last audition, but we are looking for people who *respond* to the music.

She looks over at Justin and shrugs.

"What does Annie do?" he asks.

"She plays hockey for a college in Missouri. She's a captain, I think."

"I'll bet she dominates at all brutally competitive sports."

Jane smiles. "Probably," she says. In the dark she massages her hands, which are covered in scrapes and bites. If Boris could see them now.

"It must have been lonely to be the person up there, working the light," Justin says and they both turn their faces up to the top of the lighthouse, floating uselessly in the dark.

The next day is a rest day. They take the kids to the beach. As the certified lifeguard, Jane must stay on shore while the others swim. She burrows her fingers, one by one, into the wet sand and pretends to make sure no one drowns. Only Annie and the boys are in the water anyway, engaged in a rough game of polo, dunking each other mercilessly into the sea. The girls, they huddle together in knee-deep water, covering their stomachs and thighs with their hands.

"Margot!" Jane shouts. She makes a waving motion with her arm. "Go in!" Margot stares opaquely at Jane from her spot on the shoals but Annie, who has been taking particular delight in the sport of dunking, dives toward the girls and within minutes is splashing and tugging them into the sea. Soon all the boys are engaged in the new game—get the girls wet—and the group roils the surface in a great splashing mass.

Jane watches this with a mixture of pleasure and envy. The sun is hot overhead. She, too, wants to get wet. The kids tackle each other carelessly, their thin limbs intertwining, feet jutting up through the breaking waves, hands grazing ankles, wrists, hips. So young, Jane thinks. So compact. So free. She marvels at their bodies, limber, not yet saddled by love handles or thickening thighs, unencumbered by fatty layers of experience. So full of promise, and Jane wishes, quite acutely, that she could go back to fifteen and live the time since all over again.

"Aren't you going to swim?" Justin stands above her, dripping, breathing hard.

"I have to wait until you all get out of the water," Jane explains. She blinks up at him, but the bright sunlight breaks her vision into spots. His chest, broken up by bits of light, looks broad, and the muscles in his arms, taut and lean. She rubs her eyes. He drops down beside her and folds his knees up to his chest.

"Yeah, I don't like swimming either. Gideon, he's violent. Him and Margot—he kept grabbing—"

Jane turns to look at him. "Grabbing what?" Justin stares out toward the horizon with a blank expression. He digs his hands into the sand. Jane studies his profile. "Him and Margot what? Grabbing what, Justin?"

"I don't know," he says. He looks down toward his buried hand. "I don't know why I said any of that. It's not true."

Jane rubs a trail of sweat from her forehead and presses a hand to her temple. She should pry further into this lie, or truth, or whatever it is, but she doesn't want to know. The less she knows the better. Like the piano; the more she knows the instrument, the less conceivable mastering it becomes. And as for Boris, his marriage, his family: the same.

"I don't like swimming, but I like basketball. And I like video games. I like video games where you play basketball."

"Uh-hmmm," Jane says, circling her finger around the hole in the sand. Now that she has started thinking about Boris he is there, a presence on the beach beside her. She is remembering a night in her apartment, the window open, a sweet breeze filtering in, and a moan, one not for his benefit, as moans so often were, but a moan that was hers and hers alone. It had issued from a deep, unfamiliar place inside of her and had left her dazed, as if she were an explorer stumbling upon uncharted terrain.

"I like music, too. I like rap. Some guys at school, they call me a wigger, but fuck them," Justin is saying.

"Hey." Jane's finger halts in its circle. "What'd you say?"

"I said forget them. Those guys don't know anything. I know stuff. Do you know that they used to make guitar strings out of cat guts?"

She can sense the rev in Justin's voice, that he will soon start talking with a momentum he cannot control. She checks her watch. It's time for his medication but she will wait. The others are still in the water and the meds are back at the tent and the sun has made her drowsy. Plus, right now there is something nice about having another person beside her, rambling on. "You like music, Justin?"

"I *said* that already, Jane. Yeah, I play guitar. Jimi Hendrix is the best guitarist in the world. The universe. He had a chord named after him, the Jimi Hendrix Chord. It has two notes a half step apart and that almost never happens."

"That's right," Jane says, surprised.

"That, that—" Justin takes in a deep breath and looks at her with an expression of gravity. "That almost never happens, Jane," he says.

The seriousness of his tone makes her laugh, but when she does, he seems confused, as if suddenly marooned, and so she cuts her busted laugh short. "So you take guitar lessons?" she asks, trying not to smirk. She is giddy for some reason; forced to suppress her laughter, she now feels unable to control it. It takes her back to her competition days, shut up in a stuffy room with a judge who would call out pieces for her to play from memory, choosing from a list of ten or twenty. It must have been nervousness and anticipation, waiting to hear what seconds later she would be demanded to perform. That was before performances took on such weight, back when the physical reaction to a missed trill was a giggle.

"It's just a hobby though," Justin is saying, having switched topics without Jane noticing. "I actually want to write. Novels, or something. I started one already. It's about a man who explores the deep sea, way down where it's dark, and he's down there in the dark, freezing cold water all around him and he discovers—what do you think? What do you think he discovers?"

"Tube worms?"

"Tube worms? C'mon Jane, a little credit."

Jane laughs, shakes her head. "You're funny, Justin."

"Funny? Funny how?" He grins but seems strangely intent on her answer. A strand of green seaweed is tangled in his hair, and Jane reaches for it. It is slippery and wet and as her fingertips touch it, Justin tenses. She draws her arm back quickly, flinging the seaweed into the sand. "Funny like a fifteen-year-old," she says.

"Oh," he says.

She returns her fingers to the sand, scraping her cuticles against the graininess. It had been a night like any other, she and Boris eating dinner in her apartment, because Boris couldn't risk being seen at a restaurant. Then Boris had stopped eating. He had tilted his head just to the right, a key turning in a lock, and whispered, "Listen."

Jane had been listening—to the clink of their forks against their plates, to Boris mashing each bite between his teeth in his precise, exacting way, and to his breath, maddening in its repetition, expelled out both nostrils at each and every swallow.

Is this my life? she had thought. Is this my twenty-seven-year-old life? She looked out the open window, which sometimes offered a sweet breeze, the hum of cicadas, or the deep groan of frogs. But no breeze came. The air was humid and still. When she looked back at Boris, his head was stooped and swaying, giving the impression of an old, sickly dog. He picked up his fork and held it above the edge of his plate, poised, as if to strike down. Jane could see the creases etched in intervals along his neck and the balding spot positioned like a bull's-eye atop his head. Looking at him not looking at her, entranced by his own meticulousness, obsessed by his own exactitude, controlled by his own need for control, habit, structure, practice, fastidiousness—it was a fastidiousness that starched those lapels—looking at his bald spot, Jane suddenly felt as if she were witnessing, right there at the dinner table, fork in hand, the very picture of *aging*.

"Listen," he said again, though it came out choked, as if he might be clearing his throat, or *dying*. In ten years he'll be sixty, when it's not so strange to die, Jane realized. What had she been thinking, giving up her youth for a man who was already almost lifeless? She had to end it, them, that night, after dinner, to say good night and refuse his next advance and request sessions with someone else the next semester: Majstorovitch or Goldstein.

"Do you hear it?" Boris was asking. "Listen. Do you hear?" He lifted his eyes toward the window, and Jane saw that they were not cloudy but sharp, racing with momentum. He tapped his fork on the edge of his plate with a slow ting, letting it hang, pregnant, in the air. He tapped again on the edge of the porcelain, still staring out the window, his eyes now shut, the fingers of his other hand moving up and down, climbing and then descending a ladder, another beat, and then another.

Jane held her expression of reproach, for it was a rare moment indeed when she could mock Boris, until she realized that this was not a lapse of any sort. He was not hearing things; he was hearing *something*. When he met her eyes he looked so moved that Jane felt the hair on the back of her neck stand on end.

"Do you hear them, Jane?"

Jane looked out toward the window. She tried very hard to hear. Outside was the hazy night. She tried very hard to hear, but no melody came. Only the throaty sounds of frogs from the muddied stream and, farther in the distance, traffic.

"The frogs," Boris said, closing his eyes again, humming a tune that was full of bravado: Chopin or Liszt. He opened his eyes and positioned the fork so as to resume eating. "The frogs, Jane," he said. He smiled at her. "They're mating."

Jane swallowed, felt her crotch get wet, thought: I must have some part of this man inside of me. Right now.

———

"Are you listening, Jane? You're not listening."

"I am," Jane says. She is leaning back on her elbows with her face turned up to the sky. "I just have my eyes closed."

Justin is quiet for a moment. "Aren't you supposed to be watching?" he asks. "Isn't that your *job*?"

Jane opens her eyes. Justin's face is quite close to hers, as if he has been examining her pores. "I'm watching," she says, though she obviously is not and when she surveys the group she feels something tighten in her chest. She straightens and inches away from Justin, who still regards her intently. The sea has become choppy and only half the group remains in the water. Margot, Lily, and Gideon sit in the shallow surf, letting the tide sink them inch by inch into the sand. Jane turns and sees the others already heading back across the campsite toward the showers.

"Do you have a boyfriend, Jane?" Justin asks.

Jane tugs at the knot of hair at the base of her neck.

"Don't you need a shower?" she asks.

"Do you have a boyfriend?"

"Yes. No." She tears at the knot. "He's a pianist," she says, as if this explains all.

A look flits across Justin's face like something has been momentarily lodged in his throat. "I haven't been taking my meds," he says. He slams a fist into the sand and then turns his wrist like a screw. "I've been pretending to swallow them and—"

"I don't want to know," Jane says. She forces her palm against the air.

"But you said you wanted the truth."

"I don't want to know what you've been doing with your fucking meds, Justin. This is just my job."

As he plods back toward camp, Jane scans the ocean and tries to make up for her minutes of neglect by counting heads.

———————

Back at camp the kids shower and call their parents. Jane and Annie take turns at the phones, speaking to those worried about bug bites or heat exhaustion or diet, and one mentions a troublesome child that her son says is spoiling the trip.

"We're doing what we can," Jane says. She cradles the phone between her neck and shoulder and massages the small of her back. After she hangs up she stands motionless, her forehead leaning on the pay phone box, her hand playing over the numbers. She's not ready to go back to the group. She will stay here, in this nook behind the campsite office, facing the park for RVs. Grass creeps through cracks in the asphalt, stretching back to one lone trailer. She must be at the edge of the world. She slots her money in and dials quickly. As the phone rings once, twice, three times, she knows she is calling Boris's home and she knows his wife will answer, but when the receiver rustles and she hears a muffled voice, not his, not his wife's, but the voice of a child, Jane knows nothing at all. The girl's voice is so similar to Margot's or Lily's, that same high trill, that Jane is disoriented. For a moment, she thinks the girl is one of her own charges. She blurts out something nonsensical about an auto body shop, her car needing repairs, and the girl, like Jane, is confused.

"I think, I think you have the wrong number?"

Jane runs a hand through her tangled hair and then tugs so hard that a clump gives, releasing with a sickening rip. The knot looks bestial in her palm, thicker and darker than she has ever known her hair to be. She stares down at it in horror. She cannot believe this tumorous thing has grown from her own body.

"Maybe you should talk to my mom?" comes the voice, because Jane has been unable to respond.

"No," Jane whispers. She swallows and hangs up.

———————

She sets up for dinner. The group plays ultimate Frisbee in the grass. Jane watches the disc fly through the air, wobbly, wobbly, always wobbly. Only Annie can throw straight. But they still have a good time. Thom guards Paul who whaps Gideon who yells at Margot who throws to Grier. Lily waves that she's open but the Frisbee vaults toward Nathan, caught by Jenna, passed to Bill.

"Hey," Jane calls to Annie. "Where's Henry?"

Annie jogs over, bends from the waist with her hands on her knees.

"Where's Henry?"

Annie breathes, looks up. "I thought he was with you."

And the kids are everywhere, running around and around, the Frisbee still vaulting through the air, if they would just keep still so she could get a head count, though Annie's right, he's somewhere around, maybe resting—it is a rest day, after all. But Jane has a metallic taste in her mouth, like sucking on lead, the same taste she got before a performance when she forced herself to visualize, to see it and hear the piece before playing it. Now she can visualize. Now she is having no trouble visualizing Henry's limp arm tossing in the waves, his translucent skin turned veiny and blue. In a seamless interchange of senses she can hear the marshy scent of the grass and smell the grit of sand beneath her fingernails and she can taste that moan, the one that issued from a deep, uncharted place inside her, and everything seems broken, like Justin in the sunlight. And there he stands, apart from the group, rocking back on his heels, his broad chest, the taut muscles in his arms, and the sight of him brings forth something terrible in her thoughts, in the desire that has been swimming in her stomach all day. It makes her queasy, this thought, but also powerful and tremendous, because she knows it could be so good, for once, to be the teacher, instead of the pupil.

Annie says, "The beach. The water. You saw him get out, right?"

Jane nods yes but she really means no. Her head is in her hands and the kids are buzzing around shouting, "Henry! Where's Henry?" and in the midst of their buzzing Jane hears herself and thinks: *rattled.*

She doesn't register the laughter, Justin's laughter, him rocking back on his heels, and then Henry—was he hiding?—eyes wide with trepidation and pride. Justin caws, dances, gestures, waves. "You!" he points, and then to the others: "She freaked!" Annie grabs him, shouts, drags him away, but he escapes from her grasp and runs a few paces back toward Jane.

"Jane," he shouts, his chest puffed out, his fists clenched by his sides, and all the kids are listening, they stand around stupidly, staring at their shoes, stamping their feet in the dirt, because the adult, is she crying? "Jane," he says, "you need to brush your hair."

Henry, who has been standing quite still, who looks lost and frightened, says, "I thought it would be funny. But it took you so long to notice that I was gone."

Everyone has gone back to normal and Jane is trying but she simply wants to be left alone. She is furious—how's that for Zen?—but she feels trapped inside her furor. If she were Justin she could punch things, if she were Henry she could quake, if she were Boris, she could play. She busies herself making dinner. The kids are supposed to make it themselves, but she is tired of eating soggy noodles and she bosses them around. Justin and Henry are off being punished, and so when Henry runs up, she purposely ignores his needy tugging at her sleeve. She stirs the pot of boiling water as if she doesn't notice.

"Jane, Jane," he says. Henry looks over his shoulder and Jane can vaguely see a group forming over by the showers, a tight huddle of kids. Henry sucks in some air. "Justin got cut," he says, his wide doe-eyes tearing.

"Please," Jane snaps. "It's called the boy who cried wolf. It's a story. Do you read?"

"No, but—" Henry turns again to look at the group. Jane wants very badly to curse and so she does.

"Fucking shit, Henry," she says, "Goddammit. Christ, get a clue."

Henry's eyes widen and he backs away. He offers up his palms, which are a rosy, smeary pink.

Through the twilight she spots Annie bending over, motioning her to come, and she is running across the field, Henry like a fawn at her heels, and it's true, it really is, Justin down on the ground, blood smeared across his leg, and the skin around his eyes pulled tight in fear.

She was trained for this sort of thing. She is the medic, and as she stands above him, Annie pushing the other kids away, Annie's upturned face, all their faces, waiting, waiting for her to do something, her fingers jitter and twitch.

She kneels next to him and poises her fingers over the cut. "You did this on purpose," she says. Justin cannot keep his eyes off the gash, which pulses with blood. "You did it on purpose, didn't you?"

Justin meets her gaze but his look is fearful and pleading and Jane takes a deep breath and cradles his leg in her hands. Annie has gotten the first aid kit and Jane speaks calm words as she cleans and dresses the wound. It looks worse than it is and the precision of her hands instills confidence in the group, and soon the blood has stopped pulsing and the others have gone off to dinner and it is just her and Justin in the grass. Jane tapes the last bandage around his calf and gives him a little smile.

He clears his throat but his voice still comes out as a whisper. "I didn't know," he says. "I didn't know it would hurt so bad."

That night, after the kids are sent to their tents, Annie and Jane have a conference. Jane calls the base camp, and then they stand together and look at the stars. Annie wraps her strong arm around Jane's shoulder, gives her a little shake, and heads off to bed.

On the way to her tent, Jane rustles Justin's door. He has his own tent tonight because of his leg. He opens the zipper and she pokes her head in.

"It still hurts," he tells her. "And I'm sorry I told you to brush your hair. I didn't mean it. You have nice hair."

Jane smiles. Her headlamp forms rings of light along the wall of the tent, giving it an underwater feel. She is crouched half in, half out, her feet still in the mud.

"A cut like that just toughens you up," she says. She moves to leave.

"Please," Justin says. He grabs the hem of her T-shirt. It pulls taut against the back of her neck. "Please, Jane. Don't leave me alone."

Jane looks at the bandages, which hide the cut. She knows it will scar, a thin sandbar along his calf, and that years later, when a woman finds it hidden beneath his mat of curled hair, he will remember Jane as his first love, a woman who, like his mother, he could never adequately impress.

In the tent, Jane switches off her headlamp. Like that the rings of light are gone. Jane lies down beside him, the sleeping bag slippery against her skin, his breath hot and regular. She lies down beside him because he is not yet a man.

SHARON MAY

Stanford University

THE WIZARD OF KHAO-I-DANG

Tom treats me like a servant in the day, but he invites me to drink with the Australian embassy staff in the evening. He's new on the Thai border and my least favorite of the immigration officers, arrogant and short-tempered. But I accept his offer because I consider this, too, part of my job, not only to work as a Cambodian interpreter but also to try to educate the staff, as I've been here longer than any of them. Besides, I know he'll buy the beer, and without the alcohol, I cannot sleep.

Tonight all three of them are there—Tom, Richard, Sandra—sitting at a table outside the Bamboo Garden, which caters mostly to foreigners, under a hand-lettered sign that says BAMBU GARDIN. I am the only Cambodian man—the only Cambodian here. The other two translators—Thais who speak Khmer with an accent, and who have their own families to return to in the evening—are absent. Only I have nowhere better to go.

My favorite of the three Australian officers, Sandra, looks about forty years old, pale and fleshy. She wears a red felt hat with a floppy brim, as if she must shield herself from the soft glow of the street-lights. Dark freckles dot her body, like bugs in a sack of rice, speckling her face, her neck, her arms. Of the three embassy officers, she is the kindest, and the most emotional, especially when she's drunk.

Tonight, after her fourth beer, she leans her face close to mine and says, "These poor people. How can you stand it?"

Her tears embarrass me.

I don't want pity. What I want is for them to understand. Of course this is a foolish desire. I know what the Buddha teaches: desire is the cause of suffering. And so I have tried to eradicate desire from my heart. I have tried to weaken its pull on my mind. But still it remains. A wanting. A deep lake of yearning, wide as the Tonle Sap, which expands more than ten times its size during the monsoon, only to shrink again in the dry season.

Even after we have lost everything, we still want something. Having escaped from Cambodia to Thailand, the people stuck in Khao-I-Dang camp want to get to America or Australia or England—or any country that will have them. They want this not for themselves, but for their children. I, who made it to Australia and then came back to the camps to help my people, want to go home to Cambodia. And the immigration officers, what do they want?

The next morning, Tom doesn't look at me or the Cambodian applicant, who has been bussed here from Khao-I-Dang for this interview, along with the other hundred refugees waiting outside the building for their turn. I suspect Tom is tired or hungover. He stares at the file lying on the table and absently twirls an orange Fanta bottle clockwise with his thumb and forefinger. Water drops cover the glass like beads of sweat, except near the lip, which he wipes with a handkerchief now before taking a sip. He drinks a dozen bottles of orange Fanta a day, because—as he confided to me when he first arrived a month ago, nervous and sweating—he is afraid of the water, afraid of the ice, and isn't taking any bloody chances. So every morning in the Aranyaprathet market I fill an ice chest to keep the bottles cold.

"When were you born?" Tom finally asks the applicant, who stares intently at the floor while I translate the question into Khmer. He wears the cheap, off-white plastic sandals distributed in the camp last week. One of the side straps has broken.

"I'm a Rat," the man answers, glancing up at me, not Tom.

Of course I don't translate this directly. The man, Seng Veasna according to the application, nervously holds his hands sandwiched between his knees. Seng Veasna means "good destiny." He looks about fifty, the father of the small family sitting in a half circle before the officer's wooden desk. I calculate quickly, counting back the previous Years of the Rat until I reach the one that best suits his age.

"Nineteen thirty-six," I say to Tom. He checks the answer against the birth date on the application, submitted by Seng Veasna's relatives in Australia. The numbers must match, as well as the names, or the officer will think the man is lying and reject the application. Each question is a problem with a single correct answer, except that a family's future—not an exam grade—is at stake.

It is my job to solve these problems. To calculate. To resolve inconsistencies.

I did not wish to become a translator or to perform these tricks. I had wanted to become a mathematician and had almost finished my baccalaureate when the Khmer Rouge took over in 1975. I'd planned to teach high school, but it was not my fate. Instead, I now work in this schoolhouse made of timber and tin, at the site of an abandoned refugee camp. This building alone still stands, used for immigration interviews. Inside, three tables for three teams are set in a wide triangle, far enough apart that we can see but not hear each other.

The arrangement reminds me of the triangle I have traveled from Cambodia to Thailand to Australia—and now back again, to Thailand, retracing my journey. After the fall of the Khmer Rouge in 1979, I left Cambodia, crossing the minefields to a camp like this one on the Thai border. Australia accepted me. In Melbourne, I washed dishes in a refugee hostel and took English classes. Language has always come easily to me, as have numbers. Before the war I'd studied French and some English, and like a fool I'd kept an English dictionary with me after the Khmer Rouge evacuated us from the city. For this stupidity I almost lost my life; when a soldier discovered the book, I survived by claiming I used the pages for toilet paper—very soft, I told him, ripping out a few to demonstrate.

After the Khmer Rouge, I learned some Vietnamese from the occupying soldiers. In the refugee camp, I learned a little Thai. When I first arrived in Australia, English sounded like snake language, with so many S's, hissing and dangerous. But then the words began to clarify, not individually but in patterns, like the sequence of an equation. A door opened, and I no longer felt trapped. I still felt like a stranger, though, useless, alone. I had no wife, no children to keep me there. After three years, I got my Australian passport and returned to Thailand.

First I worked in a transit camp in Bangkok, where the refugees who have been accepted must pass medical tests before they can be sent abroad. The foreign aid workers didn't trust me, because I was Cambodian. And I didn't want to be in Bangkok. After six months, I heard the Australian embassy needed translators on the border. That's where I wanted to be, where I could be useful. I jumped at the chance. One step closer to Cambodia, to home.

I had to come back. I think it is my fate to work in a schoolhouse after all.

"Why did you leave Cambodia?" Tom asks the applicant now.

Of all the questions, I dread this one the most. When I translate it into Khmer, Seng Veasna laughs, lifting his hands and opening them in the air in a wide gesture of surrender. For the first time during the interview, he looks relaxed, as if all the tension has drained from his body.

"Doesn't he know what happened in our country?" he asks me. His tone is intimate, personal. For the moment, he has forgotten his fear. He seems to have forgotten even the presence of the embassy officer, although I have not.

"You must tell him," I say in Khmer. I understand the purpose of this question is to distinguish between economic and political refugees, but I also know that this man cannot answer, any more than the last applicant, who just looked at me in disbelief. He cannot answer any more than I can. Still, I urge him, "Just tell the truth."

The man shakes his head no. He cannot speak. He can only laugh. I want to tell him I know this is a nonsense question, a question they do not need to ask.

Why did you leave Cambodia?

I've told the embassy staff many times that if they ask this question, they can never get the right answer. I've explained to the other two officers—although not yet to this new one, Tom—that nearly two million people died. One-quarter of the people in Cambodia died in less than four years. Then the Vietnamese invaded. There was no food, no medicine, no jobs. Everyone has lost family. Myself, I lost my mother and father, two brothers, one sister, six aunts and uncles, seventeen cousins. The numbers I can say; the rest I cannot.

Even now, the fighting continues in Cambodia and on the border. Sometimes in this schoolhouse the muffled boom of heavy artillery interrupts the interviews.

"Why is he laughing?" Tom asks.

"He does not understand the question."

"Ask him again. How can he not know why he bloody left the country?"

I see Tom's bottle of Fanta is almost empty. I take another from the ice chest, pop off the cap, wipe the lip with a clean handkerchief, and set it on his desk before turning back to Seng Veasna to explain in Khmer. "I know, you don't want to remember. But you must tell him what you've gone through." When the man still does not speak, I add, "Uncle, if you don't answer, he will reject your application."

At that, Seng Veasna glances quickly at Tom then back to the floor and begins to talk, without raising his eyes. I repeat his story in English, the story I have heard so many times in infinite variations, the same story that is my own. And when Seng Veasna is finally through and the interview finished, to my relief the officer Tom stamps the application ACCEPTED. One done. Ten families still wait outside. The morning is not yet half over.

Here's what I don't say to the immigration officers:

Try to imagine. The camp is like prison, nothing to do but wait and go crazy. Forget your iced bottles of Fanta and beer. Forget your salary that lets you live like a king while you make the decisions of a god.

Imagine. It is like magic. You wake up one morning and everything is gone. The people you love, your parents, your friends. Your home. Like in the film I saw twice in Australia, *The Wizard of Oz.* I watched it first with my second brother's son, who was six, who had been born on the border but raised in Melbourne and cannot even speak Khmer properly. The flying monkeys scared him so much I had to turn off the video. But those monkeys reminded me of home, of when I worked in the forest surrounding Lake Tonle Sap. They reminded me of the monkey god Hanuman and his army, who helped Rama rescue Sita. So, later, after my nephew went to sleep, I watched the rest of the movie. The next week I rented the video and watched it again alone. I didn't like the singing and dancing, so I fast-forwarded through those parts. But the girl's wanting to go home—that I understood. And I understood, too, the wizard who has no power, who cannot even help himself, although he also secretly wishes to return home.

I want to tell the immigration officers—imagine you are in that movie. Then maybe you will understand. You are the girl. Only there is no home to return to. And instead of Oz, you have woken up in a refugee camp.

Each day you have nothing to do but worry and, if you are lucky enough to have a ration card, to wait like a beggar for handouts of rice and canned, half-rancid fish. At night after the foreign aid workers leave, the soldiers who are supposed to protect you steal what few possessions you still have, and they rape your wives and your daughters. You want only to get out. To find a new home.

Every day you hope for an announcement on the loudspeaker that an embassy is conducting interviews. You hope for America but any country will do: France, England, Australia. You check the list on the wall, search for your name, squeezing your body in between the others. The people clustered around the wall have a certain rank smell, almost sweet. You wish you could wash this stink from your own body and purify yourself of this place, of this longing. On one side of you stands a husband who has waited for years, checking this same wall; on the other, a mother who's been rejected twice and so has little hope, yet still she comes to look. Behind you a father squats in the sun; he can't read, so his son checks for him while he waits. If you're lucky enough to be listed, you must be prepared to go to the interview the following day.

Imagine. The bus picks you up early in the morning, exiting the gate past the Thai guards with their machine guns, taking you out of the camp for the first time in the years since you arrived. As the bus rattles over the rutted road, your mind clenches in fear. The child in front of you presses her face to the window, enraptured. She points at the rice fields, the water buffalo, the cows, which she has never seen before because she was born in the camp. "What's that?" she asks, curious. "And that?" Her father names these things for her. You know he is thinking of the interview ahead, as you are, and how much depends on it, how her future depends on it; perhaps he is thinking, too, of how the shirt he has cleaned and pressed is already stained with sweat.

All the questions are difficult. Especially the ones that seem the simplest to the immigration officers: What is your name? Where were you born? How old are you?

Take, for example, this morning, when officer Richard asks a young man, "What is your brother's name?"

"Older brother Phal," the boy answers. He is skinny, frightened.

"What is his *full* name?" Richard, over six feet tall, has wide shoulders and a large belly like a Chinese Buddha. Although he smiles often, his height and massive torso scare the applicants, especially when he leans toward them as he does now, both elbows planted on the table, intently studying the boy. The young man stares at the floor. He looks like a real Khmer—wide cheekbones, full lips, chocolate skin. "Don't be scared," Richard says. "Take it easy. We're not going to do anything to you. Just try to answer correctly, honestly."

Still the boy hesitates. I worry Richard may take this as a sign he is lying about his relationship to the sponsor, although I've tried to explain to him that Cambodians don't call their relatives by their given names; it's not polite. You call them brother or sister, aunt or uncle, or you use nicknames, so you may not know the full given name. Then there are the names you may have used under the Khmer Rouge, to hide your background to save your family's lives, or your own. I have explained this all before, but it does no good.

In the end, Richard says, "I'm sorry," and stamps the front page REJECTED.

I can do nothing. Although siblings have lower priority, I believe the familial relationship is not the problem. Rather, the boy is dark-skinned and speaks no English. Richard, like the others, prefers the light-skinned Cambodians, who have more Chinese blood, softer features, who can speak at least some English. If they are young and pretty, and female, even better.

Just as important is the officer's mood, yet another variable I must consider. Tom is more likely to accept an applicant when he has been to a brothel the night before. Sandra is more likely to approve after she has received a letter from her children in Sydney, less likely if they happen to mention her ex-husband in Brisbane. Richard, usually in good spirits, is most dangerous when he has a hangover or digestive problems. Today, he seems to have neither trouble. He has not been running to the toilet or popping paracetamol pills for a headache, so I don't know why the day doesn't seem to get easier.

The next couple is neither young nor pretty. The wife's lips and teeth are stained red from chewing betel nut.

"When was your seventh son born?" Richard asks.

The husband and wife look at each other, confused.

"Was it eight or nine years ago?" the man asks his wife.

"Nine," she says. "No, eight."

"You sure? Wasn't it nine?"

"No, tell him eight." The wife gives her husband a scolding look, then smiles weakly at the officer, showing her stained teeth. By now Richard is laughing and shaking his head.

"Eight," I translate.

"Do they know his birth *date?*"

The husband looks again at his wife. "Dry season," she says. "I remember it had stopped raining already."

"Around December or January," I translate. Then I add, "It's not that they're lying. It's that these things aren't important. Birth dates are not registered until a child enters school, if then."

"How can you not know when your own child was born?" Richard asks me. His generous belly shakes as he laughs. He does not really want an answer, so I say nothing.

"What's wrong?" the wife asks me.

"Never mind," I say. "Don't worry."

I am forever in between.

To the people in the camp, I explain again and again, "Look, you must remember your full names and birth dates. In Cambodia it's not important, but in the West, it's very important. If you don't know, make them up. One person in the family must write all the answers down, and everyone must remember. You must practice."

They look at me funny at first, not quite believing me, like Richard watches me now, still chuckling. Because he is amused, I calculate he will accept the couple. I decide to say nothing and just smile back.

That night at the Bamboo Garden, Richard calls the owner to our table. "Your food is spot-on, very *aroy,*" Richard says, emphasizing and mispronouncing the Thai word for *delicious,* using the wrong tone. "But, mate, that sign is spelled wrong."

The owner, a slight man in his sixties, nods his head. "Yes. Thank you. Yes."

"I mean, you gotta fix that spelling." Richard points to the sign above him. "Darith, can you explain to him?"

Shit, I think, even here I have to translate. In polite language, I tell the owner in Thai that the big foreigner loves the food very much.

The owner smiles. Richard nods, happy to be understood. I think that's the end of it. But then Richard pulls a long strip of toilet paper—which is used in place of napkins—from the pink plastic container in the center of the table. In large block letters, using the pen he keeps in his shirt pocket, he writes: BAMBOO GARDEN. He underlines the double O and the E, then points again at the misspelled sign.

The owner's face darkens, without me having to explain. "Thank you. Yes, I fix," he says, as he takes the piece of toilet paper from Richard's outstretched hand.

The young woman sitting in front of the desk this morning is both pretty and light-skinned. Her hair, recently washed, is combed neatly into a shiny ponytail that falls below her narrow waist. As she passed me to take her seat, I could smell the faint sweet scent of shampoo. She wears a carefully ironed white blouse, and a trace of pink lipstick, which she must have borrowed from a friend or relative to make herself up for this occasion. Officer Tom, to whom I have been assigned today, watches the girl with interest, charmed. Her sponsor is only a cousin, so normally she would have little chance of being accepted.

"What do you do in the camp?" he asks. "Do you work?"

The young lady speaks softly. Out of politeness, she doesn't meet his eyes. "Yes, I work, but..." Her voice trails off and then she turns to me, blushing. "I don't want to say, it's a very low job."

"What is it?"

"I work in the CARE bakery, making bread."

Tom eyes me suspiciously. "Why are you talking to her?"

I could answer him straight, but I'm annoyed with him today. I did not sleep well last night. I am getting sick of this job, this place.

For all I do, it seems I have done nothing. "She was talking to me," I snap back, "that's why I talked to her."

"What did she say?"

"She says she doesn't want to tell you, because she feels embarrassed." As if on cue, she turns her head away. Her ponytail ripples down her back.

"What exactly does she *do* in the camp?" Tom says this in an insinuating way, as if he suspects she's a prostitute. I don't like the way he looks at her. Maybe he is undressing her in his mind right now. For her part, the girl waits quietly in the chair, knees drawn together, looking at her hands lying still on her knees. Her fingernails are clean, cut short. This, too, she remembered to do for the interview.

"She has a wonderful job," I say to Tom. "You know the bread from the CARE bakery in Khao-I-Dang, the French bread you eat every morning? She is the baker."

"That's very good. Why didn't you say so in the first place?" He relaxes back in his chair and takes a drink from the Fanta bottle. I don't know how he can drink this stuff, or how I can watch him drink it all day. I submerge the thought and clear my head to concentrate on the task at hand. He continues, "Ask her what she is going to do if she gets accepted to Australia."

"What are you going to do in Australia—tell him you're going to open a bakery," I say, all in one sentence.

Raising her head to face him now, she answers in a sweet, composed voice, "I want to open a bakery shop in Australia."

I translate, "She wants to work in a bakery in Australia, and when she can save enough money, to open her own bread shop."

"Good, good," he says, and stamps the application ACCEPTED.

That night at dinner with Sandra and Richard, Tom asks me out of the blue, "Why did you come back here?"

The restaurant sign is gone, creating an empty space over our heads. In response to Tom's question, I shrug my shoulders and look away, hoping he'll get distracted, perhaps by the attractive waitress waiting to refill our glasses. I glance at her and she comes forward to pour more beer for everyone.

"You came back, didn't you?" Tom persists after the waitress has stepped back into the shadows. "Your mother's Australian, isn't she? And your father is Cambodian?"

I've heard this rumor, too, mostly from foreigners. I think it is their way of explaining why I can speak English.

"No, I am all Cambodian," I say. "But I have Australian citizenship."

"So you went through the Khmer Rouge and all that?" asks Richard.

"Yes. All that."

Sandra, who knows this, watches me. Her jaw tenses under the shadow of her hat.

"I don't get it," Tom says. "Why would you come back? Seems to me everyone else is trying to get out of here." He laughs, lifting his glass. "Myself included. Cheers, mate."

I lift my glass. "Cheers," I say. I should leave it at that.

Sandra is still watching me with concern, her eyebrows drawn together. "How about that storm this afternoon?" she asks, to change the subject. "I couldn't hear a thing."

Maybe it is the beer. I don't know. I look straight at Tom. "You don't know how much the people feel," I say. He doesn't respond.

"I couldn't hear a thing," Sandra repeats, more forcefully this time. "I can't believe how loud rain is on a tin roof."

"Yeah," says Richard. "I even had to stop an interview."

"The way you treat people, you don't know anything," I say, still looking directly at Tom. He shifts in his chair and dips a spring roll into sweet red sauce. With his other hand he ticks the Formica table-top. His eyes study the waitress. As if he hasn't even heard me. I often feel this way around the immigration officers, invisible. Sometimes they talk about the Cambodians, calling them lazy or stupid, as if I am not there, or as if they have forgotten that I, too, am Khmer.

"If you ask me, these people don't really want to come to your country," I continue. "If you open the gate, they will go back to Cambodia. They won't even say good-bye." I want to stop, but I can't. "And don't ask them why they leave the country. You think they want to leave their home? They laugh when you ask them that. You should know. The real situation is that they want to survive."

Sandra has stopped talking. Richard looks into his half-empty beer glass, then takes a sip. Tom loudly crunches on another spring roll. I don't know why they are the way they are. It's not that none of them cares. There is Sandra, and others like her. And they are sent from country to country, without time to learn the difference between Cambodia and Vietnam. It's not easy for them. I tell myself that they are just worn down, but the new arrivals have the same assumed superiority, the unquestioned belief that they know everything: what is wrong, what is right—that they are somehow more *human*. I signal to the waitress for another round.

The next night, instead of beer, Tom orders me a Fanta orange soda, grinning as he slides the bottle across the table toward me. The restaurant sign is still gone.

"No, thanks," I say.

"Go ahead, mate."

"No, thank you," I say again.

"Why not?" asks Tom.

"Oh, leave him alone," says Sandra.

I stare at the orange bottle.

"It won't kill you," says Tom.

"No, not me." I try to make light of it. "I gave that stuff up a long time ago, in 1976."

Tom laughs. So does Richard in his booming voice. For all of their attention to dates from the applicants, for all their insistence that the numbers must match exactly, they ignore what those dates mean. But I am telling the truth. It was 1976, the second year under the Khmer Rouge regime. It was the rainy season, cold and miserable. I lived in a single men's labor camp on a hill in the rice fields. One night I heard the guards calling, "We got the enemy! We got the enemy!" *What enemy?* I thought. We were in the middle of nowhere. The real purpose of the guards was to keep the workers from trying to escape or steal food at night. When I opened my eyes, I couldn't see the man sleeping next to me. Clouds blocked the stars. Then I noticed the feeble flames from lit pieces of rubber tire, burned for lamplight, and got up to see what had happened.

Near the compound's kitchen, three Khmer Rouge leaders gathered around a skinny man kneeling in the mud, his elbows tied tightly behind his back. His shoulders were pulled back like a chicken's wings, tensing the tendons in his neck. He had dark skin and long hair that fell below his bound wrists. I'd heard rumors of resistance fighters, "long hairs" who lived in the forest around Lake Tonle Sap, but I had never seen one and did not believe until then that they really existed. I had thought them the product of our collective imagining, our wishing someone had the courage to fight back.

Comrade Sok kicked the man in his side, and he fell over into the mud. Sok was a big man, twice the size of the prisoner. When Sok kicked him again, the man's head hit a water buffalo yoke lying at the edge of the kitchen. One of the other leaders pulled his head up. The prisoner's eyes were closed. Comrade Sok said, "Why do you resist? Who do you struggle for?"

The man seemed only half conscious. He opened his eyes briefly, then closed them again and spoke very clearly, slowly enunciating each word, "I struggle for all of you, brothers, not for myself."

"You struggle for me? We have already liberated the country." Sok kicked him again. "We have no need of your help."

The man said once more, "I struggle for you."

Then they threw him like a sack of rice into an oxcart. Everyone was watching. We couldn't help him. We couldn't do anything.

The next day, while I was cleaning the abscesses on my feet using water boiled with sour leaves, the oxcart returned—without the man, loaded instead with bottles of soft drinks and cigarette cartons. Comrade Sok explained this was our reward for capturing the enemy: one bottle for three people, one pack of cigarettes for ten people. The next time we captured the enemy, we would receive an even greater reward.

The cigarette packets were Fortunes, with a lion insignia. The soda bottles were Miranda orange. I teased the two younger boys with whom I shared the soft drink, dividing the bottle into thirds, the top being the largest, the bottom the smallest. "What part do you want?" I asked. Of course they chose the top two portions. "Okay, I'll take the bottom," I said. "You don't mind if I drink my portion first..."

"No, that's not right," they protested together. I was only making fun. I poured the drink into three tin bowls we usually used to eat the rice ration, giving the boys most of it. They were excited about the soda, which they hadn't tasted in a long time, if ever. But all the while I was trying to make them laugh, I felt sad. A man was killed for this.

The drink was flat, not even enough liquid to fill my mouth.

The application lying on the table today in front of Sandra is a difficult case. This morning, when I dropped the files on each of the three officers' tables, I made sure this one came to her. The sponsor in Australia, a daughter, got citizenship by claiming a woman was her mother. Now that the daughter is in Australia, she claims the woman is not actually her mother, but rather her aunt, and that the woman sitting before us now is her real mother.

The mother hands me the letter from her daughter, which I translate. In it, the daughter explains that this woman is her real mother and confesses she lied before. She did not know her mother was alive then. She was alone in the camp, with no one to take care of her. That's why she decided to lie.

Sandra asks me, "Do you think they are really mother and daughter?"

"Yes," I say, and hand her the letter, which she adds to the file lying open before her, with the previous and current applications and small black-and-white photos. "You can even see the daughter looks like her."

"Well, they cannot do that," Sandra says. "She lied. The law is the law."

"I can tell you, this is a story many people face, not just these two. They do not intend to lie, but because of the circumstances they must do it, believe me. Think of your own daughter, if you were separated." And then I add, "Of course it's up to you, not me."

"She lied," Sandra says. "It's finished. I have to reject them."

"I can't tell them straight like that," I say. "Would you let me explain nicely to them the reason they are getting rejected?"

"All right, go ahead."

So I take a chance, a calculated risk. There is nothing to lose now. I know Sandra loves her own children, and also that she has a good heart. I say to the mother in a soft, even voice, "Look, your daughter lied to the embassy even though she knew what she was doing was wrong. A country like Australia is not like Cambodia. The law is the law. When you say someone is your mother, she's got to be your mother. Now she cannot change her story. So from now on, I don't think you will be able to meet your daughter anymore for the rest of your life."

Tears begin to well in the mother's eyes. I feel bad for what I am doing, but I know there is no other way. I keep my voice firm, steady, and continue, "So now, after all you've been through in Cambodia, after how hard you struggled to keep your family together, to survive, now you are separated forever."

The mother begins to wail, a long piercing sound that fills the entire room, so that the teams at the other two tables turn around to look at us. "Oh, my daughter, I will never see you again!" she cries. I translate what she says for Sandra. "After all we survived in the Pol Pot time—when you were starving, I risked my life to steal food for you. When you got sick, I looked after you. When you could not walk, I carried you in my arms. And now you lie. You lie and you are separated from me. I cannot see you for the rest of my life. *Ouey...*"

I translate it all, word for word. The father is crying now, too, but silently. He sits in a wooden chair, with his back straight. Their young son watches his mother's face and sobs as well, echoing her wails.

"Please, tell them to go now," Sandra says. She looks away and wipes her eyes with the back of her hand.

In Khmer, I dismiss the family. "Go, go. Don't cry anymore. Even if you die, nobody cares. You will never see your child anymore."

As the mother walks away, the applicants at the other tables watch her leave. The building is silent except for her voice. She cries all the way out of the building, gripping her husband's arm. Her son whimpers, too, clinging to her legs through the sarong, almost tripping her.

I start to laugh. "Well, Sandra, that's it," I say. "Send them back to the Killing Fields. Don't worry. There are more coming."

Sandra looks at me, stunned. She opens her mouth and closes it again, without saying anything, like a fish gulping seawater. The freckled skin around her eyes is red and puffy. I can see the beating of her blood beneath the translucent skin of her left temple, a small pulsing disk, like the flutter of a bird's heart. She looks away, down to the table, and starts idly shifting through the papers. She isn't really looking at them.

"I'll get the next family," I say.

She nods, her face still turned away from me. I grab the list and go call the next family from the dozens of others waiting outside the building. Some stand in the sun. Others squat in the shade of three small coconut trees, fanning away flies.

"Keo Narith," I say. No one steps forward. The crowd looks agitated, nervous. The mother is still crying, "My daughter, I can never see you again!" A group has gathered around her, asking, "What happened? What happened?"

"Keo Narith!" I call again.

Still, no one answers. I remember the name because it rhymes with my own, and I saw the family members board the bus when they were called in the morning. They must be hiding somewhere now in the crowd or behind the coconut trees or around the corner of the building. I hear a man to the left of me say, "The embassy is not happy today. They reject easily." It's true, when too many people are rejected, the next applicants don't dare answer. They'd rather wait for months or years until they get back on the list again.

After we drive back to Aranyaprathet, the embassy staff meets again for dinner at the Bamboo Garden. The owner has fixed the sign: two small, oblong O's are now squeezed into the space that held the U, and the I has been changed to an E, but the shades of paint don't quite match. Tom and Richard are talking the usual bullshit. Richard expands on his most recent stomach problems. Tom no longer talks about leaving. He has a Thai girlfriend now, a prostitute he claims is a waitress at the bar who has never slept with a man before him. "She's been saving herself," he says.

Sandra looks at him, disgusted, and interjects, "Yeah, right. You really believe that?"

As the men continue talking, Sandra turns to me and whispers, "Darith, I changed it. I changed the file, when I got back. I'm letting them go."

I say quietly, "You made the right decision."

"I know," she says, her eyes shining, urgent. "I understand."

I think, there is more than any of us can understand. I feel something I cannot express: an opening, an exit. It is like the feeling I had when I first crossed the border after the end of the Khmer Rouge regime: gratitude, mixed with weariness and hunger. The day I arrived I could still taste the foul pond water I'd drunk in darkness the night before, so thirsty, not seeing until morning the body of a woman in the pond, close to where I slept on the embankment. I didn't know then what would come, how many years I would work before returning to the border I'd fled. I wonder, does Sandra—who, out of the corner of my eye, I can see is still watching me as I glance down at my beer glass—really understand? How many families will remain stuck in the camp if I can no longer do this job? I weigh all of this: duty, desire, two halves of an equation, as I turn the glass in my hand.

All the while in my heart I am thinking, hoping, I can quit now. I can leave this place. It's time to go home.

DAVID JAMES POISSANT

University of Arizona

Venn Diagram

Every Wednesday, after dinner, we drive to the nondenominational church across town. Here, for an hour, a dozen of us sit in a circle of aluminum chairs in a small, well-lit room telling our same sad stories. Sometimes there's coffee. Sometimes there's chocolate cake. Usually, there's a tissue box that orbits the empty center of our circle like a misshapen moon.

Each week, Pam, our counselor, reminds us that it isn't a competition, that the goal of group therapy is not to outdo each other or to rank our circumstances. Misery, she assures us, cannot be measured. But our greatest comfort is in comparing. Validation awaits those who tell the best stories. And, since talk won't bring back the dead, we make do with our little game of grief. What it comes down to is the following equation: If a train leaves Chicago at sixty miles an hour and another train leaves Atlanta at eighty miles an hour, when they both collide in Kentucky and everybody's babies die, who is the saddest?

There's Lydia who had an abortion in order to finish college, then wanted the baby back after graduation. Then there are Marie and Beth with their multiple miscarriages. We pretend to feel sorry for them, but really they never had children they loved and lost. Then there's Dot and Drew, whose son was decapitated when he tried to drive home after too many tallboys. Granted, a tragedy, but at least they had him for eighteen years. And, hey, if they'd been better parents, who knows?

One week, a weepy, mascara-stained wreck of a woman stops by. She introduces herself as Jenna, then tells us her story, and, for a moment, we have a winner. Her three-month-old died without explanation, and it wasn't until a year later, after interrogation by two cops and a coroner, that the husband admitted to shaking the baby. In this way, three became two, then one. Still, my wife says, it's not the same. Jenna has someone she can be mad at. Jenna has somebody to blame.

What happened to us, Lisa says, in poker terms, is like being dealt three of a kind. You bet high and show your hand only to see that, really, all you have is a pair, and the whole time you're wondering how you ever mistook that three for an eight.

With SIDS, despair isn't tied to regret or what-ifs or whose fault. With Sudden Infant Death Syndrome, the only thing you want to know—after you wake with the shock that you slept through the night, after you sit up and stare and consider the silence, the stillness of the cradle, after you swallow your paranoia and go to the baby, only to feel the warm rush of panic again flooding your chest, after the touching, the holding, the shouting, the running, the phoning, the signing, right here, on the dotted line—after all of it, the only thing you want to know is *why?*

It's the question we all ask each Wednesday, a question for which there is no answer. So, why do any of us return, week after week? Because, at the conclusion of every session, there remains a single, blessed assurance. In the end, all satisfaction lies in the certainty of this, our shared secret: That each of us knows we have it the worst.

The divorce rate for couples who lose infant children is almost 90 percent. Most couples split up inside of a year. Our own one-year mark a week away, I've decided that Lisa and I are no exception. It's not that we've stopped loving each other exactly, only that every time I look into my wife's eyes, all I see is my little girl. Lisa is holding out for a miracle, the thing that will bring us together, unite us in our sorrow. But the only miracle here is that we've lasted as long as we have.

Lying in bed one tired Wednesday night after group, we consider what would happen if I left. This isn't the first time the subject's come up. It's not meant as a threat. I just want Lisa to be ready when I go.

Lisa hasn't bothered to wash her face, and her eyes are still red, her face puffy. Mascara has stained dark rings around her eyes, and in the lamplight she looks like a sleepy raccoon.

"Where would you go?" she asks. She takes my hand, wants me to see she's taking this seriously, but she's exhausted, drained by the meeting. This, of course, is why I waited until now. Because I can't face Lisa when she cries. Because on any given Wednesday night, with no emotion left, we can talk about separation like two strangers discussing the weather.

"I'm not sure yet," I say.

"You don't have to leave," she says.

"Actually, I kind of think I do." I rub the back of Lisa's hand with my thumb. "I mean, we tried. We gave it our best shot. It's just too much. All of it."

And this is how we've come to speak of our dead child, as though saying her name will summon what happened back into being. Say *June* and someone might say *Jinx*.

"We can make this work," Lisa says.

I don't say, "We're doomed."

I don't say, "What happened, it's going to haunt us as long as we're together."

"Maybe," I say, "but not like this."

"If we just keep going to group," Lisa says, and I wonder if she believes this. She lets go of my hand, pulls the covers up to her neck. Beside me, she seems small, a frightened animal.

"I'm not talking divorce here," I say. "What do they call it? A trial separation."

"Right. Because those always have such happy endings."

"I just think we need some time apart."

"You. You need time apart. Not me. You don't know what I need."

That shuts us both up. When I speak again, I choose my words with care. "Lisa," I say, "I need this. I need space, some time to figure things out. Solve for X, you know? I want you to be okay with this." But I think we both know the truth. When I leave, it will be the end.

Lisa sits up. She puts one hand on her pillow, as though any second she might bring it down over my face. "Listen to you. Do you even hear yourself speak? I'm not a variable, Richard. You can't just take me out of your little equation and expect it to balance on both sides."

I don't want to cry, but suddenly I do.

"Lose me, and you wind up with less than you had."

"Lisa," I say, "please."

"No. Enough. You want to leave? Leave." There are tears in her voice, but she does not cry. She fluffs her pillow a few times, dramatically, violently, then smoothes it against the headboard and lies down.

"You can't escape what's happened by leaving this house," she says, rolling onto her side. "The only thing you escape if you leave is me."

The first thing they do when you lose a newborn is pump you full of drugs so you don't kill yourself. Lisa took the antidepressants, but I refused. I had my reasons. I wanted it to hurt, was certain I deserved the pain.

Have you ever been to a baby's funeral? There's an absurdity to the pageantry: the miniature casket, the floral arrangements done up in pastels. I don't remember anything the minister said. I only remember I couldn't breathe. Lisa sat on my right, my mother on my left. Each of them leaned in. After the service, my shoulders were wet and my hands ached.

Friends and relatives followed us home after the funeral. "You shouldn't be alone right now," everyone said. Lisa nodded. She wore a smile I'd never seen before and haven't seen since. She was determined to do whatever everyone thought was best.

Something about death makes people bring food. In north Georgia, people still operate under the pretext of "southern hospitality." Neighbors whose names I'd never learned came bearing balls of aluminum foil.

"You'll never finish all this by yourselves," everyone said. Our guests set up card tables and folding chairs around the house. Our kitchen counter was transformed into a buffet. Soon, everyone was helping themselves to turkey and ham, noodle salad, little sandwiches cut into triangles.

The air was full of the aroma of rolls being warmed under the broiler, when Lisa and I began to fight. I wanted to be left alone. Lisa said she liked the company. The argument escalated quickly, our voices competing with the din of the crowded living room. I yelled something. Lisa screamed something back. Then ours were the only voices left. People drew near, surrounded us. Sentiments were whispered. Hands patted my shoulders, rubbed my back. I felt like a bird with a broken wing, the neighborhood cats closing in.

"Please," I said. "She just died. Please leave us alone."

"Oh, and now you care," Lisa said. "You didn't even want her."

At that, everyone took a collective step back.

"It's your fault!" Lisa said. Her body shook. "You didn't want her and she died!"

Lisa collapsed into me, pressed her face to my chest, heaving. A second later, I heard the words, processed the meaning of what she had said. And in that moment I hated my wife. Her very touch repulsed me.

I pushed her. I meant only to separate our bodies, to get away, but there was a miscalculation of force. Lisa fell backward onto a table, sending a plate of carrot sticks and a bowl of ranch dressing to the floor.

That could have been the end right there, except that it wasn't.

The next day we went on as though nothing had happened. I started taking the pills I'd been given, ignoring the recommended dosage.

It's true though, what Lisa said. The pregnancy was not what people call "planned," and I hadn't wanted the baby, not at first. It's not as if I told her, spoke the words aloud: *I don't want this baby.* But Lisa knew. She knew the moment she told me she was pregnant.

I was teaching when the news came. Lisa had thrown up that morning, called a sub, and gone back to bed. The high school is where we met, where I'd been teaching math to teenagers for ten years. Lisa was right out of college, the hot, new biology teacher all the boys, and some of the girls, had a crush on. The decade's difference in our age went unnoticed by both of us. We kept the relationship a secret as long as we could. Public school gossip, after all, is seldom kind. The smaller the town, the worse it is, and this is a small town. Of course, when Miss Adams returned one fall and told everyone to start calling her Mrs. Starling, it wasn't long before people put two and two together.

The voice coming through the intercom ordered me to the front office. I had a call waiting on line one.

When Lisa told me, I dropped the phone. We had been married only a year, and we had been so careful. I put a hand on the office copy machine to keep from falling over. My thumb caught the keypad, and then the copier was humming and whirring. Blank paper streamed into a tray on the floor. I watched the paper coming out, sheet after sheet. I fully expected a baby to tumble from the mouth of the machine, down the chute, and into the gray basket.

I bent over, grabbed the phone, brought the receiver to my ear. "Well," Lisa said, "aren't you excited?"

They were there, all the words I knew I should say, the words one uses for such an occasion, but none found their way to my tongue.

"Fine," Lisa said. "I'll see you when you get home."

So I feigned joy, went through the motions as I thought a better man might. I painted the spare bedroom blue, then, after the third ultrasound, repainted it pink. I helped Lisa's friends at school throw a shower. But in time real pleasure crept in. Action blossomed into belief, and belief turned to love, a love for what grew inside Lisa, love even before the baby came. I bought the baby book, the one Lisa still looks at every day, the first month the only section filled in.

Our daughter was born in June and we named her just that: *June.*

It was only after June died in July that the subject of my initial reluctance resurfaced. Lisa has not mentioned it again since the outburst following the funeral, but it has stayed with us, a green cloud hanging low in the house. When we fight, I feel her holding back, and with each argument I have waited—am waiting still—for her to throw the accusation back in my face, as though death is a thing I wished upon our daughter.

I decide to postpone the separation, again, this time with the stipulation that I no longer have to attend group. Lisa can go, but I've had enough.

After all, I'm hardly a model candidate for group therapy, especially group therapy with a spiritual component. Me, I'm a believer in the concrete. Give me statistics. Give me data. Give me a line, fat and sturdy, working its way across a grid.

I believe in a calculable world, even when the math doesn't quite make sense. Take Lisa and me, for example. We, "X," may be expressed as follows: $X = [3 - 1]$ but $[1 + 1 \neq 2]$.

Lisa and I used to be a lot alike. My world was made up of numbers, hers of biological processes. She saw everything through a scientific lens. Her outlook changed, though, after June died. When Lisa couldn't pin the blame on me, she turned to God. Suddenly, meaning attached itself like a leech to everything in her life. Everything that happened happened for a reason.

Soon, she was reading the Bible every day and memorizing scripture. *God's will* became a favorite catchphrase. Sunday mornings now find me home alone.

Lisa agrees to my terms. I can stop going to group. She also says I owe her an apology, so the Friday following our fight in bed we drive an hour south to Atlanta to the opening of a new film at the Fernbank Science Center's IMAX theater. We sit in the front row, craning our necks at the enormous screen. Lisa's just nuts for nature documentaries. This one's called *The Amazing Journey* and chronicles an annual herd migration across the Serengeti Plain. The film pretty much follows the standard African migration documentary format: Gazelle and zebra and water buffalo travel hundreds of miles, terrorized by lions and cheetahs, fording crocodile-infested waters, all so they can make it to a lush basin somewhere in Kenya. In the basin, the grass is long and green. Plant life of all kinds abounds, and there is fresh water enough for every animal. It is like a kind of heaven. Then all the animals fuck and go home.

Only here's the thing. As it turns out, they don't all go home. Every so often, a particularly astute zebra or savvy antelope will say to itself, "Hey, why not stay here?" These few remain in the basin where they live rich, long lives free of hardship.

"So, what I want to know," I say, my arm around Lisa, as the lights come up and the credits scroll down the screen, "is why don't more stay? Why would any of them leave the basin?"

"Simple," my biologist wife says. "The habitat could never sustain that degree of life. The basin only thrives as long as the resources aren't used up."

I nod. I watch the muscles in her neck move as she speaks.

"From an evolutionary perspective," Lisa continues, "the animals are drawn away so that they don't destroy what they have."

"And what about the ones that do stay?"

"Well," Lisa says, "I guess they just managed to outsmart evolution."

After the funeral, Lisa and I worked at being miserable, as though happiness might disrespect the dead.

One night, coming home late from school, I found Lisa on the sofa watching a sitcom. I sat down, and she moved in close, rested her head on my shoulder, an intimacy I had not known in weeks.

Something funny happened on the show, and without warning Lisa let out a laugh. The sound emerged sharp and loud and strangled at the end. She cupped a hand over her mouth. We watched the rest of the show just like that, refusing to laugh, Lisa keeping a hand near her face just in case.

It was six months before we made love. It wasn't planned, couldn't have been. To speak of sex would have made it impossible. Instead, having gone to bed early, unable to sleep, we held each other. I kissed Lisa on the forehead. Her body tensed and I apologized. "No," she said, taking my face in her hands. She kissed me hard on the lips, grabbed at me, tore at my T-shirt. In a few minutes it was all over. I hadn't removed my boxers.

"That was nice," she said.

"Yes," I said. I was bewildered, but Lisa seemed happy. That was what mattered. A few minutes later, from the bathroom, over the hum of the fan, the gush of the faucet, through the closed door, I heard Lisa sobbing.

"Did you enjoy the movie?" I ask once we're in bed. When it's quiet, we think about June. Most nights we fight to fill up the silence. Tonight, though, we have something to talk about.

"It was good, but hardly groundbreaking," Lisa says.

"Oh," I say. "I beg your pardon."

"No. It was fine. I only mean that the filmmakers made no new discoveries."

"Such as?"

"Well," she says, "take, for example, a documentary I saw last week. It had to do with the Nile and the animals that live there. Mostly, it was about hippopotamuses and crocodiles, how they share the river."

"They live together?"

"Sure," Lisa says. "It's the Nile. For the most part, it's no problem. Typically, the crocodiles leave the hippos alone. Nothing can take down a full-grown hippo. But, sometimes if a group of crocs is hungry enough, they'll attack one of the younger hippos."

I try to picture it, a crocodile wrestling a hippopotamus, the splashing, the waves, the water's red surface.

"But, here's the good part," Lisa says. She smiles. "What really got me was this footage they shot of a hippopotamus funeral."

"A funeral?"

"Well, sort of. Something that had never been caught on tape. See, this baby hippo had been mauled by crocodiles. It managed to pull itself onto a sandbar in the middle of the river. Then the other hippos surrounded the calf until the crocodiles swam away. After the calf died, the hippos held a kind of ceremony."

"And what did they do, these hippos?"

"They licked the baby."

"What do you mean 'licked the baby'?"

"I don't know how else to explain it," Lisa says. "The hippos made a circle around the dead baby and licked it. And they actually have these very long tongues. They must have licked every square inch of it, then they all lay down and rested their heads on the body. After a while, they stood up, walked back into the water, and swam away."

"That's wild," I say. "So, why do they do it?"

"Who knows? It's an entirely unexplored phenomenon. At the very least, it proves these particular animals have learned to mourn."

For a moment, neither of us speaks. We contemplate the complexity of nature, the mystery, the beauty of love manifested among hippos.

"That's fucked-up," I say. Lisa frowns. I have miscalculated. "I mean, it's weird, that's all. Sad hippos." But it's too late. The magic was gone as soon as I opened my mouth.

"It's not weird," she says. "It's beautiful. How can you not see that?"

"Lisa, I didn't see the show."

"But the idea! These animals, they lost one of their own, and they came together to grieve. Can't you see the beauty in that?"

"Honey, we're talking hippos, here. They don't *feel* anything. You taught me that, about animals and emotion, how they don't experience loss like we do."

"You're right," Lisa says. "They don't. And you know what else they don't do? They don't abandon their mates. And, get this, more than anything, instinctually, they know enough to care for their young."

And there it is.

I pull the chain on the bedside lamp. Lisa begins to cry. I move to the edge of the bed and squeeze my pillow to my ear to muffle the sound. But, when I close my eyes, I picture the hippos. I fall to sleep and they follow me into my dreams, chasing me with their big, pink tongues. I spend my night on the banks of the Nile, running from them, and the next morning I wake, shower, and eat breakfast, all the time unable to think of anything else.

I was the one who discovered June. It's why I don't sleep well at night, why morning sends me looking for the cradle that's no longer there.

At first, Lisa wouldn't let me disassemble the cradle. For weeks, it held only a pillow, a pacifier, and a yellow stuffed duck. One Sunday while she was at church, I took the thing apart, packed the pieces into a box, labeled the cardboard with black Magic Marker, and carried the box to the attic. When Lisa got home I was in bed. The morning had taken everything out of me. Lisa stepped into the bedroom, stopped, and for the longest time stood very still.

"What's wrong," I asked, knowing full well the thing she was missing.

"Nothing," she said.

As with everything else, it was easier to say nothing at all.

Wednesday night hurls us back into argument. Lisa comes in from gardening, one of her hobbies. Her hands are stained with Georgia red clay, but otherwise she's clean.

"I'm going to shower," she says.

"What for?" I ask.

"Group. We have to leave in less than an hour."

"We? What's this *we*? We had a deal, remember?"

We pull into the parking lot five minutes late. Lisa, who despises tardiness from both her students and herself, hurries toward the church doors.

I linger by the car. "I'll be there in a minute," I call across the lot. I look up and the night sky is an instant disappointment. From our yard, just outside of town, the night is black and the stars are bright. Here, though, electric light bounces off of everything, light commingling with light, the stars obscured by a hazy luminescence.

It will be my last night with Lisa. By morning, I decide, I will be gone.

Pam opens with the usual prayer, the one that concludes with our standard chant: "Lord, grant us peace. Let us rejoice in your glory. And give us strength, that we may rejoice in our suffering, for we know that suffering produces perseverance, perseverance character, and character the hope that springs eternal. Amen." I mouth the words but refuse to speak them.

Pam asks who would like to share and, immediately, Lisa raises her hand. I know that she is going to tell everyone about the hippos, and she does. By the end of the story everyone but me is crying, even the men.

Lisa shoots me a look that says *I told you so*. But she doesn't stop there. Next, she relates the hippos to her own grief, and someone goes for another box of tissues. Finally, she reminds the group that tomorrow marks the one-year anniversary of June's death.

Before I know what I'm doing, I stand. My chair tips, falls to the floor behind me.

"They're just hippos!" I bellow.

I have everyone's attention, but I don't know what to do with it. I'm seething, an animal myself, trapped in the circle. No one says a word.

"Don't you get it? You keep searching for reasons and meaning and signs, but there is no meaning. None of it means anything! Our kids are dead. We're not special. We just got fucked by chance, by bad luck. Everyone in this room just has really, really shitty luck."

I look at Lisa. She is pale, horrified.

"Why can't we get past this? I just want this to be over already."

Pam approaches me. "Richard," she says, "it's never over. We just keep going, and this is how. This is how we continue." She places a hand on my shoulder. "You're angry, but I promise you, it gets easier."

I can't explain what happens next, but here it is: I am laughing.

"Remember," Pam says, "God will not give you more than you can bear."

I laugh so hard I fall forward. My knees hit the floor, and I sit.

"Let's pray over him," Pam says, and suddenly I'm surrounded. My laughter is like a drawn-out roar. People speak, but the words don't reach me.

It is when I start feeling the hands all over me that everything stops seeming so funny. They come from every direction, patting me, stroking me, holding me. A hand touches my face and I know without looking that it is Lisa's. I miss most of what's said. The words are all tangled up. But the feeling of hands on my body stays with me, even after the hands are gone, long after I've left the church. And later still. That night, in bed, the feeling remains: the heat, the press of palms against my skin.

I fall right to sleep. It's not the same sleep as the last few hundred nights. Nodding off, I feel something holding me down, silent as summer rain. It's like leaving purgatory at last, being, at last, dead.

The next morning, I wake, look at the clock. It's nearly nine, impossible to make my escape now without causing a scene. I head downstairs, drawn by the smell of coffee. I pause on the bottom step, thinking about whether or not I should leave Lisa. But I cannot make up my mind.

Lisa stands at the window in the kitchen. She wears her bathrobe, a mug of coffee in one hand, the curve of her neck cradled in the other.

I go to the window. As I expected, there are deer on the lawn.

Our property is situated on an acre in the country, woods on one side, road on the other, our house and the lawn and Lisa's flower gardens in between. I've always taken a kind of maniacal delight in lawn care: the geometry of mowing, the chemistry of fertilizers, and so on. For years, the deer have come, drawn by the lush, green fescue. After June died, though, I let the grass go to shit. Now the lawn is pocked with brown spots and weedy throughout. Except for Lisa's well-groomed gardens, the yard is an embarrassment. Still, the deer come, two or three at a time, at daybreak or dusk. They eat around the dead places.

This morning, there are four of them, and it's nice. I can't remember the last time we stood at the window and watched the deer. It was before June died, I'm sure of that.

"Coffee?" Lisa says.

"Yes, please," I say.

She moves to the cupboard, the stove, returns with a second cup. I reach out and the mug is hot in my hand. I twist the mug around, hold it by the handle. Outside, the deer approach the house, coming closer than I've ever seen them come. Is the grass near the house so much better than the grass at the end of the yard?

"They must be hungry," Lisa says.

"Yes," I say.

"Richard?"

But the deer are advancing, and all of a sudden they're in Lisa's garden. One paws a tentative hoof at the mesh encircling a flower bed, then stretches its neck over the wire and nibbles at the head of a pansy.

Lisa throws open the window and leans out of the house. "Hey!" she screams. "Hey! Shoo! Get out of here! Out! Out!"

The deer lift their heads and their ears flick forward. For a moment they look like lawn ornaments, deer statues. Then, as one, they explode, scatter in every direction, run to the edge of our yard, and disappear into the thicket. Lisa falls back from the window ledge and slips to the floor. Sitting with her back to the wall, she looks up at me and her face is wet. I feel like I am meeting her eyes for the first time since the funeral, and I am scared and ashamed and full of hope.

"Lisa, I don't want to go." As soon as I say it, I know it is true. It would be the easiest thing in the world to walk out that door, but in the end it doesn't matter who's suffered most or what's been said.

There's a graphic organizer in mathematics called the Venn diagram. It's two circles, a pair of rings that run together, and the place where they intersect is called the union. For the last year, Lisa and I have traveled in circles, both of us charting our own paths around what's happened, each one pursuing an unending course. And only now have we met in the middle, in the quiet overlap, the space between.

I kneel beside Lisa and help her up. Holding each other, we stand very still and look out the window. We stand and we wait for what feels like days.

"Stay," she will say. I imagine it, try to summon the words into being.

When the invitation comes, it is as if there was never the need for a choice.

"Stay," she says, and I do.

ADAM STUMACHER

Wisconsin Institute for Creative Writing

THE NEON DESERT

I.

The highway coils through the hills, glossy as ribbon. Nathan is struck by the absence of ruts from passing tanks, bombed-out skeletons of vehicles, ditches gushing sewage. But of course, this is a settler road. On pavement this smooth, bulletproof buses can whoosh past, barreling toward the safety of fortified outposts. For the first time since crossing over into the West Bank three weeks ago, he finds himself on a clean stretch of road, and as his eyes follow the line of blacktop across the dusty landscape, he feels suddenly homesick.

Not that he has much to return home to at the moment, just an empty apartment with shades drawn, stale crumbs on the countertop, and vegetables rotting in the refrigerator, a stack of unpaid bills cascading over the edge of his desk, a to-do list tacked onto the bulletin board: file for unemployment, file for bankruptcy, file for divorce.

Still, this smooth road makes him ache with the memory of his early years with Julie. He remembers cruising along the interstate in the old Buick, squeaking the vinyl seats and laughing until tears streamed down their faces. But he can't let himself remember too much right now, so he is relieved to note the dust swirls of an approaching Israeli Jeep. Teenagers with live ammunition have a way of wiping out all other concerns, which is exactly why he needs to be in a war zone.

Namiko pulls out her notebook. "You handle this one," she says. "I'll hang back and document."

Nathan nods, glad to have somebody else making the decisions. Back at the human shield training in Bethlehem, he ended up paired with Namiko because the other new volunteers were a bunch of kids: young European couples giddy with idealism and Turkish coffee. The only other volunteers his age were those middle-aged anarchists from Newcastle, but by the second day it was clear he couldn't make out a word they were saying. At the end of the training, everybody was supposed to choose an affinity group, the people you would work with for the duration of your stay. Nathan felt like he was back in fifth grade again, the scrawny boy always picked last for kick ball. So in the end he was paired with Namiko, the woman in charge of the training. He was excited when he realized they would be together, not because she had already published three books about her experiences here (available only in the original Japanese), but because he had a bit of a thing for Asian women, and Namiko's sleek black hair and sly smile reminded him of his soon-to-be ex-wife. For the past few weeks, as they have traveled from village to refugee camp, Nathan has been gratified that everyone assumes Namiko is his girlfriend. But in fact she takes care to maintain a certain professional distance. He tells himself this is probably for the best.

As the sound grows louder, Nathan sees a shepherd in black-and-white checkered kufiyya hurrying to hide in a distant grove of olive trees, stringing sheep along the hills behind him. Then the vehicle rounds the corner, and Namiko groans. A moment later he sees why: the dark blue Jeep means border police—more of a challenge than your typical soldiers, scared eighteen-year-olds with M16s, and also the only officials in the West Bank with the authority to arrest foreigners. The Jeep skids to a standstill directly across from them.

Nathan's breath is shallow, and he feels like he's swallowed the sludge from the bottom of one of those miniature coffee cups. But he forces a brash cowboy grin onto his face and lengthens his stride. Nobody back home would have guessed it, but in the past couple weeks he has discovered he is a natural actor. Something about fear makes him come alive. Every time he approaches an army checkpoint, some external force seems to inhabit his body. Sometimes he tucks in his T-shirt and takes on a deliberate, almost professorial gait. Other times, such as now, his face opens into a toothy Texan grin and his vowels drawl. The role doesn't really matter, as long as the soldiers are thrown off balance.

"Howdy!" he shouts out as the Jeep's door opens. A machine gun muzzle trains onto him.

"How you folks doin' today?" he continues, taking it down a notch. "Anybody in there speak English?"

A helmeted face appears, but the gun stays pointed at his face.

"Why are you here?" The voice is high, thickly accented. "This is restricted area."

"Well, you see, we're medical volunteers. Just on our way into town."

The officer swings the door fully open and leaps out. Behind him, two curly haired teenagers are crammed into the backseat, rifles resting against their knees. One of them is holding what appears to be a Snickers bar.

"You are here with what group?" the officer asks.

"No group, pal. We're here on our lonesome."

"Who are you?" The officer veers his gun around to Namiko.

"So sorry no speak English," she says, as her pen scribbles furiously. Namiko is already on her second notebook since Nathan's arrival. For a moment, he imagines her back in her cramped Tokyo flat, sipping a gin and tonic as she transposes these notes into her next chapter.

The officer turns back to Nathan. "You know you should not be here."

He strides back to the Jeep and opens the driver's side door, snapping his fingers for the two-way radio. A muffled conversation in Hebrew ensues, and Nathan looks back out to the hillside.

The shepherd is still hidden in the olive trees, but he has allowed his sheep to wander and they now dot the slope. Nathan is glad the Jeep didn't pass by five minutes earlier. From what Namiko said, local villagers have to watch out when they cross the one-kilometer gap between the villages of Saalem and Beit Fureek because this means crossing the settler road. But people still walk back and forth to visit grandparents, attend weddings, or pick olive groves, which means if they're unlucky they vanish behind the walls of Hawarta military prison. Every once in a while a body is found on the road, torn up by machine gun rounds.

Settler roads don't present the same danger to foreigners, though. The worst they have to fear are some bruises on their faces at the deportation hearing. Of course back at the training, volunteers were warned that the soldiers have become more aggressive lately, and there were those stories from Rafah: a British photojournalist shot in the head, an American girl crushed by a bulldozer. But that was Gaza. In the West Bank, Americans are still more or less untouchable, Nathan heard. Just wave a navy blue passport in the air and nobody will shoot.

The officer says something quiet into his receiver, then hands the two-way back into the Jeep and looks around sharply.

"This is not your country. I see you people here, there are so many things you do not understand. For example, my brother. They killed him last year, in Beit Hanoun."

"I'm sorry, partner." Nathan shakes his head. "I wish we could all just go home."

The officer suddenly jams the barrel of his rifle toward Nathan's face. His left eyelid twitches for a long moment, and then his shoulders slump and he lowers the gun again. "You don't know our situation," he says. He hops back into the Jeep, and then leans his head out the open door. "You should leave the area before tonight. You don't want to be here, especially this night. Somebody might get hurt."

Then he slams the door and the Jeep disappears, spitting sand onto the pavement. When the dust clouds still, Namiko leads them to an olive grove, where they sip the last of their water and rest a moment, sheltered from the brutal sun. When they get up to continue on to the village of Beit Fureek, Nathan glances back to see the shepherd emerge from the trees and begin gathering together his flock, white splotches spread across the brown desert hills.

Until he began to oppose the government of Israel, Nathan never thought of himself as particularly Jewish. Of course, back in high school he was harassed for coming from just about the only Jewish family in southwestern New Hampshire. He can still remember one time in study hall when Ethan Cunningham dumped a handful of pennies behind him on his desk chair, how the coins clanged and scattered onto the floor when he stood up to sharpen a pencil, Ethan and the other football players in the back row chirping out "cheap cheap cheap" and sneezing "A *Jew*!" "A *Jew*!" "Gesundheit!"

But after moving out to California, he more or less forgot about his background. He took the Greyhound cross-country to pursue his dream of becoming a musician, and even though his career never developed beyond a brief stint at a piano bar on Lake Merritt and a few gigs in the Central Valley playing keyboard with an eighties cover band, he acquired enough of a taste for artichokes and tan lines that he stayed on and found work as a piano tuner. And so, the only time he's been inside a synagogue in the last decade was to tune a Bösendorfer at a congregation in the Berkeley hills. High holidays are now marked by his father calling up and chanting a prayer into his answering machine, then blowing the shofar. And although his grandmother's Yiddish occasionally returns to him behind the wheel ("Schlemiel! Watch where you're going!"), his wedding to Julie was distinctly pagan in flavor, the guests standing in a circle on a green hilltop up in Mendocino County, not a rabbi or a huppah in sight.

But all that changed one afternoon, the week after she finally moved out. She called up and said she wanted a day to come pick up the last of her boxes, some old books and photo albums. The sound of her clearing her throat over the phone overwhelmed him with rage and longing, but he forced his voice to sound casual: Yes, of course, tonight would be fine. I have plans anyway. And so, needing some excuse to get out of the house, he called up Raul and said he'd changed his mind: He would go with him to that Palestine presentation after all.

Everybody knew Raul represented the radical left fringe of the piano-tuning world. A longtime member of the group Bring a Piana to Havana, he'd been a participant in multiple tuning tours of Cuba. On one of those trips Nathan was talked into coming along with this crew of overweight, bespectacled warriors who wandered from back-alley clubs to crumbling concert halls, repairing some of the most neglected instruments on the planet. After work, the tuners would return to the clubs, where old musicians hunched over patched-together baby grands and beat out throbbing, feline syncopation behind the horn section. And for the first time ever, Nathan began to actually enjoy the work: the almost epic scale of these battles against creaky action, worn felt, rigid guide pin. One hand on the hammer, pulling slightly, the other hand striking the key. Pull, strike. Push, strike strike, until the perfect intervals began to shimmer. That was the first time he ever thought of tuning pianos as something noble, maybe even as a struggle against entropy itself.

Raul would confide, after a couple drinks, that he intentionally left a note sharp or flat on a Steinway up in the Piedmont hills, depending on the politics of the owner. This piano-technician gig was just a front to get into the parlors of the rich and powerful, he said, and when the revolution came he would make sure the theme song was perfectly pitched. He was always talking about some upcoming meeting or rally, but Nathan usually had an excuse handy. In theory he sympathized with the whole idea of revolution, but there was always some more pressing concern. That is, until the evening when he needed to get out of the apartment while his wife came back to gather the remnants of the previous five years, pack them up tight in cardboard sealed with layers of tape.

And so he found himself seated beside Raul in the front row of an auditorium. A woman with an explosion of curls stood up before the crowd and began to talk. Lights down, and the slides burst one after another onto the screen, like a string of firecrackers. In the darkness, Nathan discovered that he was crying for the first time in years. There was one slide with a cluster of street children waving into the camera, beaming and toothy, the collapsed remnants of a bombed-out building in the background, the one standing wall of the structure spray-painted with an enormous baby-blue Star of David. That night Nathan lay alone on the sheets, and for once he wasn't thinking about the empty space over on her side of the bed; he was pondering that blue star. This thing was being committed in his name. He lay awake until dawn, the thought reverberating through him like the clink of pennies onto linoleum.

II.

Hasan sits on the front step of his shop and rubs his chin, watching the two foreigners who somehow managed to beat the house odds, bluffing their way through the checkpoints, talking their way past the Jeeps, negotiating their way across the ditches and over the roadblocks, to find the one remaining store in the entire town of Beit Fureek. He shakes his head as they approach, noting how the man peers uncertainly around the alley and clutches his arms around himself, how the woman holds her head high, a black-and-white checkered kufiyya pulled around her shoulders. It has been months since Hasan last saw a foreigner, except for the actors on *Ally McBeal,* which he watched the other evening at his uncle's place over on the other side of the village.

"*Salaam aleichem.*" He raises his hand, motions them forward, smiling.

"*Wa aleichem salaam,*" says the woman. "Peace be with you." She gives Hasan a firm handshake and looks him straight in the eyes. The man stays silent and avoids Hasan's gaze.

He is surprised at a Chinese woman who can speak Arabic, but unsurprised at the handshake. A few times, when his uncle has been able to get a signal from that station in Tel Aviv, he has seen a show called *The Apprentice,* in which it always seems to be the women shaking hands to close the deal, smiling confidently at the cameras. Only lately his uncle mostly sticks to Al Jazeera, for the news.

"We need to buy some supplies," the woman says. "Are you open?"

"Please come in," he says. "Have some coffee." He wants to talk to them, to hear stories about the world outside this dinky little town he has been unable to leave since the curfews started two years ago. Maybe they have news of his friends in Nablus. Also, so few of his customers have shekels these days, and of course these two won't have that problem. So he decides to take a bit of a gamble himself; today he will break curfew and open the shop.

They make their way through his store, and Hasan tries to imagine how it must look to them: the dusty light from a single bulb over the counter, the half-empty shelves propped up on slabs of broken concrete, the few milk bottles neatly aligned in the refrigerator case. They will not understand how lucky he is, how much negotiation and sacrifice it has taken for him to keep his father's store open since the old man's death. In the back room, he pulls out two stools and asks them to sit, then walks over to the sink and fills the coffeemaker, careful not to spill any water. He stirs in the grounds, making a mental note that he is getting low, and lights the stove.

"Thank you for your hospitality," the woman says.

"It is nothing." Hasan lowers the flame, concentrating. "We still need to live." He watches the grounds slowly boil up, waiting for that fragile moment when they will flip over and the coffee will be ready.

He hands each of them a small cup and saucer, and the man nods silent thanks, holding the miniature handle awkwardly in his large hands. He still hasn't said a word, but Hasan decides he must be an Arab with that curly black hair.

"What country do you come from?" he asks.

"He only speaks English," the woman answers.

"He is not an Arab?"

"No, he is Jewish."

Hasan looks closely at the man. The only Jews he has ever seen up close are soldiers, and of course the ones he sees on his uncle's television set. His favorite Jew is that gangster from *The Godfather,* which seems to be playing on the Tel Aviv station every time they can catch the signal. The one in the lime green suits who owns half of Las Vegas, the dreamer who imagined a dazzling strip of lights in the desert. Hasan has always respected this Jew for his guts, and he sometimes practices his English by repeating the lines: *I'm Moe Green! I made my bones when you were going out with cheerleaders!* He doesn't understand what all the words mean, but there is something satisfying in the rhythm. This man is no Moe Green, though. He hasn't even said a word.

"He just arrived here from America," the woman says, switching to English.

"Good. A good country." Hasan's mouth feels awkward with the foreign words, as though trying to hold a grape between his teeth without breaking the skin. But he needs the practice. "New York. Las Vegas." He sighs, imagining sleek cars below neon signs so bright they blot out the moon.

Once, over at his uncle's place last year, Hasan saw another old movie with the American actor Paul Newman playing a pool hustler, and afterward he spent hours perfecting that cool, self-contained expression in the mirror. That is the face he tries to make now as he makes his way to the door, pauses to listen for the rumble of tanks. But all he hears is the drone of conversation from the upstairs apartments, so he slides up the bullet-scarred storm shutters and unlocks the door.

"What do you want to buy?"

"Some rice. Milk. Maybe a leg of lamb," the woman answers. She looks around the empty shelves. "Will that be possible?"

"Of course, we can get whatever you need."

Hasan likes it when the foreigners come to Beit Fureek because it makes him feel his town still matters, even if there isn't enough water here for them to stay. His friends from Nablus told him how the foreigners stay only with the rich families, how they eat a lot and use water to shower every day. But when they walk past, everyone still shouts and waves and offers coffee, because they know when foreigners ride on ambulances, the soldiers will let them through the checkpoints. When a tank parks beside a chicken coop at the edge of the camp, the young boy who goes to gather eggs will be allowed to approach only if a foreigner walks with him. And sometimes foreigners can arrange a student visa for your cousin. Also, foreigners carry shekels and they can afford meat.

It has been over a year since Hasan last tasted lamb himself, and of course his shop doesn't have any. Still, he knows the right people to call. And unlike many in his village, he has managed to keep his phone working, the same way he has managed to keep his gas connected, to stay informed about when a water truck has been let through the checkpoints, to keep the shop open for business. A simple matter of playing the odds. For example, he arranges to get several liters of Maccabee beer smuggled through each week, and he keeps them cold in the back of a refrigerator, pulling them out whenever a Jeep stops out front for an inspection. After all, the soldiers are just teenage boys inside those uniforms, and boys are always thirsty. After a couple bottles, they laugh and slap him on the shoulder on their way back to their Jeep, and he hardens a grin onto his face until the engine thunders around the corner.

Like a smart gambler, Hasan always manages to get by. Before the intifada, he used to deal blackjack at the Oasis Casino in Jericho, laughing politely as the same Jordanian businessmen told the same jokes night after night. Eventually he learned to spot the gamblers who approached the table with a system for calculating odds. None of them ever succeeded, but that only meant their math was sloppy. Hasan, on the other hand, was always meticulous; in university, he kept his calculations in strict formation, like a battalion. After a few months dealing blackjack at the Oasis, he was able to see an outline of the game's probabilities shimmering before him. Of course the Jericho casinos closed long ago, but not before Hasan learned how to outfox the house. Not before he figured out his destiny: to play the velvet tables in Las Vegas, where every woman has long legs and every drink chimes with clean ice, where you get a crisp new deck of cards for every hand.

As he hangs up the phone, Hasan sees the man holding open the refrigerator door, sticking his head inside, turning his face side to side to cool his sweat. He hesitates, then decides not to say anything about the cost of electricity. Better just to add the extra overhead on to the price of the lamb.

"The things you want, they are coming," he says.

"A working phone," says the woman. "You must have friends in the right places." She walks over to the refrigerator and gently pulls the man by the arm, closing the door.

The man comes over to Hasan and speaks for the first time. "You have a nice shop," he says.

"Before, yes. Now, no." English makes Hasan's jaw hurt, but he needs to practice. "When before—when my father—"

He is almost relieved to hear the soft clinking sound. At first only the glass doors of the refrigerator begin to shake, then the cans begin rattling against each other on the shelves. As the floor begins to quake beneath them, he runs to the door and slams it shut.

"The light!" he says, but the woman has already switched it off.

The three of them squat below the counter as the tanks pass in the street, loudspeakers blaring Britney Spears, interrupted by the soldiers shouting out insults in Arabic. *Your mother is a dog.* As the roar of the tank fades, Hasan hears M16 rounds, roughly three-quarters of a kilometer away judging from the sound. Then silence. After a couple minutes, he stands up and switches the light back on.

"No problem," he says. "This is normal." He looks calmly back out into the street, calculating the next hand.

Of course the first customer to enter the shop is Abu Faruq. The old man never buys anything except cigarettes, but he seems to have a nose for when the store will open. Hasan has always figured Abu Faruq comes to the shop because he's lonely. His wife and grandchildren live in Ramallah; he was in Beit Fureek for his sister's wedding when the curfews started and he hasn't been able to get back through the checkpoints to see his family for almost two years now. *"Salaam aleichem,"* the old man says, nodding at the foreigners as though completely unsurprised to find them here. He stations himself on a plastic stool by the counter, and lights up a cigarette. Each time the door jangles open, he looks up unsmiling from under his kufiyya and gives a nod in greeting. Everyone comes over to shake his hand before going about their shopping.

The next customer is Imm al-Abd from across the street. She strolls over to the bin of fava beans and pours half a scoop into a bag she has brought with her. Back before the intifada, she was a professor of linguistics at the university in Nablus. The colleges may be shut down now, but her education is still evident in the way she thoroughly examines each can on the shelf for dents. As she picks up a can of condensed milk and puts it in her bag, Hasan remembers that night during the olive harvest a few months ago, when her son didn't come home. How the whole village broke curfew to spend the night out looking for him. Then just before dawn, somebody found him over by It Mar settlement. Nobody wanted to tell Imm al-Abd how the body had been mutilated, but she must have heard because she hasn't spoken a single word since that night.

Now a group of lanky teenagers comes in laughing, racing each other to the freezer to stare with longing at the few remaining ice-cream bars. A small boy lags behind, standing outside of the group and looking glassy-eyed at the wall of their shoulders. Hasan recognizes him as Mahmoud from the other side of the village. The one whose older brother was a *marteer*, his face surrounded by paintings of machine guns and heavenly gates on posters plastered around the camp after he blew himself up on a bus last year, killing three. Hasan remembers him coming into the shop the week before he did it, a skinny fourteen-year-old boy standing rigid in the aisles for over an hour, staring at empty shelves, buying nothing. Now his little brother, Mahmoud, steps forward to get a better view of the ice cream, and one of the bigger boys jabs him hard with an elbow and he falls to the floor.

Before Hasan can get around the counter, the foreign woman is already there, standing over the small boy and reaching out to pull him onto his feet. Mahmoud's jaw is slack as he looks up at her, and his hand falls stiff down to his side. As soon as the other boys realize she is a foreign woman, they begin to crowd around her, excited.

"Hello hello I love you China girl what's your name?"

The boys press forward, one of them putting a hand on her shoulder while another makes kissing sounds. She holds herself still and looks calmly into their eyes.

"Shame!" Hasan shouts. "Leave her and go home! I will speak to your fathers!"

Immediately they quiet down and slink one at a time out the door, except for Mahmoud, who stops at the end of the aisle and turns to look back at the Chinese woman. She is standing erect with her arms crossed, and she shakes her head as her eyes follow the boys out into the street.

"I am sorry," Hasan says. "Those boys are young."

"It's okay," she smiles. "This is not the first time."

"Before, this kind of thing never happened here. In my country we should never treat a woman this way."

"No, really it's okay." She reaches out to touch his arm, and for a moment Hasan catches some strange spice in the aroma of her sweat. But then she stops suddenly and drops her hand, looking down at the floor. "Thank you for your help."

Hasan nods and walks back to the counter. Since the curfews started, the boys in Beit Fureek have changed. They have nothing to look forward to, nothing to do every day except stay inside watching the news, listening to their parents talk about the old days. So now more and more the boys are out running in the streets or studying with the imams, and nobody knows what they will do anymore. He hears his customers complain how their sons disappear for days at a time, come back silent or else talking too much, so arrogant they try to tell their own fathers how to be good Muslims. And then sometimes the boys don't come back at all.

Meanwhile the door keeps swinging open, and the shop fills with furtive laughter. Hasan offers cigarettes to all the men, smoking his own down to the filter as he writes each purchase in his ledger. After almost two years of curfew, nobody in Beit Fureek has a job anymore and very few people have shekels, so everything functions on credit. People in the village take what they need to survive, and Hasan keeps meticulous records. But of course now he has no cash to pay the farmer Abu Munir for the eggs the old man delivers whenever he can sneak them across the settler road. So the farmer keeps a ledger as well. And if Abu Munir needs to repair his work boots, Fawaz the cobbler gives him credit. All they can do is trade promises, like stacks of brightly colored chips in a casino where no one ever cashes out.

"You are a good man," the woman says. She stands over to his left, watching him work.

"It is nothing," Hasan says. He shakes his head, then looks back down at the books. What he does, what everybody does, has nothing to do with good.

III.

For weeks, Nathan has been waking up from the same dream: It starts with him naked, stuck deep inside a monstrous piano. He frantically tries to remove the instrument's action, to pull the mechanism out into the light. But the frame is stuck, and his hands are slick with sweat as he jiggles it from side to side, hoping to pry it loose. Suddenly Julie's hands are on the keyboard, and she is playing a Chopin prelude, crushing him in layer upon layer of chords. The hammers begin to rise and fall, increasing in speed and violence until they are bashing into the lid, removing chunks of wood. Blood begins pouring out of the instrument, and he holds the shattered wood against his chest until he realizes he is holding the body of a boy who looks up at him with a sideways grin. The boy begins to hum counterpoint to the melody, his voice growing higher and higher in pitch and repeating a theme that becomes louder and more insistent, until Nathan realizes it is the alarm and opens his eyes.

He finds himself wondering, not for the first time, if he shouldn't move into a new line of work. He has begun to see the world as an instrument of dense hardwood and heavy alloy, pulled into a state of constant tension, and himself as the only person capable of getting the damn thing into equal temperament. But no matter how he coaxes the pin, the strings will never quite render. A waver remains in this octave, a twang in that unison. So he has taken to constant fiddling and puttering, an endless effort to fix everybody else's problems. He might let his own bills pile up unopened on his desk, but he keeps busy repairing the people around him like so many busted D-strings.

This tendency used to drive Julie insane, and even though he knew it was pushing her away he couldn't help himself: He needed to tell her the right way to cut a grapefruit, the right tone to use when talking to her mother on the phone, the right anecdotes to tell when trying to impress her boss. The more he talked, the less she listened. Not that she had ever paid much attention to begin with; she couldn't tell a Steinway from a Hamilton if her life depended on it, never seemed to understand music. So by the end they just stopped talking. And they had been such good conversationalists in the beginning. They were that noisy couple next table over in the diner, interrupting each other's stories with laughter that sprayed root beer across the booth. Over the years, their voices quieted down, and by the end they hummed absently as they read different sections of the newspaper and passed the sugar across the table without looking up. If their fingertips accidentally brushed together, Julie shivered as if her body were fighting venom. Maybe if he had been in a different line of work, Nathan thought, maybe if he had developed a different set of habits, things might have worked out.

On the other hand, the habits of a piano technician are well suited to survival here in the West Bank. Nathan figures this place is like a beautiful old instrument: featherlight touchweight and rich sound quality, the whole contraption held together by thirty tons of pressure across rusty strings. All those years of manipulating the tuning crank have given him the patience to settle in for these more involved jobs, and patience is perhaps the most important quality in a human shield. Because he is finding life in a war zone to consist for the most part of sitting and waiting. The most common danger here seems to be boredom.

And while you wait there are the cigarettes, the countless cups of coffee, the heaping platters of food. Resources may be scarce, but people always somehow manage to fill the table for guests. In fact, as Nathan picks his way between villages, he somehow finds himself putting on weight. So, after an old man in a kufiyya walks into the shop in Beit Fureek holding his granddaughter by the hand, and as Namiko explains that this is the mayor of the village and he wants to talk to them, Nathan smiles because he is hungry, and he knows they will soon be sitting down to a feast. Sure enough, the shopkeeper disappears into the back for a time and then emerges with plates of fresh figs and grapes and flatbread, bowls of olives, creamy hummus, savory mashed fuul.

The mayor settles down at the table across from the foreigners while the shopkeeper returns to his station behind the counter, chatting with the customers as they browse the barren shelves. The mayor pats his granddaughter on the head and talks for a while in Arabic while Nathan smiles, feigning understanding. Then Namiko turns to him.

"He said his granddaughter was crying the whole time the tanks were here. Loud noises sometimes make her scream."

Nathan bites into a fig, pretending not to notice the shopkeeper watching him over by the counter. The mayor begins speaking rapidly in Arabic, and Namiko's pen scratches along the page, while Nathan tries to appear engaged without calling too much attention to himself. To pass the time, he tries making friends with the girl, but she just grips her grandfather's knee and stares vacantly out the door at the fading sunlight.

Nathan finishes his coffee, unsure where to put down the empty cup on the crowded table, so he places it discreetly on the ground under his plastic chair. He can loop a faulty string around the hitch pin, but as he maneuvers these miniature dishes his hands feel clunky as catcher's mitts. As he straightens back up, he catches the grand-daughter looking at him. He decides he will find some way to make her smile.

"He says they're almost out of water." Namiko says. "The soldiers have been stopping the tankers at the checkpoints on the way to Nablus." She shakes her head. "The farmers have to kill their live-stock because there isn't enough water to keep them alive."

Then the mayor is talking again, so Nathan nods vaguely, reaching for a grape. Over by the counter he sees a group of customers gather-ing together, laughing quietly, and he decides they are not talking about him. He has a plan: He will play peekaboo with the little girl, a strategy that never fails to get at least a giggle. So he ducks his head below the tabletop, then slowly peers over the edge at her. But her eyes seem to be focused six inches behind him, and her face is slack.

The mayor glances over and shakes his head. "She does not play," he says. Then he swivels back to Namiko and starts speaking in Ara-bic again, gesturing toward the door. Nathan notices he has barely touched the food on the table in front of him.

"Last night the tanks were here," Namiko translates. "The loud-speakers said all men between fifteen and fifty had an hour to meet at the school. Any male who stayed inside would be shot."

Nathan meets her eyes for a long moment, but her face is the same professional mask as ever. "I think we should stay in Beit Fureek tonight," she says. "The soldiers are up to something, but maybe they won't come if foreigners are here."

Nathan nods, glad as ever to have somebody else making the deci-sions. She puts down the pen and turns back around and says some-thing in Arabic. The mayor remains silent for a time, sipping his coffee.

Nathan is determined to make this little girl smile. He pulls a fig off the platter and sits back, turning it deliberately over in his hand, one final adjustment to the tuning crank. Then he bites into the fruit and opens his mouth wide, his teeth sheathed in the purple skin, eyes rolling. He looks over at the girl and laughs, shaking his head side to side. And while she doesn't exactly grin, for a moment the corners of her eyes seem to crinkle, slightly.

The mayor puts down his cup and smiles, cobwebbing wrinkles around his own eyes. "Please to stay in my home tonight," he says in English. "You are welcome."

Then the voices over by the counter grow suddenly loud, and Nathan sees a middle-aged man standing in the center of the group, smiling and passing something around. The man makes huge gestures toward the ceiling, and everyone reaches out to shake his hand, and then the group shouts and moves toward the back. When the man gets closer, Nathan sees he is missing several teeth in his wide grin, and that he has been passing around sticks of Juicy Fruit. The man hands a stick of gum to the mayor, and then one to each of the foreigners.

"Today I am a grandfather!" he says in English.

But at that moment the refrigerator doors begin to rattle faintly once again, and he lets the pack drop to the floor. Then someone shuts off the light, and the shop grows silent as the tanks rumble closer.

IV.

The echoes of cracking pavement shiver through the air, and everyone crouches down below the shelves. However many times he hears it, Hasan has never quite gotten used to the way the noise of tanks vibrates deep in the chest. But, like everyone else in the village, he has become expert in interpreting these sounds.

"At least two Bradleys," he whispers. "Maybe three."

"And that higher pitch?" Abu Ibrahim, the mayor, puts his cigarette out on the floor. "Must be an APC."

"They won't be passing here again tonight. *Insh'allah.*" Hasan looks at all the bodies crouched on his floor.

He knows the odds are against the soldiers returning to the same neighborhood twice in such a short period, but of course there is no certainty, however straight you keep those columns of numbers. Opening shop was a calculated risk, like splitting a pair in backgammon, but without risk nothing moves forward.

"You can't just leave those two pieces so far back," his father once told him, placing a hand on his shoulder as he looked at the board. "Sometimes you have to leave yourself open or you'll never gain position." Hasan remembers walking home to the shop after school and seeing his father and the neighborhood old-timers drinking coffee and crowding the tables out in the open street, laughing and gesturing up to the mountains, like men who would never dream of huddling down on the floor. To this day, when Hasan thinks through probabilities he sees the shadows of pieces on a backgammon board, he smells cardamom mixed with coffee grounds, he feels the pressure of his father's hand on his shoulder. "Wait," his father would say. "Examine the whole board before you move."

Now the two foreigners are making their way over toward where Hasan and Abu Ibrahim are squatting behind the counter. The woman is in front, her face pale in the light coming in from the streetlamp, and Hasan can just make out the man wheezing softly in the background.

"If they come, let us talk to them," the woman says. "They won't shoot if they know foreigners are here."

"No. They will pass by." Hasan shakes his head. "This is only normal."

"We want to help," the man says in English. "This is why we are here."

As Hasan is forming his mouth into the awkward shapes of English once again, he notices the roar of the tanks has grown louder, and the rumble tells him the vehicles are approaching the mouth of his alley. He looks over at Abu Ibrahim, but the mayor's eyes are closed, his granddaughter clutched tight to his chest. Then the sound grinds even closer, and Hasan knows the tanks are in front of the shop. He is distinctly conscious of himself not breathing, aware that nobody in the entire shop is allowing air to escape. Then the engines go silent.

"This is an illegal gathering," the loudspeaker booms. "You are in violation of curfew."

Then Hasan hears the quick snap of rifle fire, and three bullets thud into the front of the building, one of them breaking the front window.

The strings of dried garlic hanging across the aisle swing back and forth, and Hasan finds himself thinking back to the day he came home from school and there was no clatter of dice or conversation in the street. The shutters were drawn, and only his mother sat behind the counter, holding her head in her hands. She didn't answer when he asked where baba was. She only leaned against the countertop with her shoulders shaking, which is exactly what Hasan will not let himself do right now.

"Come out with hands over your head and your ID card out."

A bright glare shines in through the front windows, and the customers in the aisles cringe, faces on the floor. Then Hasan sees a shape moving to his left, and it is the foreign woman standing. She begins making her way, slowly and calmly, toward the door. Hasan nods and stands, and all around him the other customers start standing as well. Everybody begins slowly filing outside, holding aloft bags of groceries and orange identification cards. Hasan takes a final look around his shop, making a mental note to restock the milk if he can get word to Abu Munir. Then he pulls out his card and joins the others walking toward the door, toward the loudspeaker and the gleaming spotlight.

Just outside the door, the crowd has stopped. Desert stars hang thick above them and a cool breeze crosses Hasan's face as he stands blinking into the light.

"Put down the bags and hold both hands up!"

Hasan reminds himself those soldiers are just teenage boys, and he can hear from the voice on the loudspeaker how scared they are. The thing to do now is to stay very calm and very quiet and to follow every instruction.

But the foreign man seems to have lost his mind, walking to the front of the group and waving something blue in the air. "Don't shoot. I'm an American."

Then Hasan sees a movement off to one side. It is Imm al-Abd, his neighbor from across the street, the one who has not spoken since her boy's funeral. She reaches into her shopping bag, calmly pulling out that flawless, undented can of condensed milk and turning it over in her hand. The foreign woman makes a noise in her throat and reaches toward Imm al-Abd.

"Hands over your head! Put both hands where we can see them!"

Imm al-Abd's face has the same look of concentration as when she eyes the shelves, measuring the fava beans. It's the same look she had at her son's funeral, when she didn't cry, didn't even make a noise. She pushes aside the foreign woman's outstretched arm and hurls the can straight at the spotlight. Then there is only the sound of shattering glass, and the light goes out.

Dealing blackjack back at the Oasis, Hasan reached a point of precision in his calculations where he could clearly picture the face of the next card before it was turned over. And something like this happens now, so he knows to jump to one side, to throw his body to the ground and cover his head with his hands. He is dimly aware of other people diving down as well, the foreign woman off to one side, to the other, Abu Ibrahim covering his granddaughter with his body.

"Wait," the foreign man says. "They're only shopping."

Hasan buries his face in the dirt, trying to remember the number of rounds in each clip.

Morning comes over Beit Fureek, not so much sunrise as a vague lift in the gray overhead. Hasan leans back against the doorway, looking down at the crushed glass, scattered spices, and cracked bottles that used to be his father's shop.

Very high probability the soldiers will be back soon, this time with the bulldozers, and no quantity of Maccabee beer bottles will make things different this time. One of the foreigners was shot, so they will be thorough. Hasan can still see the body shivering on the stretcher as they pulled the foreign man into an ambulance, that Chinese woman sitting in the back of a Jeep holding her head in her hand-cuffed hands. He wished he could say something to her then, but of course he could not approach.

The soldiers will be here soon, before the reporters can make it through the checkpoints. So Hasan needs to leave. Maybe he can stay with his uncle on the other side of the village, which at least will give him a chance to catch up on *The Apprentice* and practice his English with old movie lines: *Tonight the Corleone family settles all accounts.* Of course, part of him wants to stay at his father's store to the very end, to hold on just a little longer to the smell of dried dates, the half-recalled weight of a hand on his shoulder. But only the most disciplined gamblers are able to walk away from the table after losing a hand to the house, and Hasan has always been one of those players—

the smart ones, the ones who always hold a little something back and bide their time before returning, head held high, to lay twenty-one down on the tabletop. So the bulldozers can have his shop; he knows it is only a matter of time before he builds it back.

For just a moment, though, he squats down in the wreckage and closes his eyes. He will allow himself one final cruise down the Vegas strip in that red Mustang, the neon signs flashing on his face. Magic names swirl past him: Caesars Palace, Riviera, Stardust, Mandalay Bay. He chooses the biggest, brightest entrance he can find and swings his car under the awning, tossing his keys to the valet. Then he glides in through the front door and makes his way over to the tables, where the dealer nods at him through the ching of slot machines and the rumble of roulette. All the women have long legs and all the tumblers chime with clean ice, and everything slows down for a moment as Hasan shakes the dice, smiling as he listens to them rattle together in his cupped hands. Then he lets them fly.

STEFAN McKINSTRAY

New Mexico State University

No One Here
Says What They Mean

Joe leaned his bike against the wooden rail of the porch and went around the corner of the log building of Jedediah's House of Sourdough. It was early, the dew on the grass fragrant, wetting the bottoms of his pant legs and the leather moccasins he wore. Most of the businesses lining the street were still closed. Birds rioted in the trees, their morning songs blasting from the foliage lining Broad Street. He wore a pale blue T-shirt, the material fraying at the sleeves, the bellicose image of Uncle Sam glaring across the front, jabbing a menacing finger, the letters F_CK in bold blocks above his red, white, and blue top hat, and written below, THE ONLY THING MISSING IS U. At the foot of the steps Joe picked up the newspaper. He shook water from it, holding the end of the plastic bag it came wrapped in as if dangling a small animal by the tail.

"Morning," said Emily Saulsberry, wiping one of the bakery's wooden tables with a rag. She stood barely above five feet, and was pretty, in a round, healthy glad-faced sort of way. She'd lived in Pinnacle along with her husband, Remy, for almost two years now, since they finished graduate school in North Carolina and moved to Pinnacle to start the bakery. Her hair was long, brown, with light streaks of blond. She wore it pulled back in a way that highlighted her oval face. She dressed in cutoffs, a flowered blouse rolled up to her elbows, and blue canvas tennis shoes with no socks. A wide, copper-studded leather band around her left wrist was her only jewelry. Neither she nor Remy wore wedding bands, but instead on the fourth fingers of their left hands, each had a simple tattoo with both their names entwined in a circle.

"Morning, Emily." Joe loved this hour of the day. No customers, the smell of baking bread permeating everything, the strong scent of brewing coffee and cinnamon rolls just out of the oven. Music played from speakers set high in the corners of the little dining area at the front of the bakery. He recognized the song, though he couldn't recall the name of the singer. The singer had a funny name. He liked the song. Something about a lonely man threatening sundown that he'd knock the hell out of it if he caught it creeping around his back stairs. He waved the paper at Emily and walked over to the counter and laid it next to the cash register.

"Newspaper," he said.

"Why's she insist on reading that?" Emily replied looking up from the table. She blew a strand of hair from her face. "Tell her, Joe. She wants to know *why.*" She moved from the table she'd finished cleaning to the next. "Poorly written articles, mean-spirited and overly religious conservative editorial bias. Nothing but livestock reports and articles about vandals defecating in public. It is *not* a good newspaper." Emily went on making slow circles over the table. "She dislikes it, *really* dislikes it, yet she reads it front to back, every word. Tell her why." Joe got a kick out of the way she referred to herself in the third person.

He went around the counter to the coffeepot and took a cup down, poured in brown sugar and nearly a third of a cup of milk, before adding coffee and mixing it with a spoon. "He doesn't know," Joe answered blowing on his coffee. He couldn't pinpoint the exact day when he'd begun answering her in the third person.

"She must be an idiot then," Emily said finally. She moved to the window, the rag draped over her shoulder, and raised the bamboo shade, letting in thick ropes of sunlight. Joe discreetly shook a handful of NoDoz into his hand and popped them quickly into his mouth, washing them down with sips of coffee.

"Remy baking?" he asked.

"Oh, he's baking."

"You need anything?"

"Ketchup and moose-turd," she replied. "Butter, creamer, top the sugar bowls, clean towels in the pooper."

"I'm on it."

"Finish your coffee, Joe McKuhn, one thing every fifteen-year-old needs is copious amounts of sugar and caffeine in the morning."

"My dad won't let me touch the stuff."

"Whatever happens at Jedediah's, *stays* at Jedediah's," she replied in mock seriousness.

"Hey, Remy," Joe said a moment later, stepping out the back door of the kitchen and sitting down on the steps next to Emily's husband.

"Little big man," Remy said. Remy Sullivan was twenty-nine and long-boned with a thick shock of black hair. A joint dangled between his bearded lips, which appeared supernaturally red and small in the midst of his dark beard. The smell of marijuana was sweet and thick in the morning air.

"You baking?"

"I am baked, and I am baking." Remy took the joint from his lips and held it out for Joe. Joe looked for Emily over his shoulder. "I almost killed myself yesterday," Joe said taking a drag. "Spaced out. Way, *way* out. Things were not as they appeared." If his dad found out he smoked pot he'd ground him for life. He reminded himself he didn't care; reminded himself to *keep* reminding himself of that until the knowledge was automatic. New things were happening, the world was different now. His mom had changed the shape of the world when she'd removed herself from it. Remy was speaking. Joe put the thought of her—wherever she was now—out of his mind. "You must let your unconscious *mind* take over, Grasshopper. You must meet the grass as the grass meets wind . . ." This was what Remy did. Emily referred to herself in the third person and her husband got stoned and spoke like the narrator in *Kung Fu*. "Grass bends in the face of wind," Remy said. "It does not meet it head-on. When Wind blows, Grass *bends*." Now it was Remy's turn to look over his shoulder. "You should be writing this down," he said. "This kind of wisdom only presents itself in bus stations."

From the radio, Van Morrison gave way to Herb Alpert and the Tijuana Brass white-grooving their way into "A Taste of Honey."

"What was that last thing?" Joe asked.

"When? Just now?"

"Yeah, I think so."

They looked at each other and laughed. "Something about the weather, maybe. You better give that back," Remy said holding out his fingers for the doobie. He wore a pair of blue jeans patched so many times that seven or eight different textures of material overlapped where he'd mended them. Remy was rail thin, the muscles long and ropelike on his arms and legs. He and Emily had an old green Volvo, but most days they rode their bikes into town from their little house in Pylson Grove, five miles southwest of Pinnacle.

Joe said, "My unconscious mind finds it difficult counting out correct change."

"You see?" Remy said. "Then you were listening."

They sat facing a small wooded lot. Emily and Remy were hoeing the ground in order to start an organic vegetable garden for the bakery. Next to the lot, a small stone footbridge spanned a barely existent creek that ran into a metal drainpipe flowing beneath DeLoney Street to the west. The trickle ran into a bigger creek called Flat Creek, and Flat Creek eventually ran into the Snake River; the Snake sidewinding its way, finally, to the ocean. There was a saying his mom had, he remembered: *Does the ocean become the drop, or the drop the ocean?* He liked that, enjoyed thinking that one day the water running through his hometown would pour more than a thousand miles to California and the Pacific. It tied things together, connected Pinnacle to a place he didn't need to *see* in order to know it was out there.

They sat, each absorbed in his own thoughts. He wondered if she'd gone back to California. Thought probably she had. They passed the doobie; Remy called it "kicking the gong around." After a while Remy said, "You're lucky to have been born here, man. I love this place."

Through the trees, thin black shadows curved along the ground as the light brightened. "I don't feel all that lucky about it," Joe replied. "I've lived here my whole life."

"'San Diego Serenade,'" Remy said. He sang something Joe didn't recognize and the sound surprised him. The tune Remy sang was slow and sad, but his voice was nice:

Never saw my hometown until I stayed away too long.
Never heard the melody, until I needed the song.

A long moment went by after Remy stopped. Joe listened to the sound of Remy's breathing, the sound of his own breath mixed in. The shadows traced along the ground. His body vibrated, like a tree with a nest of bees buzzing inside the trunk.

"Should we get on with it?" Remy suggested finally.

Joe got up, held his hand out. "You're the boss," he said.

"Feel lucky," Remy said, letting Joe help him up. "It's free."

For the rest of the morning Cammy Higgins, the high-school girl hired to help out behind the counter and serve as a second waitress, worked alongside Joe and Emily out front. Joe bussed tables, made sure the women had everything they needed, while also assisting Remy in the kitchen. Joe lost himself in the repetition, the sounds of work: small tinklings of silverware against coffee cups, Remy's singing along with the radio offset by the sound of oven doors closing and refrigerator doors opening; the little dings of the old-fashioned cash register as Emily or Cammy rang up customers; and the louder sounding jangle of the bell on the door as people entered and left Jedediah's. Pot helped him focus on each movement of his body, while the NoDoz juiced him full of a frenetic energy he felt throughout his entire body, but in his rib cage especially—a sort of winged sensation, a lifting.

After the morning rush was over, Joe readied for his afternoon deliveries. He secured the saddlebags to the harness over the back tire of his bike. Next, he fastened the breadbasket to the clips on his handlebars. In it he put items like rolls or homemade sandwiches, but it was large enough for cakes and pies, too. Emily prepared a change bag while Joe made his delivery list, the best tippers at the top.

"You know," she said handing him the bag, "you keep taking breaks with Remy out back . . ." She didn't finish, but made a face Joe knew completed her thought.

"I'm okay," he said, stuffing the bag in his hip pocket. The grin on his face felt goofy, lopsided. "My mental clarity," he said, "is razor sharp."

"You're spending far too much time with my husband," Emily replied. "*He* imagines his mental clarity is razor sharp. Sadly, he is mistaken in this."

"I live in Pinnacle, Wyoming. What could possibly happen?"

"*Everything* can happen," she replied. "Hit Mrs. Hanson first, okay? You know what a blank-in-the-blank she is. And be careful in town. There's more tourists through here every day. And don't cruise through stop signs for goodness' sake, this isn't California. Emily worries. Please do not make her worry."

"She doesn't need to," Joe said. "Her friend is like grass. He *bends.*"

"Just don't break him."

He was glad to be back on the bike, the morning warming. He worked fast—the NoDoz helped that—wanting to get everything to their customers on time. He knew the streets by heart, felt his bike was leading *him* most of the time. On-time delivery reflected well on the bakery. He was on his way back a few hours later, his deliveries finished, when he passed a beaten-up little red house. A white truck was parked in the middle of the street in front of it, the driver's side door hanging open as if daring another car to come along and take it off. On the door was stenciled HOPKUIN'S HOSPITAL SUPPLIES. The truck had large side panels on both sides of the bed and stacked in the middle were large cylindrical tanks, like the kind seen on the backs of deep-sea divers from old movies, only bigger. The tanks were painted green and white. A man rolled two tanks on a dolly over the weedy yard toward the house's front door where a woman stood holding the screen door open. Beside the woman stood a girl about Joe's age. Both woman and girl were smoking cigarettes. The girl had a faraway look, like she stared at nothing because nothing was all there ever was to look at.

The woman was maybe in her thirties. There were curlers in her hair, though it was nearly two o'clock in the afternoon. Her skinny white legs were uncovered and pale and looked sickly, clad only in a pair of old shorts and a T-shirt with an image of Mickey Mouse flipping the bird. Both females wore expressions like they knew something the rest of the world didn't, but this secret knowledge seemed to bring neither of them any pleasure.

The man wheeled the tanks onto the porch and nodded at the woman as he disappeared inside. Just then the woman glanced over at Joe and their eyes met. His face warmed suddenly and he waved, feeling as though he'd been caught at something. She took the cigarette from her mouth and flipped it into the dirt yard, then went into the house. She hadn't smiled, or acknowledged his wave; she only stared—the sullen, ugly turn of her mouth unchanging, as if ratcheted there since birth.

Joe was thinking about the woman when he noticed the girl was now looking at *him*. This time he told himself *not* to wave. The girl began laughing at something, and though he couldn't hear it, it was obvious there was no humor in her laughter. In fact, her expression made her look ugly, as though she actually hated him, though they'd never before laid eyes on each other. She continued laughing as she disappeared inside the house, the screen door banging closed behind her.

As he rode away something stuck in his gut. He wanted to turn around and go back. Maybe it was the intrigue of the guy wheeling the tanks into the house? But then maybe this desire had something to do with the woman, whose refusal to respond to his gesture struck Joe as more sad than unpleasant. Most likely, though, it was the girl. Her ugly laughter struck him like an insult, like a sucker punch delivered from thirty yards away.

He tried pushing her from his mind, but she was still there the following morning, and when it happened that the woman and the girl stepped into the bakery around 9:30, the punch she'd delivered the day before pained him all over again. Today the woman was dressed in a pair of bright red shorts and a cotton T-shirt cut off at the shoulders. Though the morning was chilly, neither she nor the girl wore jackets. The woman's arms were red and dimpled with goose bumps. Though her arms were thin, her skin was flabby and her fingers and hands looked plump, as though swollen by years of menial labor. She received her order from Emily silently.

The girl remained standing by the door to the left of the entryway, her attention again fastened on something invisible before her. One of her skinny knees was exposed by the bent angle of her leg as she propped her foot against the wall. He bussed a clean table at the front of the store so he could be near her. It felt like the room had tilted, pulling him toward her. She wasn't pretty; she was skinny to the point of unhealthiness, and like her mom she was pale. She wore a black skirt that hung like a sack, a Black Sabbath T-shirt, and plastic sandals. The outfit only accentuated the sickly pallor of her skin and the shapelessness of her body. He wondered if she really thought she was as ugly as she tried to appear.

She's acting, he thought. When she caught him staring, she recognized him instantly, and just like yesterday his face burned when her eyes hit him. At least she didn't laugh. She turned without a word and swung out the door of the bakery. He couldn't get her out of his head as he made his afternoon deliveries. She was laughing again and he couldn't get her to stop. As he rode, different things flitted across his mind: her ugly ill-fitting clothing, the way her indifferent gaze actually accomplished the opposite of her intentions, seemed to covet attention rather than dismiss it. He remembered her skinny knees, the left one with the big purple bruise that bloomed like an insult of the flesh. Several times angry horns from drivers kept him from cruising into intersections without stopping.

After his last delivery, to Jack Davis Sporting Goods right off Pinnacle's busy town square, he walked past his bike and turned into an alley that led behind the building, where he ducked behind a large Dumpster and masturbated, a vision of the girl stuck at the center of his mind. His eyes were shut tight, his jaws clenched. She sneered at him; he couldn't make her stop. She laughed and kept laughing but he couldn't hear it, only saw her face twisted into that ugly expression of hers. She wouldn't stop laughing and he couldn't make her.

Instead of offering release, his ejaculation only confused and repulsed him more. Feeling disgusted, he reached into the Dumpster, grabbed a filthy newspaper, and used it to clean himself. He slumped against the alley wall, the decaying odor of garbage making his head swim. His tennis shoe was in a puddle of dirty water. The remains of what looked like a slice of tomato floated there, along with a couple of cigarette butts and candy wrappers. He felt so light-headed he thought he might pass out and for a long time sat breathing through his mouth. His heart was sore, beating dully in his chest. He tapped at his pockets for his Inderals, but he didn't have his beta-blockers with him. He had the box of NoDoz, so he swallowed a handful. With his heart condition, a congenital flaw called atrioventricular septal defect, taking speed was not only stupid, but could be lethally toxic. But he liked the "floaty" feeling he got when he mixed it with his medication.

When he walked through the bakery's doors twenty minutes later it took him a second to realize Emily had spoken. Her worried expression made him suddenly angry all over again, though he couldn't understand *why* the feeling bubbled up in him so quickly, why it felt so good to *feel* it. "I'm not high, okay?" he said, though in fact he hadn't really heard what she'd said. "I just don't feel . . . *right*."

"Come here." She put the back of her hand to his forehead. "You're warm."

"I've been riding," he replied.

She drew a glass of water from the faucet and Joe drank it off. "Better?"

"Yeah," he said. "Thanks. Sorry."

"Listen, Joe...," she began but stopped. She shook her head. "Gimme your bag," she said, "go ahead and knock off."

"I'm fine."

"Go," she said. "We're slow."

He was home nearly an hour before he realized he'd forgotten to say so long to Remy, and this oversight, which meant nothing, made him furious. He slapped himself hard across the face and enjoyed the stinging pain that covered the right side of his cheek. When he struck himself a second time, he felt even better. For the third blow, instead of slapping himself, he balled his hand into a fist and swung as hard as he could. The pain was bright and traces of light whirled before his eyes. He lay on his bed and rolled into a tight ball. His heart raced from the speed he'd taken, but he didn't get up and take an Inderal. He lay there a long time, his eyes open.

On Friday morning when he walked into the bakery Emily met him as usual.

"How you feelin'?"

"Sorry about the other day," he told her. "I guess I was a jerk."

"You were."

"You mad?"

"Nah."

"So we're okay?"

"I know *I am*," she said. "You okay?"

He went into the kitchen and said hello to Remy, told him he was sorry about not saying good-bye before leaving on Wednesday. He fixed himself coffee and then spent the next twenty minutes kneading dough while Remy explained his recipe for Russian rye while alternately discussing the inner workings and capitalist processes of service-based economies, the benefits of solar power—which, Remy stated, by 1984 would power the entire country—and who the better guitar player was between Jimi Hendrix and Django Reinhardt.

Outside the sky was overcast, the peaks of the mountains surrounding Pinnacle obscured behind a heavy, lowering roof of swollen clouds. Joe loved gray days, how fractures of lightning parted the sky, the booms of thunder, which Remy said sounded "like God moving furniture." He loved the way air smelled of electricity before rain; like something sweetly decaying afterward. When Emily handed him the slip of paper for the delivery of a birthday cake, Joe didn't recognize the address until he'd already biked through the streets of the Gill Addition and come to a stop in front of the run-down red house with the weedy, garbage-strewn yard. The hospital truck was gone. He carefully lifted the cake from the basket and walked to the front door. He felt the first light drops of the rain that had been threatening all day.

The girl opened the door. She didn't say anything. Finally, to ease his growing discomfort at her silence, he held up the cake. His grin felt awkward, leaden. His face grew warm and then increasingly hot. "It's a cake," he managed.

She was in a flowered dress, old and gauzy. The dress was held at her pale shoulders by two thin straps and fell over her flat chest all the way to her white, pronounced ankles. Her feet were bare, her toes long and thin, the nails painted a painful shade of purple. Her hair dangled to her shoulders, a dirty blond color with darker streaks of black and more purple dyed through. Her hair framed her face like slack curtains.

"It's a cake," he repeated when she still hadn't said anything.

"A revelation," she said finally. She pushed the screen door open and Joe stepped back so it didn't hit and topple the cake he held to her like an offering. He stepped around the door and went by her into the house, so close he smelled her. Ivory soap and cigarettes, something sweeter beneath that. "It's my birthday," she said dully, letting the door slam behind him. She said it as though she were challenging him to say otherwise.

"Yeah," Joe said. His voice sounded high-pitched. "Happy birthday."

"It's been glorious." She went past him. He looked at her shoulders, his eyes roaming down her back, over the small curve of her ass. Through the dress material, he saw she wasn't wearing panties. The feeling flamed in him so quickly it made him weak. His eyes traveled down her legs. He couldn't catch his breath.

"Can I put this down somewhere?"

"No, you should keep holding it," she replied, turning a corner.

He followed but stopped abruptly at the entrance to the living room. Instead of regular furniture—couch, chairs, end tables, coffee table—a hospital bed sat in the far corner of the room, the metal restraining bars on its sides raised and shining in the light cast by the TV. A woman lay on the bed with a white sheet pulled to her throat. Her arms were outside the sheet, held straight down at her sides. Her chest rose slightly, fell, then rose again. Her eyes were closed, and it appeared she was sleeping, though Joe found that hard to believe with the volume of the TV. Moments before, standing face-to-face with the girl, he hadn't noticed how the sound blared. An oxygen mask was affixed over the woman's face, one of the big white and green tanks plunked down solidly next to the bed. There was a machine next to the tank. Every now and then it emitted a beep he could just make out beneath the sound of the TV. He held up the cake again.

"Birthday cake," he said to the sleeping woman.

He turned and moved down the hallway, his legs heavy beneath him. At the end of the hallway was the kitchen. He placed the cake on the table. The room was dismal, dirty. It smelled awful. Pots and pans, plates, glasses, Tupperware piled high in the sink and all over the countertops. An open box of cereal and a carton of milk sat beside the sink. Something reeked and Joe, without thinking, went over and put his nose to the milk carton, drawing back and making a face. He poured the remainder into the sink, watched the white gloop swirl around and down the drain while he ran water from the faucet to wash it away.

He left the kitchen and turned in the direction she'd gone moments before. It was another hallway, this one darker than the first, leading to a staircase. He took the creaking stairs slowly and stopped just before the landing at the top.

"In here," a voice said.

"Hey," Joe said, stepping into the doorway. The room was low lit and empty, save for a dresser and the bed the girl was lying on. A lamp beside the bed glowed red from a red bulb, and a single candle flickered every few moments as tiny gusts of wind pushed through the curtained windows. Her narrow feet were drawn together, her arms placed behind her head. She lay perfectly still, her attention fixed on the ceiling above her.

"I don't know where my mom is," she said not looking at him, "so I can't pay you for the cake. *Typical.*"

"I can come back," he suggested. She didn't reply. "Who's that downstairs?" He immediately regretted asking the question.

"My aunt," the girl replied. "She's dying." She said it so matter-of-factly he was dumbstruck by the directness of her words.

"Jesus," he replied, then shook his head at how stupid that reply had been. "I mean, I'm sorry. It's none of my business, I guess." His head felt loose on his neck.

"You're right," she said fixing her eyes on him for the first time since he'd entered the house. "It *isn't*. So why'd you ask?"

He didn't know how to answer. She went on before he got the chance.

"She got cancer," she said again in that toneless way of hers.

He couldn't think of anything to say. He wanted to go over to her and sit next to her on the bed, but he felt just as powerfully the desire to leave, to flee without another word and hopefully never set eyes on this girl or her mean-faced mother or her dying aunt ever again, but his legs seemed poled to the floor.

"I should get going," he said finally, and for the third time since he'd been there, he felt disgusted by the *wrongness* of everything that came from his mouth.

"Oh, no more questions? How terribly sad," she said. "The day won't be the same."

"I can come back for the money."

"Oh, yes, please do," she replied staring once again at the ceiling. "The party's going nonstop around here. Come for the cancer and stay for the cake."

"Yeah, okay," he said. "So I'll see you."

She didn't reply. His heart bothered him, and he closed his eyes and took a couple of deep breaths. When he was once again on the ground floor he went down the first hallway and then turned and went down the second, longer one, moving quickly past the living room entrance and the dying woman. He didn't look. Through the screen door the afternoon shadows had deepened and in the distance came booms of thunder. He stopped. Rain slashed white lines through the air.

The red house was no more than a few minutes' bike ride from his own. It had probably been right here his entire life. Yet he'd never known. If he'd passed the house—which he *must have,* dozens of times—he couldn't recall having done so now, and he thought how strange it was that he couldn't remember. Things could be practically in your own neighborhood, yet you never really knew. And then they could be gone. Just like that. Some people get this thing called cancer. Other people could just leave their home one day and never return. They didn't say good-bye. They never called to say they were okay. This woman a few feet away from him was going to die. Her life—*her life*—was going to be over because of *this thing* she had wrong with her.

He stepped out of the dying woman's house. It was the most fantastic thing he'd ever heard of. One moment you're alive and the next . . . He looked back at the house. He was already soaked. The light from the TV flickered.

"You're gonna die," he said out loud this time. What was strange was that he didn't feel anything about what he'd said. It was just something that was going to happen.

All the following morning Joe waited with anticipation, wondering if she'd come into the bakery. It rained steadily. *Maybe,* he reckoned, *that's why she hasn't come.* When he'd told Emily what happened, omitting everything other than the girl not having any money to pay for the cake, Emily told him not to worry.

"Poor kid," she said. It seemed to Joe that Emily had been on the verge of saying something else, but stopped herself.

"I'll go by there and pick it up," Joe said.

"Don't sweat it, man," Remy replied. He sat atop the counter with a glass of water in his hand, his legs swinging back and forth slowly. "They'll pay. If they don't we'll send Em over to lop their heads off with a cleaver."

"Right," Emily said brightly.

"We got one in the back we keep special."

"Right."

"It's no problem," Joe pressed.

"Why don't you like the cleaver idea?" Remy asked. "It shows strength, *purpose.* They don't pay, they sleep with the trout."

"It's my responsibility," Joe said.

"Don't sweat it," Remy said. "It'll keep. Look at the weather." Here,

Remy changed his tone, pronouncing the next words with a deep, theatrical tenor. *"It was raining,"* he said, *"and it was going to rain."*

Emily smiled at her husband. "Thank you, Wallace Stevens."

On his way home, Joe took a left on Sweetgrass instead of staying on Brandeis, and a few minutes later he pulled up in front of the red house. It was badly in need of a paint job, and weeds smothered what was left of the grass. Dandelions slumped at their necks as though they couldn't bear the sight of the bare patch of earth they were forced to grow from. He was still straddling his bike when she came to the door. Something happened. She held her hand to the side of her face. She looked like a painting of a girl waving, the way the doorway framed her. Joe waved back. He tossed his leg over the bike, then let the bike fall to the ground and walked across the yard. He stepped onto the porch and went in through the door she held open for him.

She said, "Here you are."

"Here I am."

Her aunt was sitting up in the hospital bed, smoking a cigarette. Between drags, she held the oxygen mask to her face. Across from her sat the woman Joe figured to be the girl's mother. She sat on a folding lawn chair a few feet away from the woman in the bed. She was also smoking. The room swam in gray swirls made visible by the light from the TV. The curtains were open, yet none of the windows were cracked, and the air in the place was as clogged and stifling as the day before.

"Mom, Aunt, this is . . ." She stopped, holding her hand toward Joe. "Name?"

"Joe."

"Joe," the girl repeated. "He brought the cake."

Both women looked at him with faces devoid of expression. The girl's aunt removed the mask from her face and took a drag from her cigarette. She coughed—a wet, awful sound. Joe looked at the girl, who was studying him. He thought he saw something other than sullenness in her gaze. She was sad, he guessed, maybe even a little embarrassed.

"There's money in my purse," her mother said. Joe and the girl waited, but when it became apparent the woman wasn't going to elaborate, the girl motioned to Joe for him to follow her.

"Nice meeting you," Joe said to the women, who didn't look up.

"Welcome," the girl said theatrically, turning and holding her arms out, once they were in her room. She sat down on the edge of the bed, her hands in her lap. She was dressed in the familiar torn sundress, but her hair was clean today. Her neck, her thin white throat, looked fragile. One of her feet was pulled up and held against her thigh. Joe saw the smooth white flesh of her leg. She didn't speak for a time, but sat looking at him. A book lay on the bed beside her, its pages thrown open like the wings of a dead bird resting facedown.

He sat next to her on the bed. The curtains swayed. A pack of cigarettes sat on the ledge in front of the window, a book of matches on top. When he turned from the window, she was staring at him again. He got up and walked around the room, tried looking as though he were deeply interested in everything. He felt her eyes on him. He picked up a wooden statue, turned it over in his hands. A small stack of novels sat on the dresser. He scanned their titles; he'd read none of them.

"What's your name?" he asked, setting the statue down.

"Hulga," she said. When Joe stared, she laughed. "Just kidding." She picked up the book beside her, momentarily letting her eyes wander over the pages. "She's a woman in this book," the girl explained. "She has a wooden leg she's ashamed of, but it seems like she secretly treasures it, too. It's like this weapon she has that no one understands," she said. "It's about secrets, I guess. Hers and everybody else's."

Her name was Faith. Knowing she had a name like that made her seem prettier to him. She looked at her hands in her lap. Joe walked around the edge of the bed and sat on the opposite side from her.

"How come you laughed at me?" He hadn't planned on asking the question. The words tumbled from his mouth and suddenly the question was in the air between them. She let herself fall backward on the bed. "Tell the truth," he said.

"I was going to," she replied defiantly. "I *so* value truth above all things."

You're just acting nasty, he thought.

She moved so that her back leaned against the bed's headrest. He caught another glimpse of her legs, the diamond-shaped shadow between. If she'd noticed him looking, she gave no indication. It felt as if his entire body were rushing toward her, while his head stayed behind and watched.

"You were looking at me," she said.

"I wasn't," he said quickly.

"Yes, you were. You were standing in the middle of the street, staring."

"Oh, yeah," Joe replied. He nodded, comprehending. *The street. The other day.* She wasn't talking about right now. This minute. "I guess you just looked..." He couldn't find the words, couldn't believe he was beside her on her bed. A vibration went through his body and he remembered the other day, when his body had felt like a nest of bees buzzing.

"Why'd you stop?" she asked. "The other day."

He thought about it. He didn't know why, exactly. "I thought I recognized you," he said.

"But you've never seen me before."

"It wasn't *you,* exactly," he told her. "It was the way you looked. I thought. I don't know what I thought."

"Come here," she said.

When he left hours later he was dazed, his body charged, his head filled with the memory of her white body beneath his hands. Her mouth had been wet with the strong odor of smoke. She'd undone his pants wordlessly, slipped her hand into his shorts, and taken hold of him in her fist. When she'd lain down on her side, her head resting in her hand, Joe felt himself falling, and then her arms were around his neck and her mouth opening, her tongue slipping into his mouth. It wasn't until he arrived home that he realized he'd forgotten to collect the money for the cake again.

"It's free," he thought.

He returned every day for the next two weeks, either showing up on the doorstep, or else going around the side of the place and climbing onto a rusting metal barrel and using that to pull himself into a tree, then climbing that and letting himself in through the window. She greeted him as though she was neither excited nor surprised to find him there. But she wasn't disappointed, either. They stayed in her bedroom. Where her mother was, Joe had no idea. The woman never came upstairs, never checked after her daughter to see what she was doing.

He had no idea what they were doing. Both seemed to be occupying a space the other needed filled. Though she hadn't attained anything like beauty in his eyes, her presence, the sullen face and sneering turn of her mouth, the thin pale body, seemed to hover before him every waking moment. She was *necessary* in a way impossible to explain. They barely spoke, or told each other anything personal about themselves. He didn't even know her last name. Faith was enough. He hadn't mentioned his mom's disappearance and wasn't going to; hadn't probed her as to why a woman withering from cancer spent her final days smoking cigarettes. It was so hopeless Joe didn't want to know the reasons why. He didn't want to care. People did what they did because they didn't know how to do anything else. That was good enough. He only wanted to feel the warmth of her beneath him, and feel himself inside her.

"Faith," he said.

"Hey, buddy, step on over here a sec." They were in Jedediah's kitchen. He stood before Remy and Emily feeling fidgety, wanting only to count out his change bag and do his afternoon prep so that he could go to her room and hurl himself against her. *Faith.*

"Take it easy, man," Remy said. "Why you so jumpy?"

"I'm not," Joe replied. He heard the excited pitch in his voice, willed himself to slow down. "I'm sorry. Shit."

"What is it, Joe?" Emily asked. Her concern was obvious. They waited. But he didn't want to explain. He knew he couldn't have anyway, so what would've been the point? And anyway, how was *his* business theirs? He just wanted to go to her. He wanted to feel things. Or *not* feel them. What he didn't want to do was *explain.*

"It's nothing."

"It's *some*thing," Remy said. "You've been a freak, man."

"We've had complaints, Joe." She let the words sink in. "That you've been rude." Her expression wasn't angry. There was only concern. And it was this *concern* that pissed him off. It welled up in him as if it'd been lying in wait for the right occasion. He was so fucking tired of people's concern. *Fuck them,* he thought. He didn't need their concern, didn't want it. It came with a price. The price for their concern was more than he could pay.

"It's not like you," Emily said, but he cut her off.

"How do you know what I'm like? You don't know!" He'd been about to go on, but he was tired suddenly, and didn't want to be there. He'd had to drag even those few words from himself, as if they'd weighed a ton.

"We know *you*," Remy said.

"How?" Joe asked turning to the older man. "How's anyone know anyone unless they see them every day and know exactly what's going on with them?" He didn't give Remy time to respond. "Who complained?" he demanded.

"Is that really so important?" Emily replied.

"No," he said. "Anyway I don't care. It doesn't matter."

"Joe," Emily began.

"I don't wanna talk, okay? Please don't make me."

They looked at each other, Joe at them and the two of them at him. Remy shrugged, made a face that seemed to say, *This is the kind of shit we men do. We are a wondrous, mercurial species.*

"Am I fired?"

"What're you talking about?" Remy asked.

"Joe," Emily began.

He took the bag and dropped it on the table. "I quit anyway."

"The hell you do. We're not going to accept your resignation." Joe opened his mouth to say something else, but Emily cut *him* off this time. "Stop there," she said. "You interrupted me. Something's bugging you and you don't feel like talking about it. Fine, no problem. But," she continued, "now you're speaking rashly and people who do that end up saying things they regret, so instead of quitting, which I really hope you don't mean, I think you should take a couple of days to think it over. In the meantime, Remy and I don't have to lose our friend because of some stupid misunderstanding."

"What she said," Remy said.

"I'm sorry," Joe said. He couldn't think of anything else to say, so he said that. He *was* sorry. He didn't know about what, exactly, just that he was. The words sounded stupid, but sometimes you had to say something. People *expected* you to. Whether you meant what you said or not.

He went in through her bedroom window. She wasn't there. He went to her bed and lay across it, pushed his face into her pillow. He lay for a long time, breathing in the smell of her. When she didn't come after ten minutes he went downstairs, stopping at the entrance to the living room. The bed was empty, just as he'd known it would be. The place had a deserted, forlorn feel to it. There was such an awful sadness about the place; it crept into him. The lawn chair was turned on its side; the ashtray on the floor beside it overflowed. Cigarette butts spilled onto the carpet. He glanced at the empty walls, at the stains on the carpeting, at old plates left here and there, remains of old meals congealing on them. With the TV off the room was so silent it occurred to Joe that the TV had been the only sound of life in the room. The women were shells, as unreal as the images on the TV. They meant nothing to him. She'd been the only living thing in the house and now he couldn't even fucking find her.

He felt ridiculous being in that awful place by himself. He stared about the room, but couldn't imagine the circumstances in a life that would lead it to a place like this. The oxygen mask was on the floor and he picked it up and held it to his face. He twisted the handle at the top of the tank. There was a small hiss. He took several deep breaths. His eyes closed. His head swam. He didn't know how long he'd been laughing before it dawned on him that he was.

When he opened his eyes again the room tipped slightly, as if it were a room on a boat with the sea swaying beneath it. He took another deep breath, removed the mask from his face and tossed it on the bed. He stood there a few minutes longer, letting his weight lean against the metal frame. He shook a handful of NoDoz from the box, shook out a couple of Inderals, and stood chewing the pills. Their chalky, bitter taste coated his tongue. He turned off the oxygen tank and left the room and went back down the two hallways, stopping in the kitchen and going to the sink and leaning his head underneath the faucet. He swallowed mouthfuls of water. A reek rose up from the sink and he gagged. He went back to her room, lay down on her bed.

When Faith hadn't arrived by the time the first hour of his vigil ended, he waited a second hour, and when *that* hour passed and she didn't come, he reluctantly pushed himself from her bed and forced himself to crawl out her bedroom window. He had the weirdest feeling and had to get off his bike and walk along beside it most of the way home. Everything around him stood out greenly, with a vividness that made it look unreal—like the world was actually a photograph with overdeveloped colors.

That night he tried to watch a movie with his dad, but every couple of minutes he needed to get up and move around. In his room, he put on headphones and listened to music, but the songs couldn't hold his concentration. When he crawled out his window, thinking he was just going to get outside for a few minutes, get some fresh air, he was back on his bike before realizing what he was doing.

Her light was on. He hopped on the barrel, pulled himself into the tree. At her window, he paused. She was lying on her bed, her legs straight and rigid, and as always, her feet were pointed like the feet of a diver entering water. She wore a dress, tattered, as all of them seemed to be. He felt sorry for her that all her dresses were like that. He told himself he should've bought her something. A dress maybe? That would've been a good thing to do, and he was sorry he hadn't thought of it until now.

She jumped when he said her name. Her head swung around. "What the fuck, man?"

He crawled through the window. The candle flickered. The lamp's red light illumined the room, but shadows remained crouched in the corners like shapeless animals.

"Where were you today?"

She shook her head, turned her attention toward the ceiling again.

"I came by," he said going over and sitting beside her on the bed. "Where were you?" he asked again after she still hadn't replied. "I came by and you weren't here. Where were you?"

"Oh, go away," she said tiredly.

"I waited two hours," he said. He put his hand on her knee, watched with a weird, detached curiosity as it moved up her leg. It didn't seem to be a part of him. When the hand reached the inside of her thigh she slapped it. The violence surprised and awakened him.

"Can you not paw me all the time!"

"Where were you?"

"We were at the hospital, okay." Her eyes sparkled. "She died." Her lower lip trembled. "Jesus, it was gross. She threw up all over herself," she said speaking to the ceiling. "All this gross green shit, and blood. All this bile like she was throwing up all her insides. Oh, my god. And then she was just dead," she finished softly.

"Who?"

"Who the fuck do you think?" she turned on him hatefully. "Are you fucking retarded?"

When the truth of what she said registered, he was surprised at how little he felt it.

"When?"

"What's it matter when?" she snapped. "She's dead. That's it. *Dead.*"

He couldn't make himself understand. He kept hearing the word— *dead, dead*—but it didn't mean anything. "What do you mean?"

She looked at him like he was something stuck to the bottom of her shoe. The curtains brushed into the room, making a soft sound. He liked the sound they made. His mouth was open slightly, giving him a stunned expression. When several minutes passed in silence, she made a face and then shook her head, and he knew she was seeing something distasteful, while at the same time trying to push it away and remove herself completely from it. He recognized the look. He wanted to touch her, but she was surrounded by something he didn't want to feel. It was *pain*. It was interesting to see what *hers* looked like. His looked different.

After a while she raised herself into a sitting position so that their faces were nearly on the same plane. She pulled her legs into the lotus position. When she put her arms around him, he tensed a little. It'd been instantaneous, nothing more than a spasm. He didn't think she noticed. She pulled him against her and Joe allowed himself to be held. He relaxed when he realized it was going to be okay. He thought he'd feel it on her, but he didn't. Her pain was hers and didn't have anything to do with him.

"Not tomorrow." She was lying on her side, watching him dress. "I have a bunch of shit I have to do with my mom. We have to make funeral arrangements. She can't do anything on her own," she said. "She's a complete veg."

"I'll come tomorrow night."

"Busy."

"All day *and* night?"

"Yeah. All day and night."

"What about the day after?"

"Funeral."

"I'll come," he suggested.

"What is your damage? You *won't* come. You aren't invited. You don't know her."

"*Didn't.*"

"What?"

"Didn't," he repeated. "I *didn't* know her. She's dead. Past tense." She contemplated him. "You're one cold little fucker."

He didn't like the way she looked at him. "People should say what they mean," he said. "Nobody ever does and they should. How's anyone supposed to know then?"

"Look," she said, "there's a reception after, okay? Or a wake or what the fuck, it doesn't fucking matter. My mom will probably be there most of the night getting drunk and asking for gas money. Come by around five, I'll probably definitely be back by then."

"Okay." He made a movement toward her.

"Just please go now, okay? *Please?*"

"I wanna stay," he said.

"I don't give a shit what you want!"

At the window he stopped. "What was her name?"

"Can you please please please leave?"

He was half in, half out the window when he heard her. She spoke it softly. "Her name was Sarah. I don't want you to say anything," she said. "Don't you dare say it's nice. *Don't you dare.*"

For two days he didn't leave his house. He still hadn't gone back to the bakery or even bothered to contact Remy or Emily. He spent most of the time lying with his hands clasped behind his head. While his dad was at work, he went upstairs and nicked one of his dad's *Playboy*s. He took the magazine into the bathroom and masturbated, emptying himself into the toilet, his forehead pressed against the wall. By three o'clock the day of the funeral, he couldn't wait any longer and threw on some clothes and rode to her house, let himself in through the window.

Empty. He dropped on her bed and fell instantly asleep. She was shaking him awake in what seemed like only minutes.

"What are you doing?"

"I fell asleep."

"No. What are you doing in my room? This is my room! You don't live here! You don't go breaking into people's houses!"

"I was waiting for you," he said.

"I don't want you to wait for me! I didn't ask you to!"

"You said to come today."

"Change of plan," she replied. "Now I'm telling you to leave." Her fists were balled at her sides. She wore a black dress and a white necklace barely whiter than her throat. She was finally beautiful. He couldn't believe how beautiful. He knew she'd be like this one day.

"I don't wanna leave," he said.

"Tough shit!"

He raised himself to a sitting position. "Look, I'm sorry. Okay? I'm sorry. I didn't know what else to do," he said. He thought if he could slow everything down, an answer that made sense would come to him. At his apology, she calmed a little. She lay down on her side at the foot of the bed, drew her knees in, and wrapped her arms around them, holding herself.

"I have to pack," she said.

"Why?"

"We're leaving in the morning."

"Tomorrow?" He lifted himself from the bed with an effort and stood before her.

"Yeah. Tomorrow."

"You're leaving?"

"Look, I told you," she said dully. She didn't finish the thought.

"Do you want to? Could we?"

"No," she replied. She said the next words with deliberate slowness. *"I want to leave."*

He swallowed. It was hard to hold it down. He patted his pockets, but he'd forgotten his Inderals at home. He hadn't asked if she wanted to *live* there. That wasn't the question. It'd been something else that he'd meant. *She'd* answered wrong. He put his hand on her shoulder and she didn't move. He moved his hand up to her throat. When she didn't respond to that he slipped his hand over her breast.

"Please don't." She didn't sound angry, so he ignored her. "Knock it off, I said!"

"Why?"

"Because I said so."

"You're leaving," he said. "I'll never see you again."

Her eyes were lit with a wild brightness, cast by the red light from the lamp.

"That's all you want," she said. The sound of her voice sounded like it amazed even her. "Isn't it? All you want is to fuck me."

He didn't know how to answer, but he wanted to say something true. He needed to say something true or else he might never get the chance again.

"Please," he said.

When she raised her dress she did so violently, hiking it up so that he could see her skinny thighs, pale as milk kicking free of the dark fabric of the dress. She raised her legs, ripped at her panties and tore them down, kicking them to the floor at his feet.

"Come on," she said. "Do it and get it over with then you motherfucking coward!"

He knew she hated him then. He didn't need to look in order to see. He could hear it. If he looked, he'd be able to see it clearly, but he didn't want to look. He didn't seem to *care.* The truth of this amazed him. He thought if there were going to be a moment when he began to care again, it would've been a moment like this one, but the feeling wouldn't come.

He unbuckled his pants, let them drop. He pushed himself onto her. Her body received him with a wooden resistance. She didn't move or struggle; didn't utter a sound. Her eyes stayed open, but it didn't seem like she was *seeing* anything. She lay with only her upper body on the bed, her legs hanging over the side. Every now and then the heels of her feet lifted from the floor as he worked himself against her. He heard himself as if from a long distance, a sound unrecognizable coming from deep inside him. When he finished, he pushed himself up and stood before her. She stared at him unblinking. She didn't attempt to cover herself, but instead left her legs open.

"You know what you are now?"

He knew. He was through talking about it. Her eyes were bright and still filling with light. He pulled his pants up, deliberately taking his time buckling his belt. He willed himself to meet her eyes. He knew what he was. He didn't need her to remind him. He thought how strange it was that he couldn't seem to *feel* it.

"I hope you remember this," she said. "I hope you remember what you are."

When he started for the door she stopped him. "Leave the way you came in."

Light surrounded her. She was dazzling in it. At the window he ducked and threw his leg over the ledge and then swung out onto the branch and in a moment, dropped to the ground. It was over now. *He'd* been the one who decided. Not her, *him*. And as he walked across the yard he felt nothing. And for the rest of that night he felt nothing. And in the morning, the same. And all throughout that day and the day after, nothing happened and nothing moved the least bit inside him. It could go on like that forever.

CONTRIBUTORS

JEDEDIAH BERRY is a graduate of the English MFA Program at the University of Massachusetts, Amherst, where he was awarded the Harvey Swados Fiction Prize. His stories have appeared in *3rd Bed* and *Fairy Tale Review,* as well as in the anthologies *Salon Fantastique* and *Coyote Road.* He recently completed work on a novel, *The Manual of Detection.*

TUCKER CAPPS was born in Humboldt County, California, in 1980, and grew up in rural Oregon. He has studied at Yale University, where he received the Louis Sudler Prize for Excellence in the Arts; at FAMU, the Czech national film academy in Prague; and most recently at the Iowa Writers' Workshop, where he taught undergraduate fiction workshops as a Teaching-Writing Fellow. He lives in Los Angeles, teaches summer filmmaking workshops in Putney, Vermont, and travels regularly to Venezuela, where he is cowriting a Spanish-language feature film. He is currently at work on a novel.

ORIANE GABRIELLE DELFOSSE was born and raised in Virginia. She is a graduate of the University of Virginia and Sarah Lawrence College. She lives in Brooklyn, where she is at work on her first novel.

LAUREN GROFF was born in 1978 in Cooperstown, New York, and educated at Amherst College and the University of Wisconsin–Madison, where she received her MFA in Fiction. Her stories have appeared in a number of journals, including the *Atlantic Monthly* and *Ploughshares,* and she held the Axton Fellowship in Fiction from the University of Louisville. Her first novel, *The Monsters of Templeton,* will be published by Voice, an imprint of Hyperion, in the spring of 2008.

GARTH RISK HALLBERG holds an MFA from New York University. His stories have appeared, most recently, in *Glimmer Train, Canteen, Evergreen Review, h2so4,* and *Em.* An illustrated novella, *A Field Guide to the North American Family,* is available from Mark Batty Publisher. Please visit www.afieldguide.com. The author is indebted to

Tad Friend, whose reportage for the *New Yorker* suggested several of this story's daffier turns of phrase.

LESLIE JAMISON grew up in Los Angeles. She is a graduate of Harvard College and the Iowa Writers' Workshop. During the summer of 2006, she was a Work-Study Scholar at the Bread Loaf Writers' Conference. She is currently working on a novel.

ELIZABETH KADETSKY spends much of her time in New York's East Village, France, and India. She has been awarded fellowships to Camargo Foundation and MacDowell, a Fulbright to India and a Dodge Foundation grant for writers affected by September 11, and has won a fellowship to the Wesleyan Writers Conference and scholarships to Sewanee and Bread Loaf. Her short stories have appeared in *The Pushcart Prizes Anthology, Gettysburg Review, Santa Monica Review,* and elsewhere, and her manuscript was the top selection in the 2004 AWP Grace Paley Prize in Short Fiction. Her memoir set in India, *First There Is a Mountain,* was published by Little, Brown in 2004. She has an MFA from the University of California, Irvine, and teaches at Sarah Lawrence College and the Columbia School of Journalism. She is working on a novel set in India.

RAZIA SULTANA KHAN was born in Dhaka, Bangladesh. Her short stories have appeared in anthologies of Bangladeshi writing, including *From the Delta* and *The Daily Star Book of Bangladeshi Writing,* as well as in the *Daily Star Weekend Magazine.* She has just finished her first collection of short stories and is working on a novel about the lives of rural women in Bangladesh, centered on the Grameen Bank. She is also a poet and is putting together her poems for her first collection. She is working on her Ph.D. at the University of Nebraska, Lincoln.

Born to an Iranian mother and an American father, SHARON MAY worked in Cambodian refugee camps, researching the Khmer Rouge for the Columbia University Center for the Study of Human Rights. She coedited *In the Shadow of Angkor: Contemporary Writing from Cambodia.* Her stories have appeared in the *Chicago Tribune, Tin House, StoryQuarterly, Mānoa, Alaska Quarterly Review,* and elsewhere. She is the recipient of the 2005 Robie Macauley Award for Fiction, and two finalist prizes in the Nelson Algren Award for short fiction. She received her MFA in Creative Writing from California State University, Chico. Currently she is a Wallace Stegner Fellow at Stanford University, where she is completing a collection of stories that centers around Cambodia.

STEFAN MCKINSTRAY was born in Jackson, Wyoming. In the last dozen or so years he has lived in Tucson, Seattle, Austin, and Homer, Arkansas. He received his MFA from New Mexico State University in Las Cruces, New Mexico, in 2006. His short story "No One Here Says What They Mean" is from his novel-in-stories, *Wave Backwards As You Go.* He lives in Roslyn, Washington.

JORDAN MCMULLIN grew up in northeastern Ohio. She graduated from Vassar College in 1999, then received an MA from Miami University and an MFA from the University of Maryland. She is the 2006 recipient of the Ohioana Library Association's Walter Marvin Rumsey Grant. She teaches at a public high school in Maryland and is currently at work on a novel and a memoir.

PETER MOUNTFORD earned an MFA from the University of Washington, where his thesis, a novel called *Alistair Wright,* won the 2006 David Guterson Award. While at the University of Washington, Peter also won the Richard Blessing Scholarship and the Mary Rouvelas Prize. The story "Horizon" also appeared in the fall 2007 issue of *Michigan Quarterly Review.* George Saunders picked one of Peter's stories as the runner-up for the *Boston Review*'s 2007 Fiction Contest and it appeared in that magazine's March/April 2007 issue. In 2006, Peter was one of two finalists for the *Florida Review*'s Editor's Prize. After graduating from Pitzer College in 1999, Peter spent a few years working as an adjunct scholar for the Alexis de Tocqueville Institution, a think tank based in Arlington, Virginia. He has lived in Ecuador, Sri Lanka, France, Mexico, and Scotland, but currently resides in Seattle, where he is at work on a new novel, *Jupiter's Range.*

DAN PINKERTON lives with his wife and son in Des Moines, Iowa, where he works at a financial services company. His stories and poems have appeared, or are set to appear, in *New Orleans Review, Poetry East, Rhino, Indiana Review, Subtropics, Minnesota Review, Quarterly West,* and *Lake Effect.* His reviews have appeared in *American Literary Review, Shenandoah,* the *Chattahoochee Review,* and *Pleiades.* He is the recipient of two Academy of American Poets prizes and an AWP Intro Journals award.

DAVID JAMES POISSANT received an MFA in Creative Writing from the University of Arizona, where he also served as coeditor of *Sonora Review.* His stories have appeared in the *Chicago Tribune, Willow Springs,* the *Chattahoochee Review,* and *Orchid.* He won second prize in the *Atlantic Monthly*'s 2005 Student Writing Contest. He has won the George Garrett Fiction Award and been a finalist for the Nelson Algren Award. He has attended the Sewanee Writers' Conference as a Georges and Anne Borchardt Scholar and twice been nominated for the Pushcart Prize. He is currently at work on a collection of stories and a novel.

SUZANNE RIVECCA is a 2005–2007 Wallace Stegner Fellow in fiction at Stanford University. She grew up in Kalamazoo and Grand Haven, Michigan. Her short stories have appeared in *StoryQuarterly, Fence, Artful Dodge, ACM, Blackbird, Third Coast,* and the *Journal,* and received Special Mention in volumes XXX and XXXI of the Pushcart Prize anthology.

CHRISTOPHER STOKES currently attends the University of Mississippi, in Oxford, where he is completing his MFA in Fiction and working on his first novel.

ADAM STUMACHER holds degrees from Cornell University and Saint Mary's College of California, where he was recipient of the Jeanine Cooney and Agnes Butler Fellowships, and he was the Carol Houck Smith Fiction Fellow at the University of Wisconsin Institute for Creative Writing. He was winner of the 2005 Raymond Carver Short Story Award, and his work has appeared in the *Sun* and *Carve.* He recently completed a short story collection and is working on a novel.

PARTICIPANTS

The Advanced Fiction Workshop
with Carol Edgarian & Tom Jenks
2115 California Street
San Francisco, CA 94115
415/346-4477

American University
MFA Program in Creative Writing
Department of Literature
4400 Massachusetts Avenue, NW
Washington, DC 20016
202/885-2973

The Banff Centre for the Arts
Writing Studio
Box 1020, Station 34
107 Tunnel Mountain Drive
Banff, AB TIL 1H5
403/762-6269

Binghamton University
Binghamton Center for Writers
P.O. Box 6000
Binghamton, NY 13902-6000
607/777-2713

Boise State University
MFA Program in Writing
1910 University Drive
Boise, ID 83725
208/426-1002

Boston University
Graduate Creative Writing Program
236 Bay State Road
Boston, MA 02215
617/353-2510

Bowling Green State University
Department of English
Creative Writing Program
Bowling Green, OH 43403-0215
419/372-8370

The Bread Loaf Writers' Conference
Middlebury College—P&W
Middlebury, VT 05753
802/443-5286

Brown University
Program in Literary Arts, Box 1923
Providence, RI 02912
401/863-3260

California College of the Arts
1111 8th Street
San Francisco, CA 94107
415/703-9500

California State University, Long Beach
MFA Program in Creative Writing
Department of English
1250 Bellflower Boulevard
Long Beach, CA 90840
562/985-4225

California State University, Sacramento
6000 J Street
Department of English
Sacramento, CA 95819-6075
916/278-6586

The City College of New York
English Department NAC 6/210
Convent Avenue at 138th Street
New York, NY 10031
212/650-6694

Colorado State University
Creative Writing Program
English Department, 359 Eddy Hall
Fort Collins, CO 80523-1773
970/491-2644

Columbia University
Writing Division, School of the Arts
2960 Broadway, 415 Dodge Hall
New York, NY 10027
212/854-4391

Concordia University
1455 de Maison Boulevard West
Department of English
Montreal PQ H3G 1M8
514/848-2340

Cornell University
English Department
Ithaca, NY 14853
607/255-6800

Eastern Washington University
Creative Writing Program
705 W. First Avenue MS#1
Spokane, WA 99201-3900
509/623-4221

Emerson College
Writing, Literature, and Publishing
120 Boylston Street
Boston, MA 02116
617/824-8750

Fine Arts Work Center in
Provincetown
24 Pearl Street
Provincetown, MA 02657
508/487-9960

Florida International University
Department of English
Biscayne Bay Campus
3000 NE 151st Street
Miami, FL 33181
305/919-5857

Florida State University
Creative Writing Program
Department of English
Tallahassee, FL 32306-1580
850/644-4230

George Mason University
Creative Writing Program
English Department—MS 3E4
Fairfax, VA 22030
703/993-1180

Georgia State University
Department of English
University Plaza
Atlanta, GA 30303-3083
404/651-2900

Grub Street
160 Boylston Street, 4th Floor
Boston, MA 02116
617/695-0075

Hollins University
Department of English
Roanoke, VA 24020
540/362-6317

The Humber School for Writers
3199 Lakeshore Boulevard West
Humber College
Toronto, ON M8V 1K9
416/675-6622

Indiana University
Department of English
Ballantine Hall 442
1020 East Kirkwood Avenue
Bloomington, IN 47405-6601
812/855-8224

Johns Hopkins University
The Writing Seminars
3400 North Charles Street
Gilman 136
Baltimore, MD 21218
410/516-7563

Johns Hopkins Writing Program—
Washington
1717 Massachusetts Avenue, NW
Suite 101
Washington, DC 20036
202/452-1970

Louisiana State University
MFA Program in Creative Writing
Department of English
Allen Hall
Baton Rouge, LA 70803-5001
225/578-5922

McNeese State University
Department of Languages
P.O. Box 92655
Lake Charles, LA 70609-2655
337/475-5326

Miami University
Creative Writing Program
356 Bachelor Hall
Oxford, OH 45056
513/529-5221

The Michener Center for Writers
University of Texas at Austin
702 East Dean Keeton Street
Austin, TX 78705
512/471-1601

Mills College
Creative Writing Program
5000 MacArthur Boulevard
Oakland, CA 94613
510/430-3309

Minnesota State University, Mankato
English Department
230 Armstrong Hall
Mankato, MN 56001
507/389-2117

Mississippi State University
Department of English
Drawer E
Mississippi State, MS 39762
662/325-3644

Napa Valley Writers' Conference
1088 College Avenue
Napa Valley College
St. Helena, CA 94574
707/967-2900

Naropa University
Program in Writing and Poetics
2130 Arapahoe Avenue
Boulder, CO 80302
303/546-3508

New Mexico State University
Department of English
Box 30001—Department 3E
Las Cruces, NM 88003-8001
505/646-3931

New York University
Graduate Program in Creative Writing
Lillian Vernon Writers House
58 West 10th Street
New York, NY 10011
212/998-8816

Northwestern University
Master of Arts in Creative Writing
School of Continuing Studies
405 Church Street
Evanston, IL 60208-4220
847/491-5612

Ohio State University
English Department
421 Denney Hall
164 West 17th Avenue
Columbus, OH 43210
614/292-2242

Oklahoma State University
Creative Writing Program
English Department—205 Morrill Hall
Stillwater, OK 74078
405/744-9474

Pennsylvania State University
MFA Program in Creative Writing
117 Burrowes Building
University Park, PA 16802
814/863-0258

Purdue University
Department of English
Heavilon Hall
West Lafayette, IN 47907
765/494-3740

Roosevelt University, Chicago Campus
School of Liberal Arts
430 South Michigan Avenue
Chicago, IL 60605-1394
312/341-3710

Sage Hill Writing Experience
Box 1731
Saskatoon, SK S7K 3S1
306/652-7395

Saint Mary's College of California
MFA Program in Creative Writing
P.O. Box 4686
Moraga, CA 94575-4686
925/631-4762

San Francisco State University
Creative Writing Department
1600 Holloway Avenue
San Francisco, CA 94132-4162
415/338-1891

Sarah Lawrence College
Graduate Writing Program
1 Mead Way
Slonim House
Bronxville, NY 10708-5999
914/395-2371

The School of the Art Institute of Chicago
MFA in Writing Program
37 S. Wabash Avenue
Chicago, IL 60603
312/899-5100

Sewanee Writers' Conference
123 Gailor Hall
735 University Avenue
Sewanee, TN 37383-1000
931/598-1141

Southern Illinois University, Carbondale
MFA in Creative Writing
English Department
Carbondale, IL 62901
618/453-6814

Stanford University
Creative Writing Program
Department of English
Stanford, CA 94305-2087
650/725-1208

Stonecoast Writers' Conference
The University of Southern Maine
English Department
311 Luther Bonney Hall
P.O. Box 9300
96 Falmouth Street
Portland, ME 04101
207/780-5517

Syracuse University
Program in Creative Writing
401 Hall of Languages
Syracuse, NY 13244-1170
315/443-2173

Taos Summer Writers' Conference
Department of English
MSC03 2170
University of New Mexico
Albuquerque, NM 87131-0001
505/277-5572

Temple University
Creative Writing Program
Anderson Hall, 10th Floor
Philadelphia, PA 19122
215/204-1796

Texas State University
MFA Program, Creative Writing
Department of English
601 University Drive
San Marcos, TX 78666-4616
512/245-7681

Tin House Writers Conference
P.O. Box 10500
Portland, OR 97210
503/219-0622

University of Alabama
Program in Creative Writing
Department of English
103 Morgan Hall
P.O. Box 870244
Tuscaloosa, AL 35487-0244
205/348-5065

University of Alabama at Birmingham
Creative Writing Program
Department of English
Room 215, Humanities Building
1530 3rd Ave. S.
Birmingham, AL 35294-1260
205/934-5293

University of Alaska, Fairbanks
Creative Writing Program
English Department
P.O. Box 755720
Fairbanks, AK 99775-5720
907/474-7193

University of Arizona
MFA Program in Creative Writing
445 Modern Languages Building
P.O. Box 210067
Tucson, AZ 85721-0067
520/621-3880

University of Calgary
Department of English
Calgary, AB T2N 1N4
403/220-5484

University of California, Davis
Graduate Creative Writing Program
Department of English
One Shields Avenue
Davis, CA 95616
530/752-2281

University of Cincinnati
Creative Writing Program
Department of English & Comparative
Literature
ML 69
Cincinnati, OH 45221-0069
513/556-5924

University of Colorado at Boulder
MFA in Creative Writing
Department of English
Campus Box 226
Boulder, CO 80309-0226
303/492-1853

University of Denver
Creative Writing Program
English Department
Sturm Hall
Denver, CO 80208
303/871-2266

University of Florida
MFA Program
Department of English
P.O. Box 117310
Gainesville, FL 32611-7310
352/392-6650 Ext. 225

University of Houston
Creative Writing Program
Department of English
R. Cullen 229
Houston, TX 77204-3015
713/743-3015

University of Idaho
Creative Writing Program
Department of English
P.O. Box 441102
Moscow, ID 83844-1102
208/885-6156

University of Illinois at Chicago
Program for Writers
Department of English M/C 162
601 South Morgan Street
Chicago, IL 60607-7120
312/413-2239

University of Iowa
Program in Creative Writing
102 Dey House
507 N. Clinton Street
Iowa City, IA 52242
319/335-0416

University of Kansas
MFA Program
3114 Wescoe Hall
Lawrence, KS 66045
785/864-2516

University of Maryland
Creative Writing Program
Department of English
3119F Susquehanna Hall
College Park, MD 20742
301/405-3820

University of Massachusetts
MFA Program for Poets and Writers
Department of English
130 Hicks Way
Amherst, MA 01003-9269
413/545-0643

University of Memphis
The Writing Program
Memphis, TN 38152-3510
901/678-2651

University of Miami
Creative Writing Program
Department of English
P.O. Box 248145
Coral Gables, FL 33124
305/284-2182

University of Michigan
MFA Program in Creative Writing
Department of English
3187 Angell Hall
Ann Arbor, MI 48109-1003
734/936-2274

University of Minnesota
MFA Program in Creative Writing
222 Lind Hall
207 Church Street
Minneapolis, MN 55455
612/625-6366

University of Mississippi
MFA Program in Creative Writing
English Department
Bondurant Hall C128
Oxford, MS 38677-1848
662/915-7439

University of Missouri–Columbia
Creative Writing Program
Department of English
107 Tate Hall
Columbia, MO 65211-1500
573/884-7773

University of Missouri–St. Louis
MFA Program
Department of English
One University Boulevard
St. Louis, MO 63121
314/516-6845

University of Montana
Creative Writing Program
Department of English
Missoula, MT 59812-1013
406/243-5231

University of Nebraska, Lincoln
Creative Writing Program
Department of English
202 Andrews Hall
Lincoln, NE 68588-0333
402/472-3191

University of Nevada, Las Vegas
MFA in Creative Writing International
Department of English
4505 Maryland Parkway
Las Vegas, NV 89154-5011
702/895-3533

University of New Hampshire
Creative Writing Program/MFA
Department of English
Hamilton Smith Hall
95 Main Street
Durham, NH 03824-3574
603/862-1313

University of New Orleans
Creative Writing Workshop
College of Liberal Arts
Lakefront
New Orleans, LA 70148
504/280-7454

University of North Dakota
Creative Writing Program
English Department
P.O. Box 7209
Grand Forks, ND 58202
701/777-3321

University of North Texas
Creative Writing Division
Department of English
P.O. Box 311307
Denton, TX 76203-1307
940/565-2050

University of Notre Dame
Creative Writing Program
Department of English
356 O'Shaughnessy Hall
Notre Dame, IN 46556-5639
574/631-4799

University of Oregon
Creative Writing Program
144 Columbia Hall
P.O. Box 5243
Eugene, OR 97403-5243
541/346-0509

University of Pittsburgh
Creative Writing Program
English Department
526 Cathedral of Learning
4200 Fifth Avenue
Pittsburgh, PA 15260-0001
412/624-6506

University of San Francisco
MFA in Writing Program
Program Office, Lone Mountain 340
2130 Fulton Street
San Francisco, CA 94117-1080
415/422-2382

University of South Carolina
MFA Program in Creative Writing
Department of English
Columbia, SC 29208
803/777-4203

University of Southern Mississippi
Center for Writers
118 College Drive, #5144
Hattiesburg, MS 39406-0001
601/266-5600

University of Tennessee
Creative Writing Program
Department of English
301 McClung Tower
Knoxville, TN 37996
865/974-5401

University of Utah
Creative Writing Program
255 S. Central Campus Drive,
Room 3500
Salt Lake City, UT 84112
801/581-7131

University of Virginia
Creative Writing Program
219 Bryan Hall
P.O. Box 400121
Charlottesville, VA 22904-4121
434/924-6675

University of Washington
Creative Writing Program
Box 354330
Seattle, WA 98195-4330
206/543-9865

University of Wisconsin–Madison
Program in Creative Writing
English Department
6195F Helen C. White Hall
600 N. Park Street
Madison, WI 53706
608/263-3800

University of Wisconsin–Milwaukee
Creative Writing Program
Department of English
Box 413
Milwaukee, WI 53201
414/229-6991

University of Wyoming
MFA in Creative Writing
English Department
P.O. Box 3353
Laramie, WY 82071
307/766-2867

Vermont College of Union Institute &
University
MFA in Writing
36 College Street
Montpelier, VT 05602
802/828-8840

Virginia Commonwealth University
MFA in Creative Writing Program
Department of English
P.O. Box 842005
Richmond, VA 23284-2005
804/828-1329

Washington University
The Writing Program
Campus Box 1122
One Brookings Drive
St. Louis, MO 63130-4899
314/935-5190

Wesleyan Writers Conference
Wesleyan University
294 High Street, Room 207
Middletown, CT 06459
860/685-3604

West Virginia University
Creative Writing Program
Department of English
P.O. Box 6269
Morgantown, WV 26506-6269
304/293-3107

Western Michigan University
Graduate Program in Creative Writing
Department of English
Kalamazoo, MI 49008
269/387-2572

Wisconsin Institute for Creative Writing
University of Wisconsin–Madison
Department of English
Helen C. White Hall
600 N. Park Street
Madison, WI 53706
608/263-3374

Wright State University
Creative Writing Program
Department of English
3640 Colonel Glenn Highway
Dayton, OH 45435-0001
937/775-2196